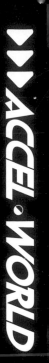

ACCEL·WORLD

08

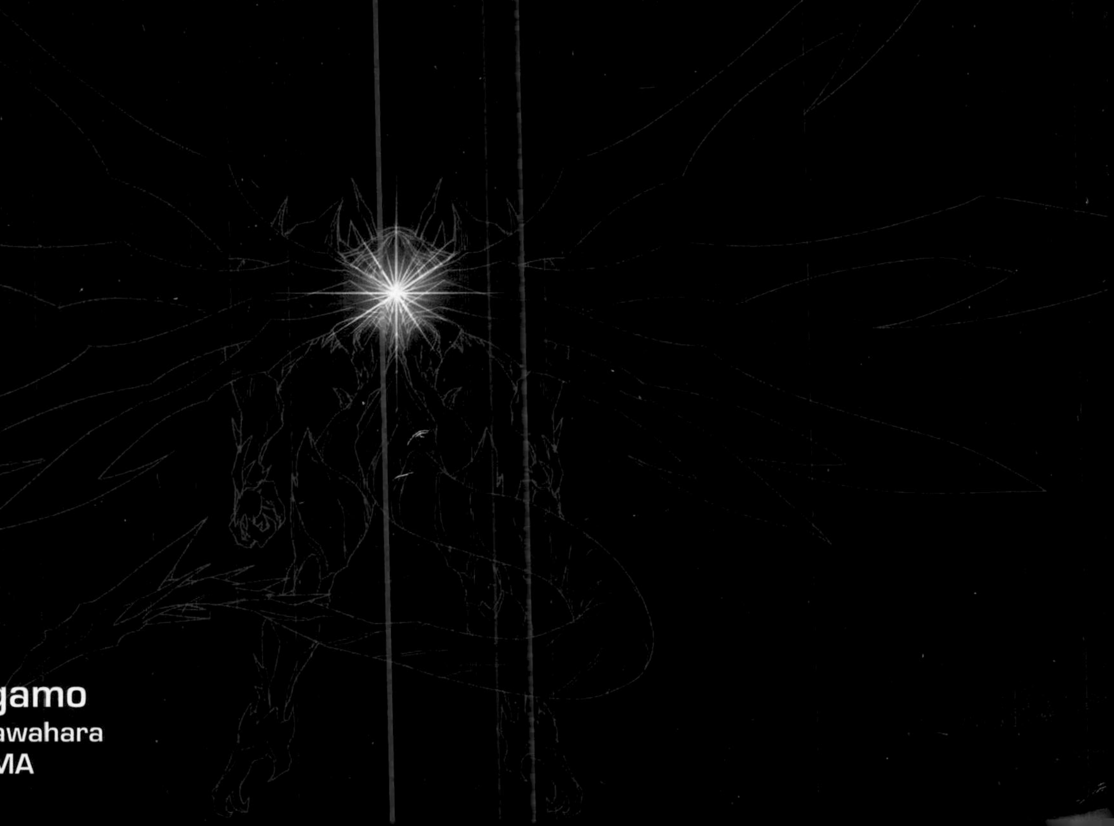

Art: **Hiroyuki Aigamo**
Original Story: **Reki Kawahara**
Character Design: **HIMA**

characters

■ Kuroyukihime = Umesato Junior High School student council vice president. Trim and clever girl who has it all. Her background is shrouded in mystery. Her in-school avatar is a spangled butterfly she programmed herself. Her duel avatar is the Black King, Black Lotus.

■ Haruyuki = Haruyuki Arita. He's good at games but is shy. His in-school avatar is a pink pig. His duel avatar is Silver Crow.

■ Chiyuri = Chiyuri Kurashima. Haruyuki's childhood friend. A meddling, energetic girl. Her duel avatar is Lime Bell.

■ Takumu = Takumu Mayuzumi. A boy Haruyuki and Chiyuri have known since childhood. Good at kendo. His duel avatar is Cyan Pile.

■ Niko = Yuniko Kozuki. Grade Five girl who pretended to be Haruyuki's cousin to get in direct contact with him. Her real identity is the Red King, ruler of the Red Legion. Her duel avatar is Scarlet Rain.

■ Fuko = Fuko Kurasaki. Taught Haruyuki the deep mysteries of the Incarnate System when he was in trouble. A war comrade of Kuroyukihime's in the old Nega Nebulus.

key words

■ Neurolinker = A portable Internet terminal that connects with the brain via a wireless quantum connection and enhances all five senses with images, sounds, and other stimuli.

■ Brain Burst = Neurolinker application sent to Haruyuki by Kuroyukihime.

■ Duel avatar = Player's virtual self, operated when fighting in Brain Burst.

■ Burst points = Points required to use the power of acceleration. To obtain them, players must win in duels against other duel avatars. A player losing all their points forces Brain Burst to uninstall.

■ Legions = Groups composed of many duel avatars with the objective of expanding occupied areas and securing rights. The Six Kings of Pure Color act as the Legion Masters.

■ In-school local net = Local area network established within Umesato Junior High School. Used during classes and to check attendance; while on campus, Umesato students are required to be connected to it at all times.

■ Global connection = Connection with the worldwide net. Global connections are forbidden on Umesato Junior High School grounds, where the in-school local net is provided instead.

■ Enhanced Armaments = Items such as weapons or personal armor owned by duel avatars.

■ Normal Duel Field = The field where normal Brain Burst battles (one-on-one or tag matches) are carried out.

■ Unlimited Neutral Field = Field for high-level players where only duel avatars at Level Four and up are allowed. The game system is of a wholly different order than that of the Normal Duel Field.

Ø8

accel world

art:
hiroyuki aigamo
original story:
reki kawahara
accel world 05:
the floating starlight bridge
character design:
hima

contents

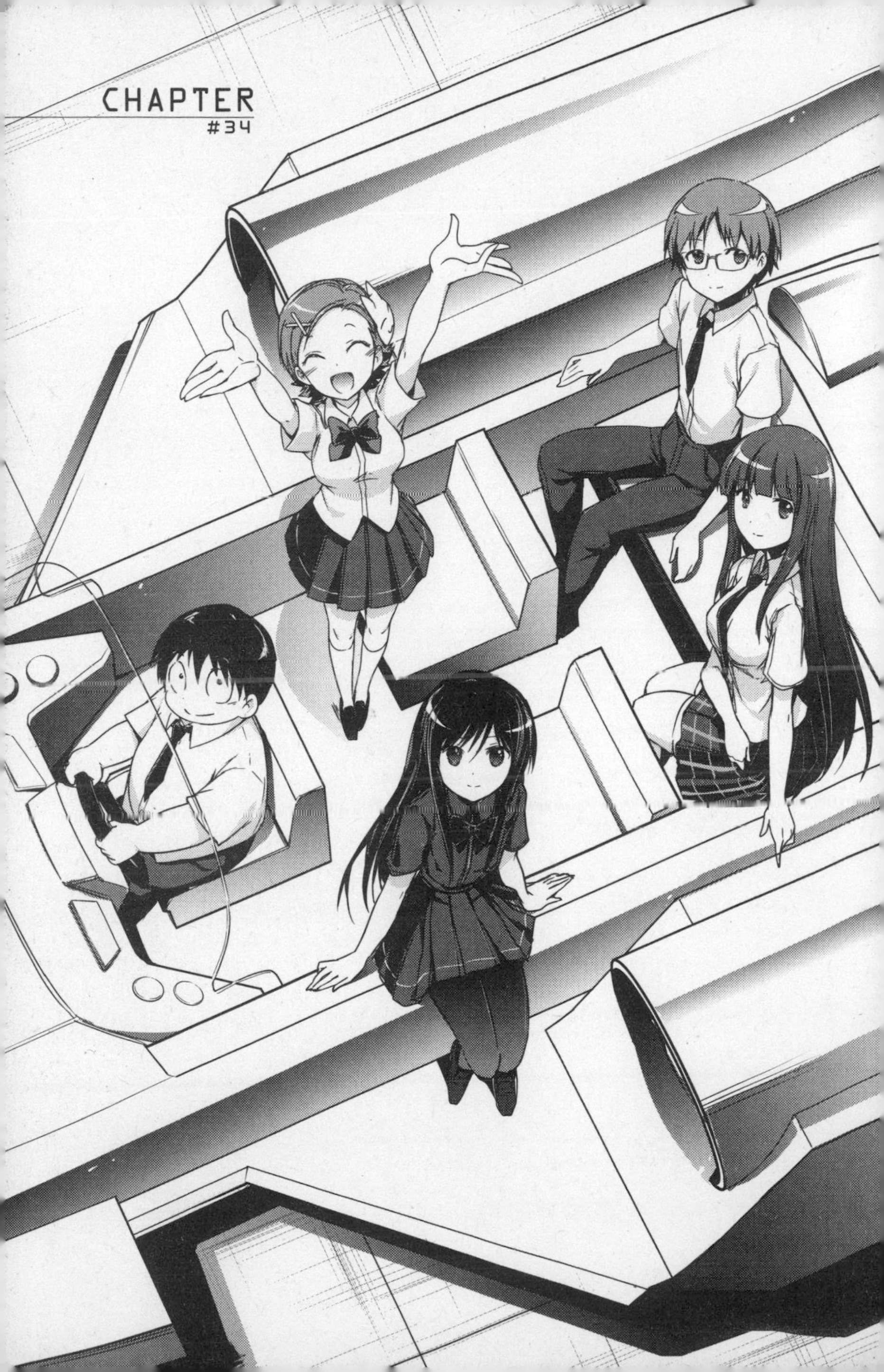
CHAPTER
#34

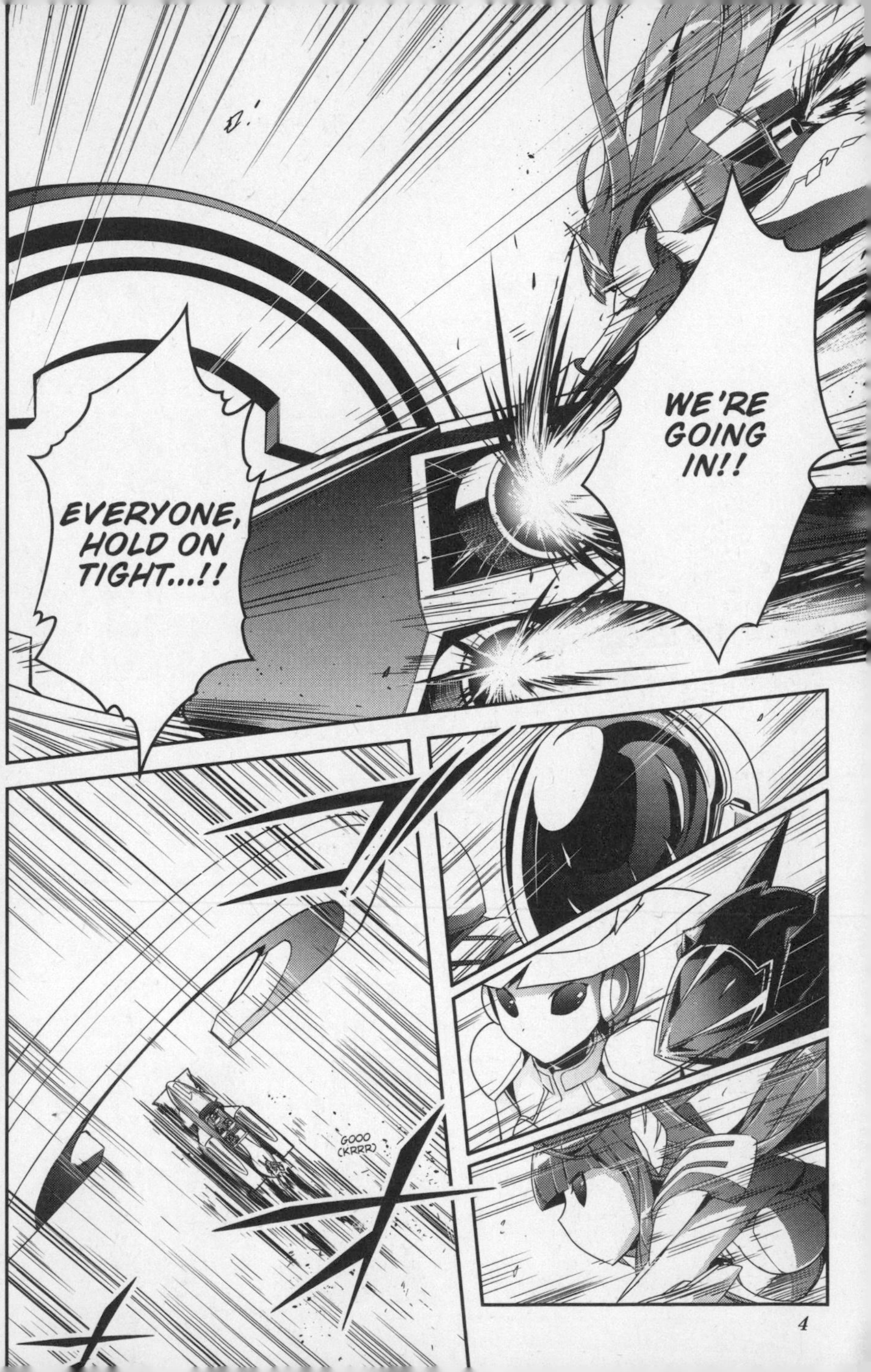
WE'RE GOING IN!!
EVERYONE, HOLD ON TIGHT...!!
GOOO (KRRR)

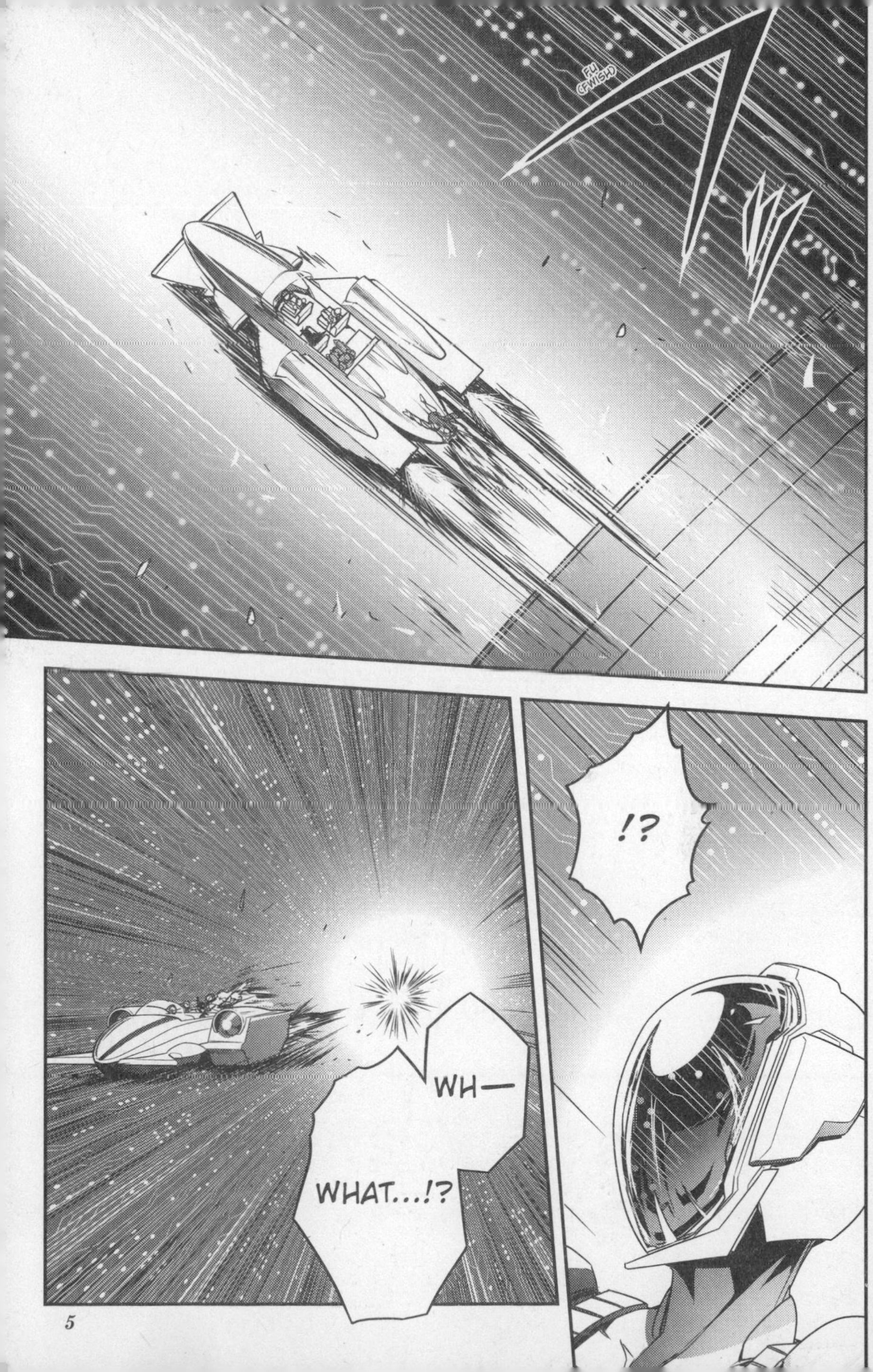
FU
(FWISH)
!?
WH—
WHAT...!?

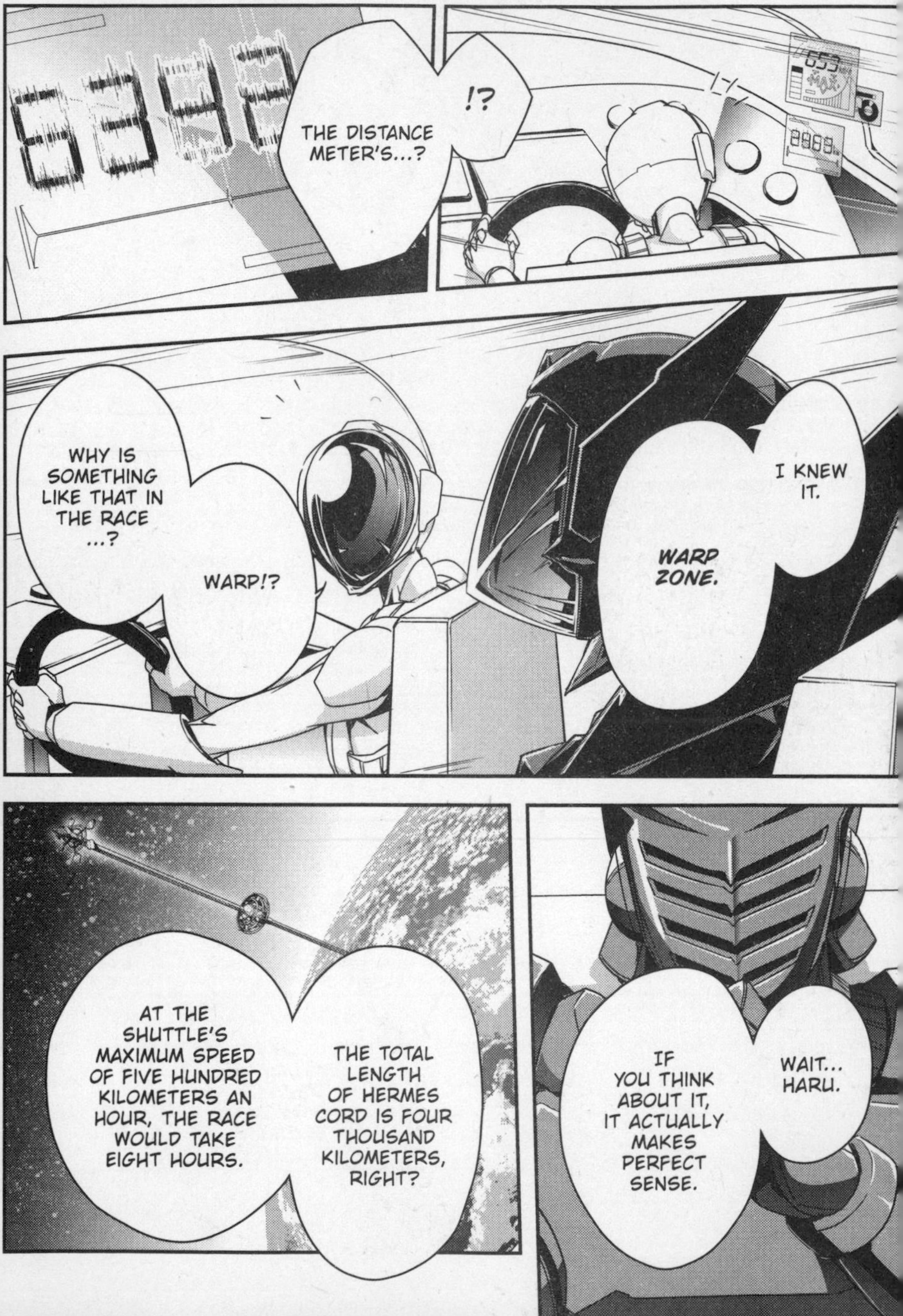
!?
THE DISTANCE METER'S...?
I KNEW IT.
WARP ZONE.
WARP!?
WHY IS SOMETHING LIKE THAT IN THE RACE ...?
WAIT... HARU.
IF YOU THINK ABOUT IT, IT ACTUALLY MAKES PERFECT SENSE.
THE TOTAL LENGTH OF HERMES CORD IS FOUR THOUSAND KILOMETERS, RIGHT?
AT THE SHUTTLE'S MAXIMUM SPEED OF FIVE HUNDRED KILOMETERS AN HOUR, THE RACE WOULD TAKE EIGHT HOURS.

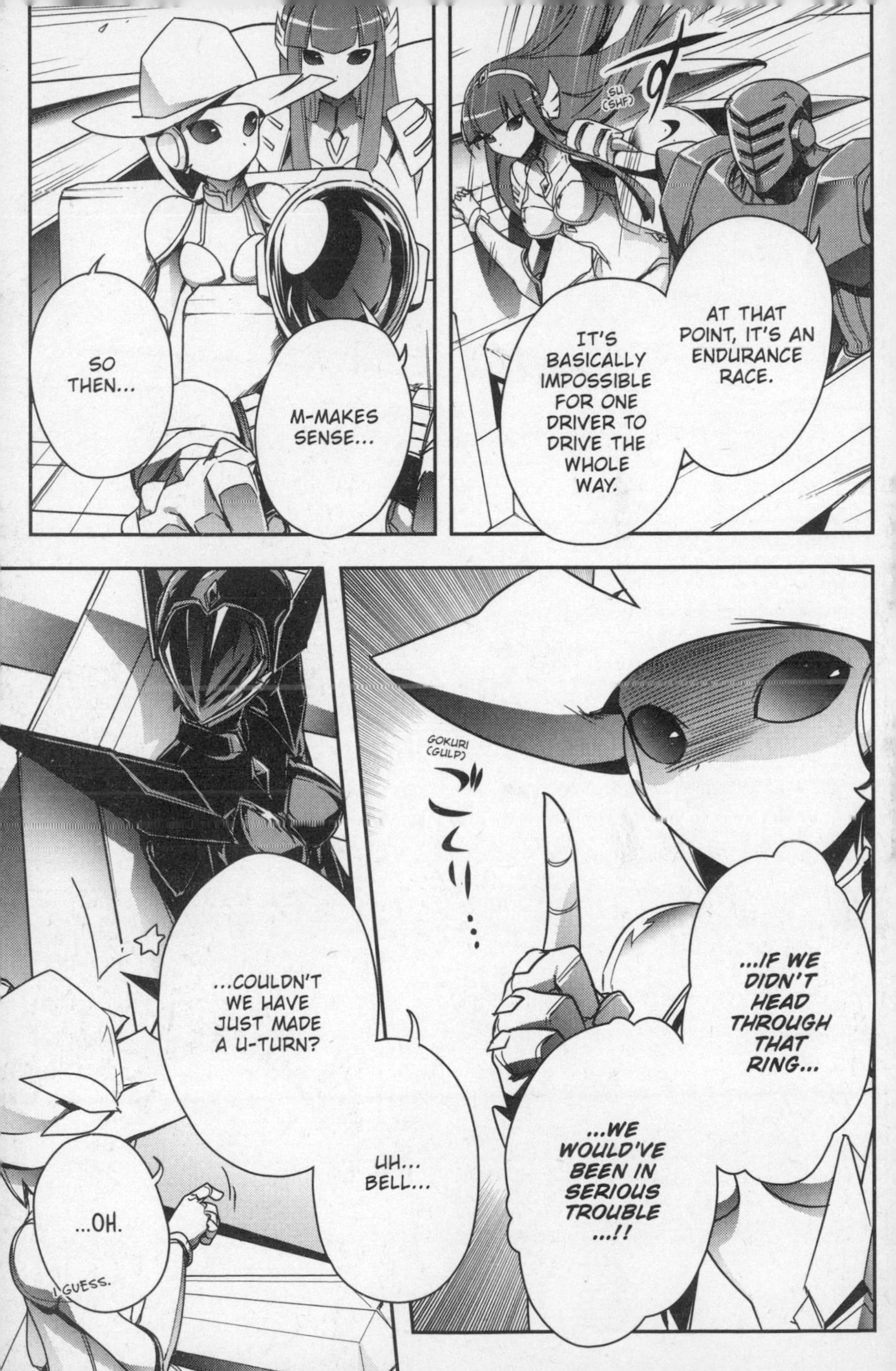
SU (SHF)
AT THAT POINT, IT'S AN ENDURANCE RACE.
IT'S BASICALLY IMPOSSIBLE FOR ONE DRIVER TO DRIVE THE WHOLE WAY.
M-MAKES SENSE...
SO THEN...
GOKURI (GULP)
...IF WE DIDN'T HEAD THROUGH THAT RING...
...WE WOULD'VE BEEN IN SERIOUS TROUBLE...!!
...COULDN'T WE HAVE JUST MADE A U-TURN?
UH... BELL...
...OH.
I GUESS.

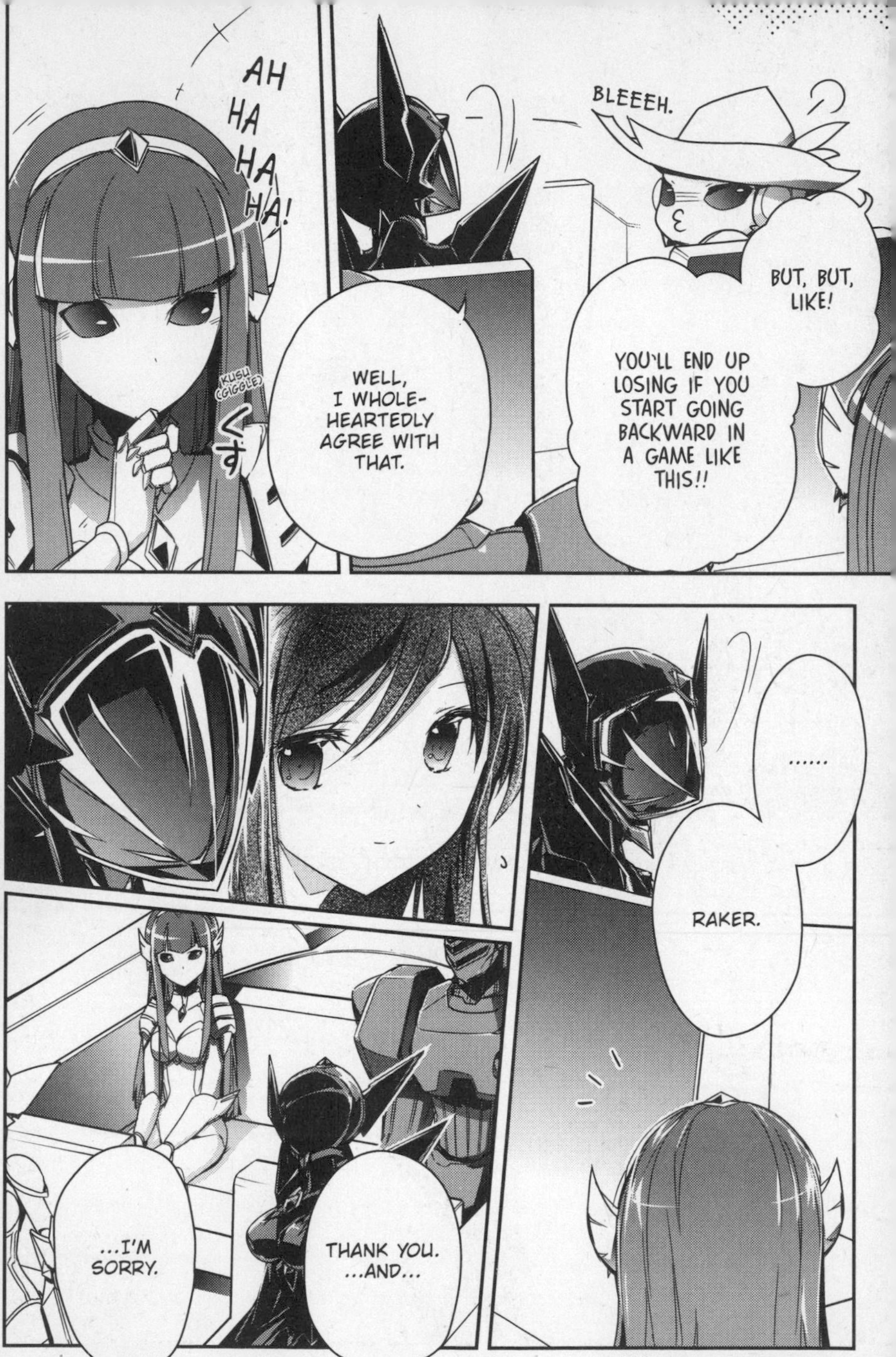
BLEEEH.
BUT, BUT, LIKE!
YOU'LL END UP LOSING IF YOU START GOING BACKWARD IN A GAME LIKE THIS!!
WELL, I WHOLE-HEARTEDLY AGREE WITH THAT.
AH HA HA HA!
KUSU (GIGGLE)
くす
......
RAKER.
THANK YOU. ...AND...
...I'M SORRY.

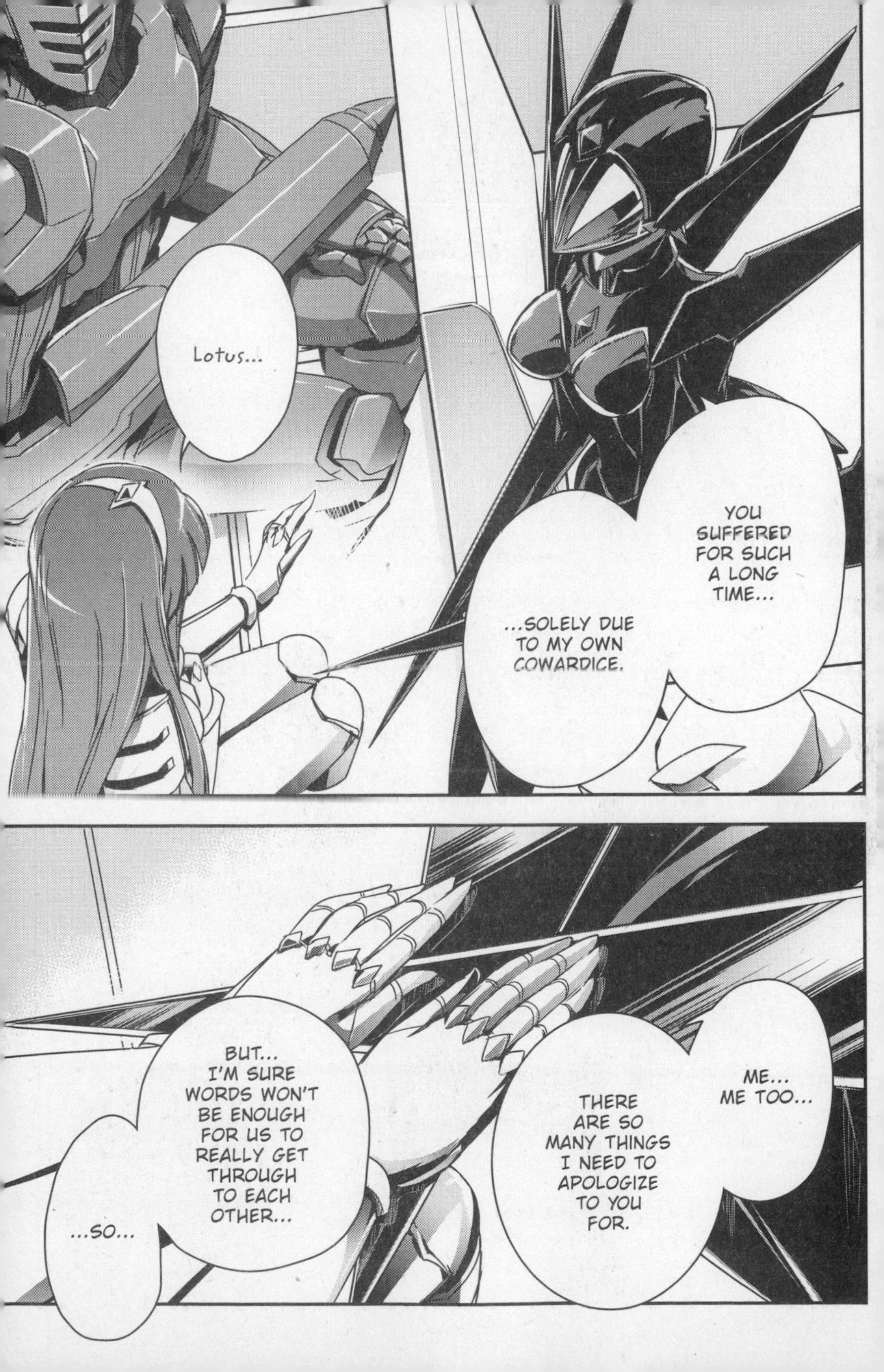
Lotus...
YOU SUFFERED FOR SUCH A LONG TIME...
...SOLELY DUE TO MY OWN COWARDICE.
ME... ME TOO...
THERE ARE SO MANY THINGS I NEED TO APOLOGIZE TO YOU FOR.
BUT... I'M SURE WORDS WON'T BE ENOUGH FOR US TO REALLY GET THROUGH TO EACH OTHER...
...SO...

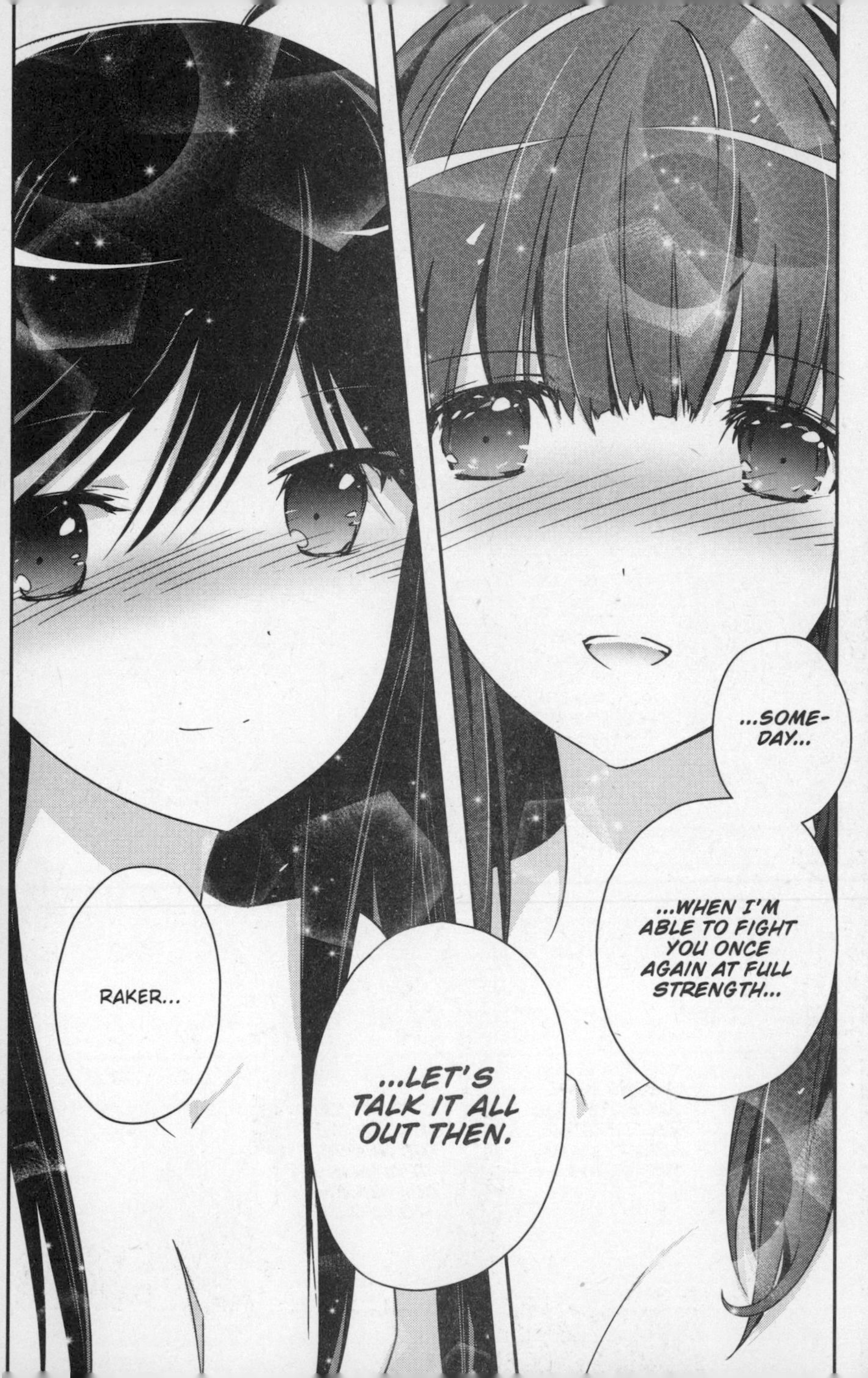
...SOME-DAY...
...WHEN I'M ABLE TO FIGHT YOU ONCE AGAIN AT FULL STRENGTH...
...LET'S TALK IT ALL OUT THEN.
RAKER...

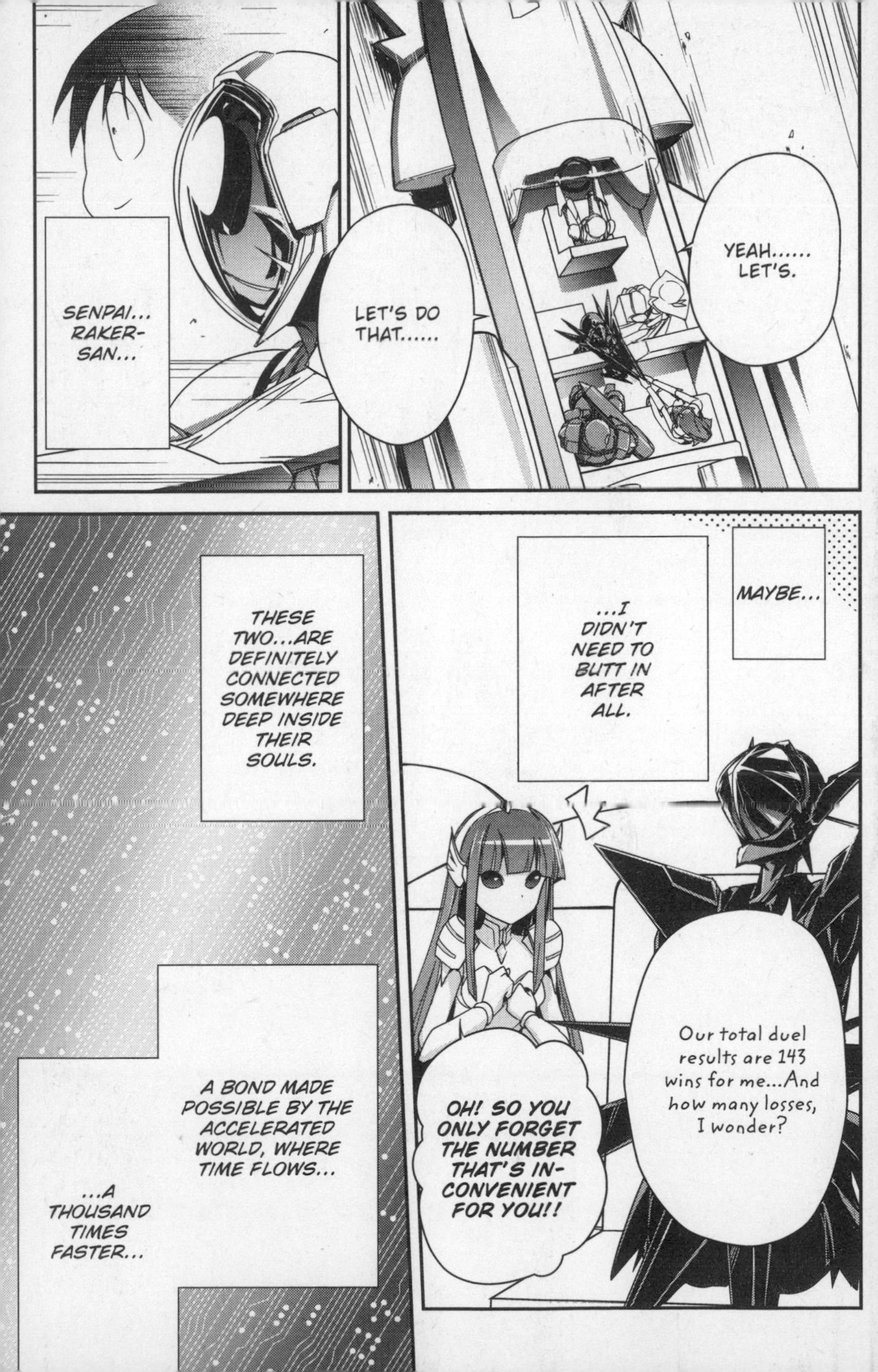
YEAH...... LET'S.
LET'S DO THAT......
SENPAI... RAKER-SAN...
MAYBE...
...I DIDN'T NEED TO BUTT IN AFTER ALL.
Our total duel results are 143 wins for me...And how many losses, I wonder?
OH! SO YOU ONLY FORGET THE NUMBER THAT'S IN-CONVENIENT FOR YOU!!
THESE TWO...ARE DEFINITELY CONNECTED SOMEWHERE DEEP INSIDE THEIR SOULS.
A BOND MADE POSSIBLE BY THE ACCELERATED WORLD, WHERE TIME FLOWS...
...A THOUSAND TIMES FASTER...

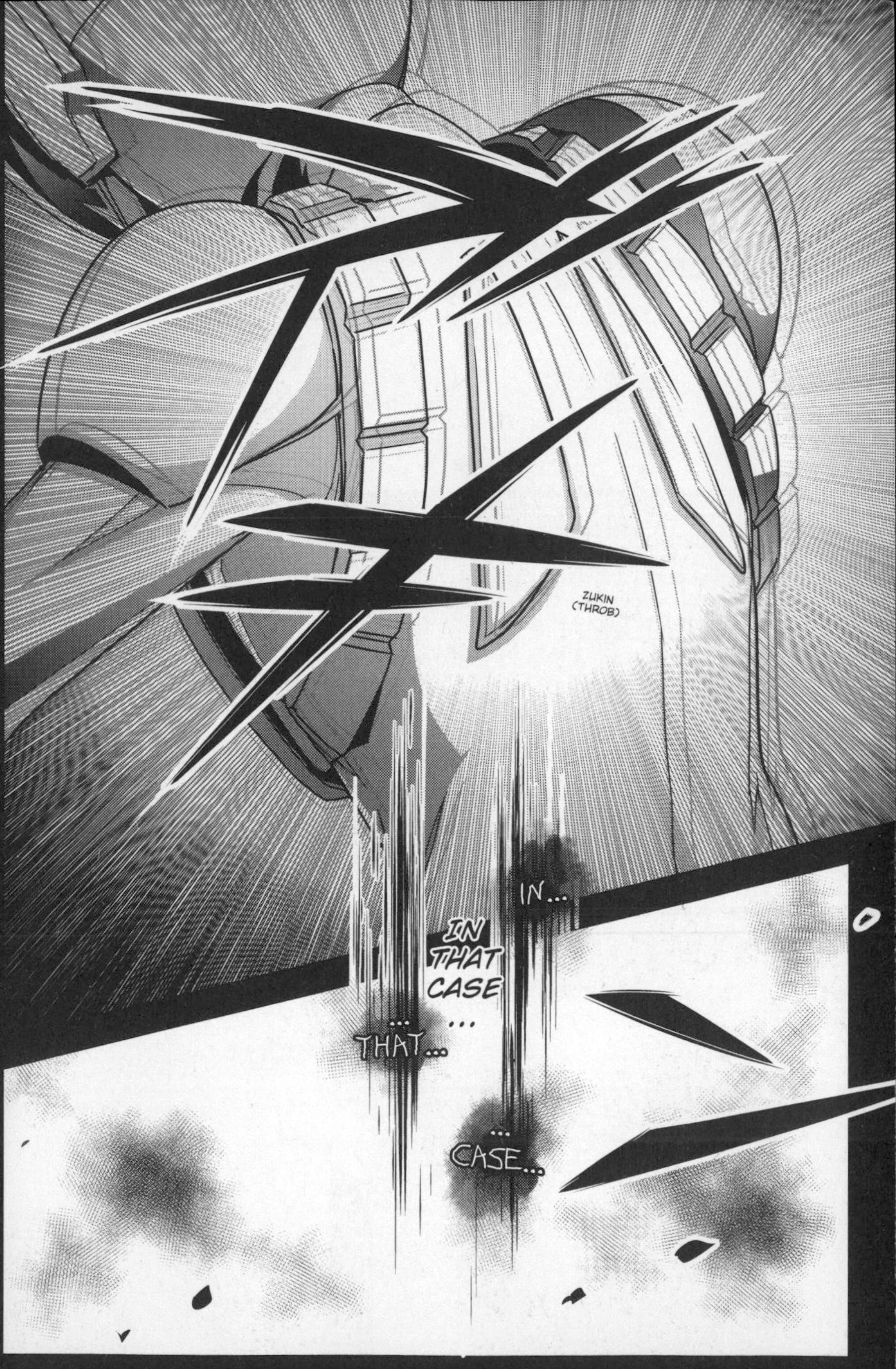
ZUKIN
(THROB)
IN...
IN THAT CASE
...
...THAT...
...CASE...

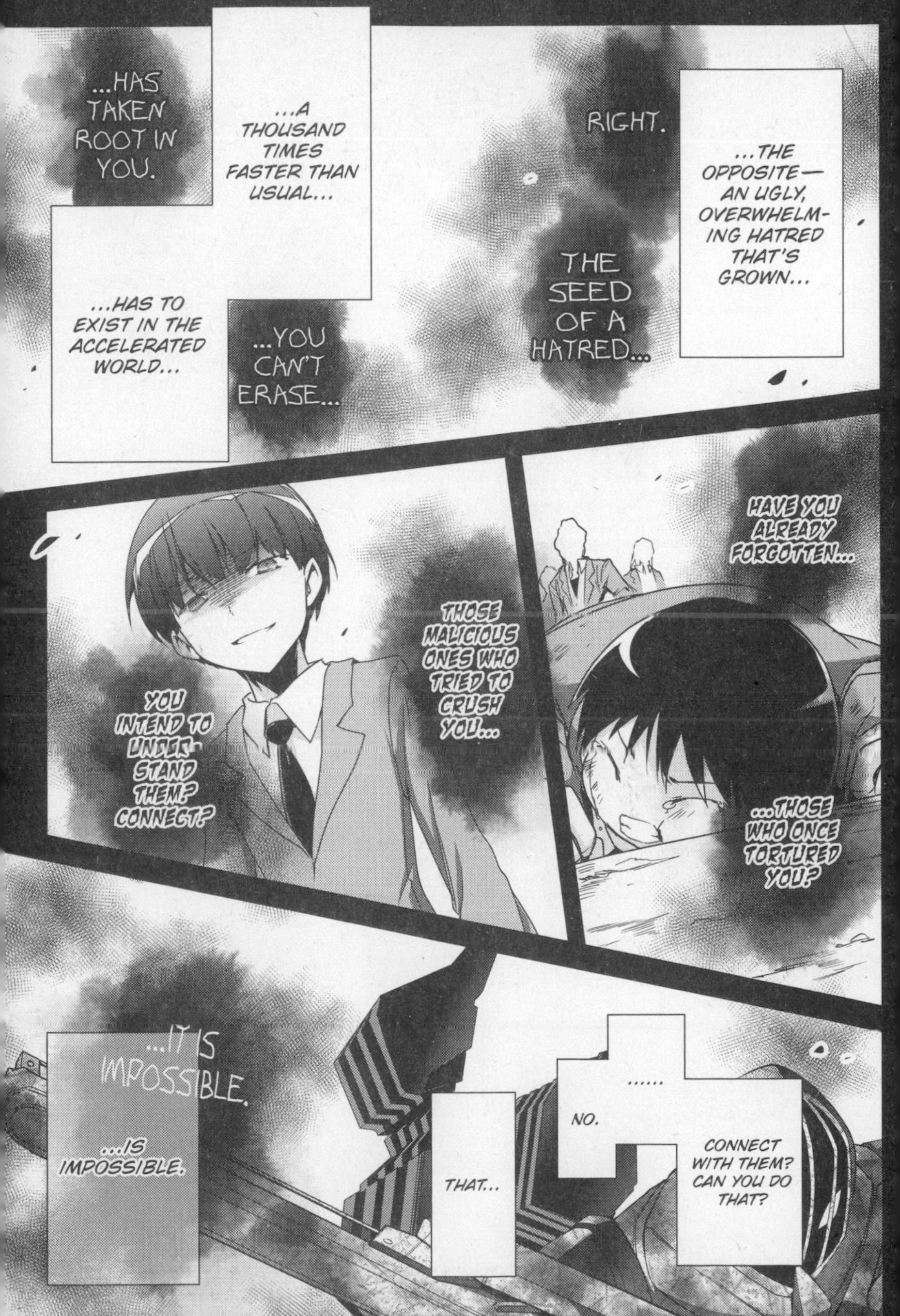
...THE OPPOSITE—AN UGLY, OVERWHELMING HATRED THAT'S GROWN...
RIGHT.
THE SEED OF A HATRED...
...A THOUSAND TIMES FASTER THAN USUAL...
...YOU CAN'T ERASE...
...HAS TAKEN ROOT IN YOU.
...HAS TO EXIST IN THE ACCELERATED WORLD...
HAVE YOU ALREADY FORGOTTEN...
...THOSE WHO ONCE TORTURED YOU?
THOSE MALICIOUS ONES WHO TRIED TO CRUSH YOU...
YOU INTEND TO UNDERSTAND THEM? CONNECT?
CONNECT WITH THEM? CAN YOU DO THAT?
......
NO.
THAT...
...IT IS IMPOSSIBLE.
...IS IMPOSSIBLE.

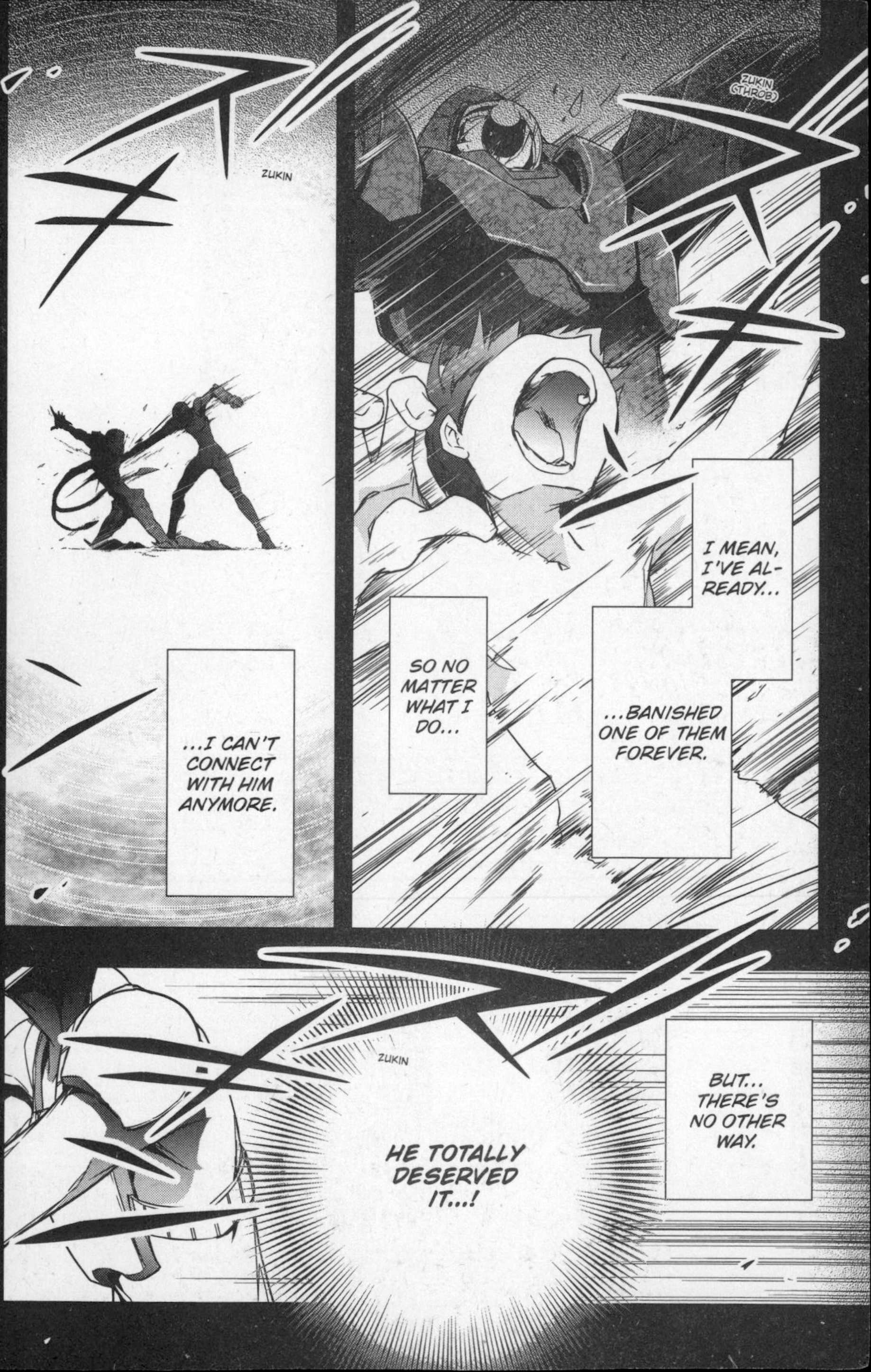
ZUKIN (THROB)
I MEAN, I'VE AL-READY...
...BANISHED ONE OF THEM FOREVER.
SO NO MATTER WHAT I DO...
ZUKIN
...I CAN'T CONNECT WITH HIM ANYMORE.
BUT... THERE'S NO OTHER WAY.
ZUKIN
HE TOTALLY DESERVED IT...!

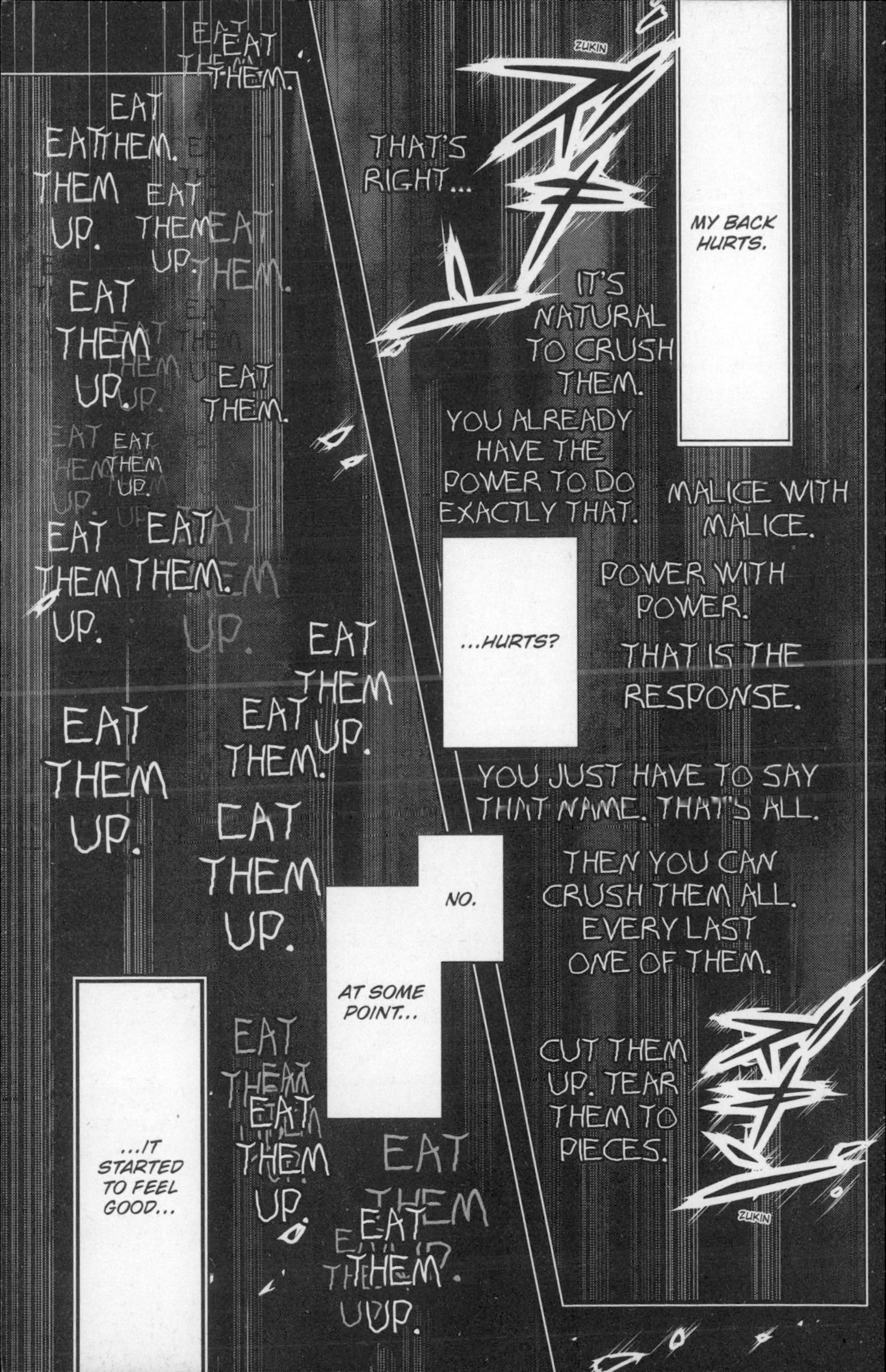
ZUKIN
MY BACK HURTS.
THAT'S RIGHT...
IT'S NATURAL TO CRUSH THEM.
YOU ALREADY HAVE THE POWER TO DO EXACTLY THAT.
MALICE WITH MALICE.
POWER WITH POWER.
...HURTS?
THAT IS THE RESPONSE.
YOU JUST HAVE TO SAY THAT NAME. THAT'S ALL.
THEN YOU CAN CRUSH THEM ALL. EVERY LAST ONE OF THEM.
NO.
CUT THEM UP. TEAR THEM TO PIECES.
ZUKIN
AT SOME POINT...
EAT THEM.
EAT THEM.
EAT THEM UP.
EAT THEM UP.
EAT THEM UP.
EAT THEM.
EAT THEM UP.
EAT THEM.
EAT THEM UP.
EAT THEM UP.
EAT THEM.
EAT THEM UP.
EAT THEM UP.
EAT THEM UP.
EAT THEM UP.
...IT STARTED TO FEEL GOOD...

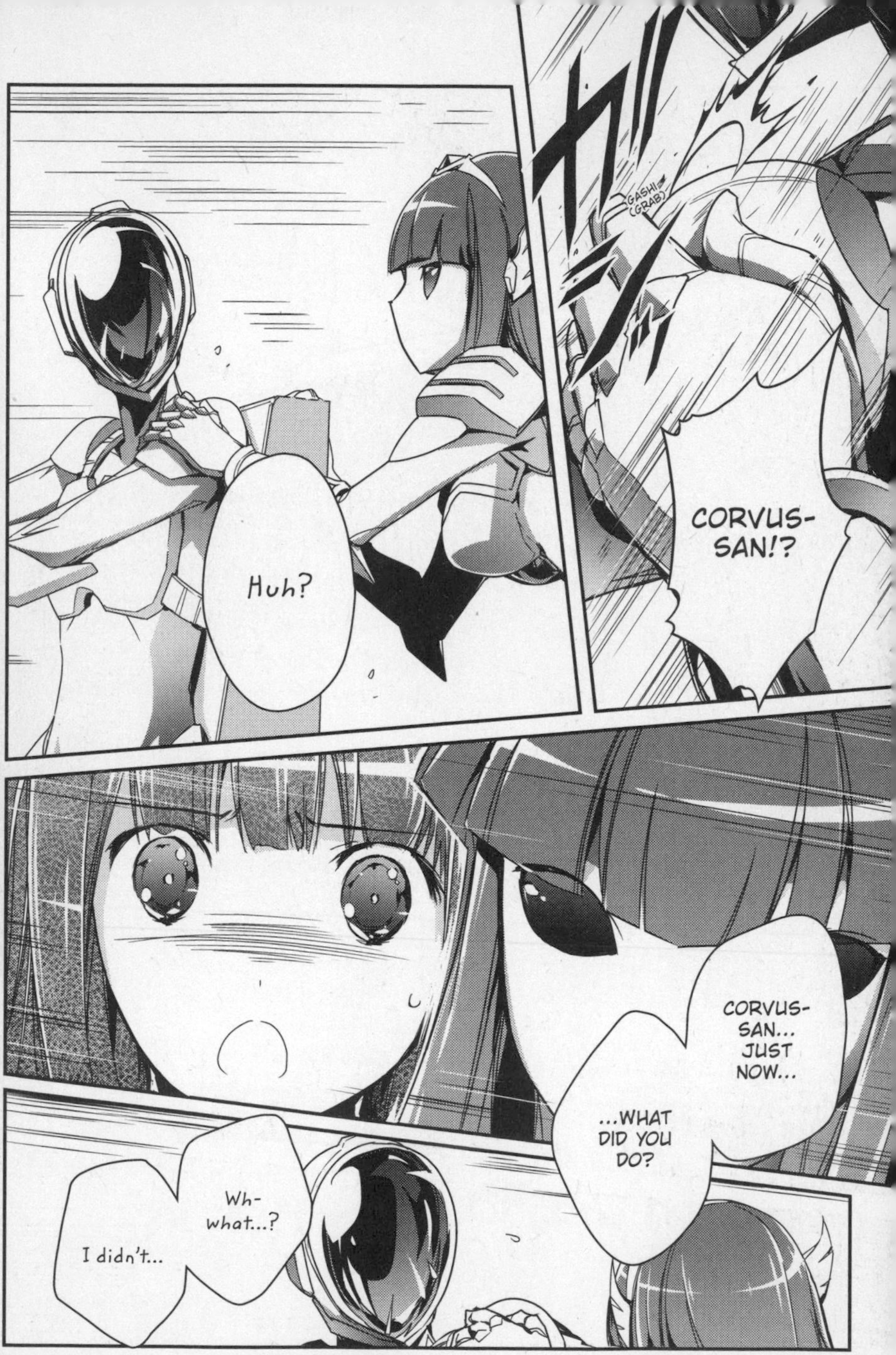
GASHI (GRAB)
CORVUS-SAN!?
Huh?
CORVUS-SAN... JUST NOW...
...WHAT DID YOU DO?
Wh- what...?
I didn't...

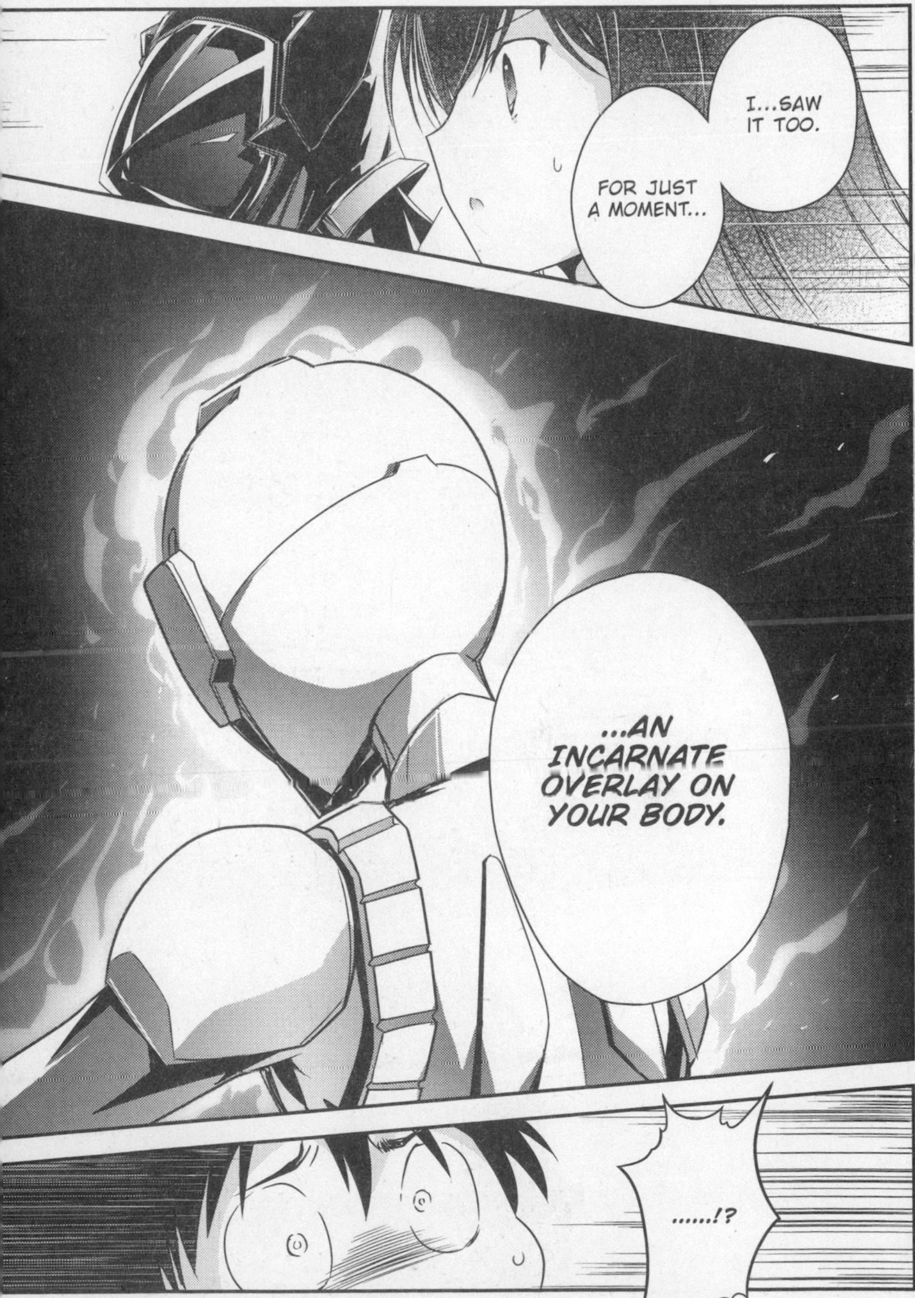
I...SAW IT TOO.
FOR JUST A MOMENT...
...AN INCARNATE OVERLAY ON YOUR BODY.
......!?

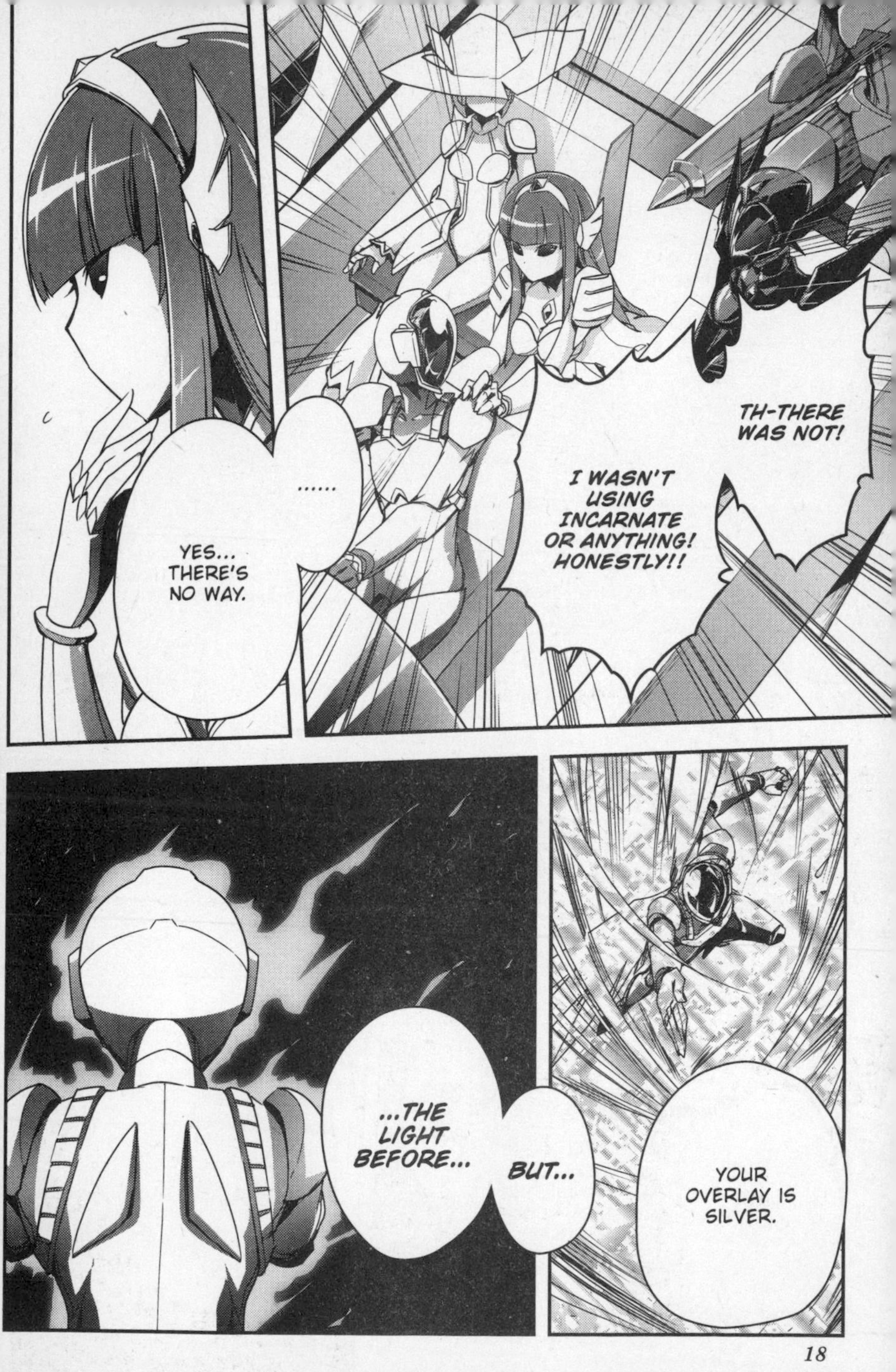
TH-THERE WAS NOT!
I WASN'T USING INCARNATE OR ANYTHING! HONESTLY!!
......
YES... THERE'S NO WAY.
YOUR OVERLAY IS SILVER.
BUT...
...THE LIGHT BEFORE...

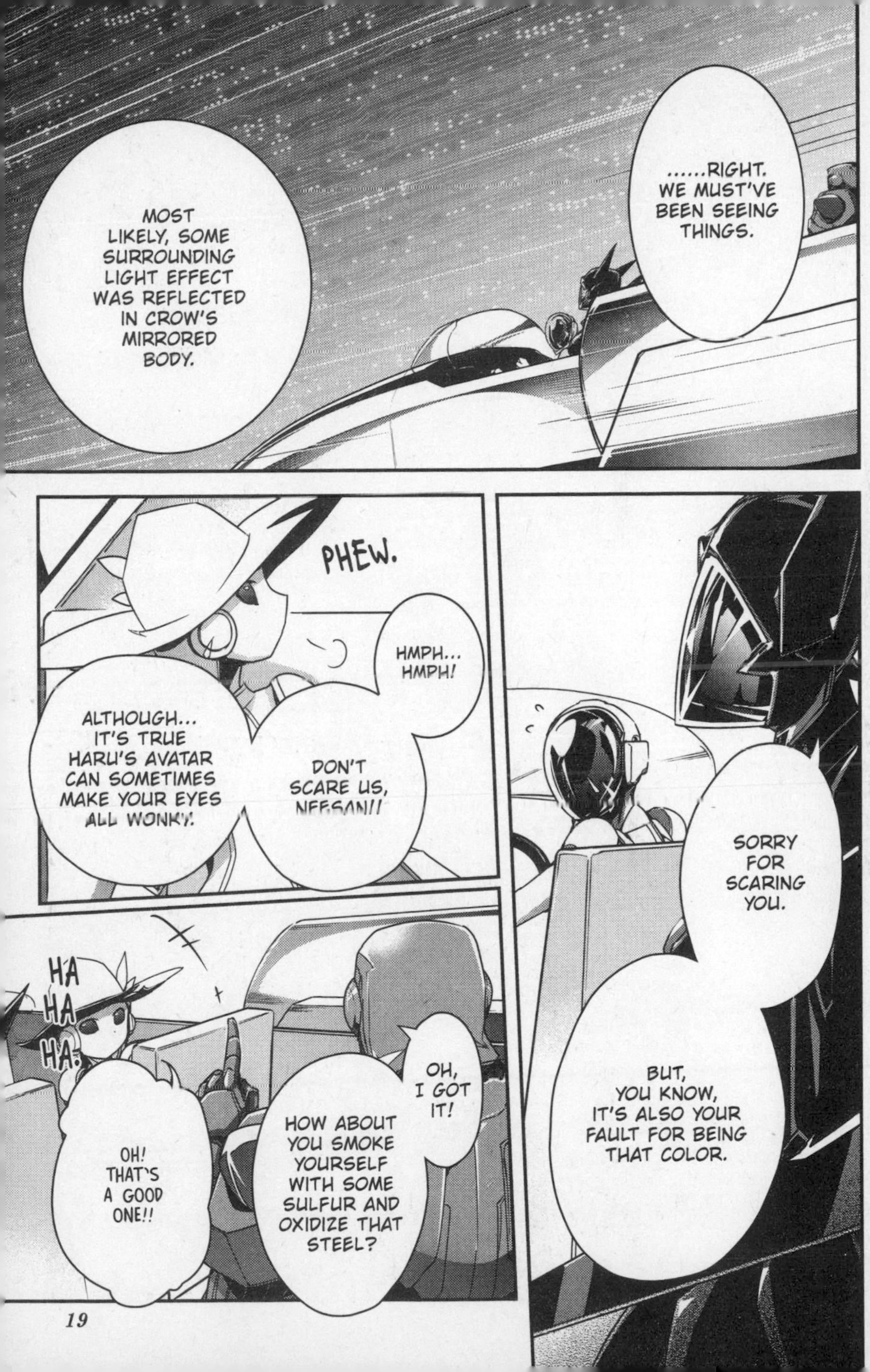

......RIGHT. WE MUST'VE BEEN SEEING THINGS.
MOST LIKELY, SOME SURROUNDING LIGHT EFFECT WAS REFLECTED IN CROW'S MIRRORED BODY.
SORRY FOR SCARING YOU.
BUT, YOU KNOW, IT'S ALSO YOUR FAULT FOR BEING THAT COLOR.
PHEW.
HMPH... HMPH!
DON'T SCARE US, NEESAN!!
ALTHOUGH... IT'S TRUE HARU'S AVATAR CAN SOMETIMES MAKE YOUR EYES ALL WONKY.
OH, I GOT IT!
HOW ABOUT YOU SMOKE YOURSELF WITH SOME SULFUR AND OXIDIZE THAT STEEL?
HA HA HA.
OH! THAT'S A GOOD ONE!!

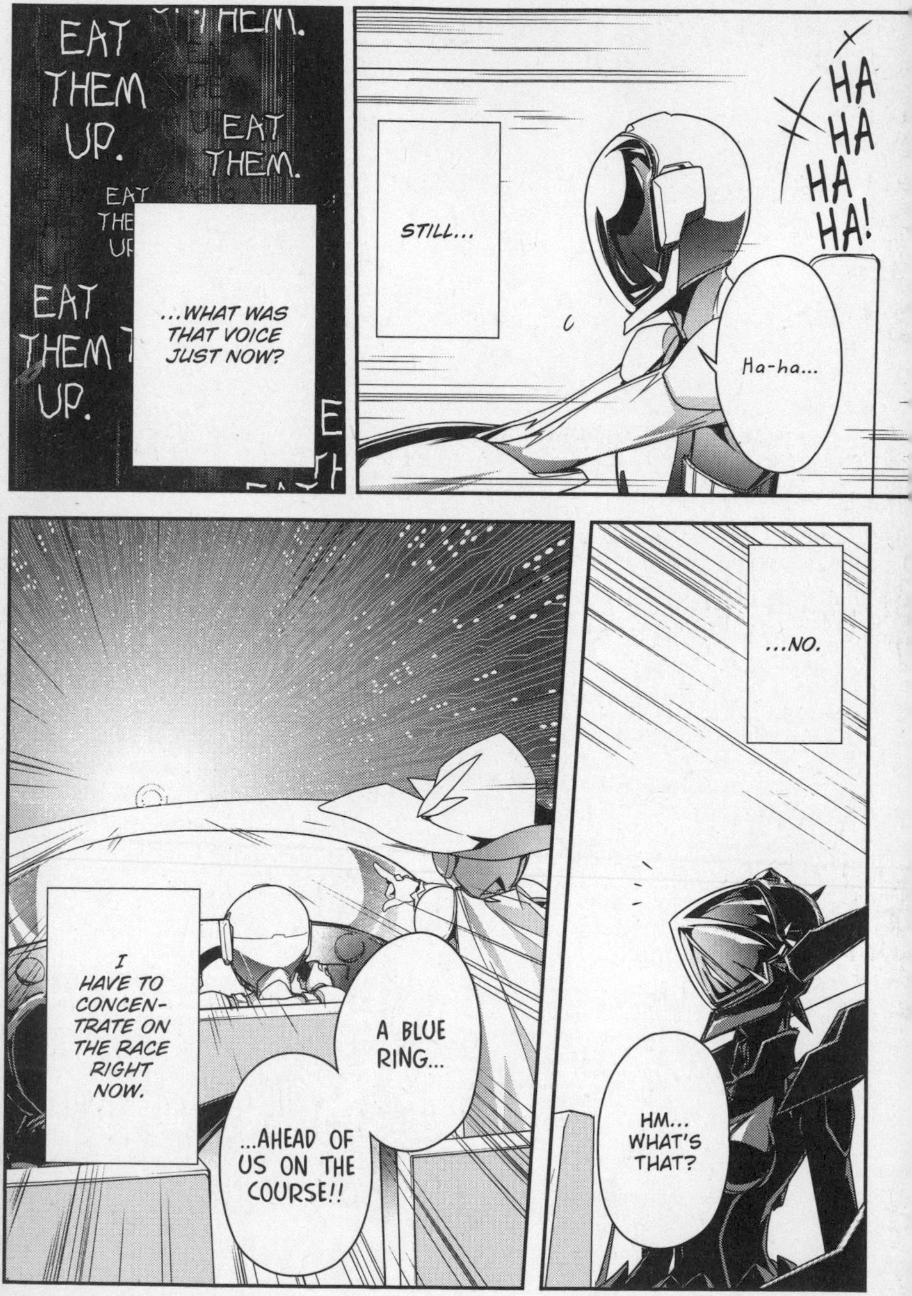
HA HA HA HA!
Ha-ha...
STILL...
EAT THEM UP.
EAT THEM.
EAT THEM UP.
...WHAT WAS THAT VOICE JUST NOW?
...NO.
HM... WHAT'S THAT?
A BLUE RING...
...AHEAD OF US ON THE COURSE!!
I HAVE TO CONCENTRATE ON THE RACE RIGHT NOW.

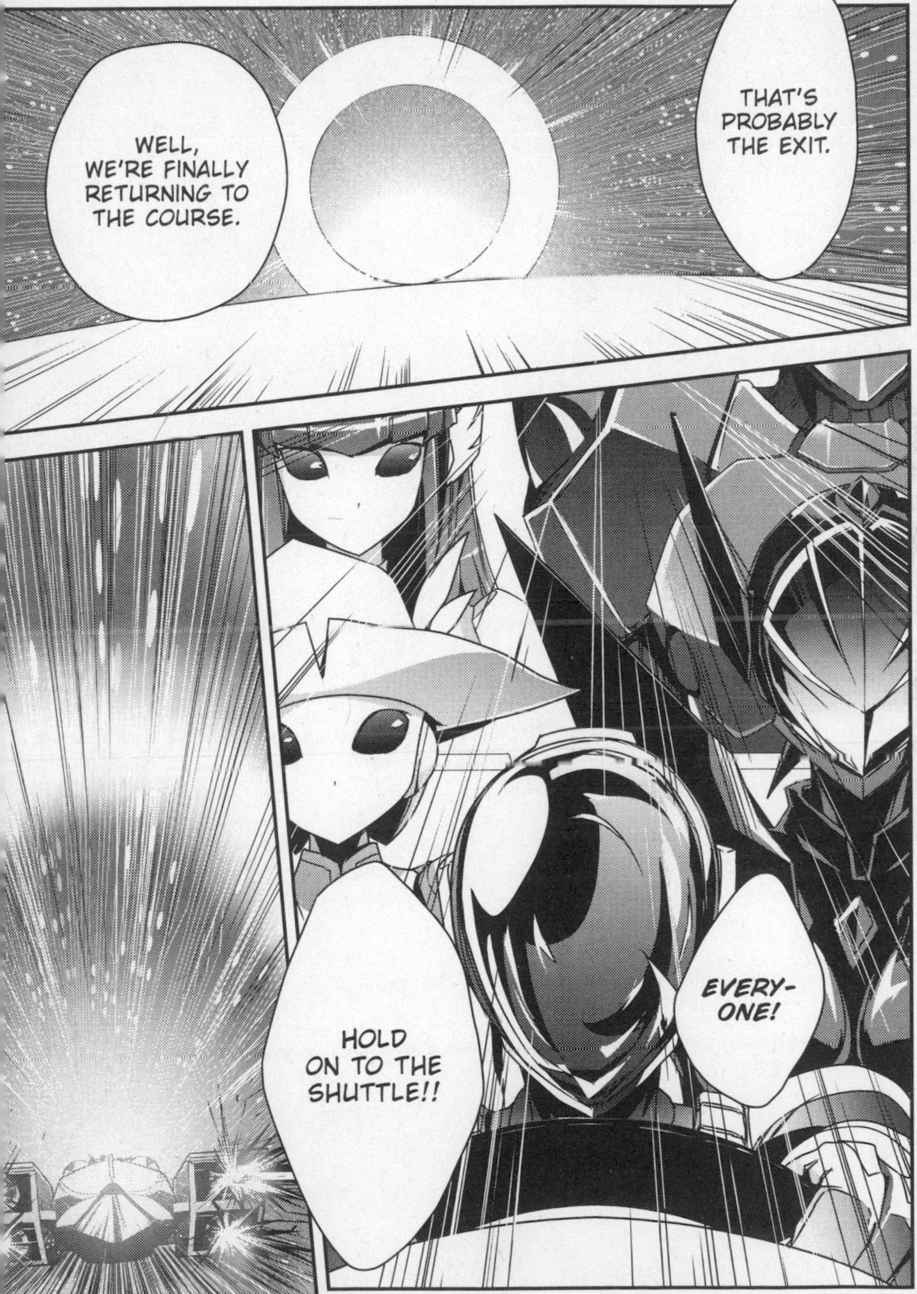
THAT'S PROBABLY THE EXIT.
WELL, WE'RE FINALLY RETURNING TO THE COURSE.
EVERY-ONE!
HOLD ON TO THE SHUTTLE!!

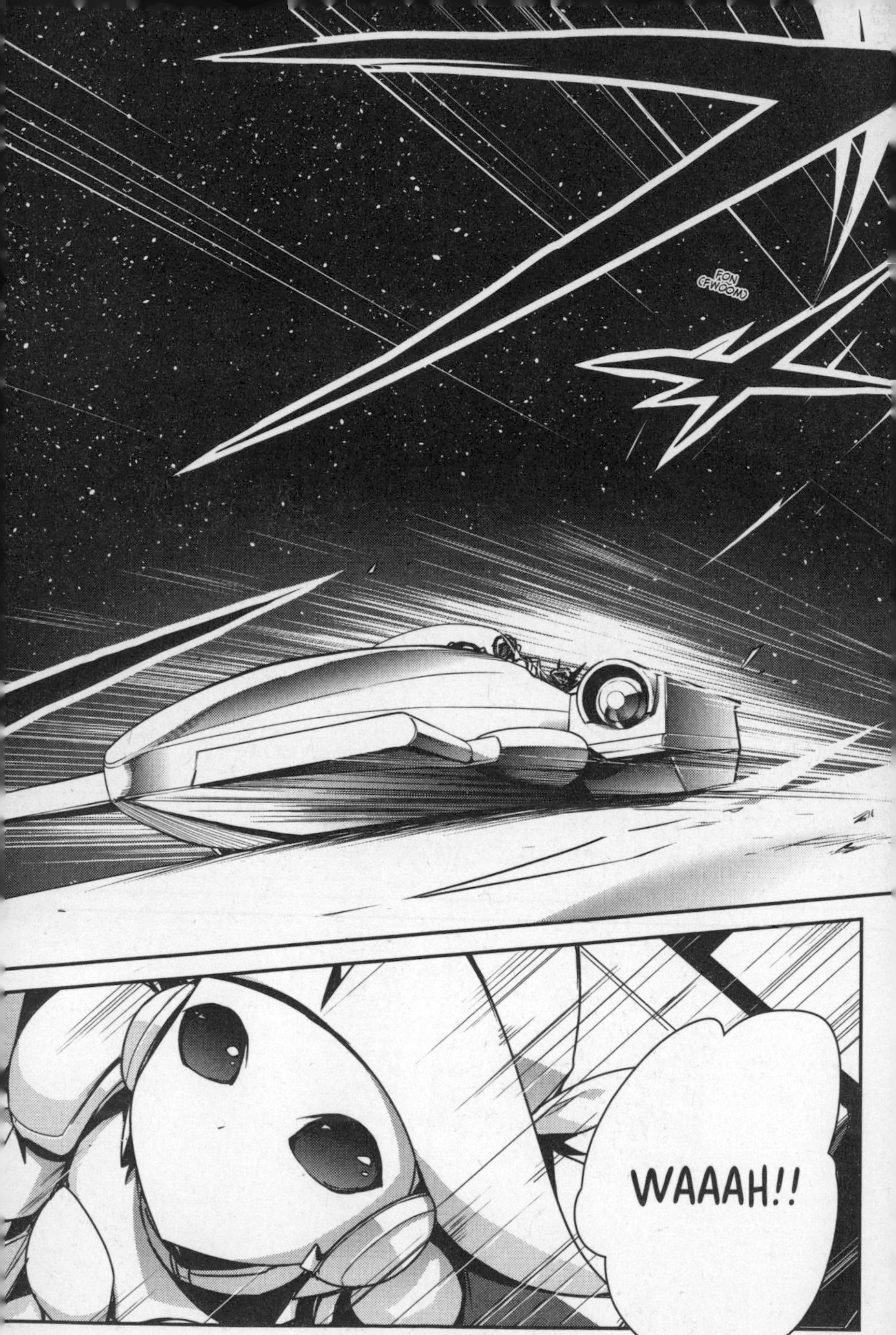
FON (FWOOM)
WAAAH!!

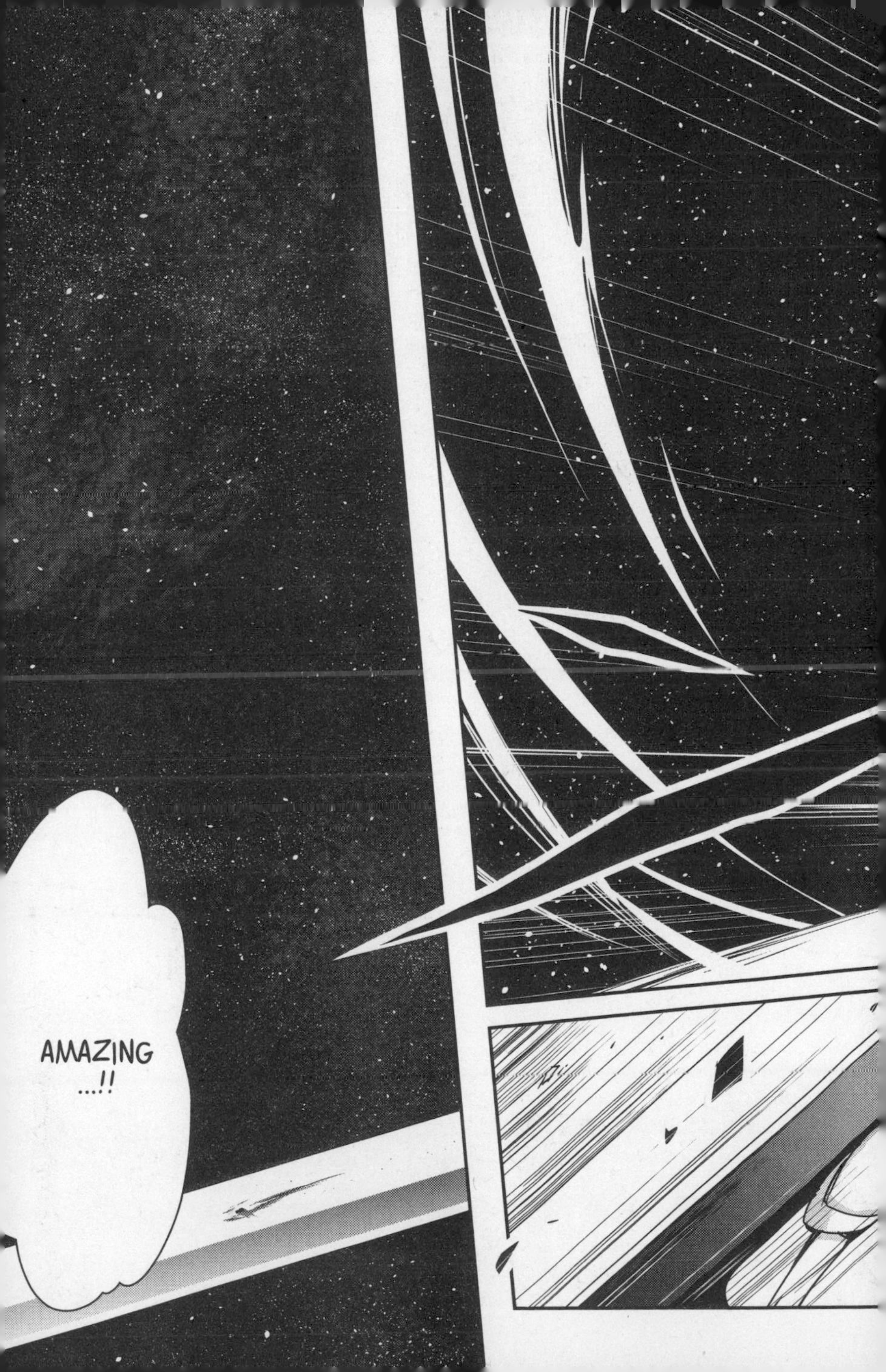
AMAZING
...!!

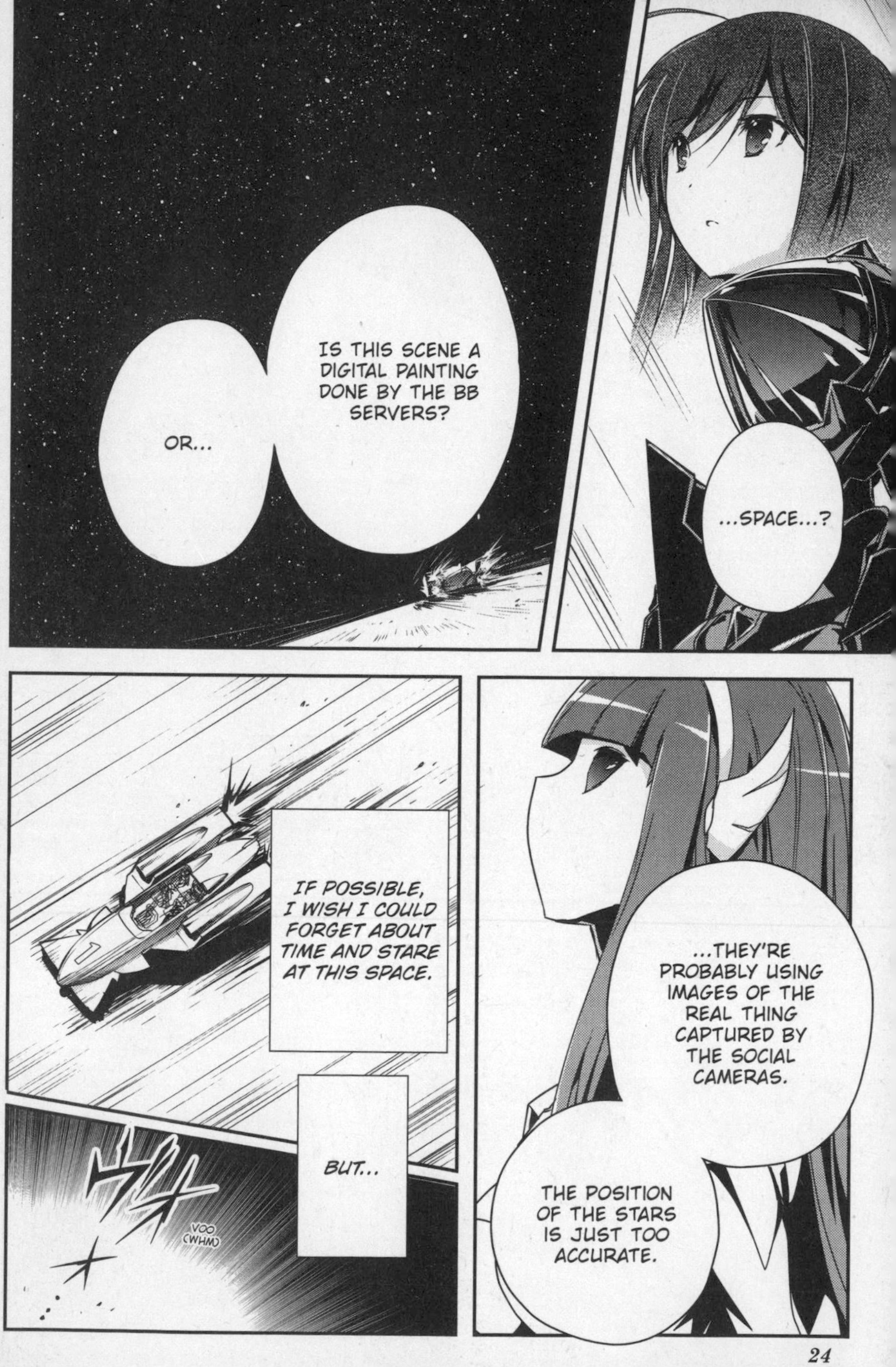
...SPACE...?
IS THIS SCENE A DIGITAL PAINTING DONE BY THE BB SERVERS?
OR...
...THEY'RE PROBABLY USING IMAGES OF THE REAL THING CAPTURED BY THE SOCIAL CAMERAS.
THE POSITION OF THE STARS IS JUST TOO ACCURATE.
IF POSSIBLE, I WISH I COULD FORGET ABOUT TIME AND STARE AT THIS SPACE.
BUT...
VOO (WHM)

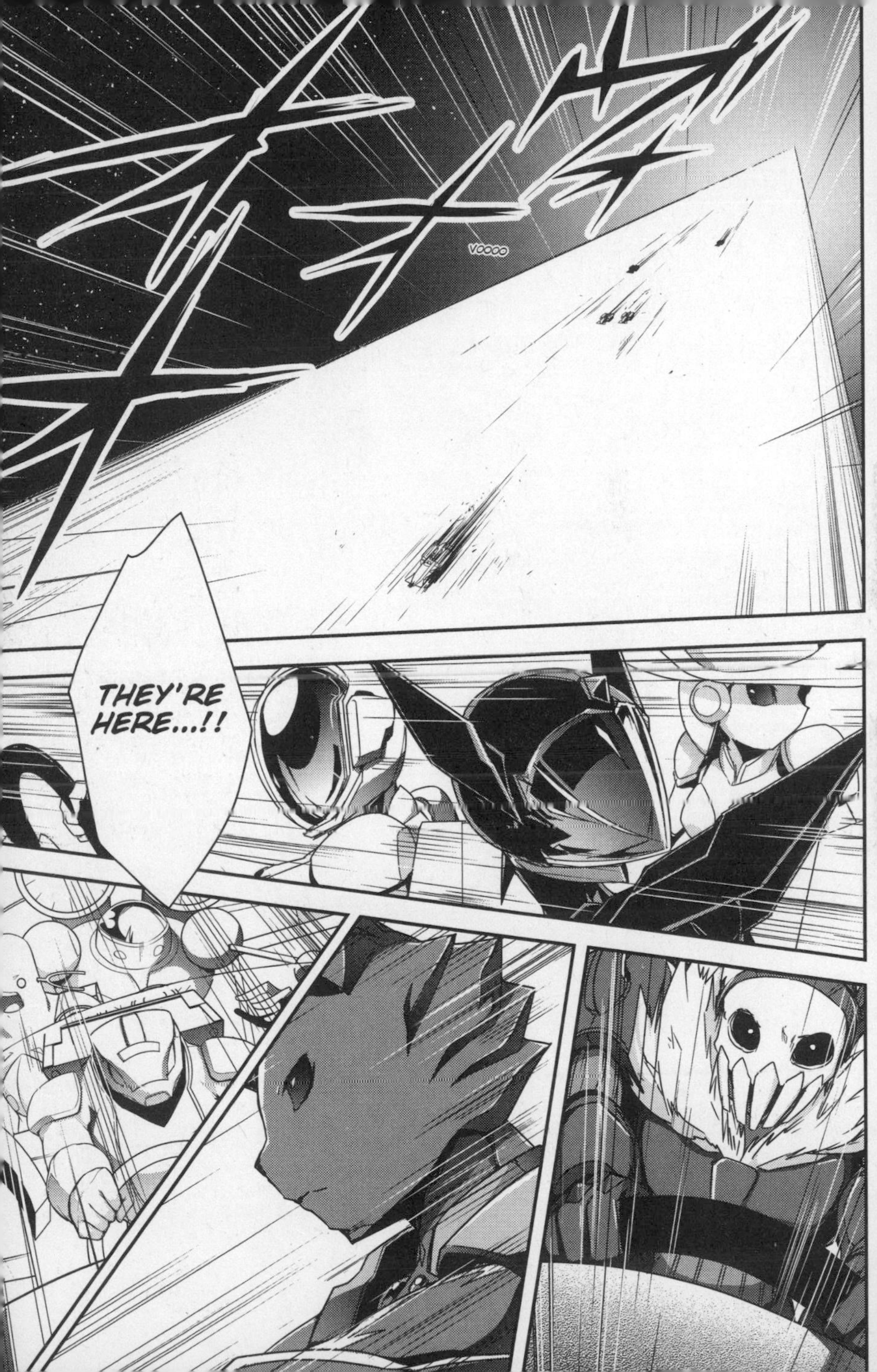
VOOOO
THEY'RE HERE...!!

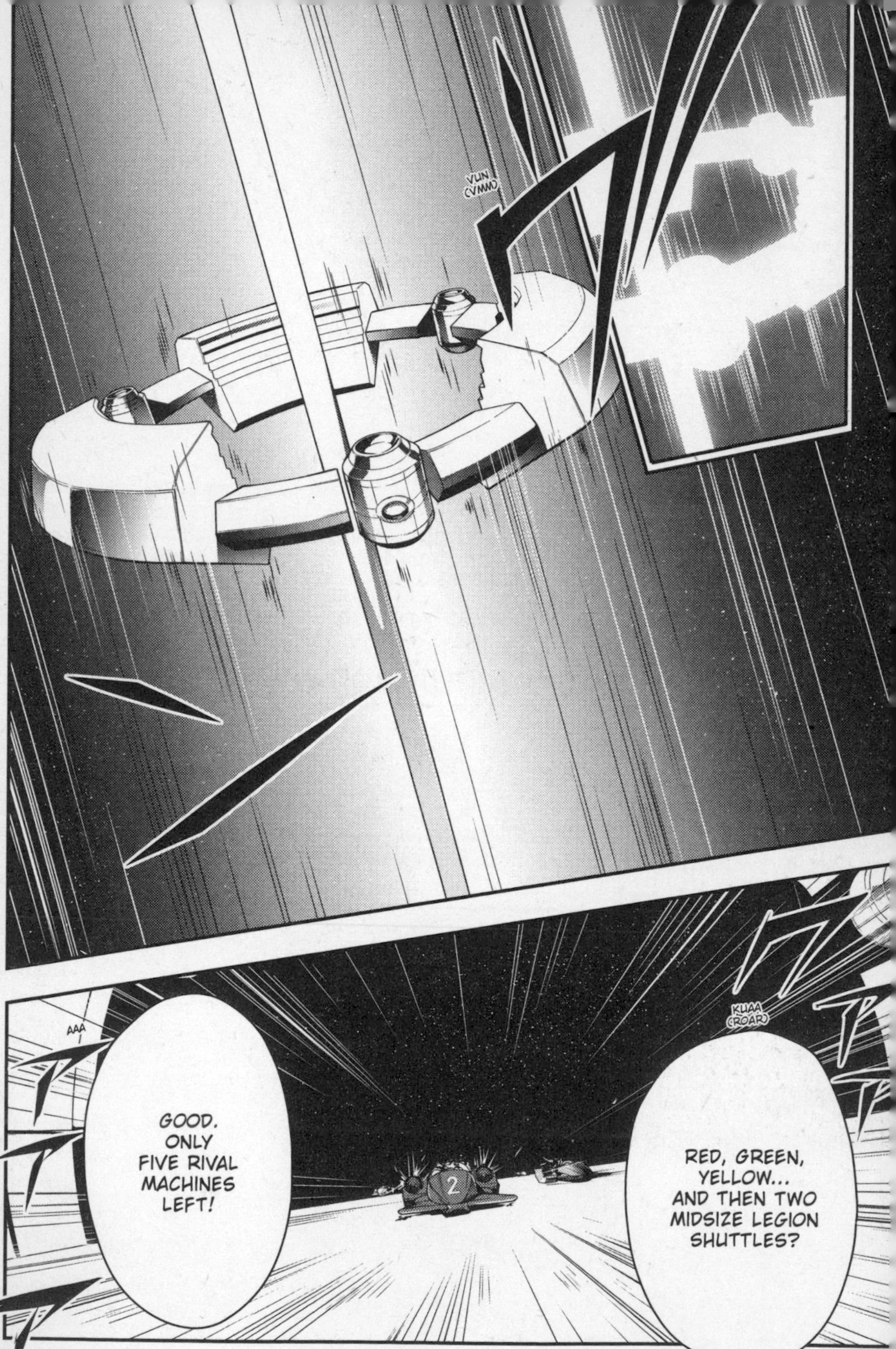
VUN (VMM)
KUAA (ROAR)
RED, GREEN, YELLOW... AND THEN TWO MIDSIZE LEGION SHUTTLES?
AAA
GOOD. ONLY FIVE RIVAL MACHINES LEFT!

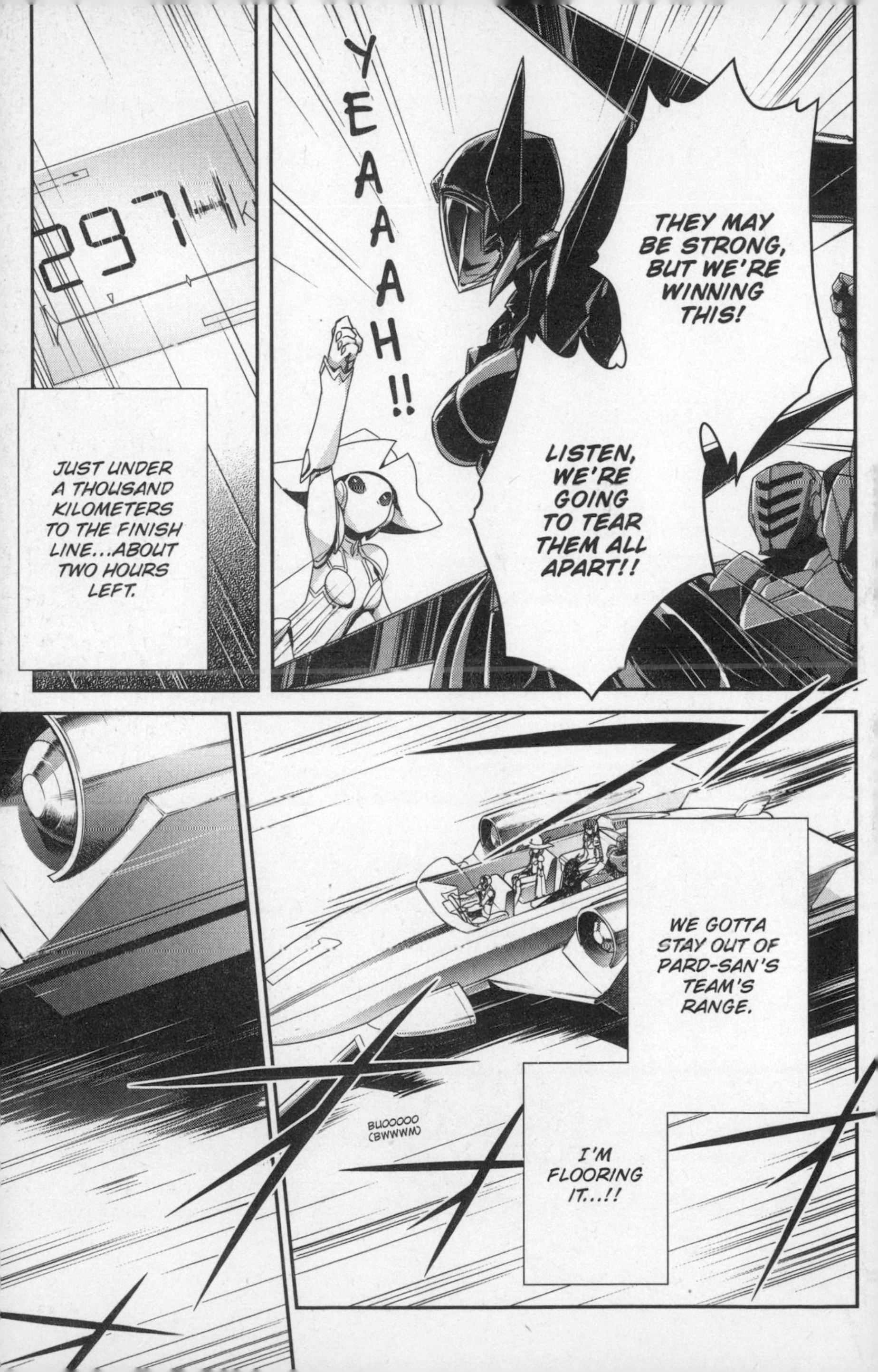
THEY MAY BE STRONG, BUT WE'RE WINNING THIS!
LISTEN, WE'RE GOING TO TEAR THEM ALL APART!!
YEAAAAH!!
2971
JUST UNDER A THOUSAND KILOMETERS TO THE FINISH LINE...ABOUT TWO HOURS LEFT.
WE GOTTA STAY OUT OF PARD-SAN'S TEAM'S RANGE.
BUOOOOO (BWWWM)
I'M FLOORING IT...!!

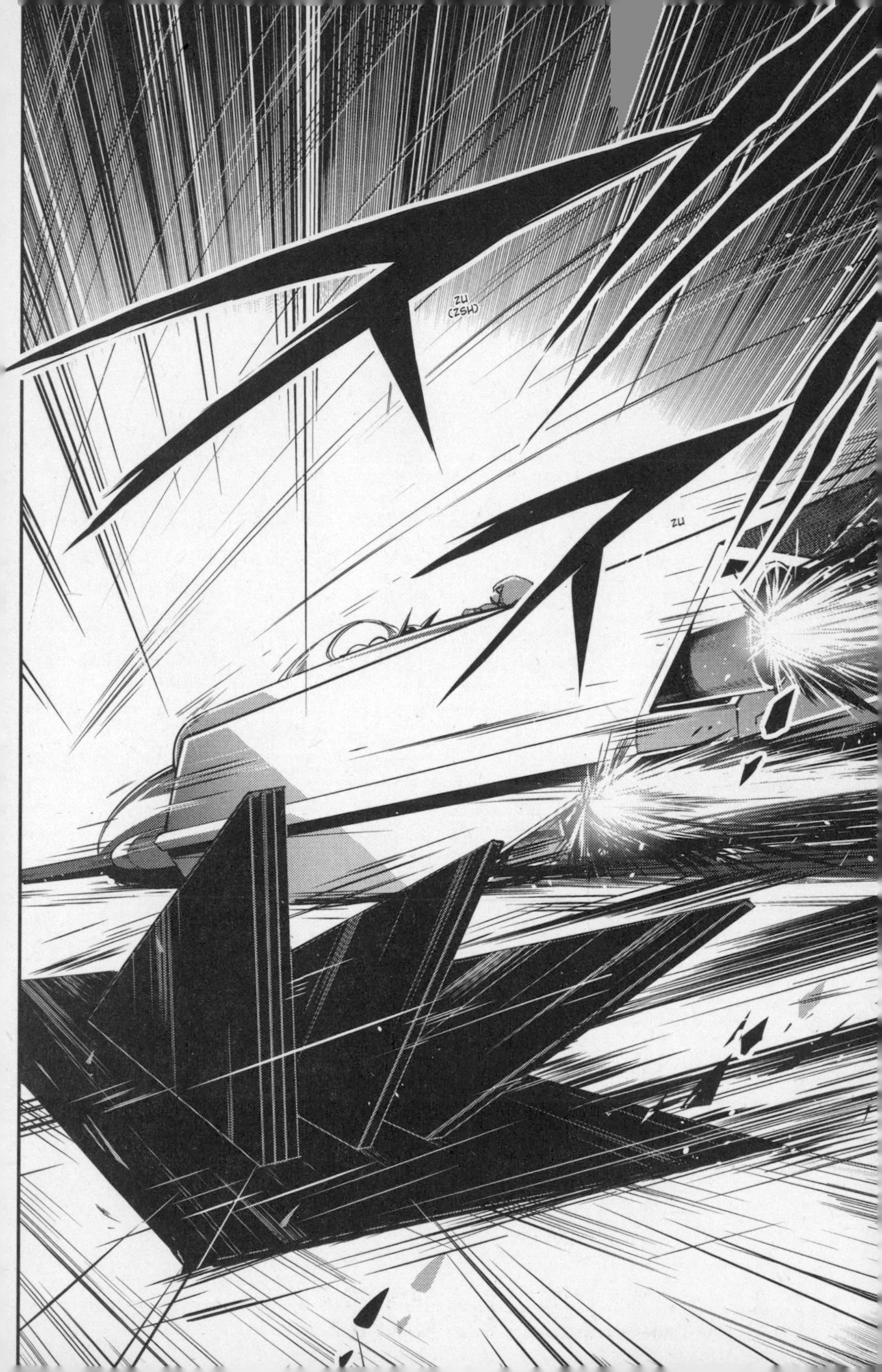
ZU
(ZSH)
ZU

ACCEL·WORLD

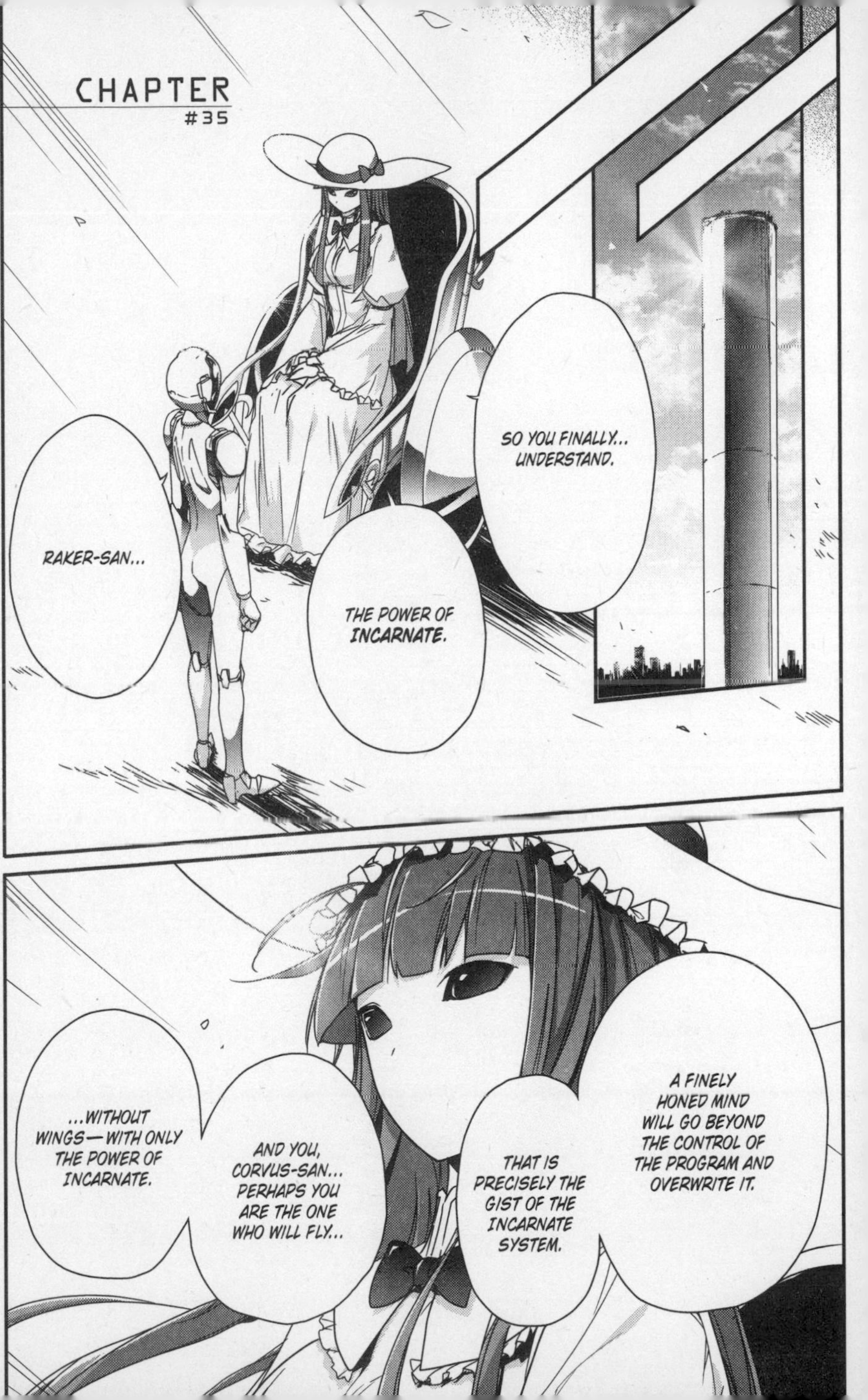
CHAPTER #35
SO YOU FINALLY... UNDERSTAND.
THE POWER OF INCARNATE.
RAKER-SAN...
A FINELY HONED MIND WILL GO BEYOND THE CONTROL OF THE PROGRAM AND OVERWRITE IT.
THAT IS PRECISELY THE GIST OF THE INCARNATE SYSTEM.
AND YOU, CORVUS-SAN... PERHAPS YOU ARE THE ONE WHO WILL FLY...
...WITHOUT WINGS—WITH ONLY THE POWER OF INCARNATE.

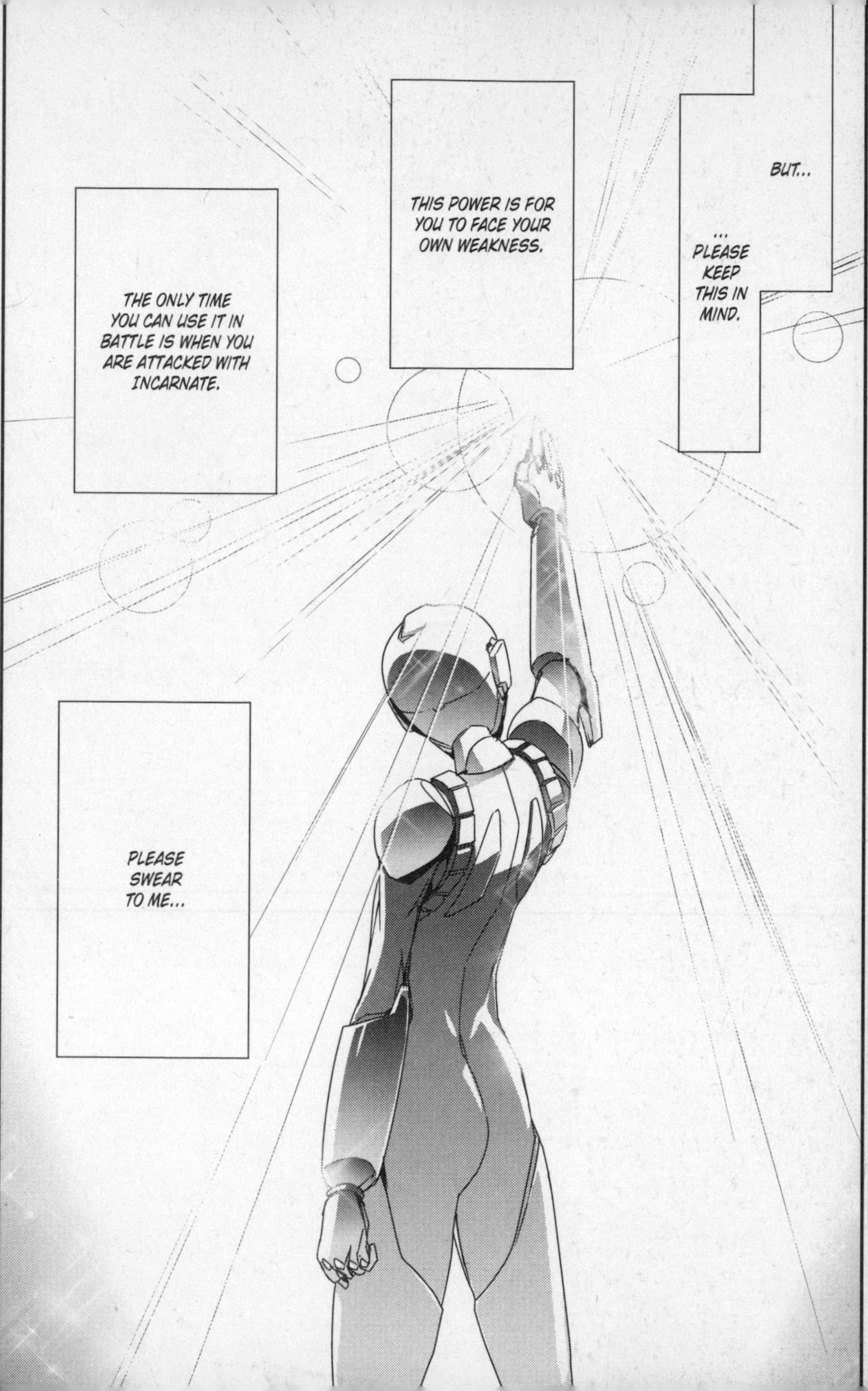
BUT...
... PLEASE KEEP THIS IN MIND.
THIS POWER IS FOR YOU TO FACE YOUR OWN WEAKNESS.
THE ONLY TIME YOU CAN USE IT IN BATTLE IS WHEN YOU ARE ATTACKED WITH INCARNATE.
PLEASE SWEAR TO ME...

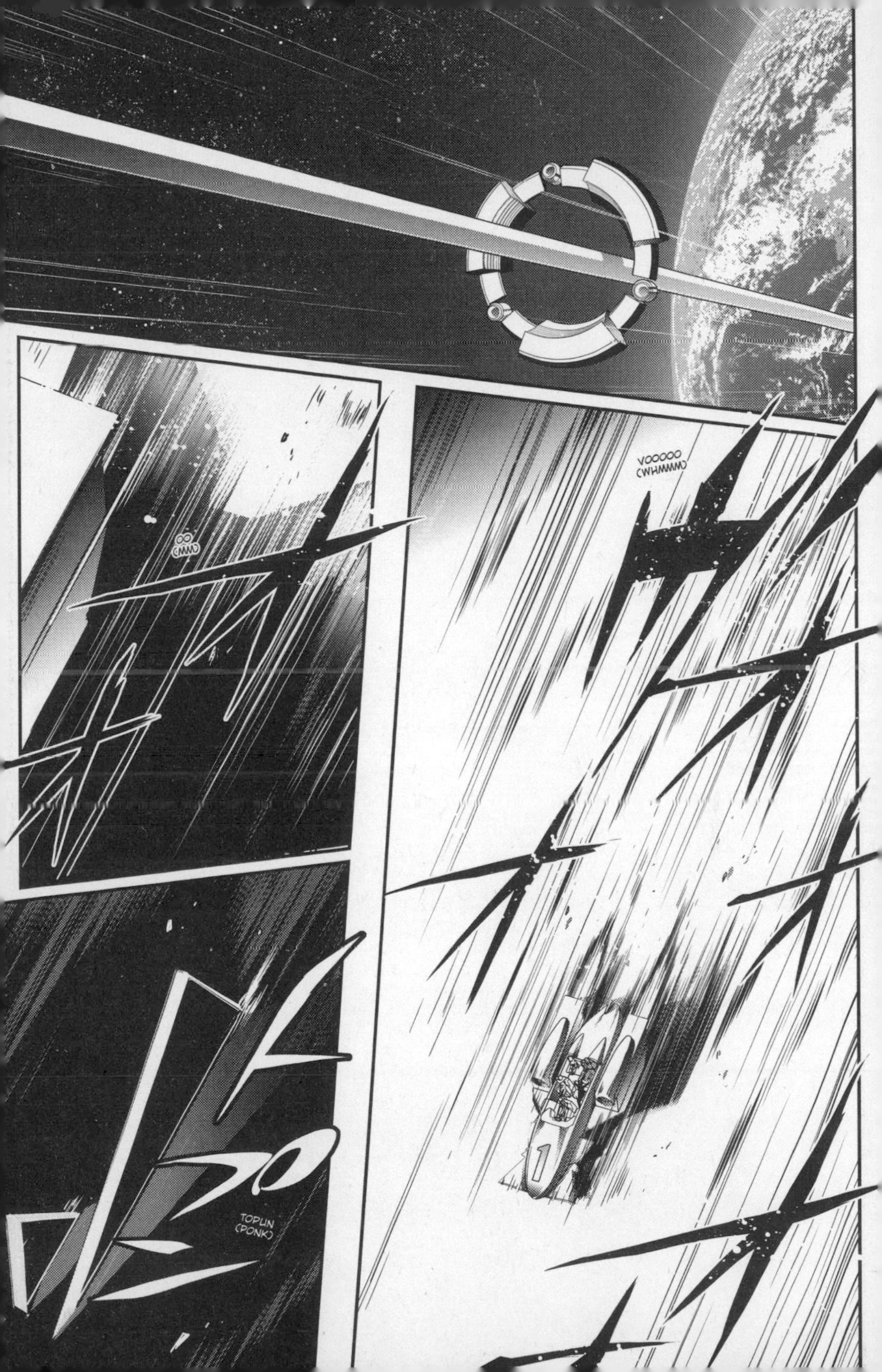
VOOOOO
(WHMMMM)
OO
(MMM)
TOPUN
(PONK)

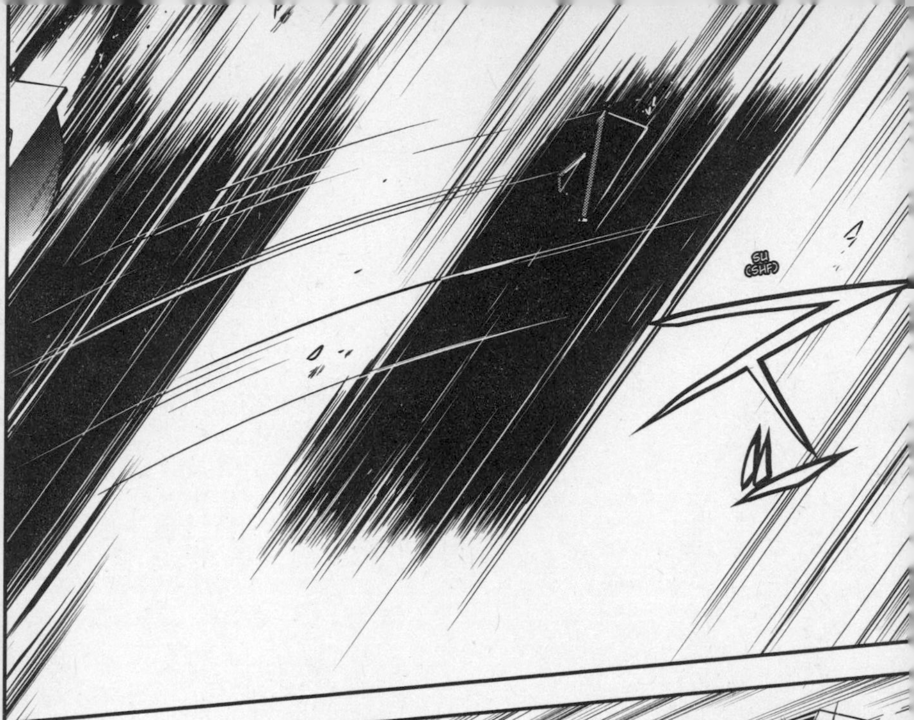
SU
(SHF)

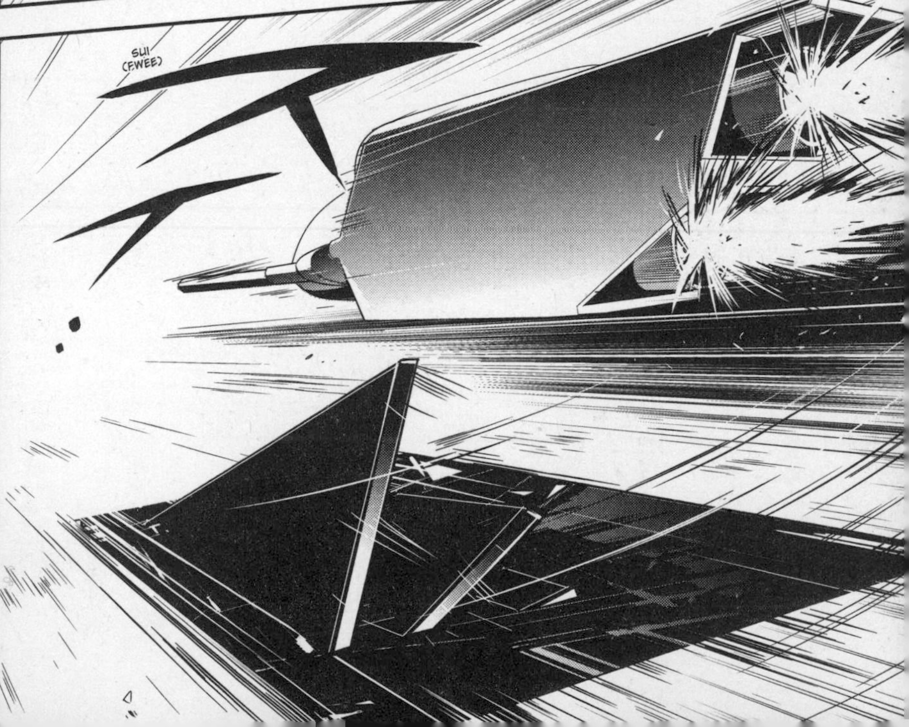
SUI
(FWEE)

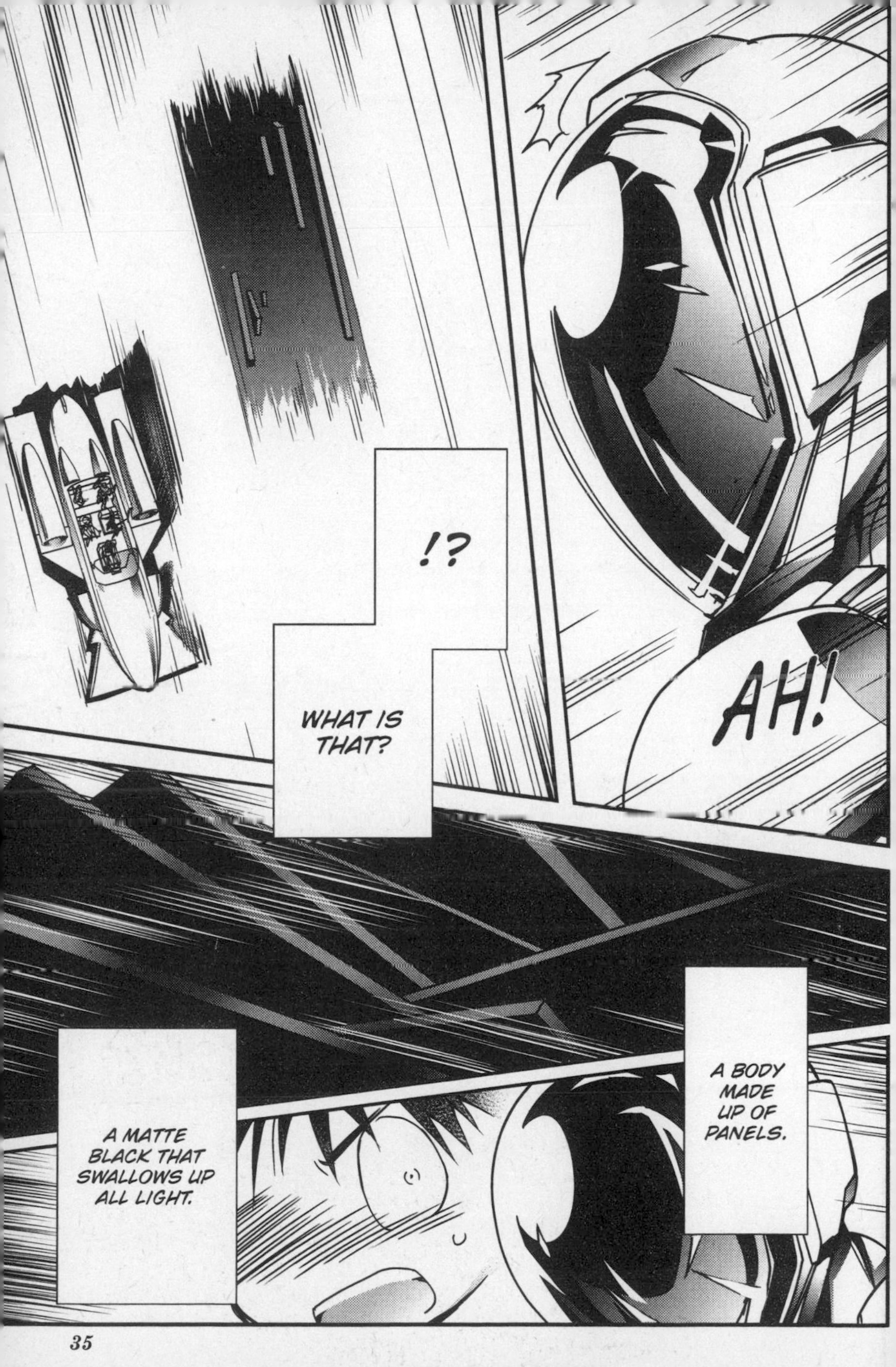
AH!
!?
WHAT IS THAT?
A BODY MADE UP OF PANELS.
A MATTE BLACK THAT SWALLOWS UP ALL LIGHT.

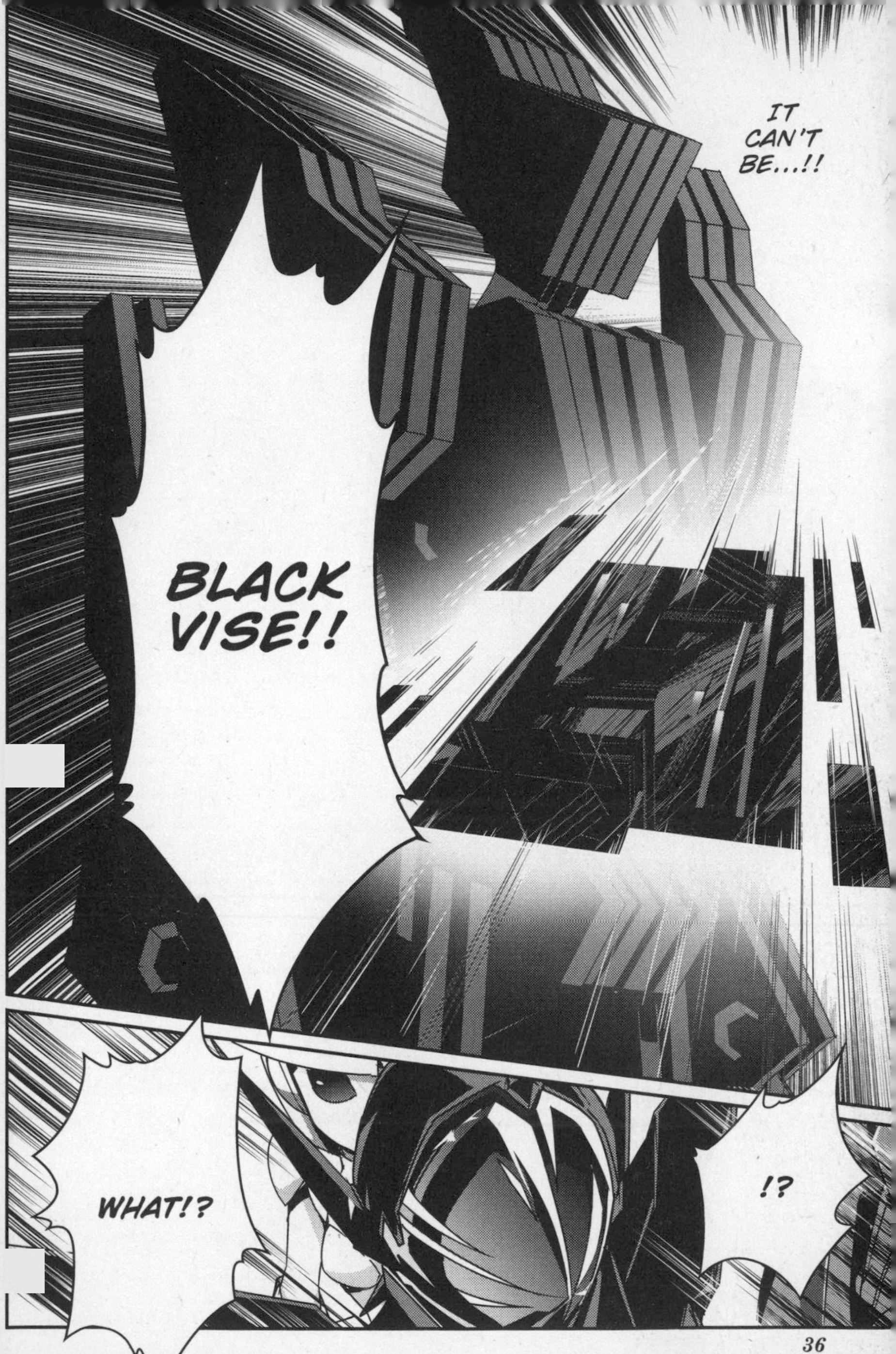
IT CAN'T BE...!!
BLACK VISE!!
!?
WHAT!?

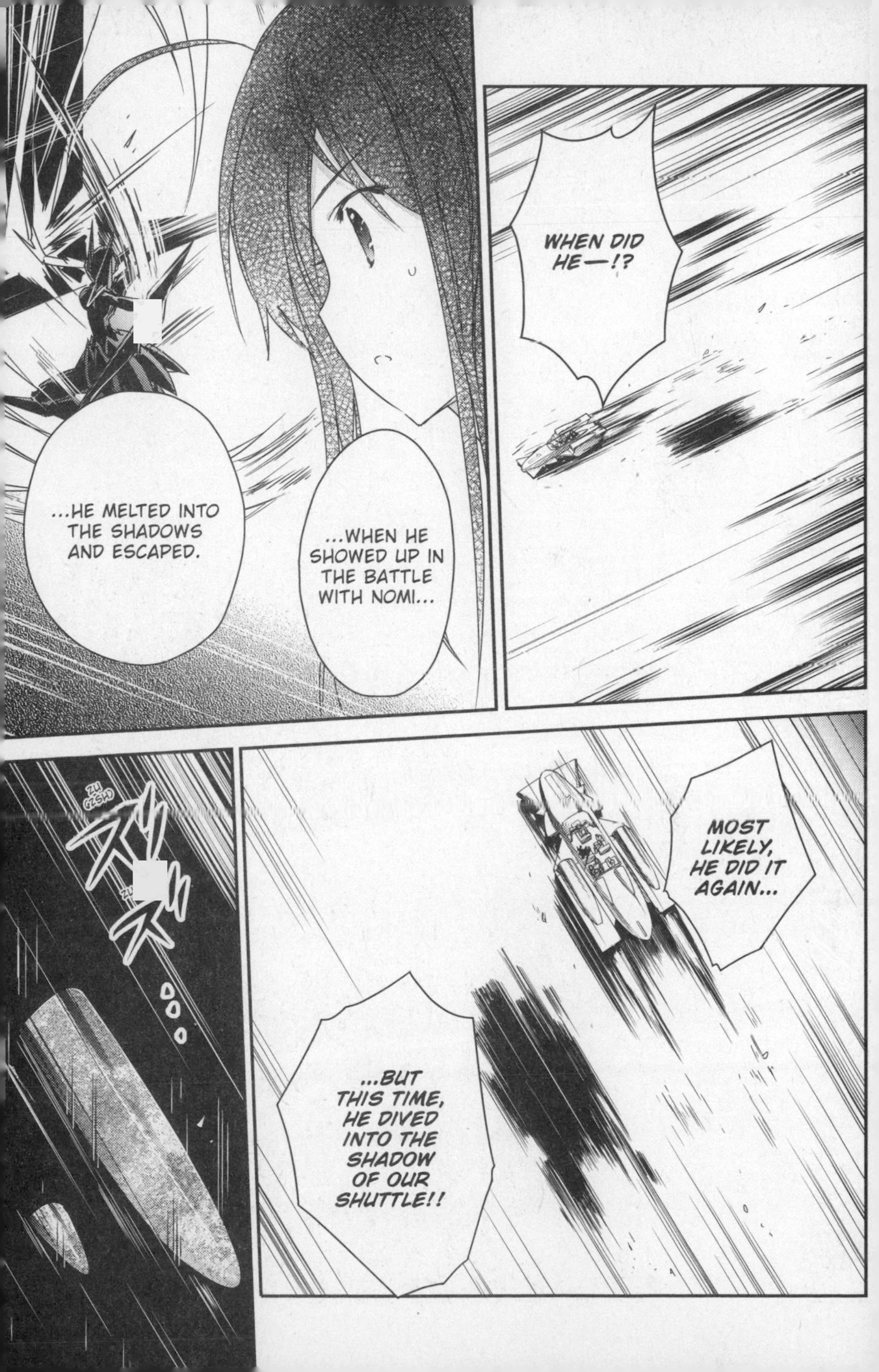
WHEN DID HE—!?
...WHEN HE SHOWED UP IN THE BATTLE WITH NOMI...
...HE MELTED INTO THE SHADOWS AND ESCAPED.
MOST LIKELY, HE DID IT AGAIN...
...BUT THIS TIME, HE DIVED INTO THE SHADOW OF OUR SHUTTLE!!

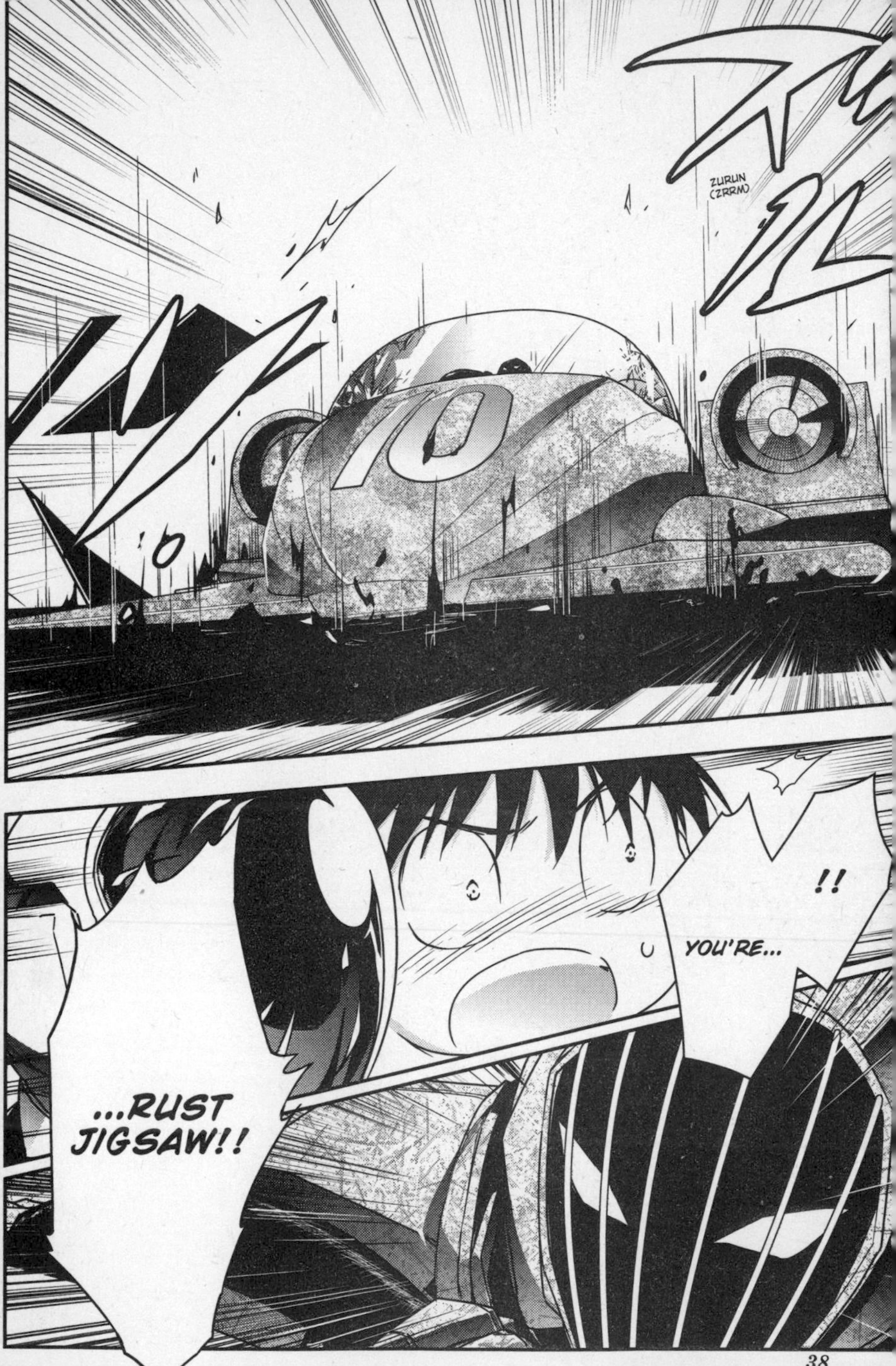
ZURUN (ZRRM)
!!
YOU'RE...
...RUST JIGSAW!!

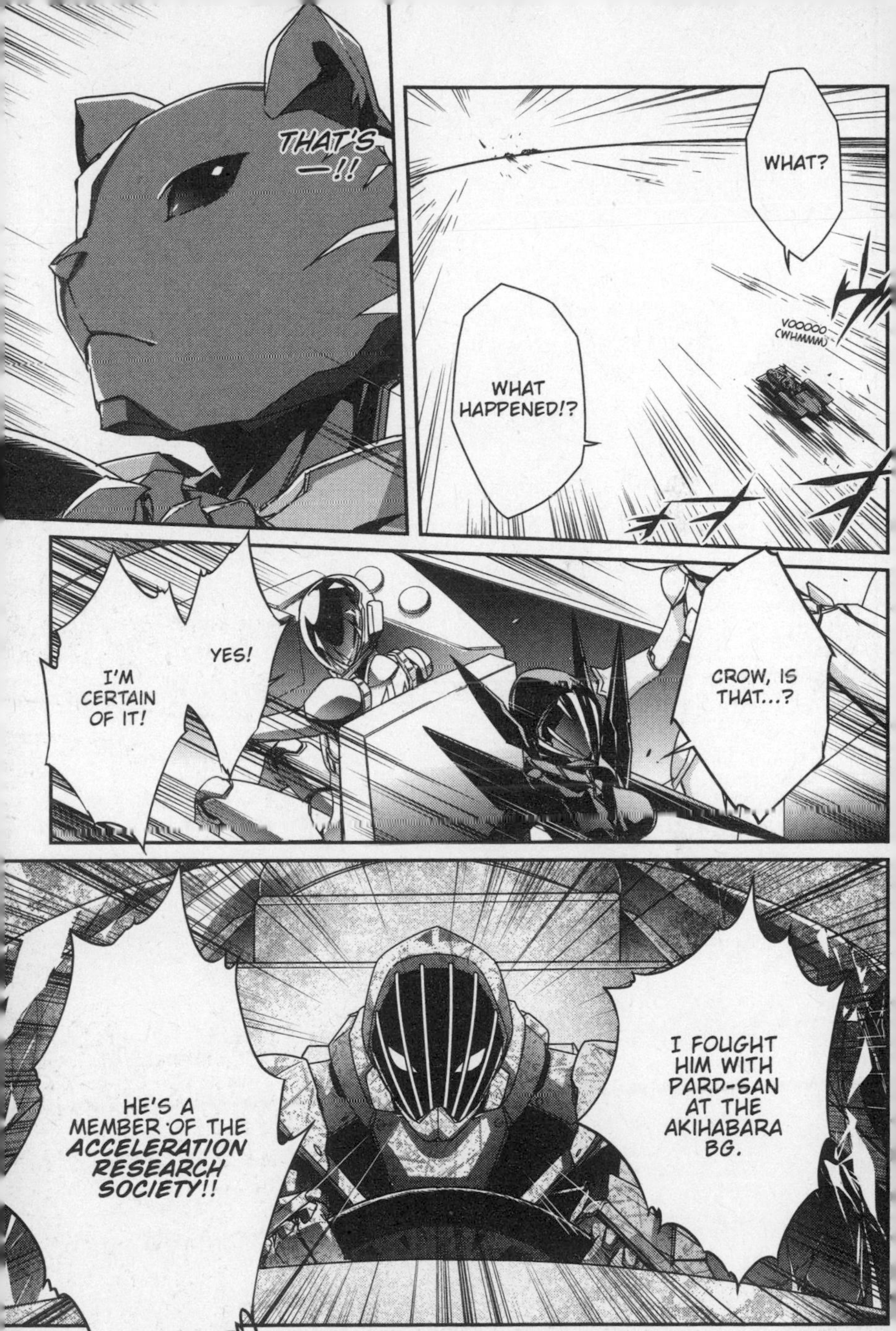
WHAT?
WHAT HAPPENED!?
VOOOOO (WHMMMM)
THAT'S—!!
CROW, IS THAT...?
YES!
I'M CERTAIN OF IT!
I FOUGHT HIM WITH PARD-SAN AT THE AKIHABARA BG.
HE'S A MEMBER OF THE ACCELERATION RESEARCH SOCIETY!!

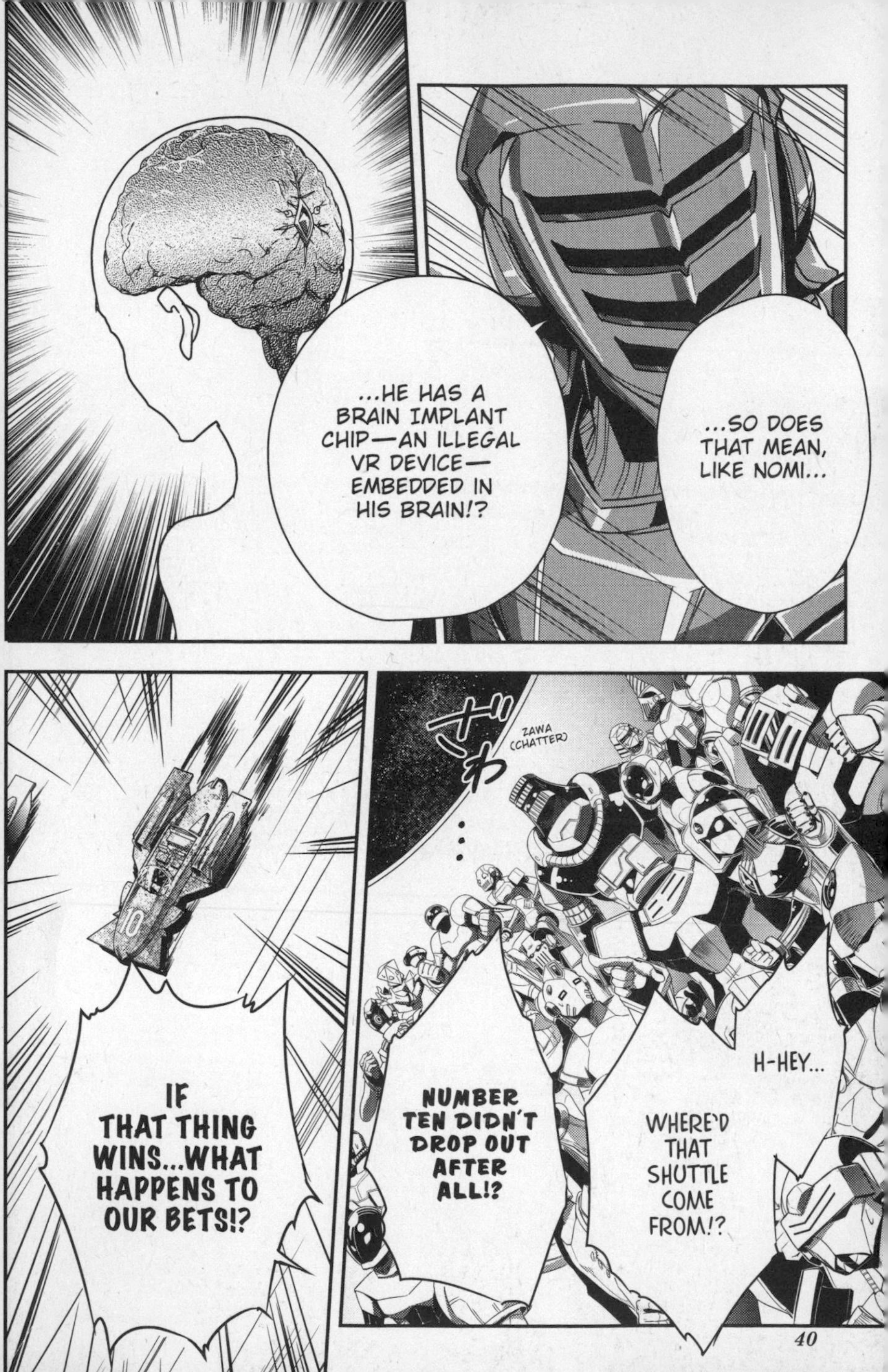
...SO DOES THAT MEAN, LIKE NOMI...
...HE HAS A BRAIN IMPLANT CHIP—AN ILLEGAL VR DEVICE—EMBEDDED IN HIS BRAIN!?
ざわ...
ZAWA (CHATTER)
H-HEY...
WHERE'D THAT SHUTTLE COME FROM!?
NUMBER TEN DIDN'T DROP OUT AFTER ALL!?
IF THAT THING WINS...WHAT HAPPENS TO OUR BETS!?

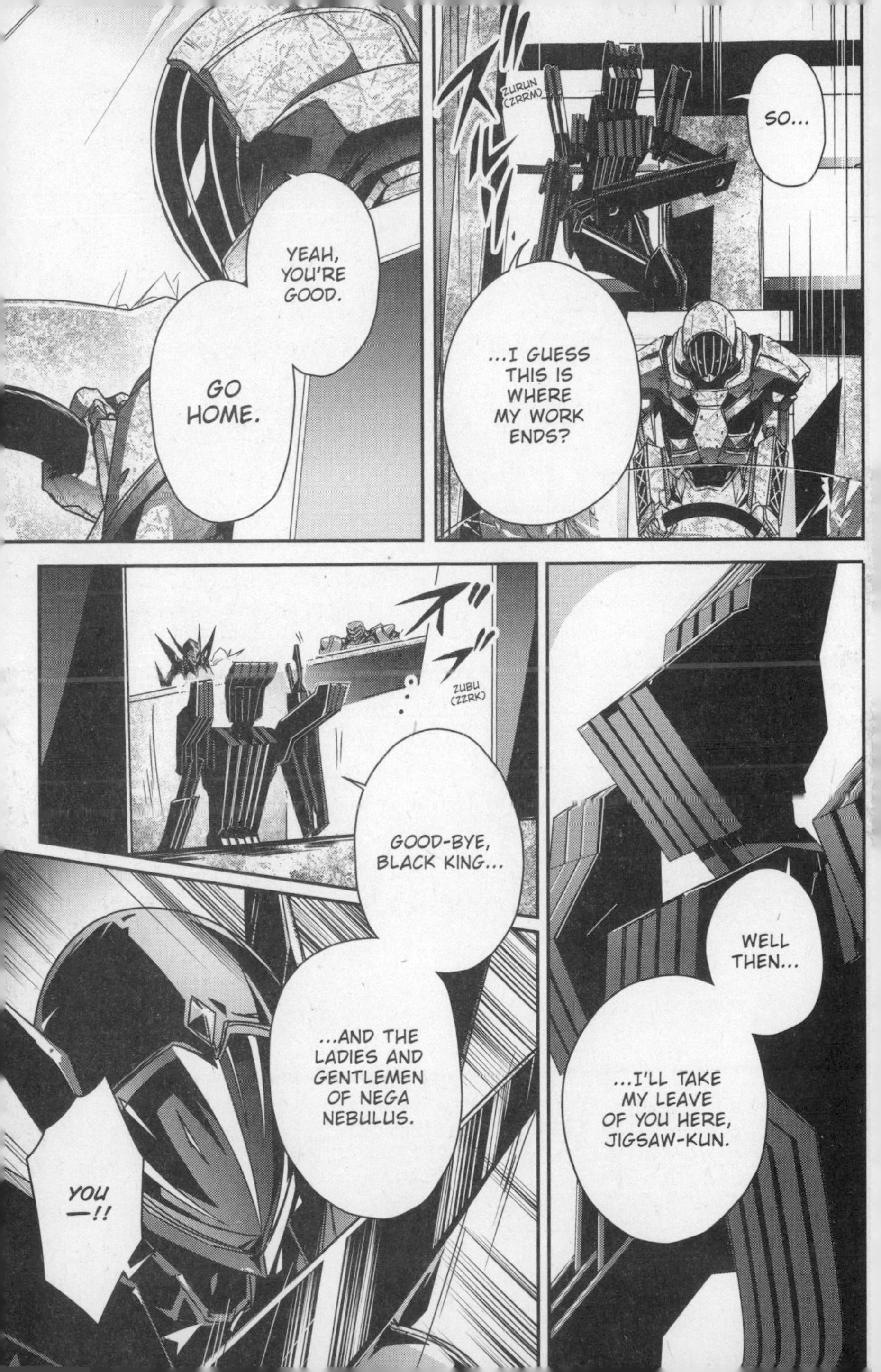
SO...
ZURUN (ZZRRM)
...I GUESS THIS IS WHERE MY WORK ENDS?
YEAH, YOU'RE GOOD.
GO HOME.
WELL THEN...
...I'LL TAKE MY LEAVE OF YOU HERE, JIGSAW-KUN.
ZUBU (ZZRK)
GOOD-BYE, BLACK KING...
...AND THE LADIES AND GENTLEMEN OF NEGA NEBULUS.
YOU—!!

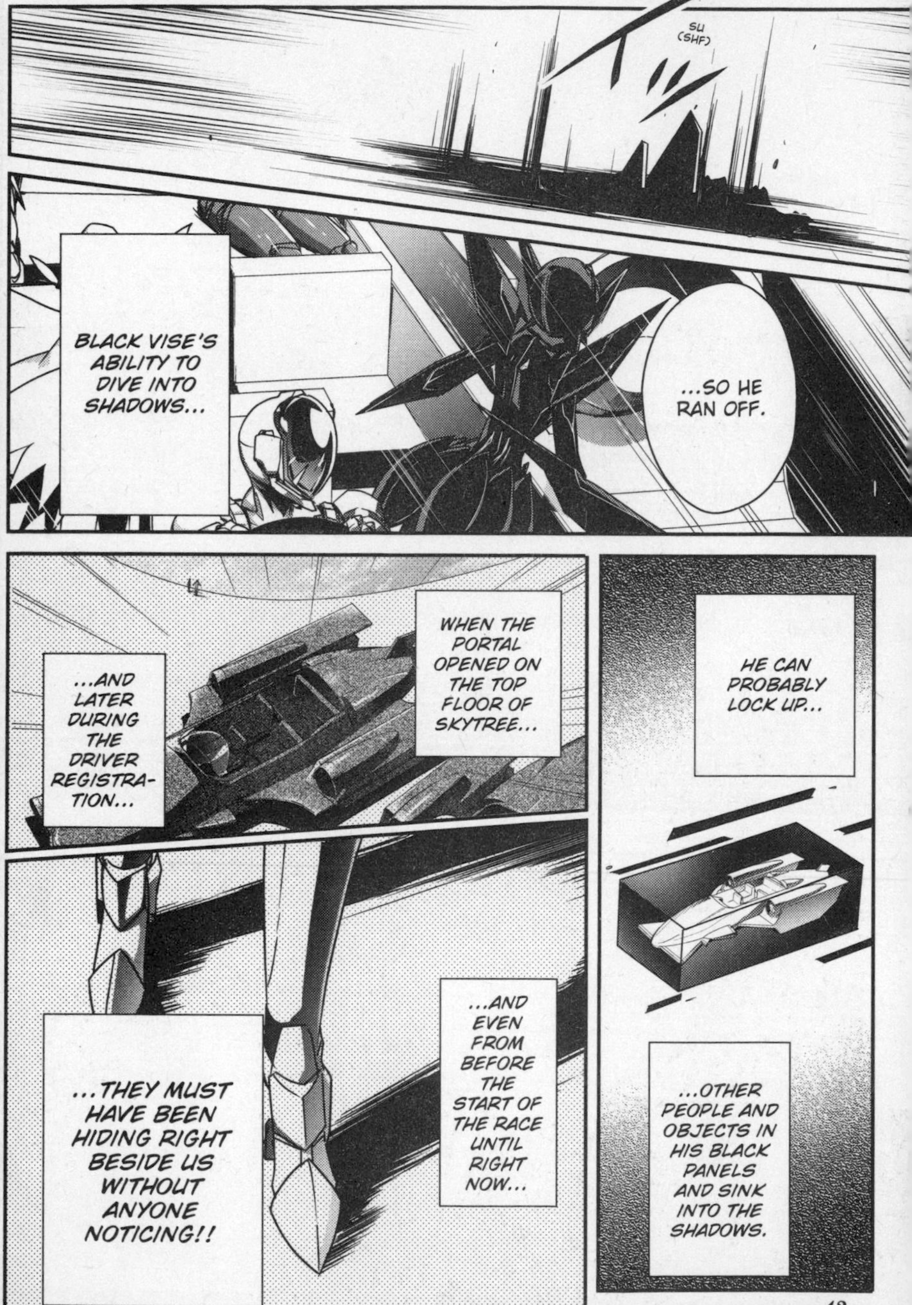
SU (SHF)
...SO HE RAN OFF.
BLACK VISE'S ABILITY TO DIVE INTO SHADOWS...
HE CAN PROBABLY LOCK UP...
...OTHER PEOPLE AND OBJECTS IN HIS BLACK PANELS AND SINK INTO THE SHADOWS.
WHEN THE PORTAL OPENED ON THE TOP FLOOR OF SKYTREE...
...AND LATER DURING THE DRIVER REGISTRATION...
...AND EVEN FROM BEFORE THE START OF THE RACE UNTIL RIGHT NOW...
...THEY MUST HAVE BEEN HIDING RIGHT BESIDE US WITHOUT ANYONE NOTICING!!

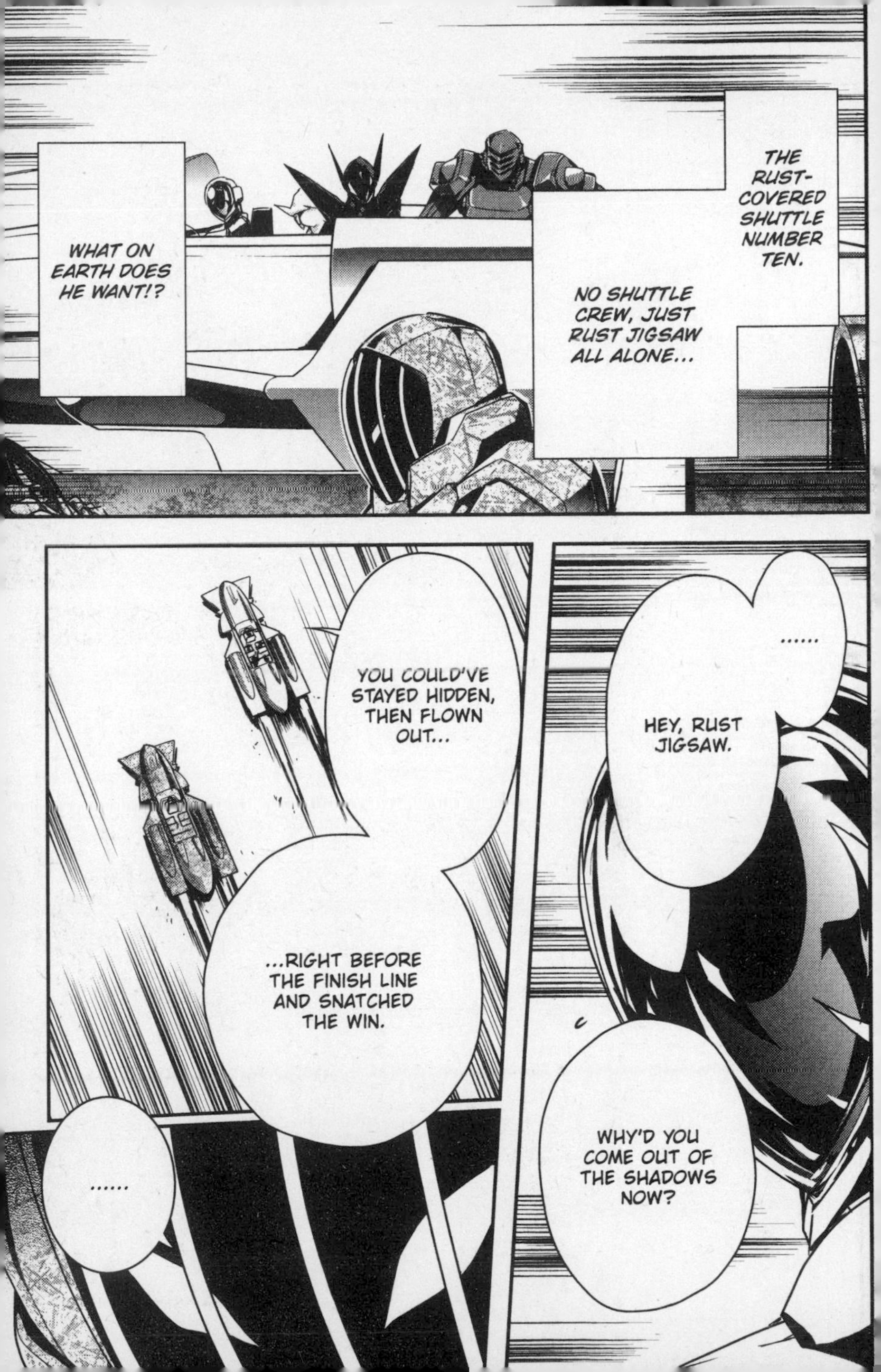
THE RUST-COVERED SHUTTLE NUMBER TEN.
NO SHUTTLE CREW, JUST RUST JIGSAW ALL ALONE...
WHAT ON EARTH DOES HE WANT!?
......
HEY, RUST JIGSAW.
WHY'D YOU COME OUT OF THE SHADOWS NOW?
YOU COULD'VE STAYED HIDDEN, THEN FLOWN OUT...
...RIGHT BEFORE THE FINISH LINE AND SNATCHED THE WIN.
......

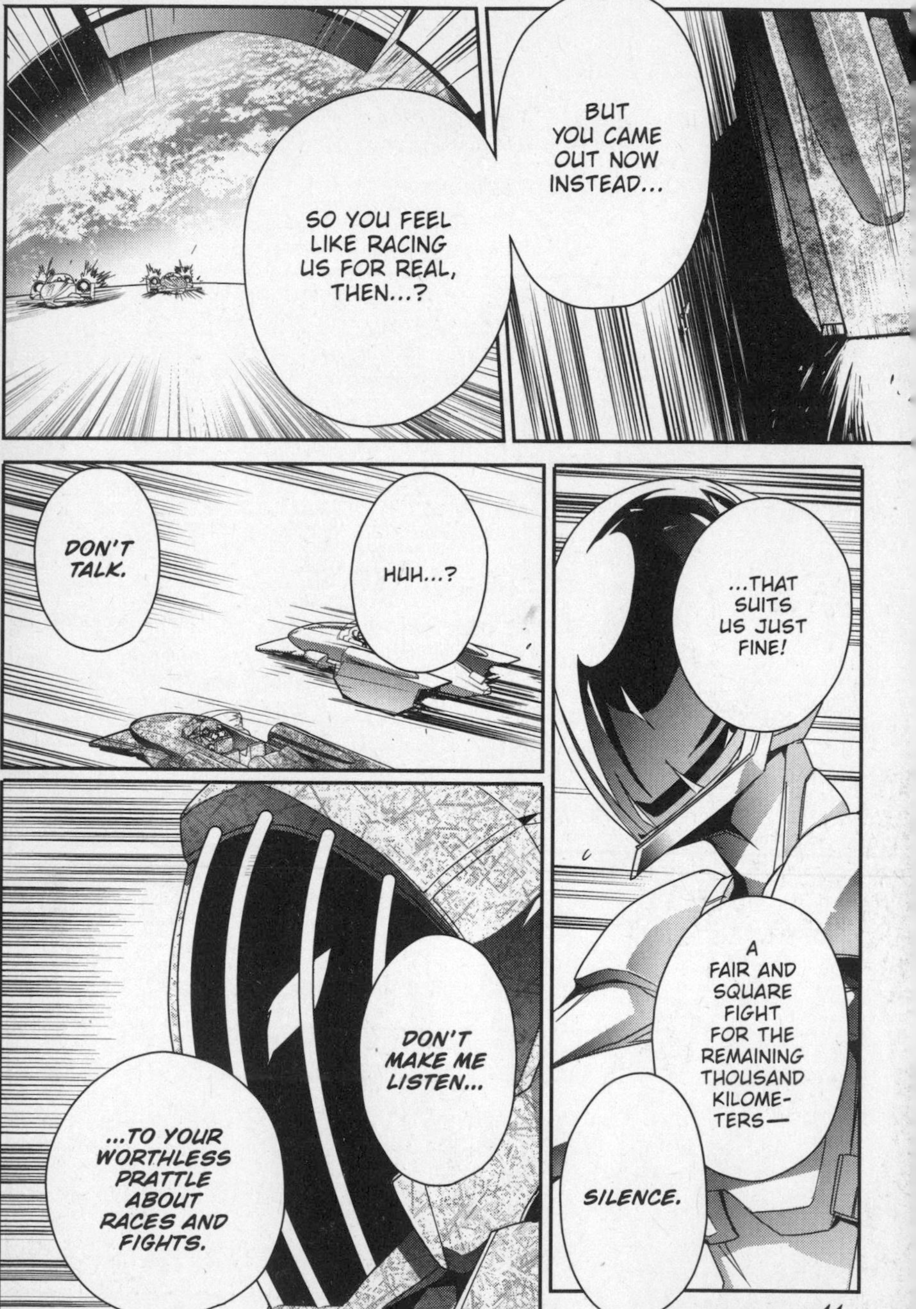
BUT YOU CAME OUT NOW INSTEAD...
SO YOU FEEL LIKE RACING US FOR REAL, THEN...?
...THAT SUITS US JUST FINE!
A FAIR AND SQUARE FIGHT FOR THE REMAINING THOUSAND KILOMETERS—
SILENCE.
HUH...?
DON'T TALK.
DON'T MAKE ME LISTEN...
...TO YOUR WORTHLESS PRATTLE ABOUT RACES AND FIGHTS.

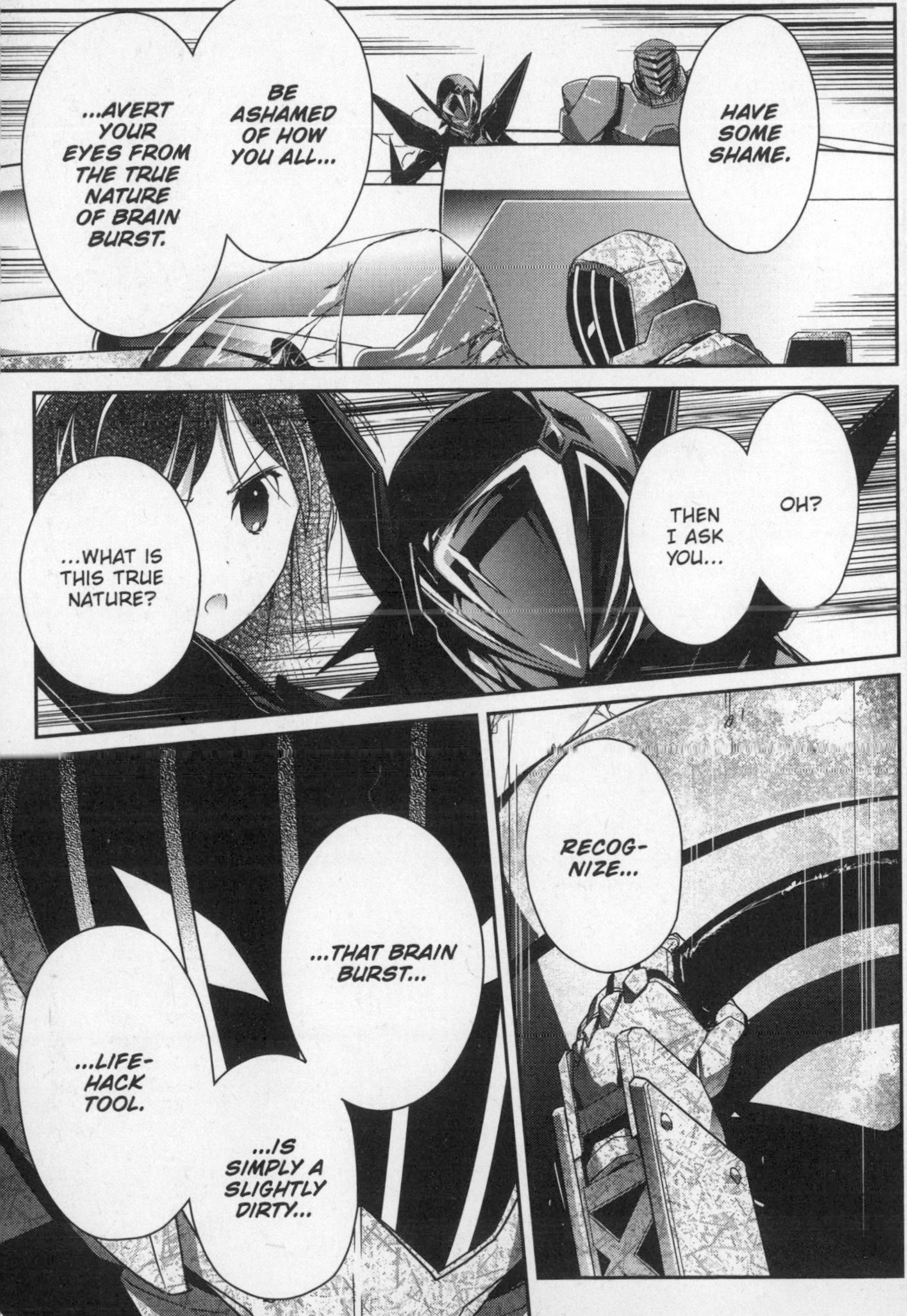
HAVE SOME SHAME.
BE ASHAMED OF HOW YOU ALL...
...AVERT YOUR EYES FROM THE TRUE NATURE OF BRAIN BURST.
OH?
THEN I ASK YOU...
...WHAT IS THIS TRUE NATURE?
RECOG-NIZE...
...THAT BRAIN BURST...
...IS SIMPLY A SLIGHTLY DIRTY...
...LIFE-HACK TOOL.

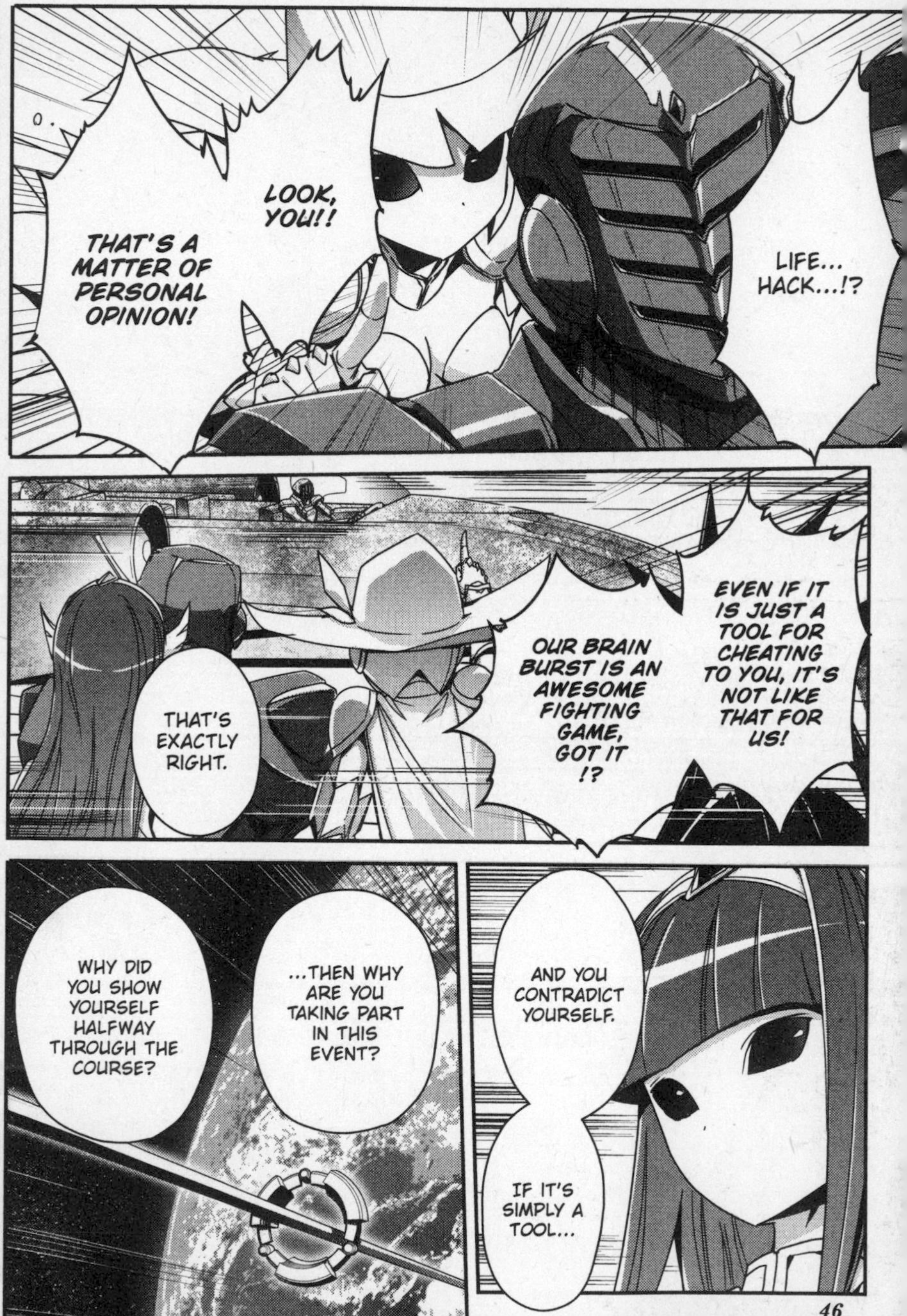
LIFE... HACK...!?
LOOK, YOU!!
THAT'S A MATTER OF PERSONAL OPINION!
EVEN IF IT IS JUST A TOOL FOR CHEATING TO YOU, IT'S NOT LIKE THAT FOR US!
OUR BRAIN BURST IS AN AWESOME FIGHTING GAME, GOT IT!?
THAT'S EXACTLY RIGHT.
AND YOU CONTRADICT YOURSELF.
IF IT'S SIMPLY A TOOL...
...THEN WHY ARE YOU TAKING PART IN THIS EVENT?
WHY DID YOU SHOW YOURSELF HALFWAY THROUGH THE COURSE?

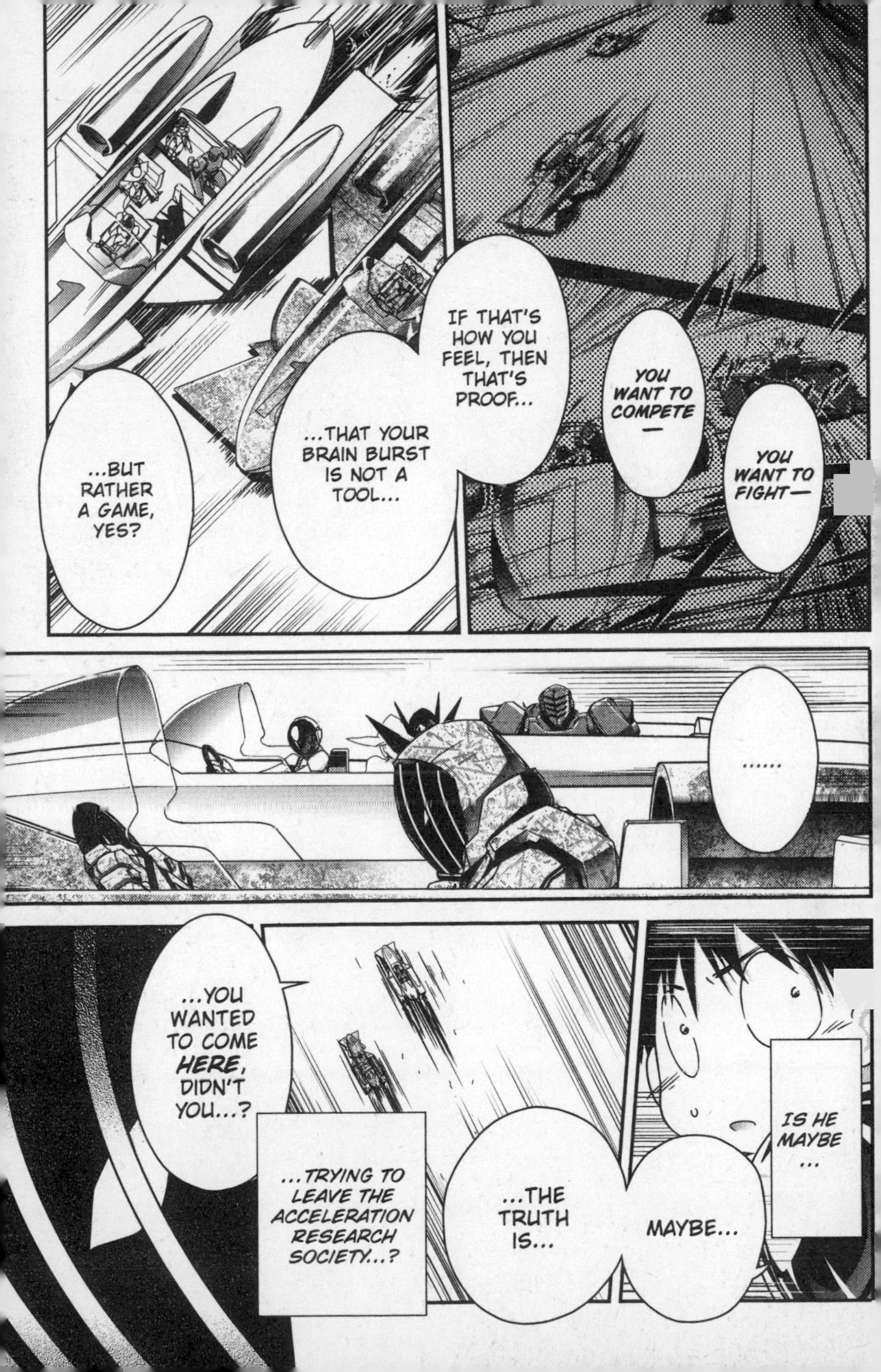
YOU WANT TO FIGHT—
YOU WANT TO COMPETE—
IF THAT'S HOW YOU FEEL, THEN THAT'S PROOF...
...THAT YOUR BRAIN BURST IS NOT A TOOL...
...BUT RATHER A GAME, YES?
......
IS HE MAYBE ...
MAYBE...
...THE TRUTH IS...
...YOU WANTED TO COME *HERE*, DIDN'T YOU...?
...TRYING TO LEAVE THE ACCELERATION RESEARCH SOCIETY...?

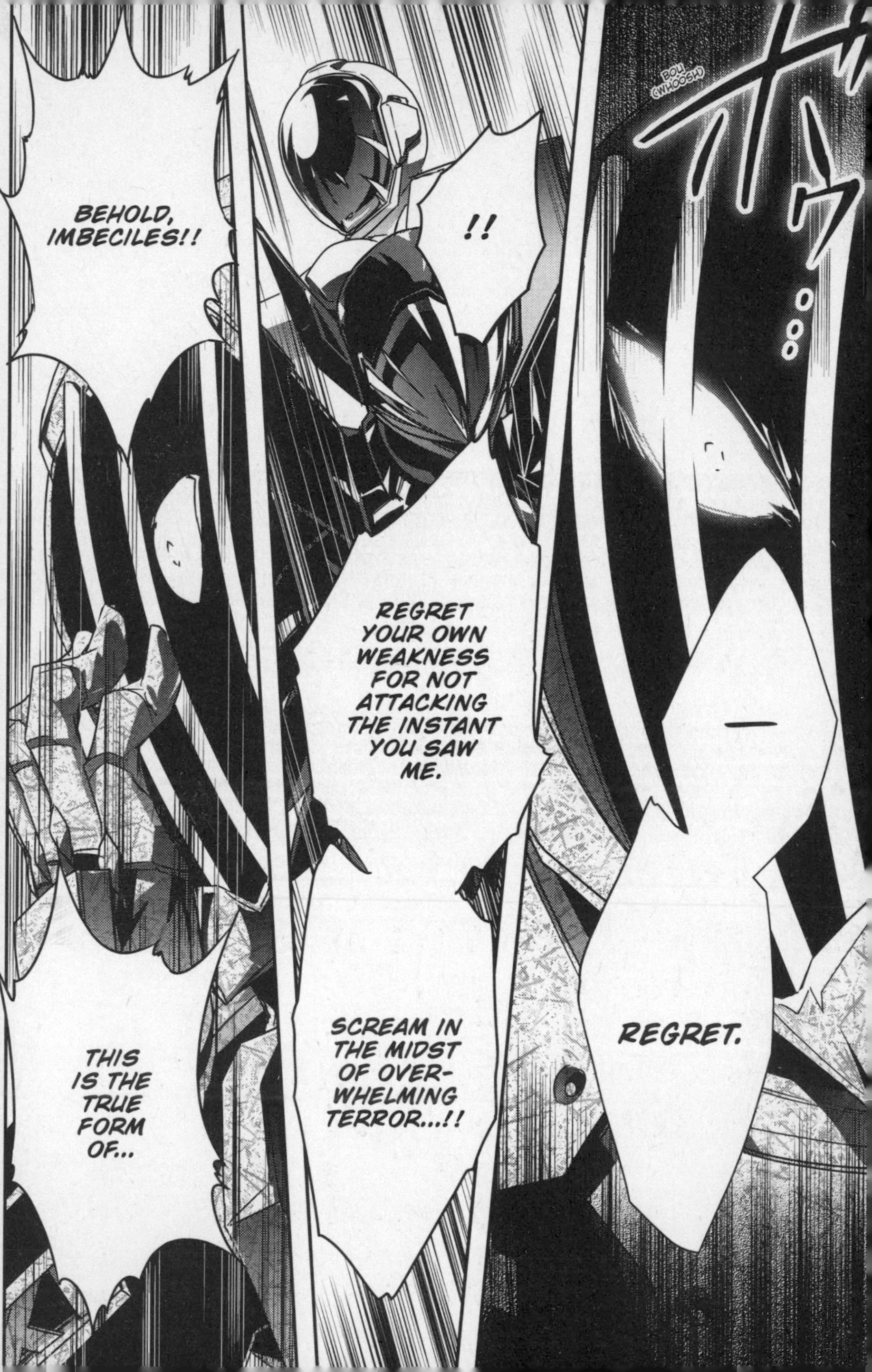
BOU (WHOOSH)
—
REGRET.
!!
REGRET YOUR OWN WEAKNESS FOR NOT ATTACKING THE INSTANT YOU SAW ME.
SCREAM IN THE MIDST OF OVER-WHELMING TERROR...!!
BEHOLD, IMBECILES!!
THIS IS THE TRUE FORM OF...

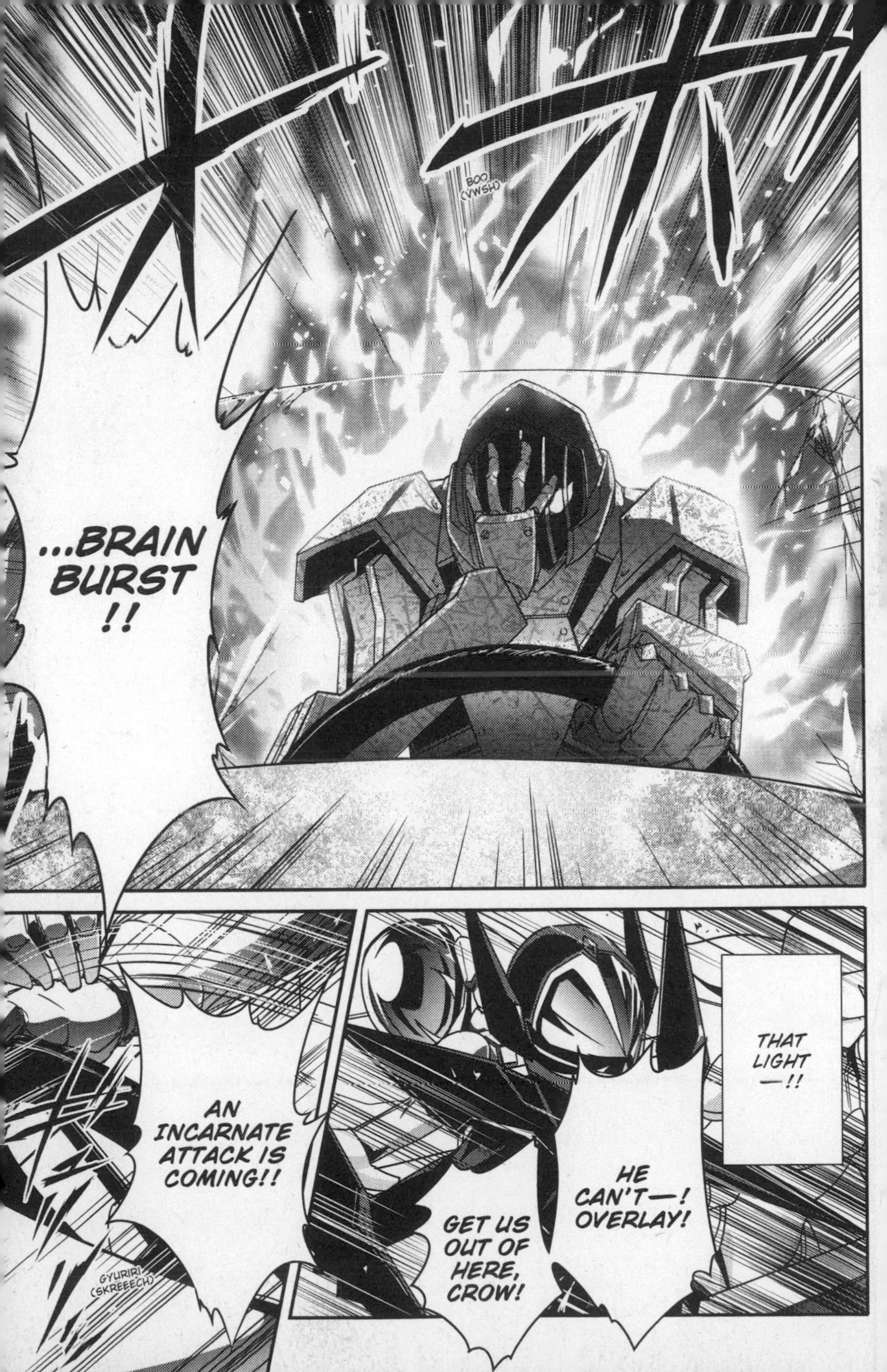
BOO (VWSH)
...BRAIN BURST!!
THAT LIGHT—!!
HE CAN'T—! OVERLAY!
GET US OUT OF HERE, CROW!
AN INCARNATE ATTACK IS COMING!!
GYURIRI (SKREEECH)

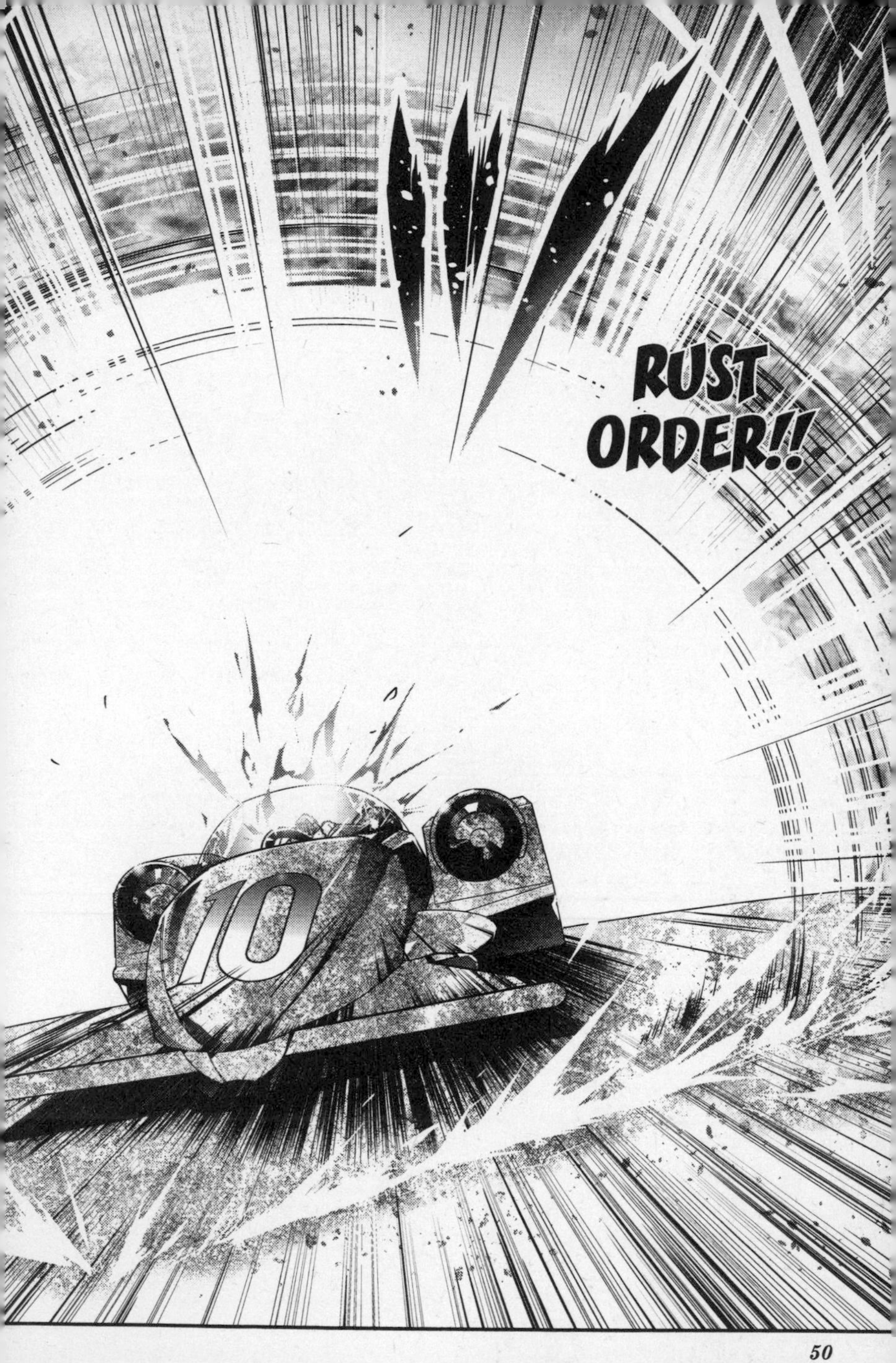
RUST ORDER!!
10

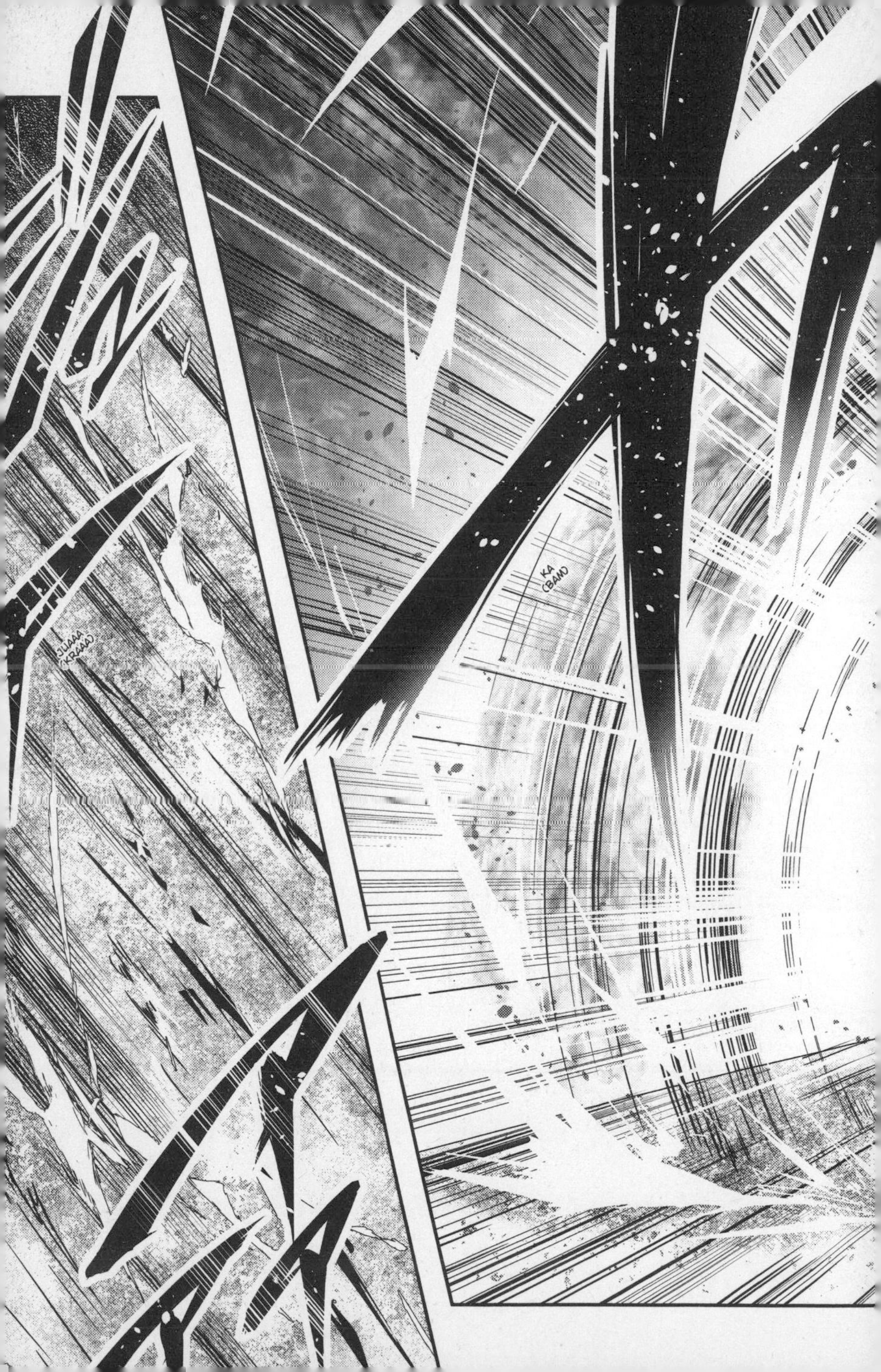
KA (BAM)
JUAAA (KRAAA)

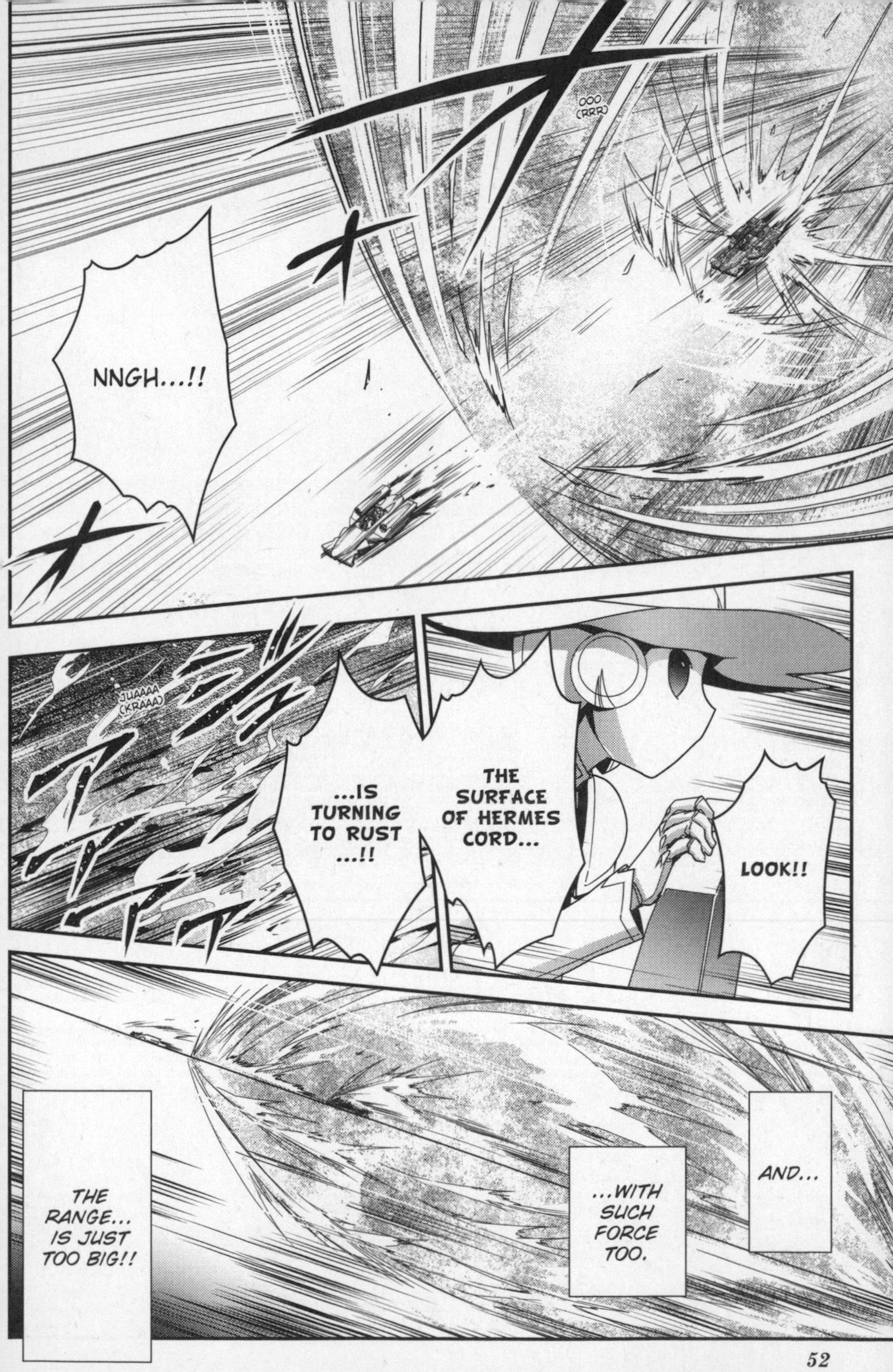
OOO (RRR)
NNGH...!!
LOOK!!
THE SURFACE OF HERMES CORD...
...IS TURNING TO RUST ...!!
JUAAAA (KRAAA)
AND...
...WITH SUCH FORCE TOO.
THE RANGE... IS JUST TOO BIG!!

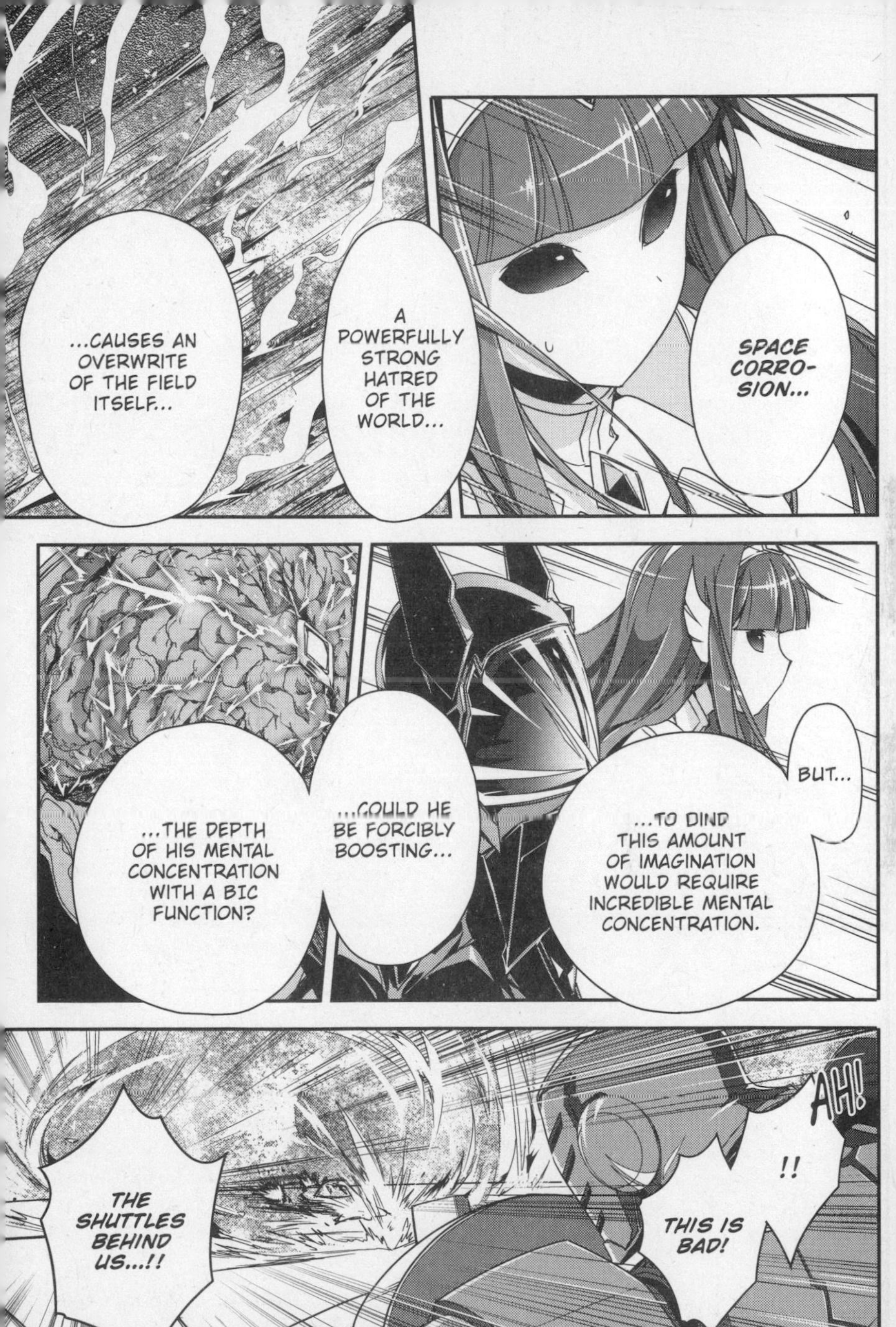
SPACE CORROSION...
A POWERFULLY STRONG HATRED OF THE WORLD...
...CAUSES AN OVERWRITE OF THE FIELD ITSELF...
BUT...
...TO DIND THIS AMOUNT OF IMAGINATION WOULD REQUIRE INCREDIBLE MENTAL CONCENTRATION.
...COULD HE BE FORCIBLY BOOSTING...
...THE DEPTH OF HIS MENTAL CONCENTRATION WITH A BIC FUNCTION?
AH!
!!
THIS IS BAD!
THE SHUTTLES BEHIND US...!!

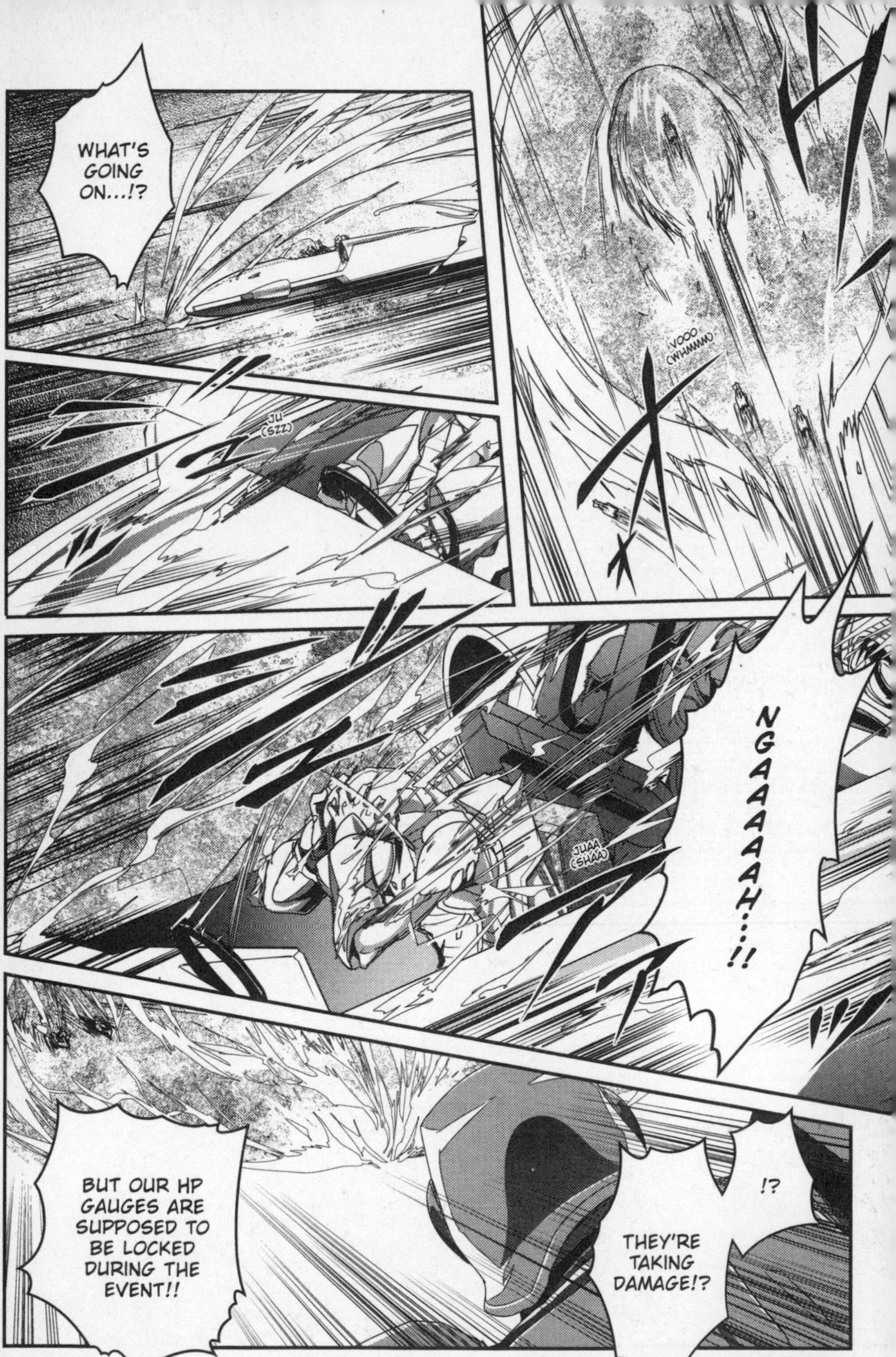
VOOO (WHMMM)
WHAT'S GOING ON...!?
JU (SZZ)
NGAAAAAH...!!
JUAA (SHAA)
!?
THEY'RE TAKING DAMAGE!?
BUT OUR HP GAUGES ARE SUPPOSED TO BE LOCKED DURING THE EVENT!!

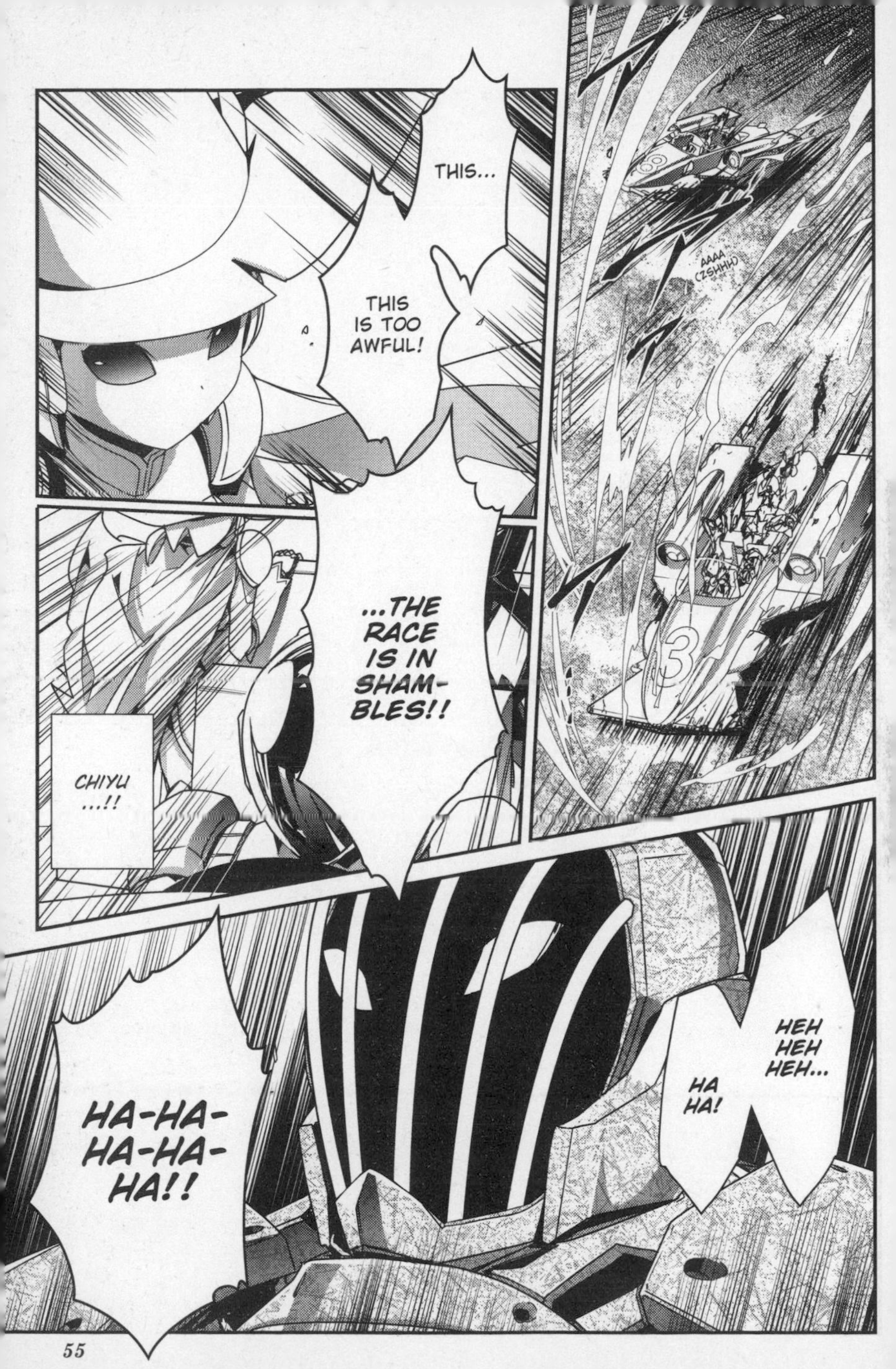
AAAA (ZSHHH)
THIS...
THIS IS TOO AWFUL!
...THE RACE IS IN SHAM-BLES!!
CHIYU ...!!
HEH HEH HEH...
HA HA!
HA-HA-HA-HA-HA!!

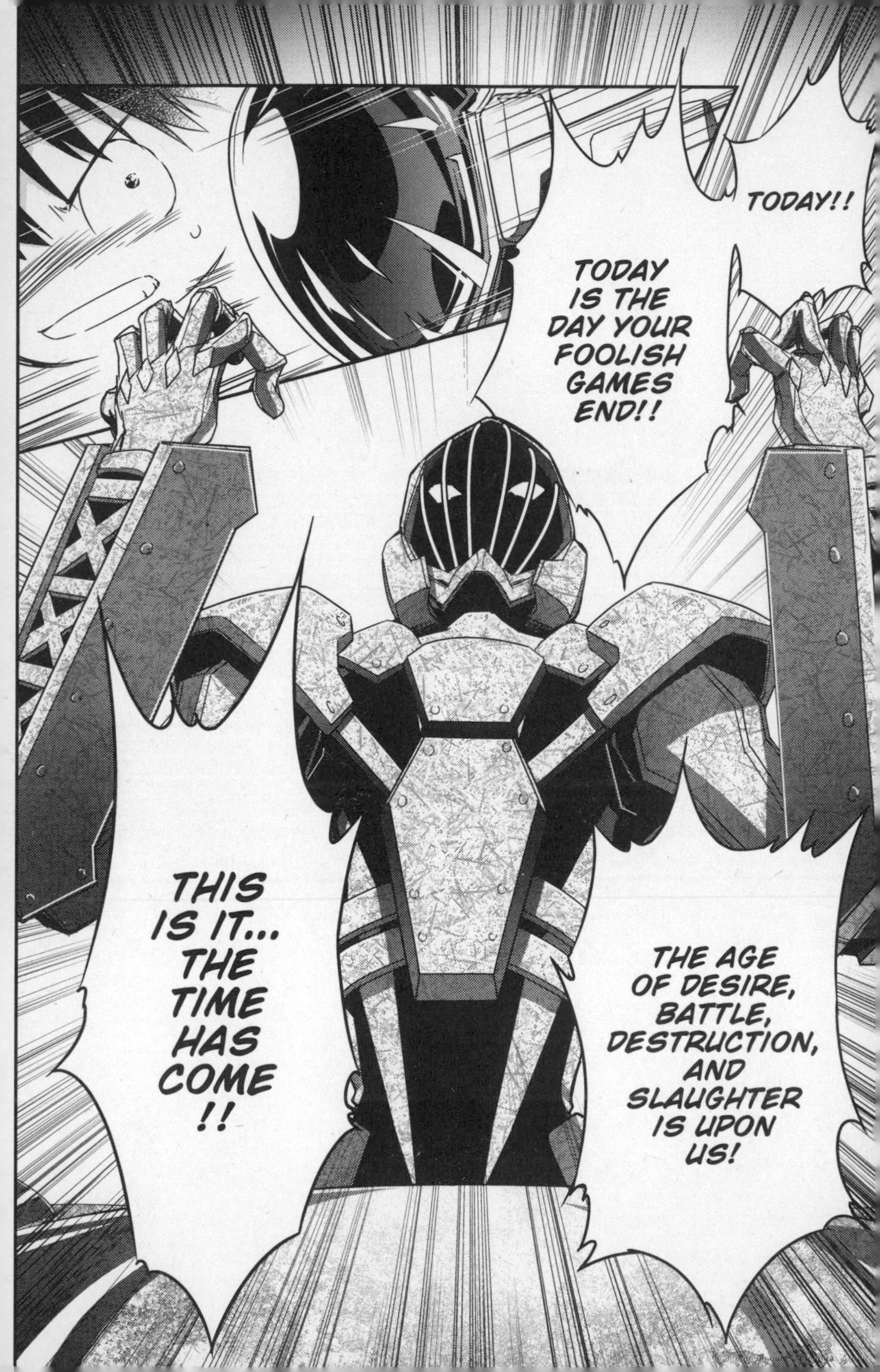
TODAY!!
TODAY IS THE DAY YOUR FOOLISH GAMES END!!
THE AGE OF DESIRE, BATTLE, DESTRUCTION, AND SLAUGHTER IS UPON US!
THIS IS IT... THE TIME HAS COME!!

►►► *ACCEL·WORLD*

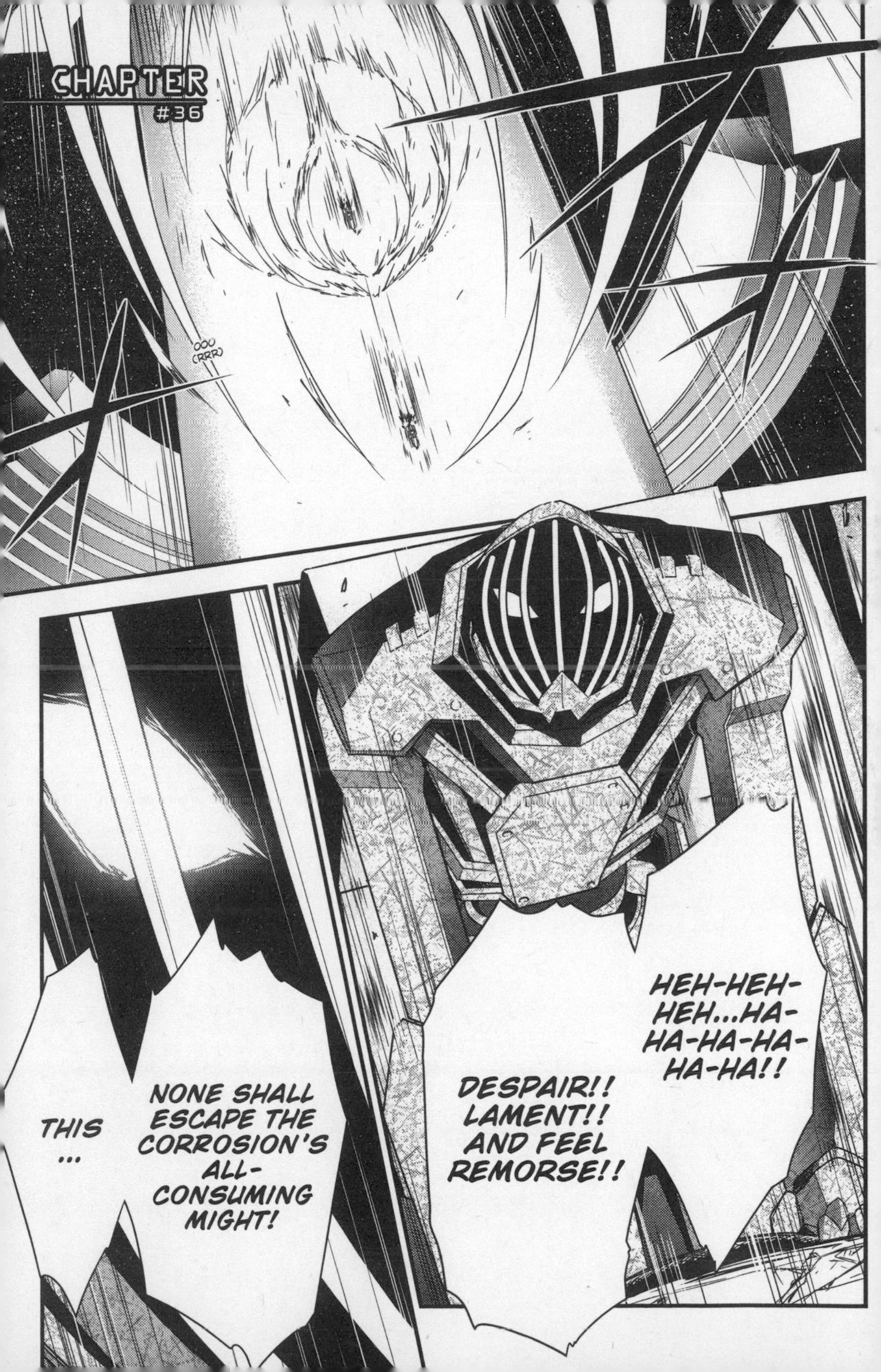
CHAPTER #36
OOO (RRR)
HEH-HEH-HEH...HA-HA-HA-HA-HA-HA-HA!!
DESPAIR!! LAMENT!! AND FEEL REMORSE!!
NONE SHALL ESCAPE THE CORROSION'S ALL-CONSUMING MIGHT!
THIS ...

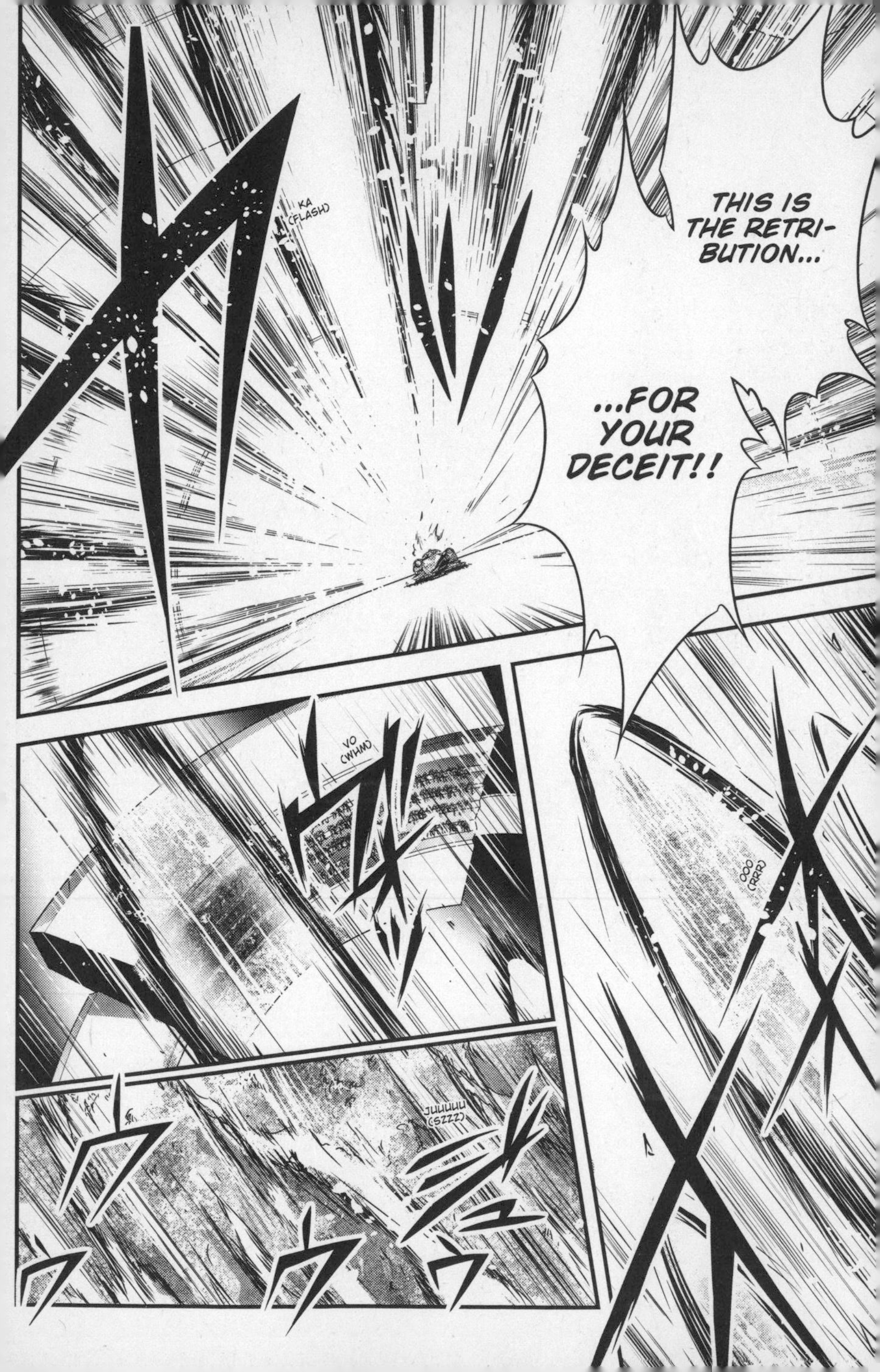
THIS IS THE RETRIBUTION...
...FOR YOUR DECEIT!!
KA (FLASH)
OOO (RRR)
VO (WHM)
JUUUUU (SZZZ)

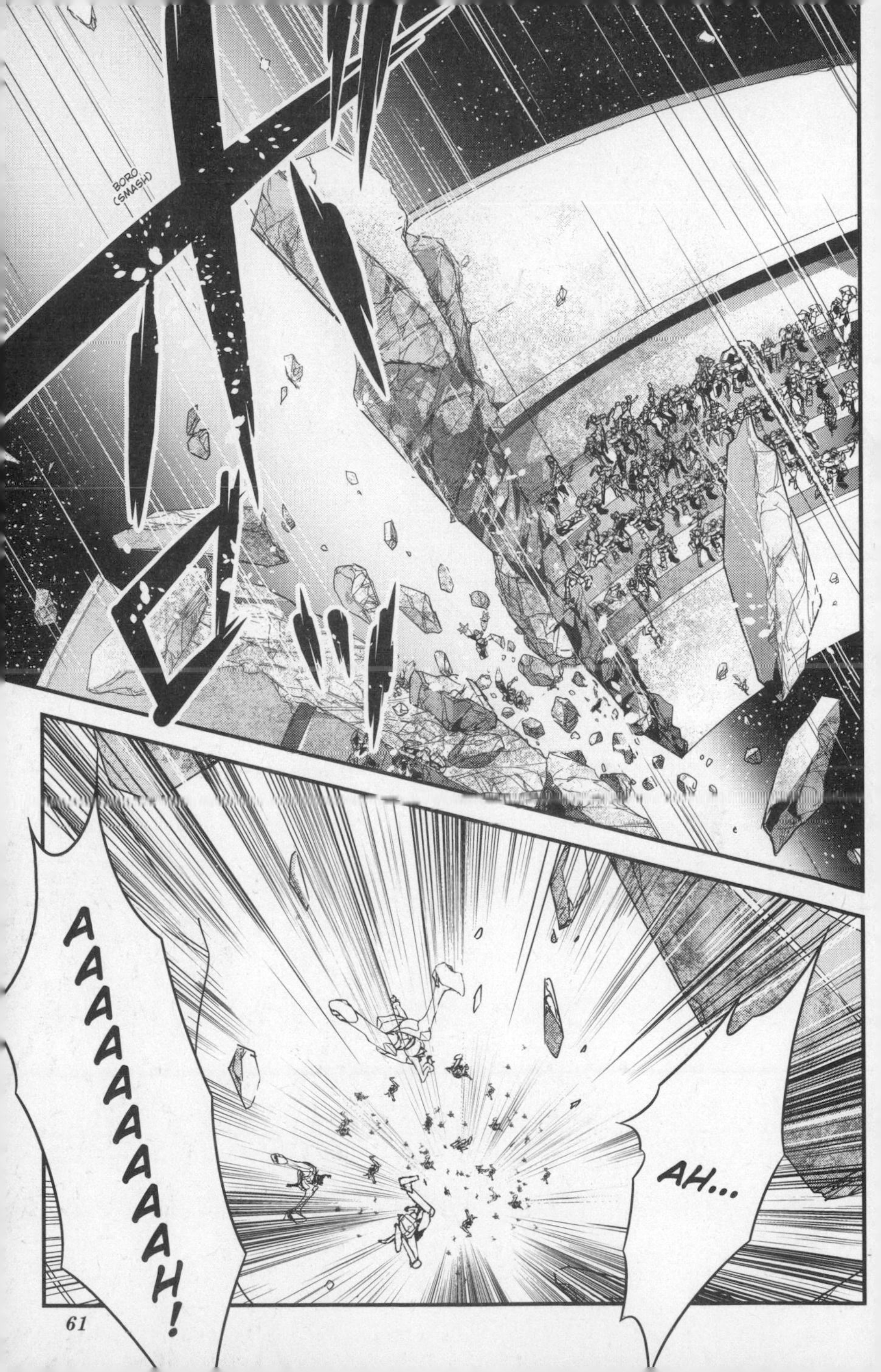
BORO
(SMASH)
AAAAAAAAAAAH!
AH...

GOING THIS FAR...

THE GALLERY WILL MOST CERTAINLY REALIZE IT TOO.

I—

INSANITY...

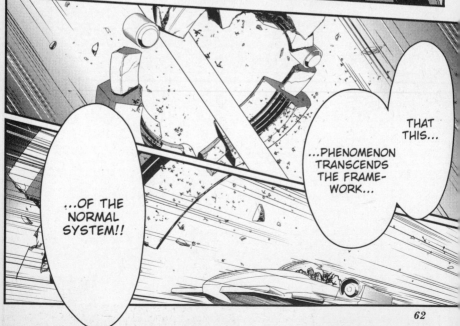

THAT THIS...

...PHENOMENON TRANSCENDS THE FRAME-WORK...

...OF THE NORMAL SYSTEM!!

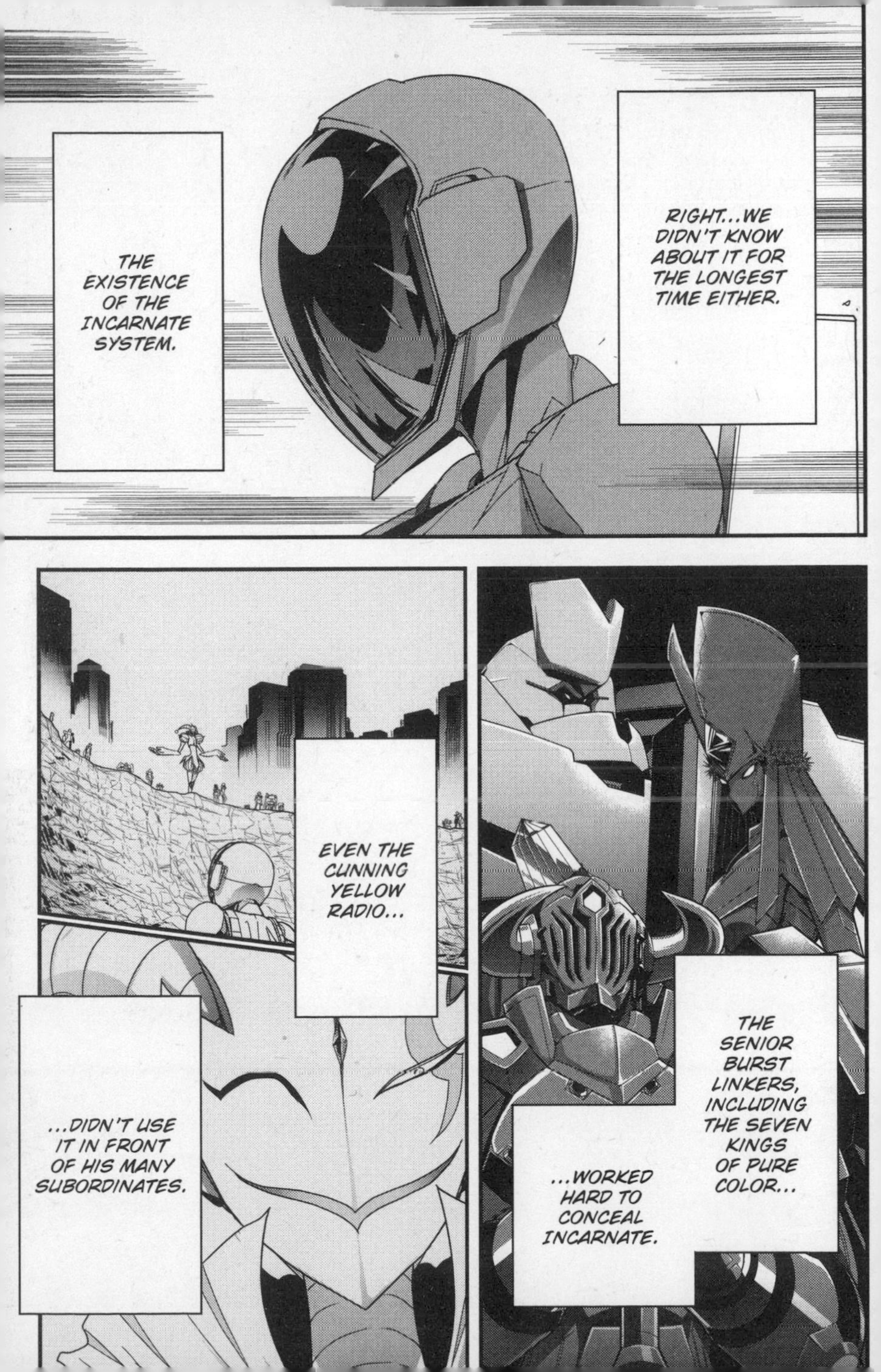
RIGHT...WE DIDN'T KNOW ABOUT IT FOR THE LONGEST TIME EITHER.
THE EXISTENCE OF THE INCARNATE SYSTEM.
THE SENIOR BURST LINKERS, INCLUDING THE SEVEN KINGS OF PURE COLOR...
...WORKED HARD TO CONCEAL INCARNATE.
EVEN THE CUNNING YELLOW RADIO...
...DIDN'T USE IT IN FRONT OF HIS MANY SUBORDINATES.

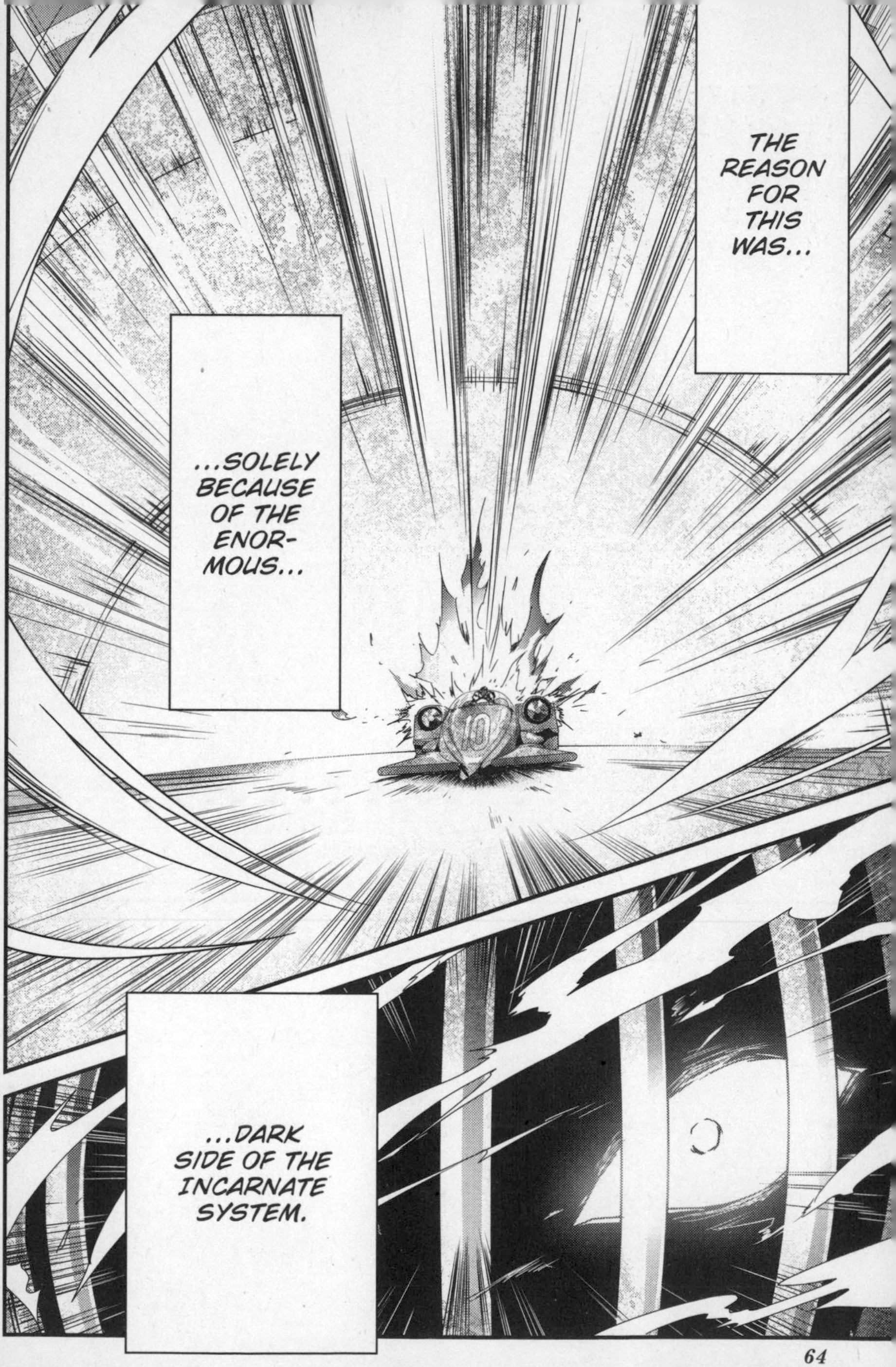
THE REASON FOR THIS WAS...
...SOLELY BECAUSE OF THE ENOR-MOUS...
...DARK SIDE OF THE INCARNATE SYSTEM.

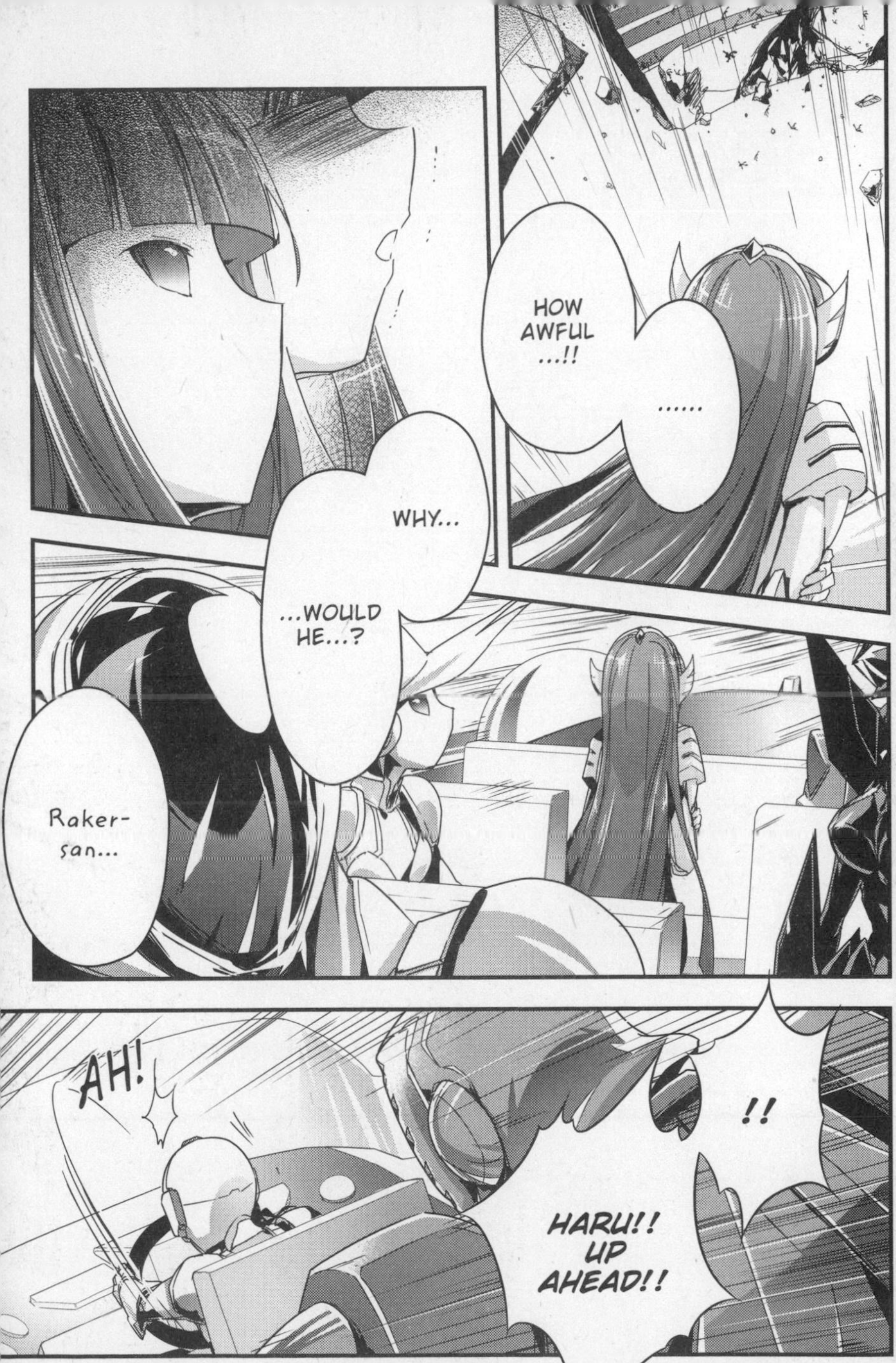
HOW AWFUL ...!!
......
WHY...
...WOULD HE...?
Raker-san...
!!
HARU!! UP AHEAD!!
AH!

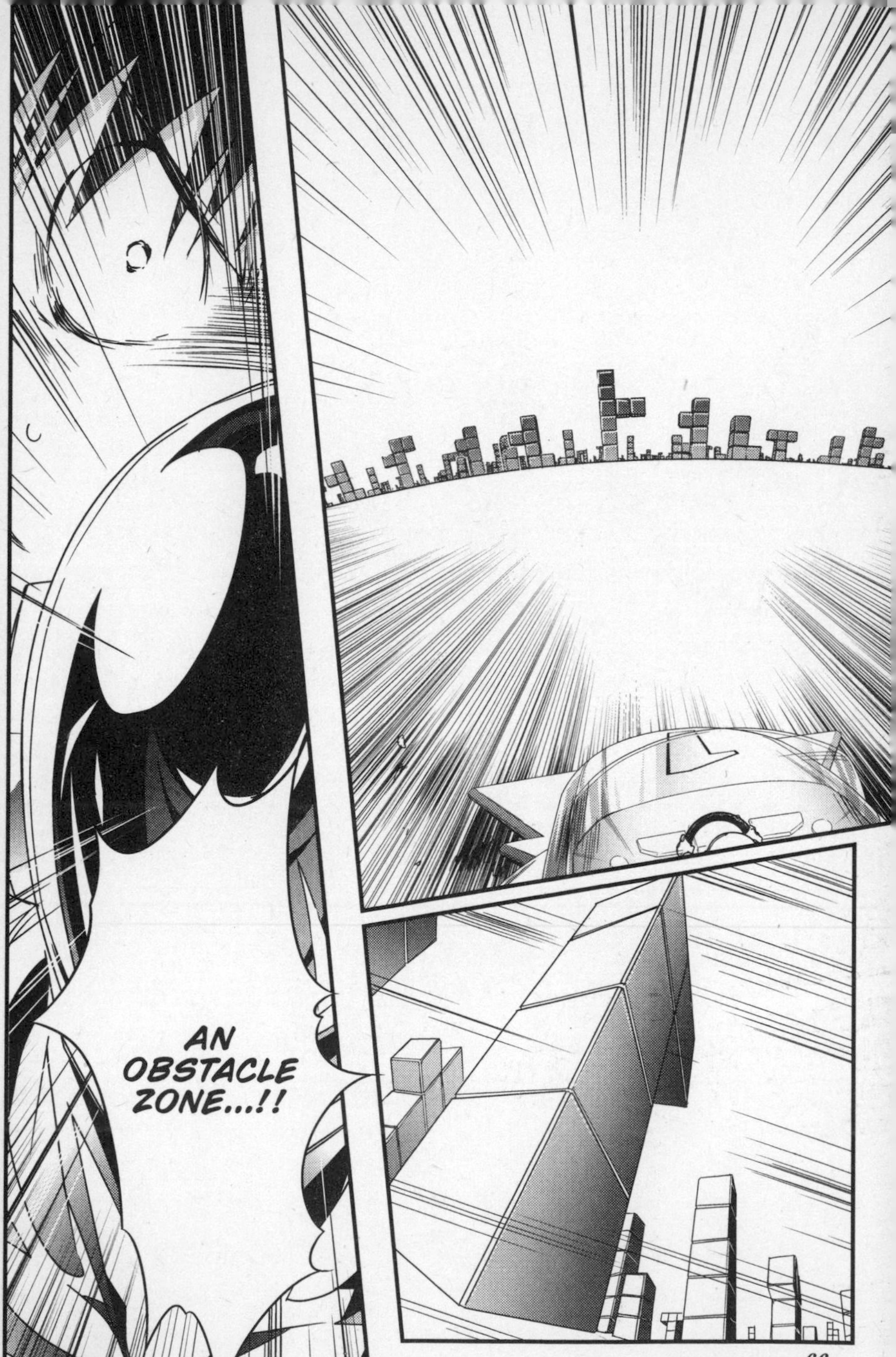
AN OBSTACLE ZONE...!!

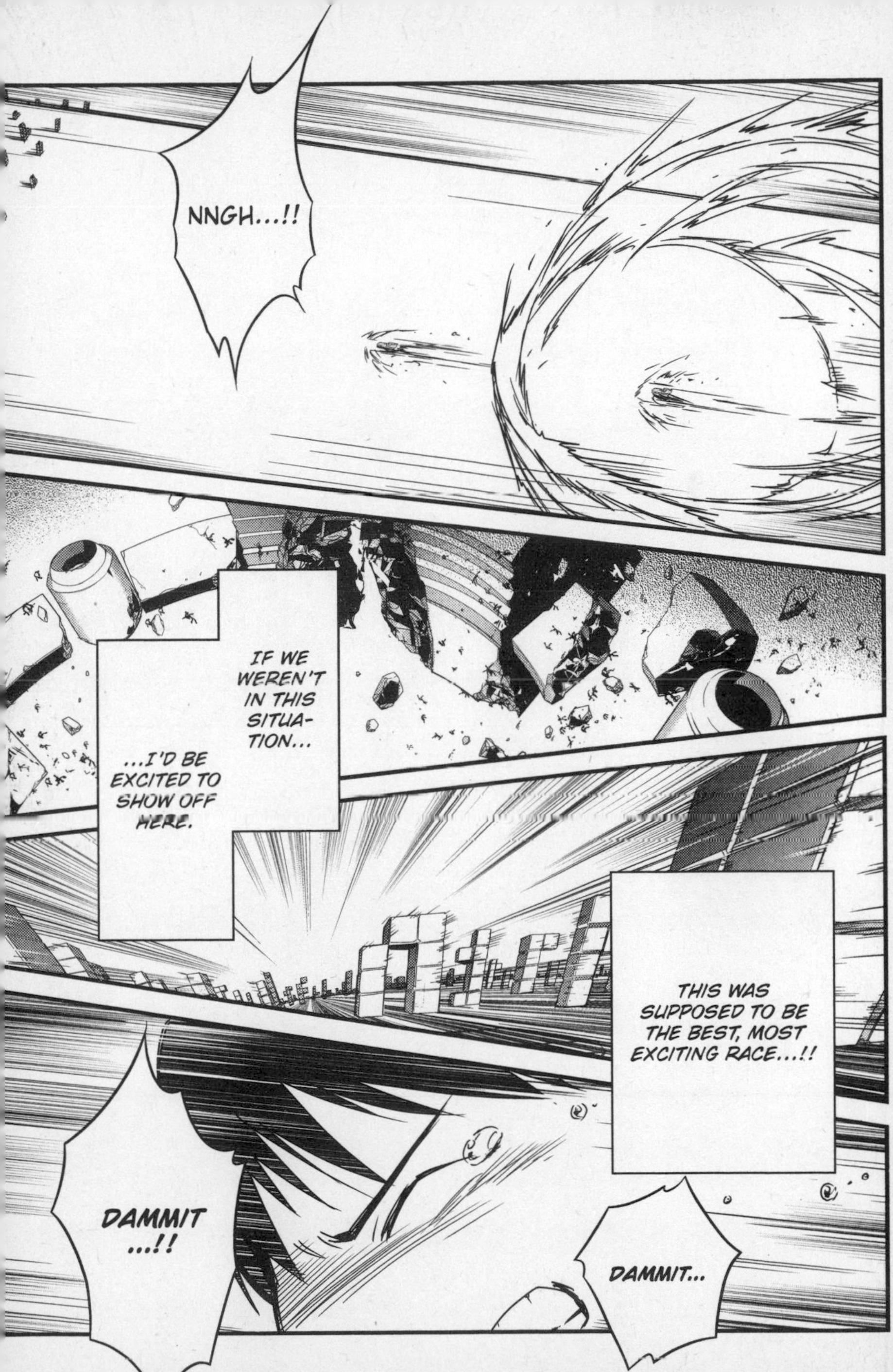
NNGH...!!
IF WE WEREN'T IN THIS SITUATION...
...I'D BE EXCITED TO SHOW OFF HERE.
THIS WAS SUPPOSED TO BE THE BEST, MOST EXCITING RACE...!!
DAMMIT...
DAMMIT...!!

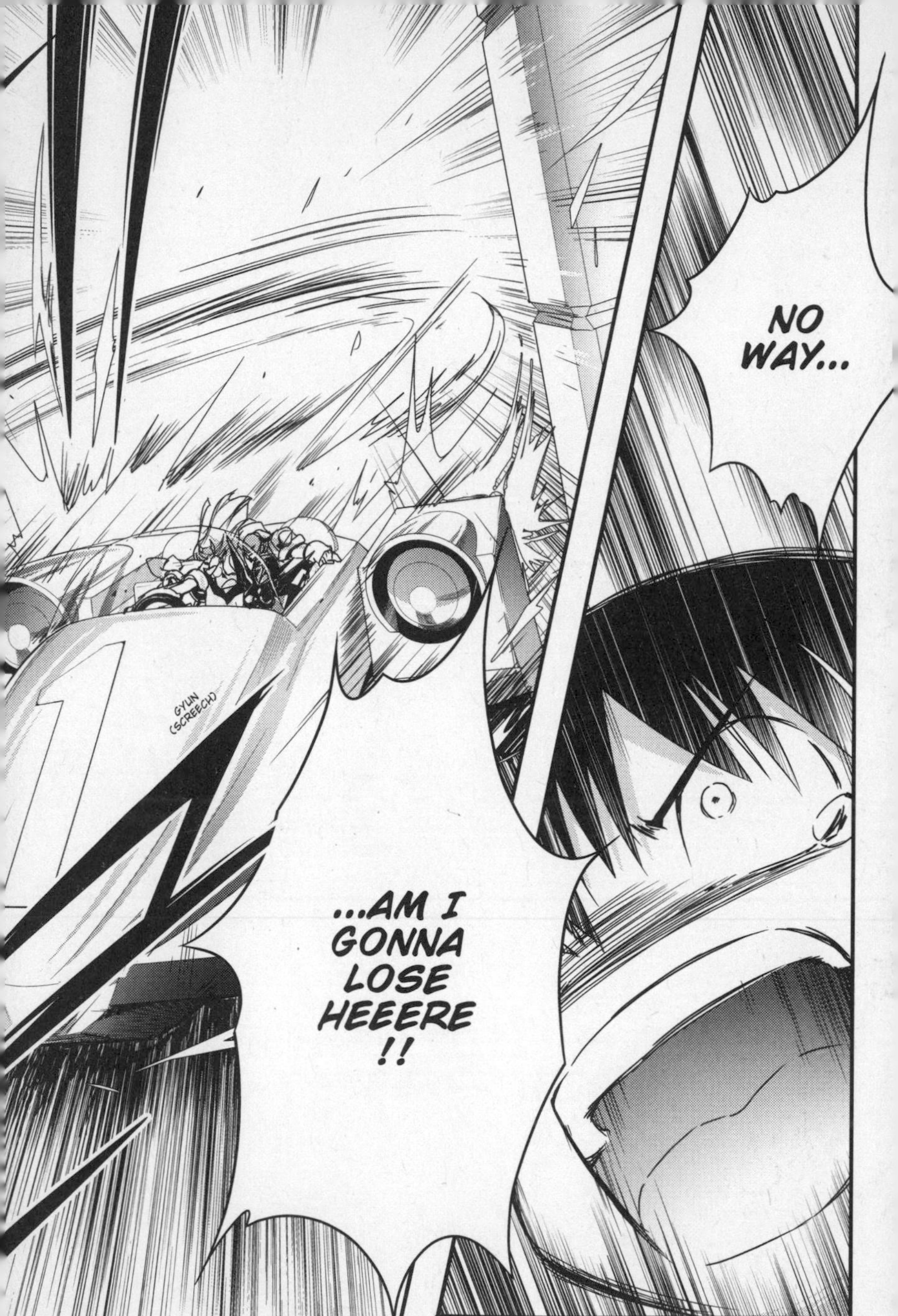

NO WAY...
...AM I GONNA LOSE HEEERE !!
GYUN (SCREECH)

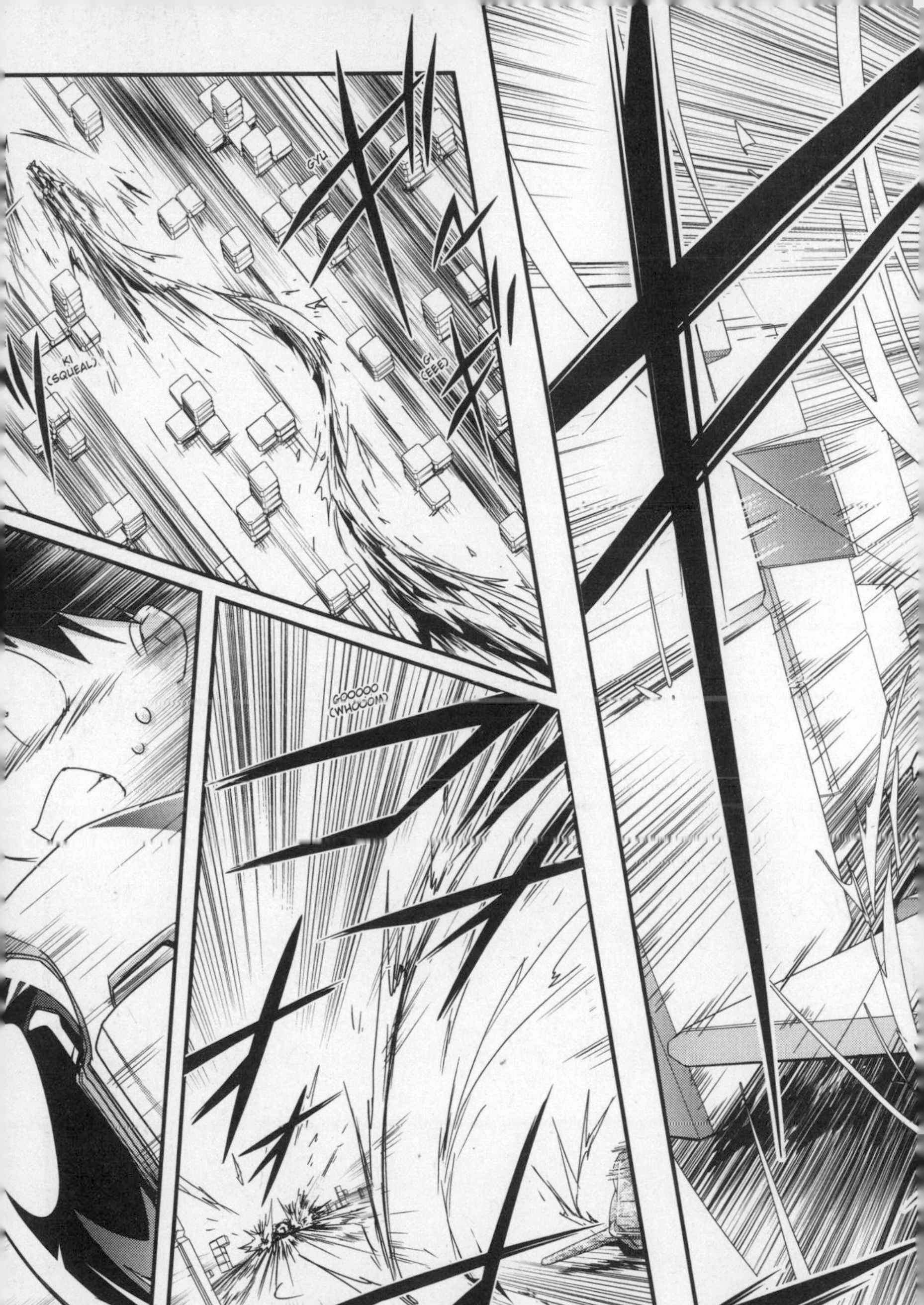
GYU
GI (EEE)
KI (SQUEAL)
GOOOOO (WHOOOM)

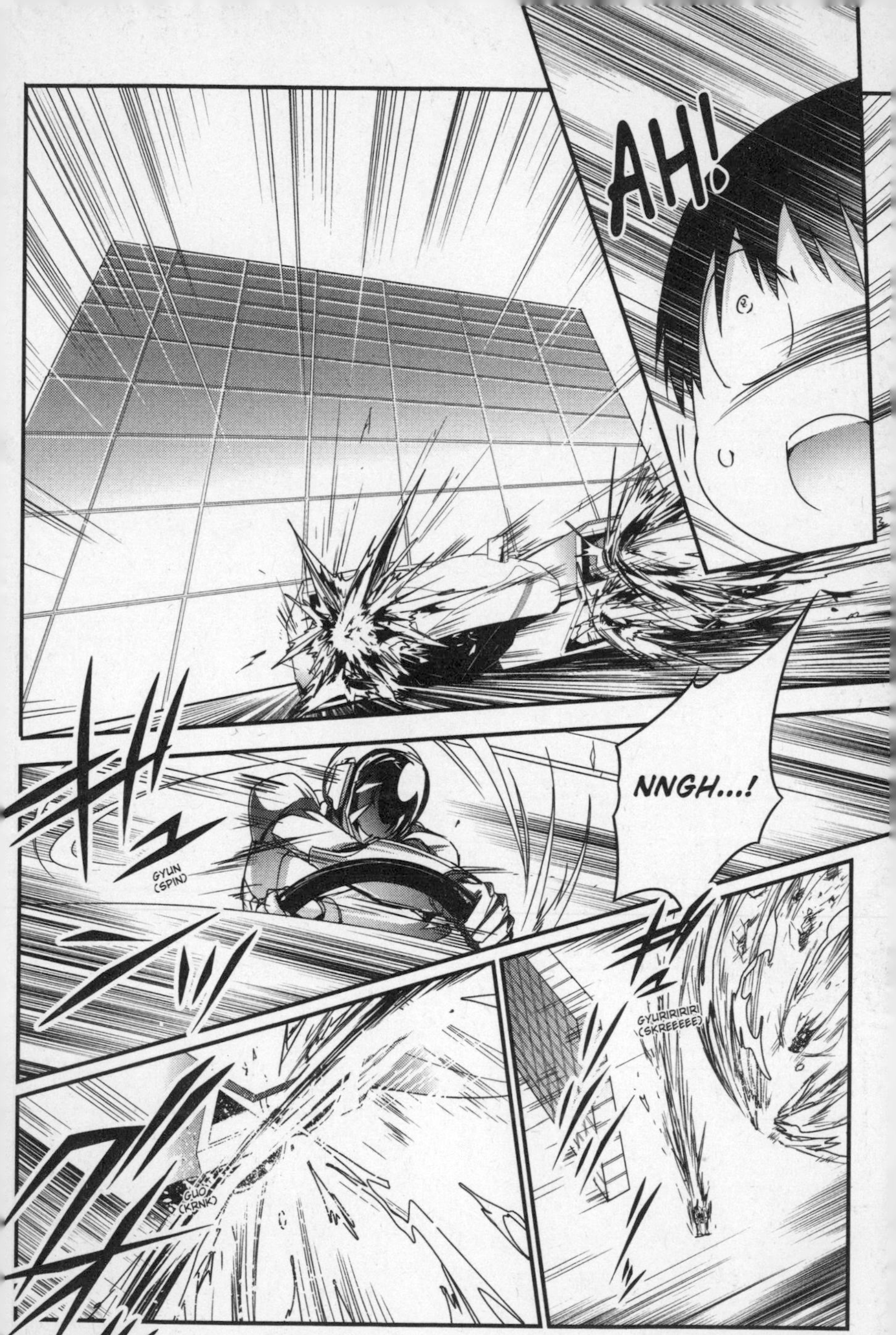
AH!
NNGH...!
GYUN (SPIN)
GYURIRIRIRI (SKREEEEEE)
GUO (KRNK)

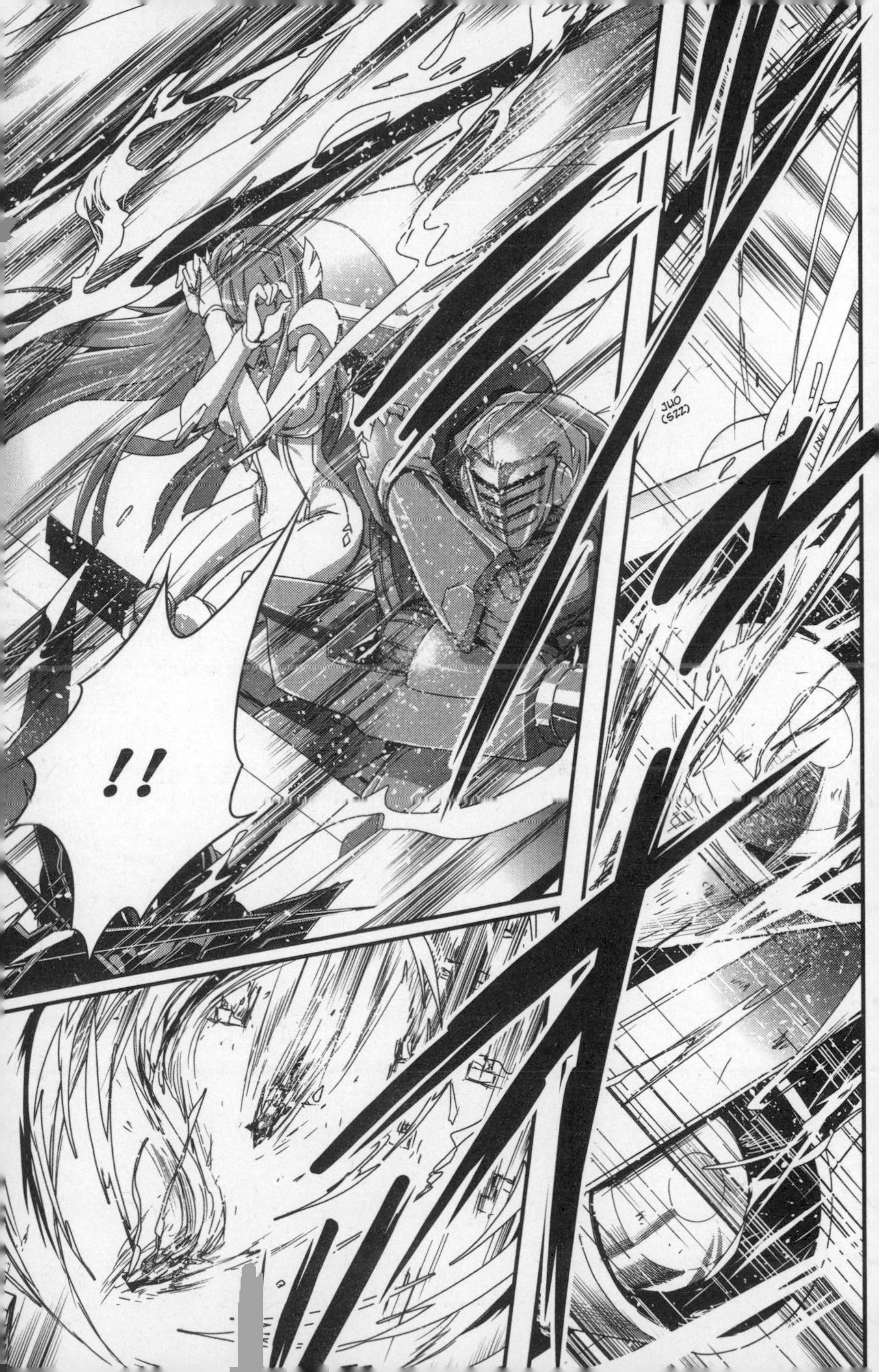
JUO
(SZZ)
!!

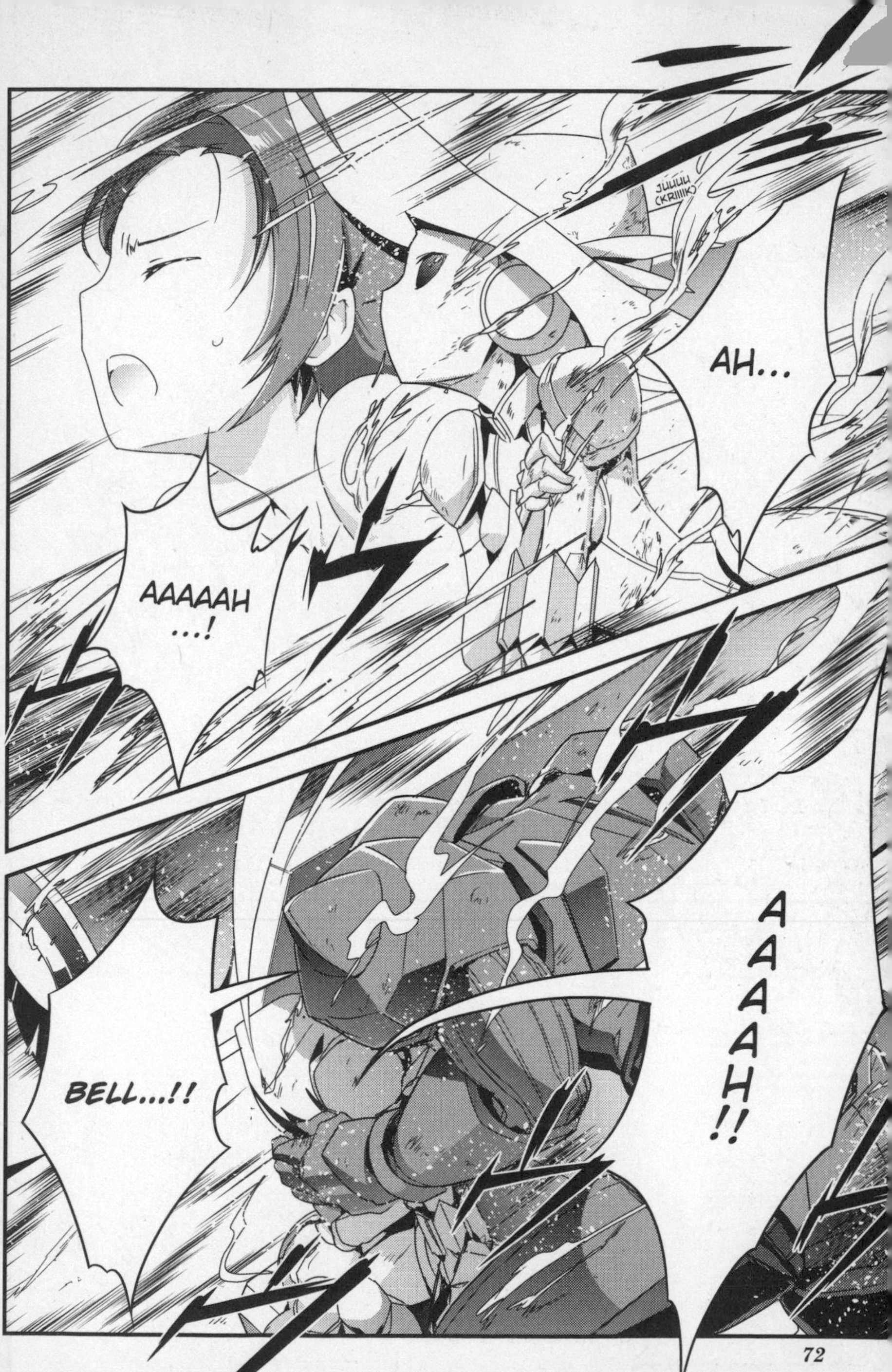
JUUUU (KRIIIIK)
AH...
AAAAAH...!
AAAAAH!!
BELL...!!

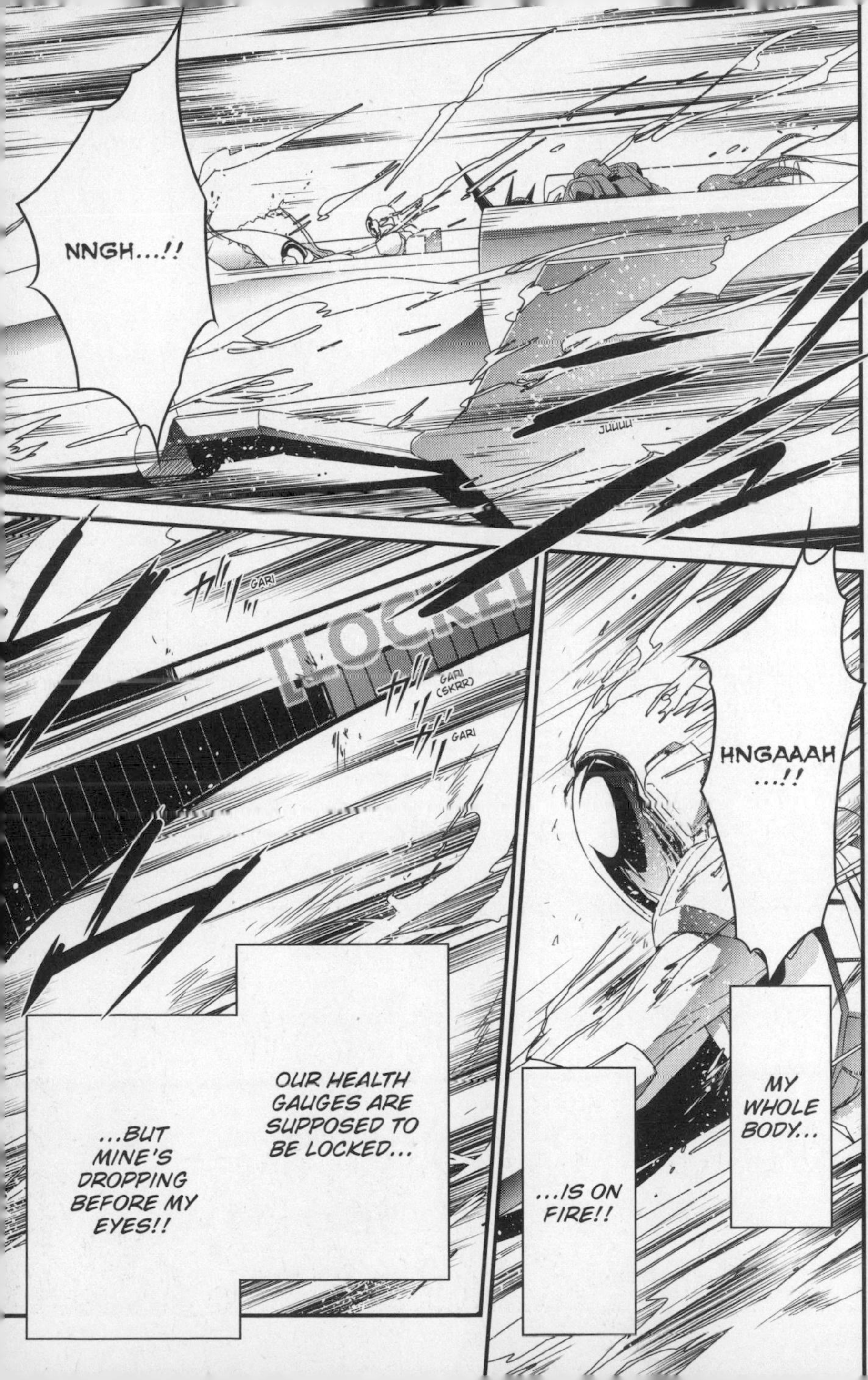
NNGH...!!
JUUUU
HNGAAAH ...!!
MY WHOLE BODY...
...IS ON FIRE!!
GARI
GARI (SKRR)
GARI
OUR HEALTH GAUGES ARE SUPPOSED TO BE LOCKED...
...BUT MINE'S DROPPING BEFORE MY EYES!!

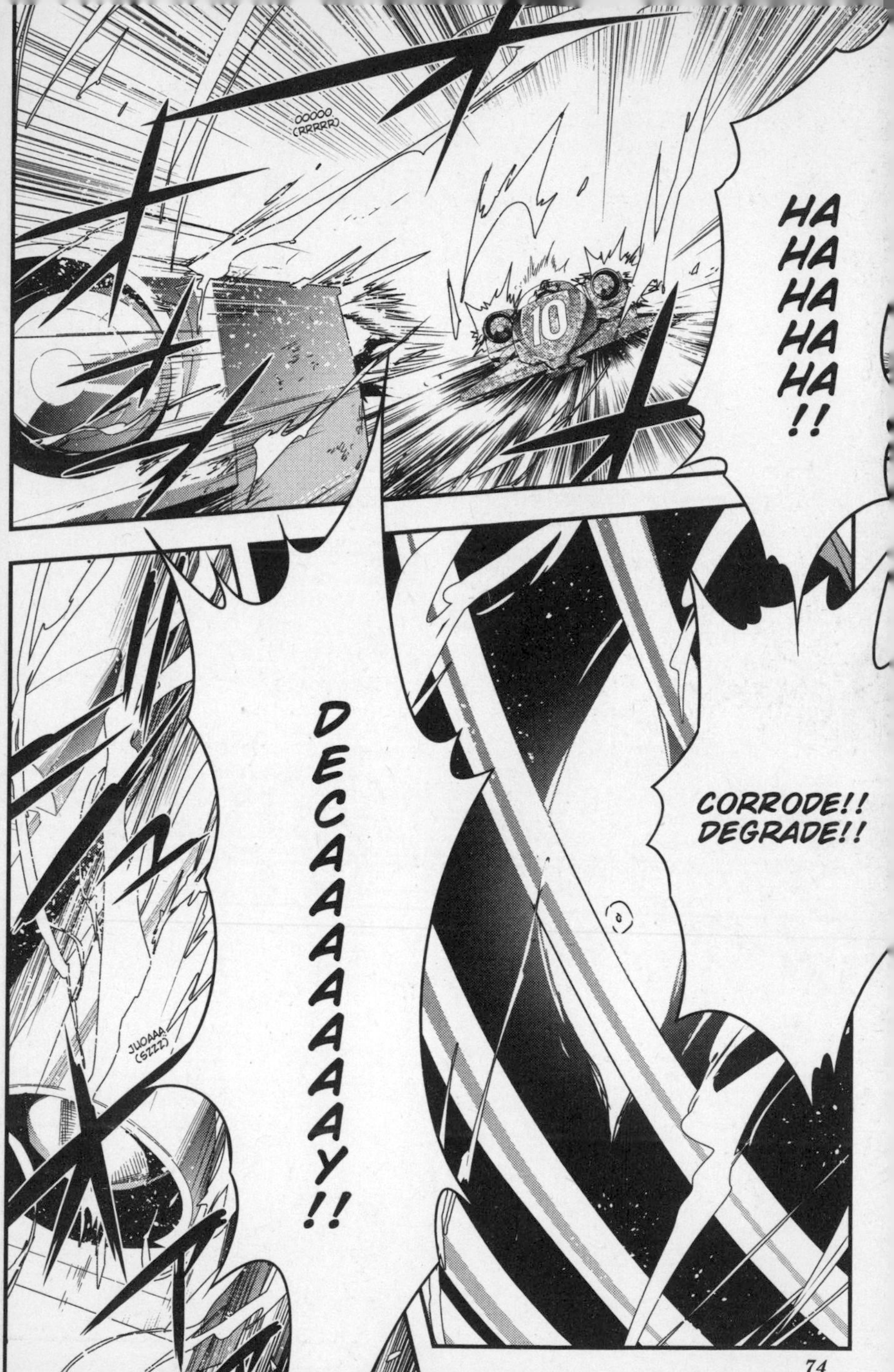
HAHAHAHAHA!!
OOOOO (RRRRR)
CORRODE!! DEGRADE!!
DECAAAAAAAAY!!
JUOAAA (SZZZ)

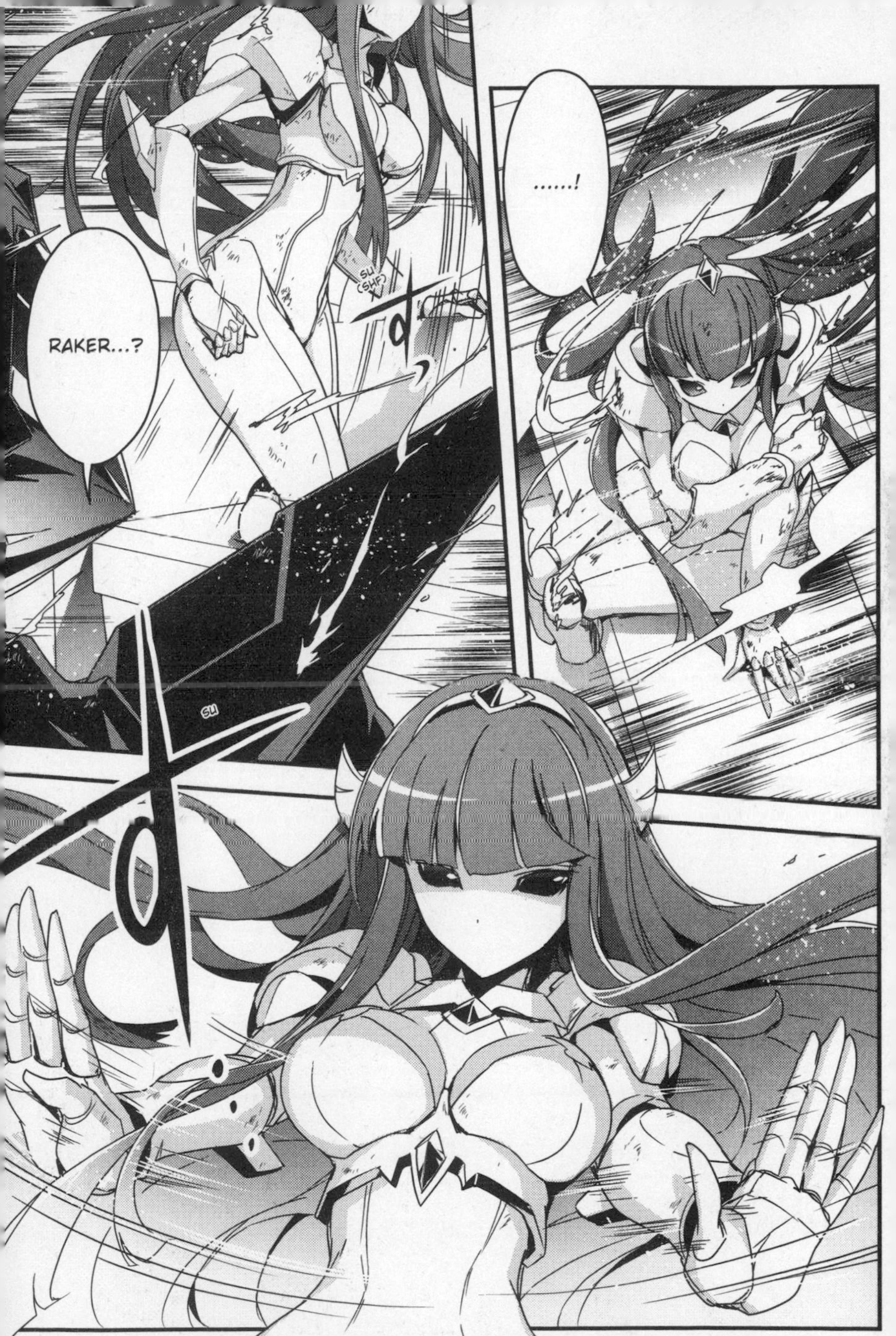
......!
SU (SHF)
RAKER...?
SU

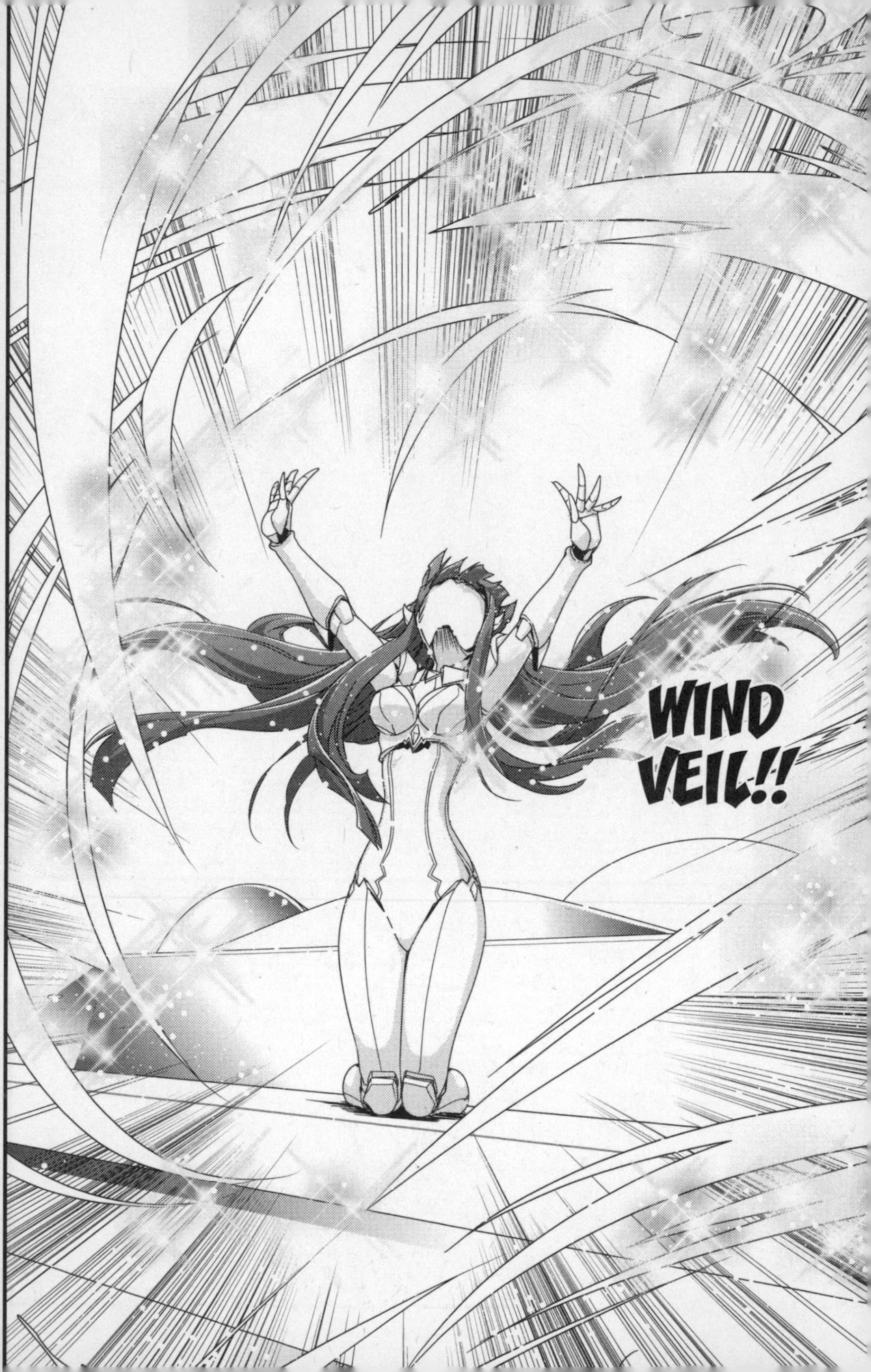
WIND VEIL!!

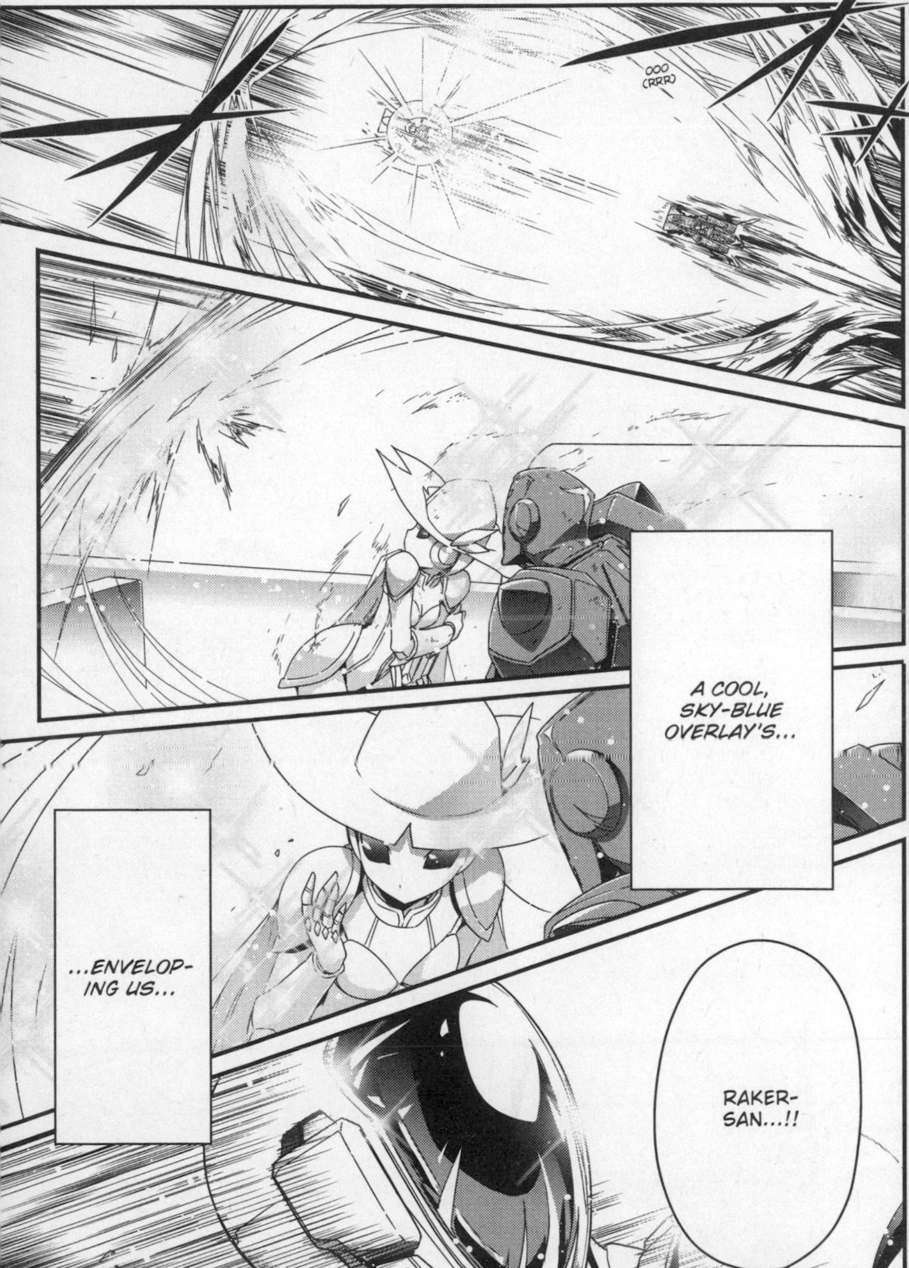
OOO
(RRR)
A COOL, SKY-BLUE OVERLAY'S...
...ENVELOP-ING US...
RAKER-SAN...!!

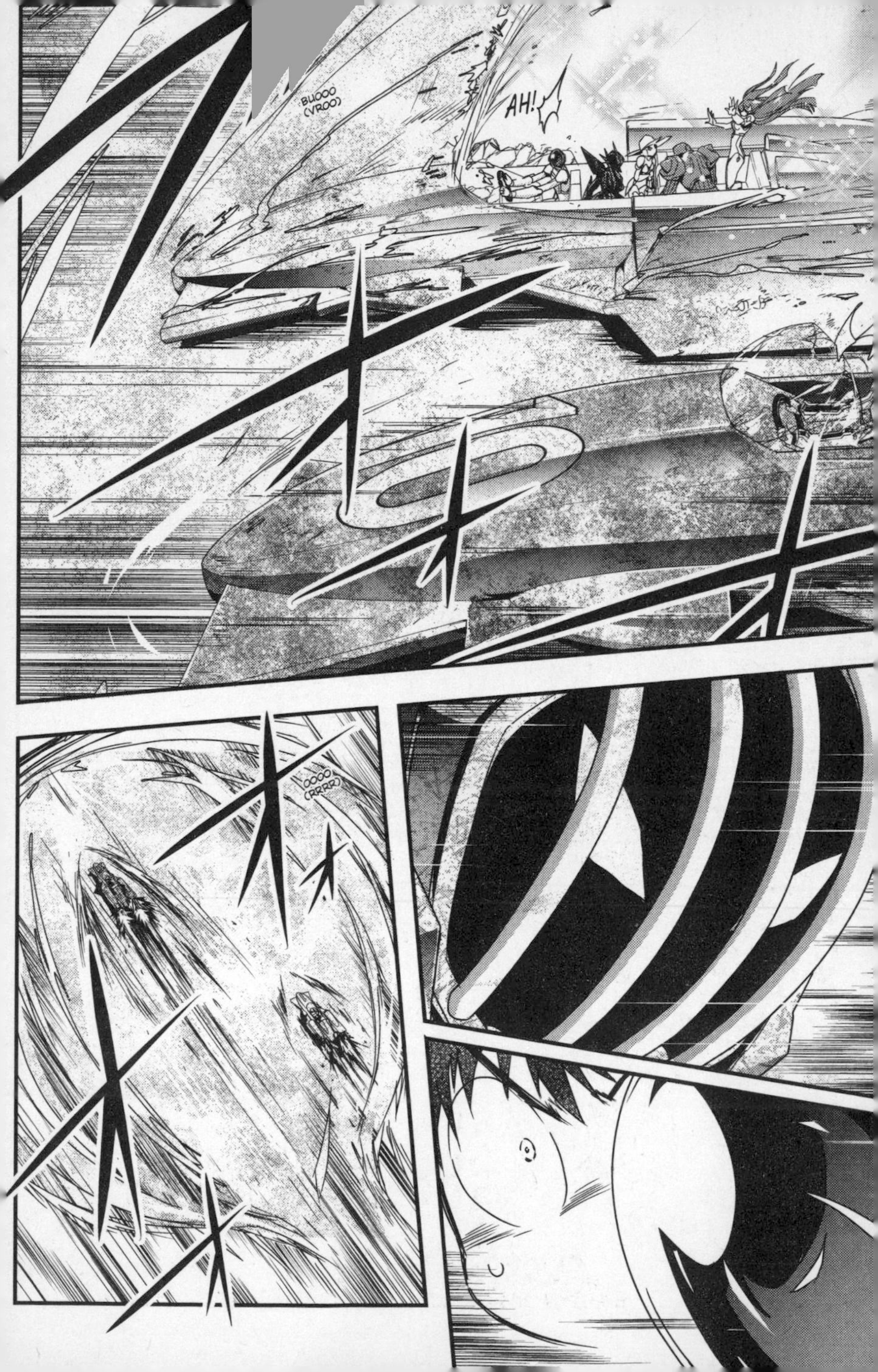
AH!
BUOOO
(VROO)
OOOO
(RRRR)

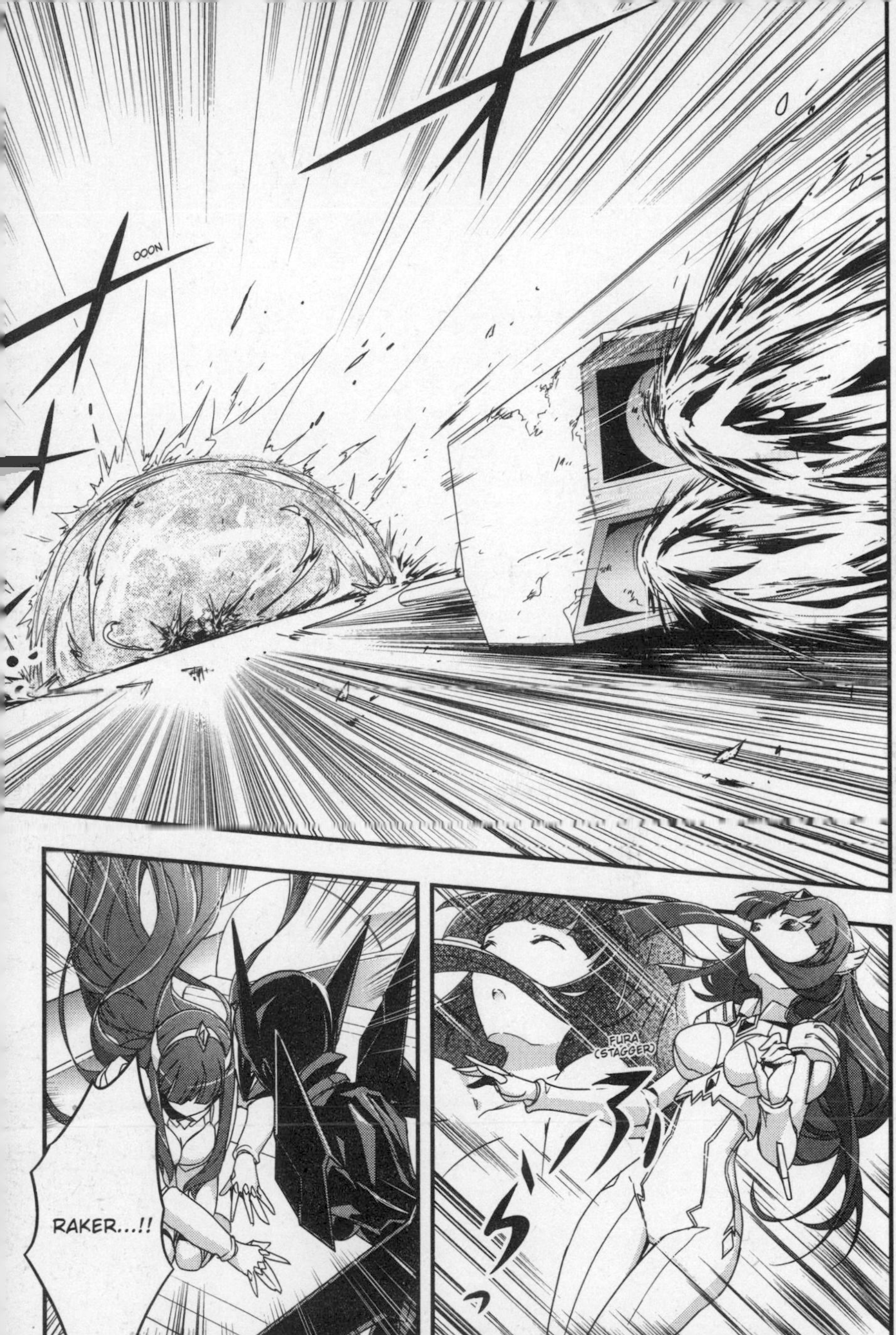
OOON
FURA
(STAGGER)
RAKER...!!

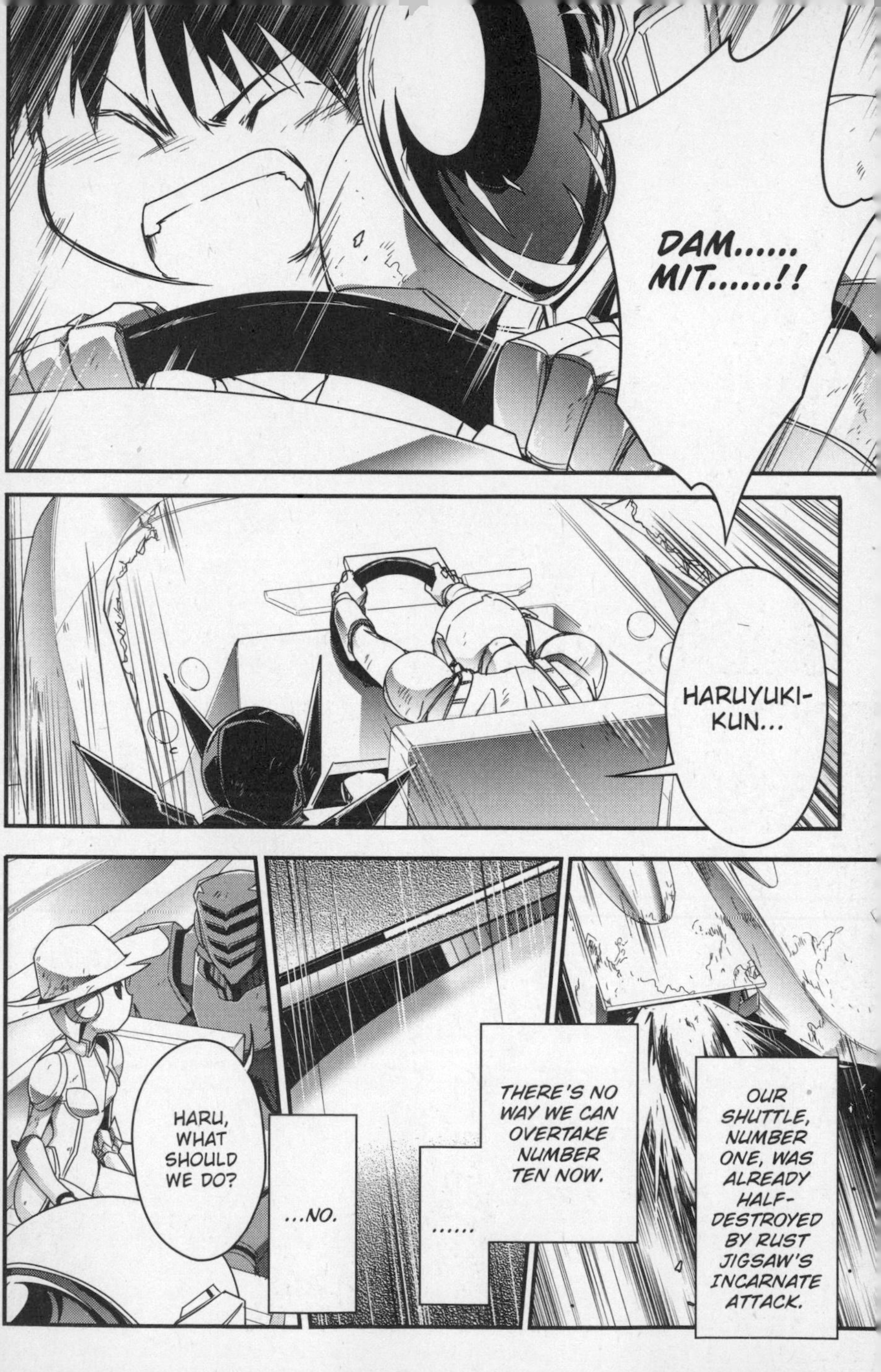
DAM...... MIT......!!
HARUYUKI-KUN...
OUR SHUTTLE, NUMBER ONE, WAS ALREADY HALF-DESTROYED BY RUST JIGSAW'S INCARNATE ATTACK.
THERE'S NO WAY WE CAN OVERTAKE NUMBER TEN NOW.
......
...NO.
HARU, WHAT SHOULD WE DO?

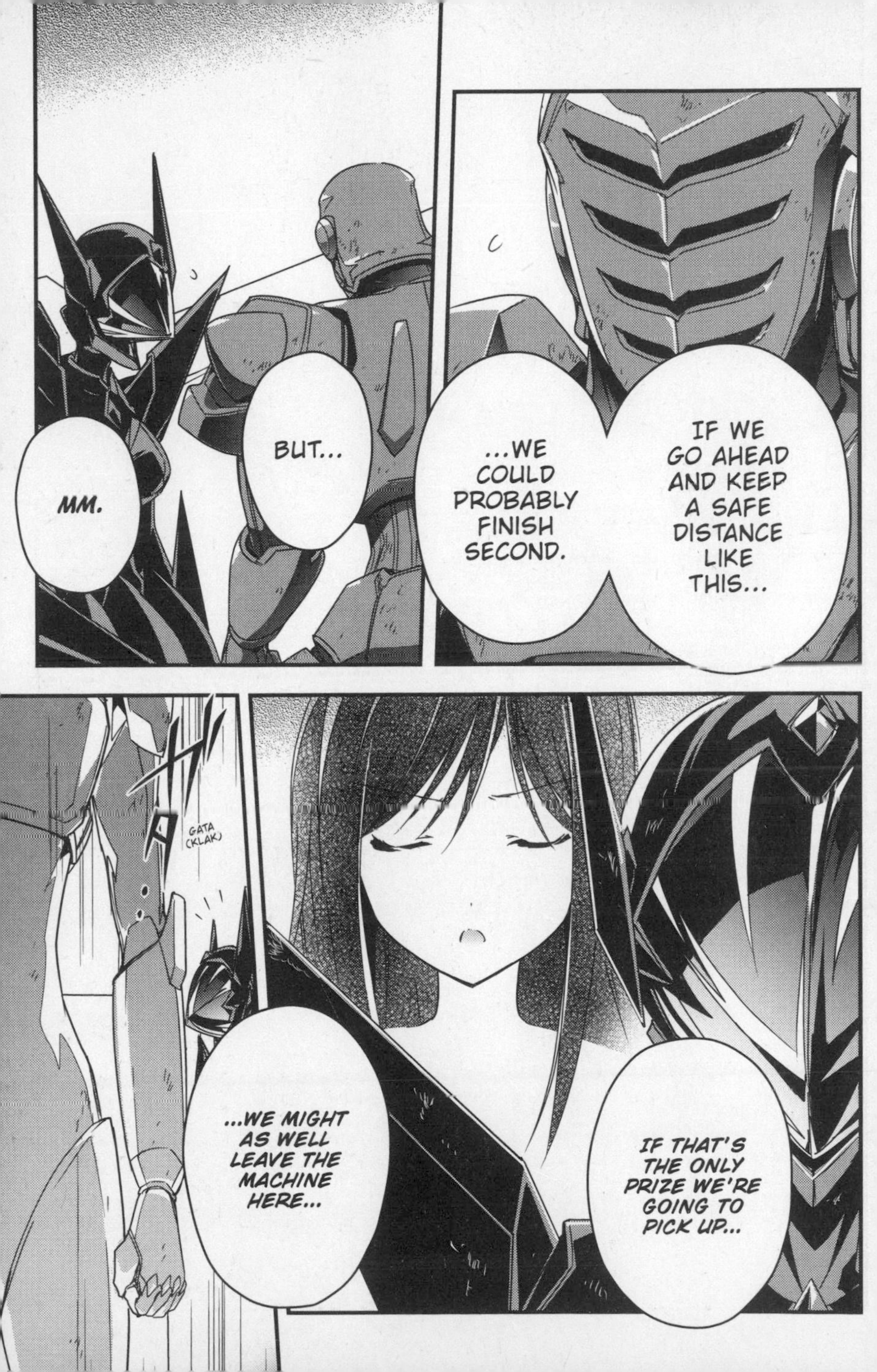
IF WE GO AHEAD AND KEEP A SAFE DISTANCE LIKE THIS...
...WE COULD PROBABLY FINISH SECOND.
BUT...
MM.
IF THAT'S THE ONLY PRIZE WE'RE GOING TO PICK UP...
...WE MIGHT AS WELL LEAVE THE MACHINE HERE...
GATA (KLAK)

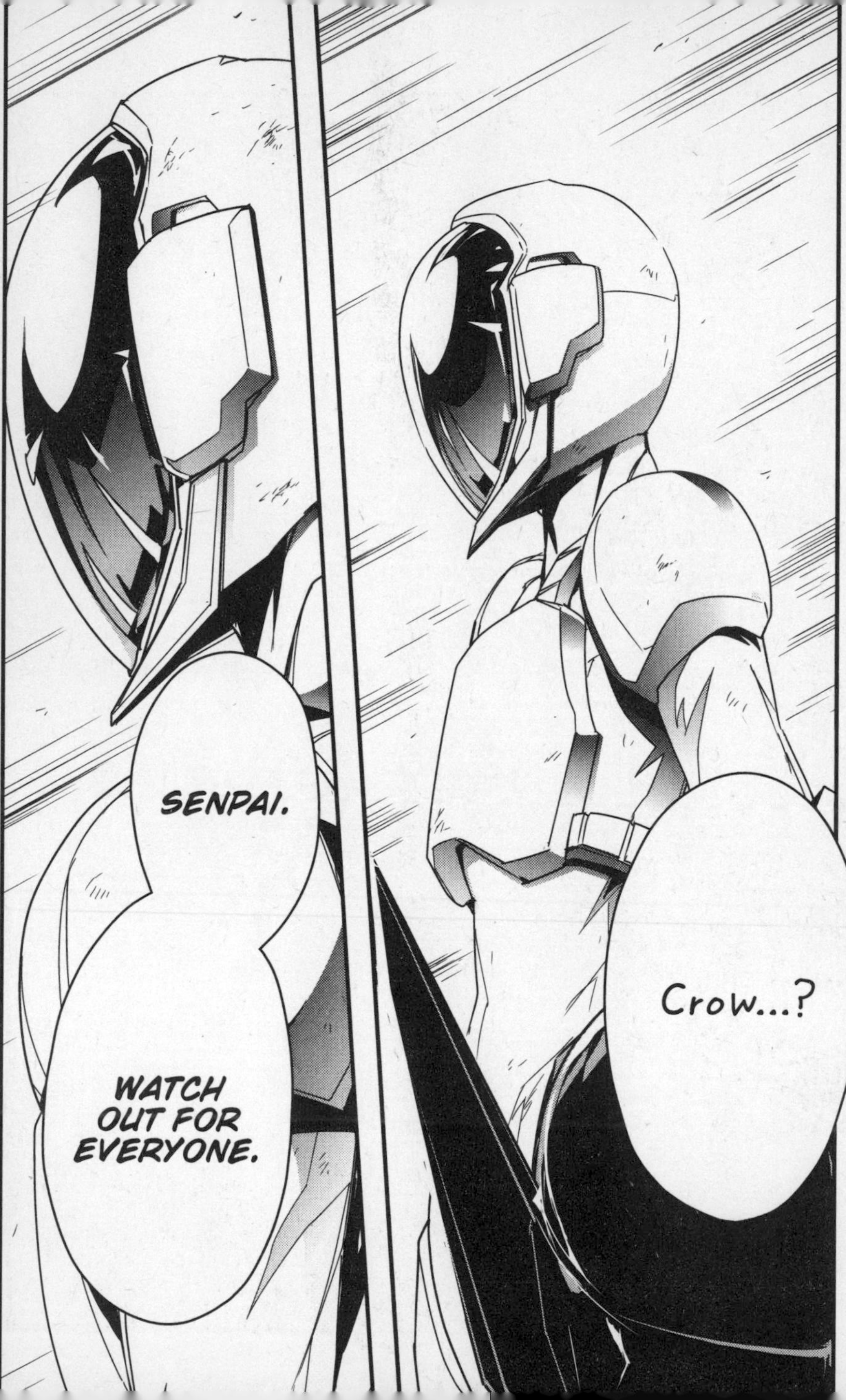
Crow...?
SENPAI.
WATCH OUT FOR EVERYONE.

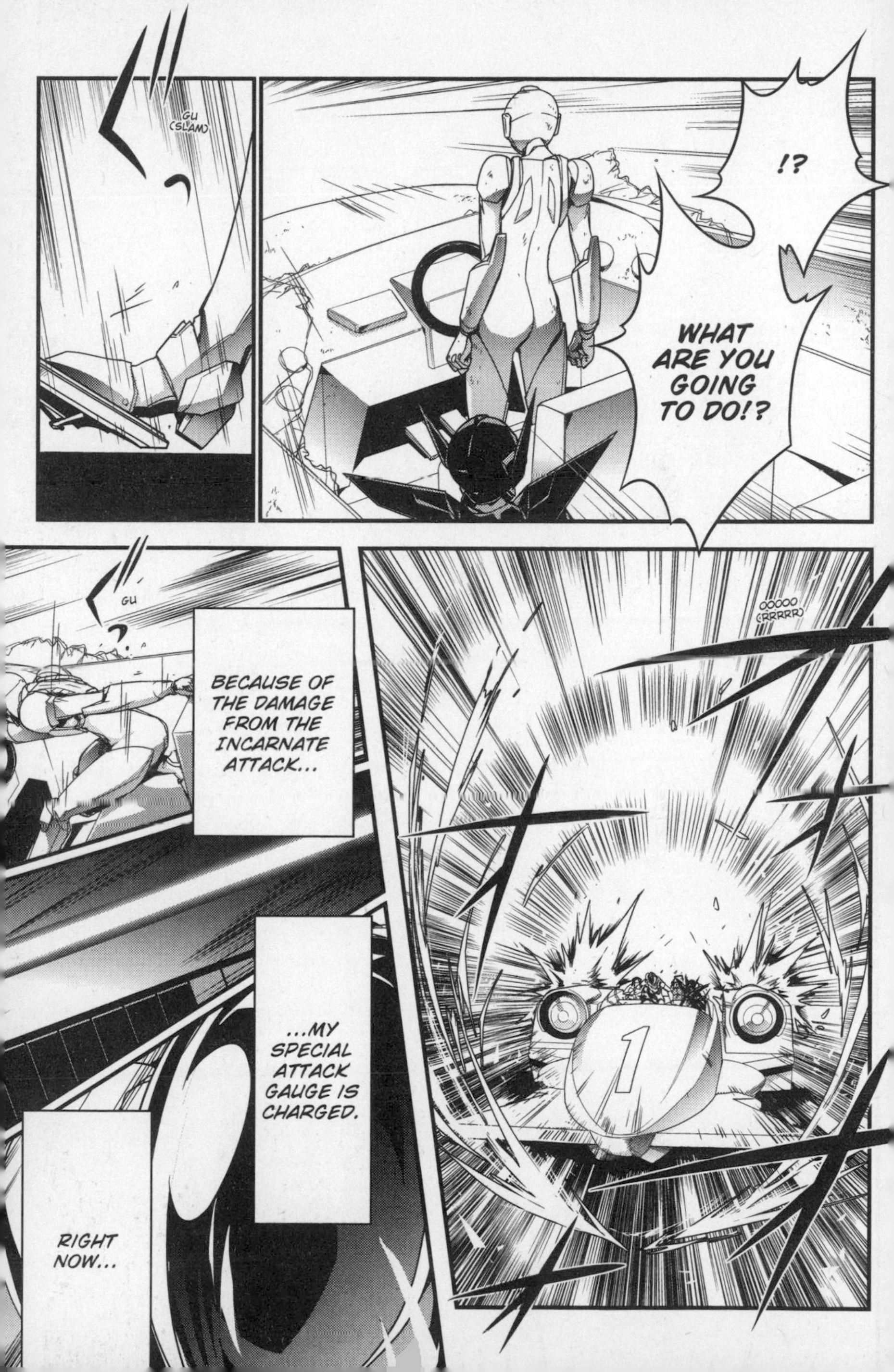
!?
WHAT ARE YOU GOING TO DO!?
GU (SLAM)
OOOOO (RRRRR)
GU
BECAUSE OF THE DAMAGE FROM THE INCARNATE ATTACK...
...MY SPECIAL ATTACK GAUGE IS CHARGED.
RIGHT NOW...

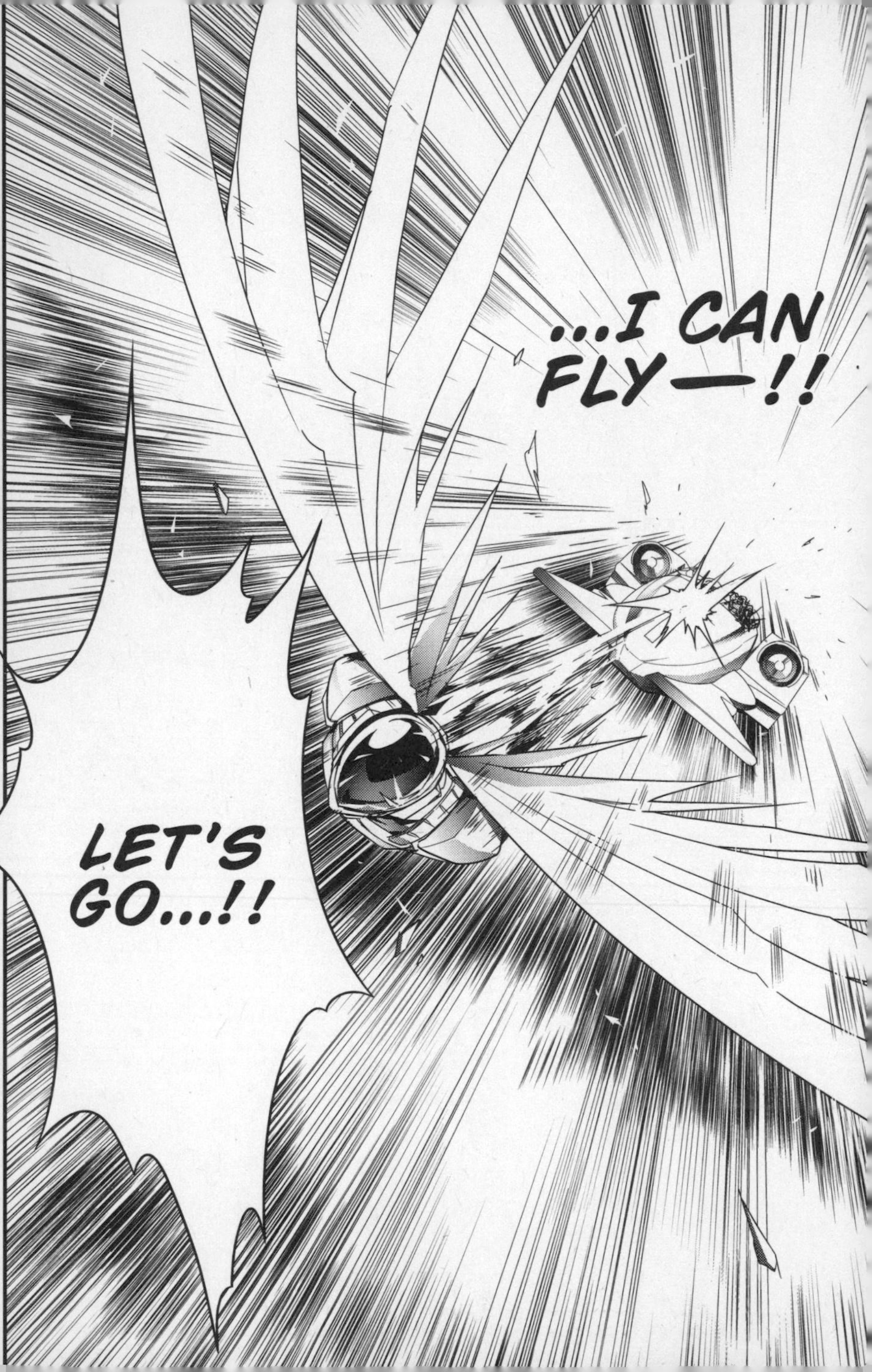
...I CAN FLY—!!
LET'S GO...!!

►►► *ACCEL•WORLD*

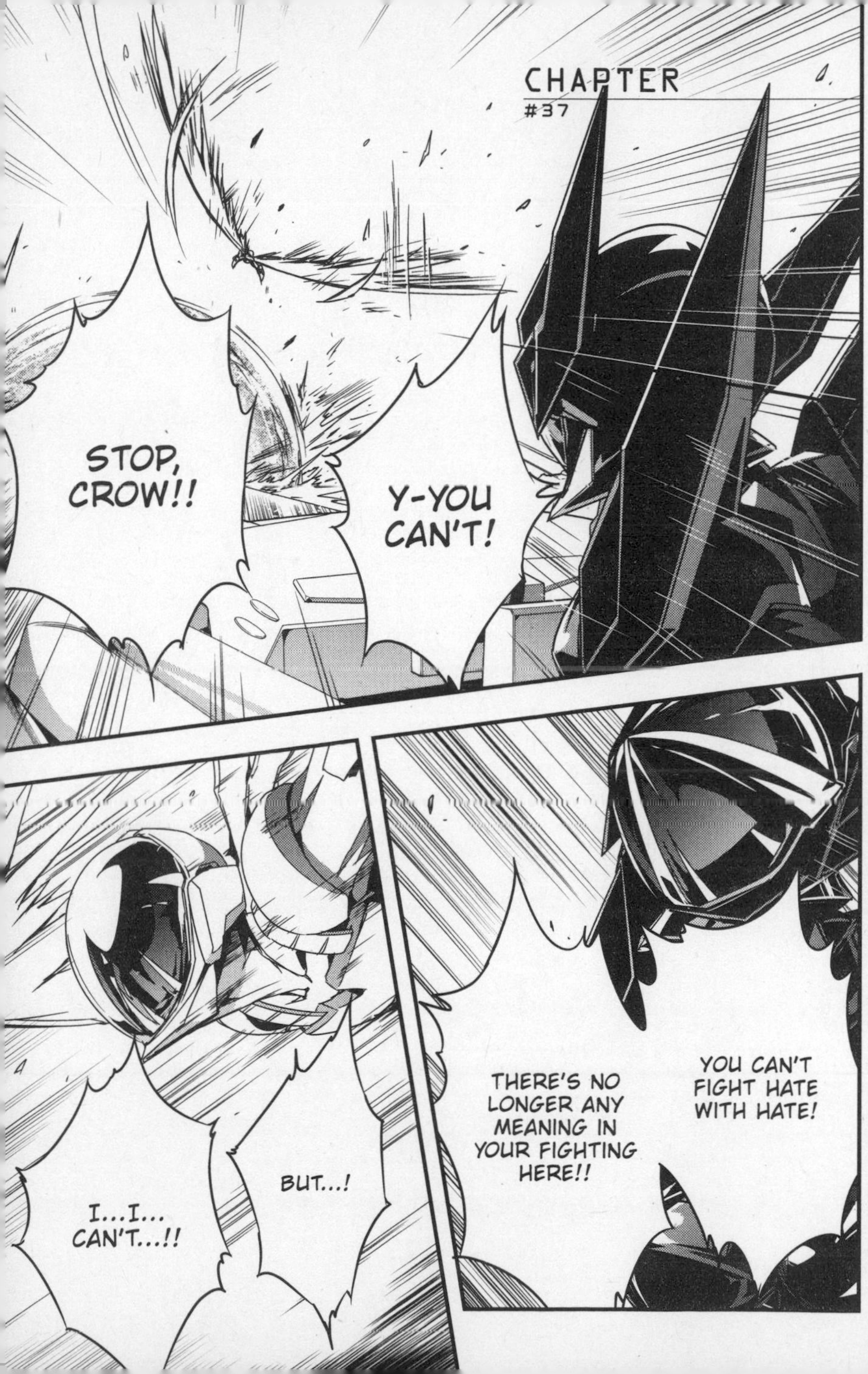
CHAPTER #37
Y-YOU CAN'T!
STOP, CROW!!
YOU CAN'T FIGHT HATE WITH HATE!
THERE'S NO LONGER ANY MEANING IN YOUR FIGHTING HERE!!
BUT...!
I...I... CAN'T...!!

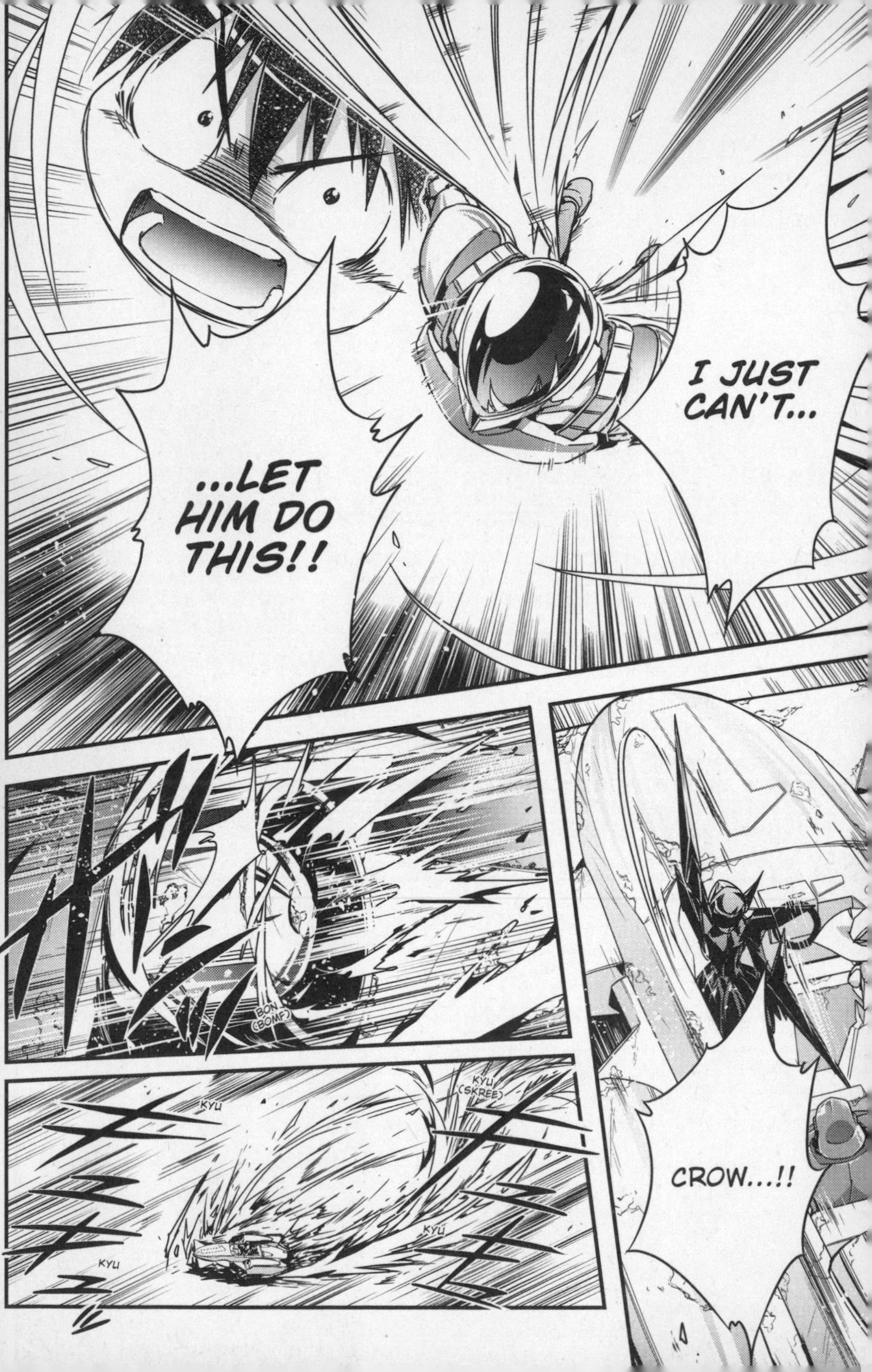
I JUST CAN'T...
...LET HIM DO THIS!!
CROW...!!
BON (BOMF)
KYU (SKREE)
KYU
KYU
KYU

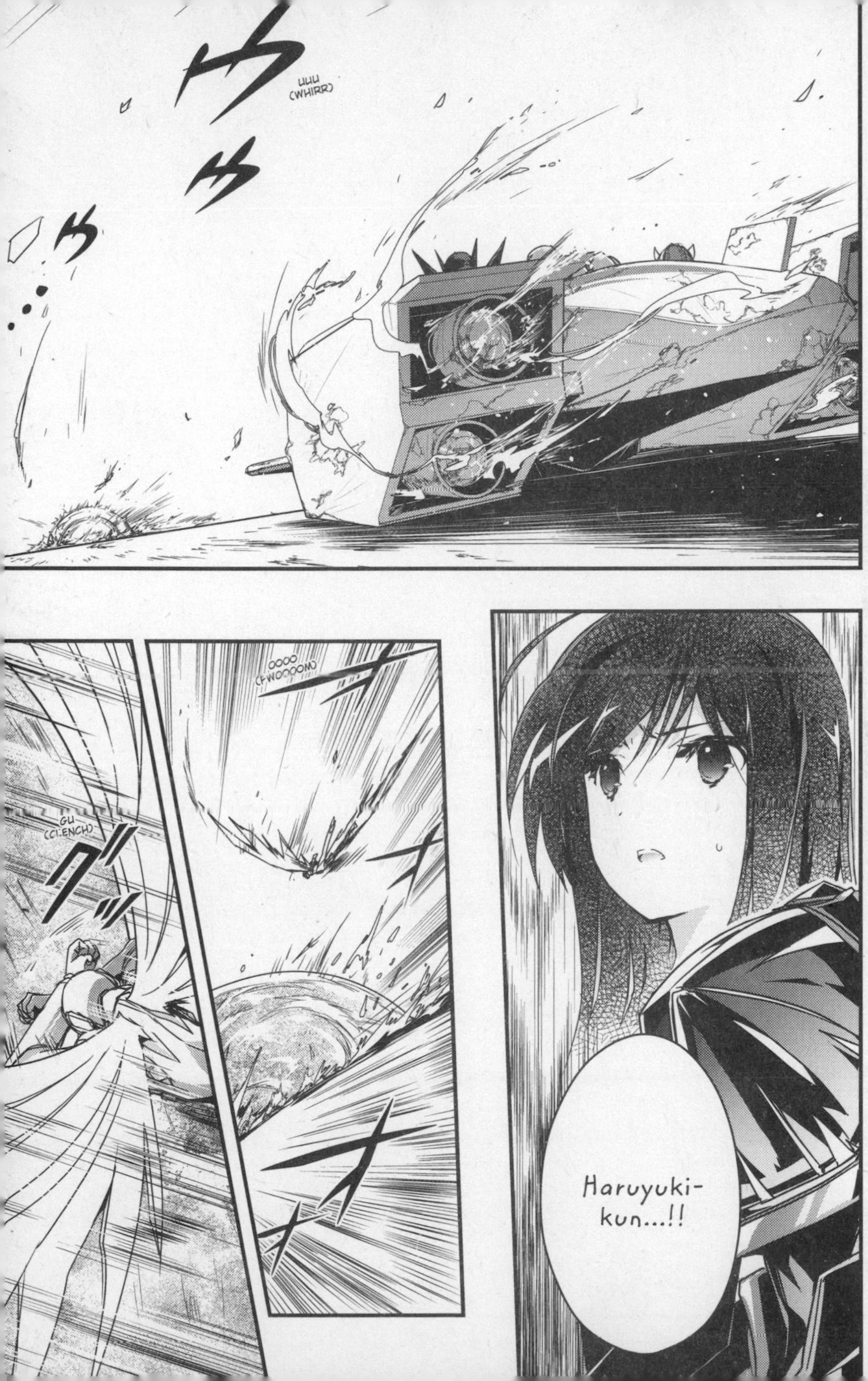
UUU
(WHIRR)
Haruyuki-kun...!!
OOOO
(FWOOOOM)
GU
(CLENCH)

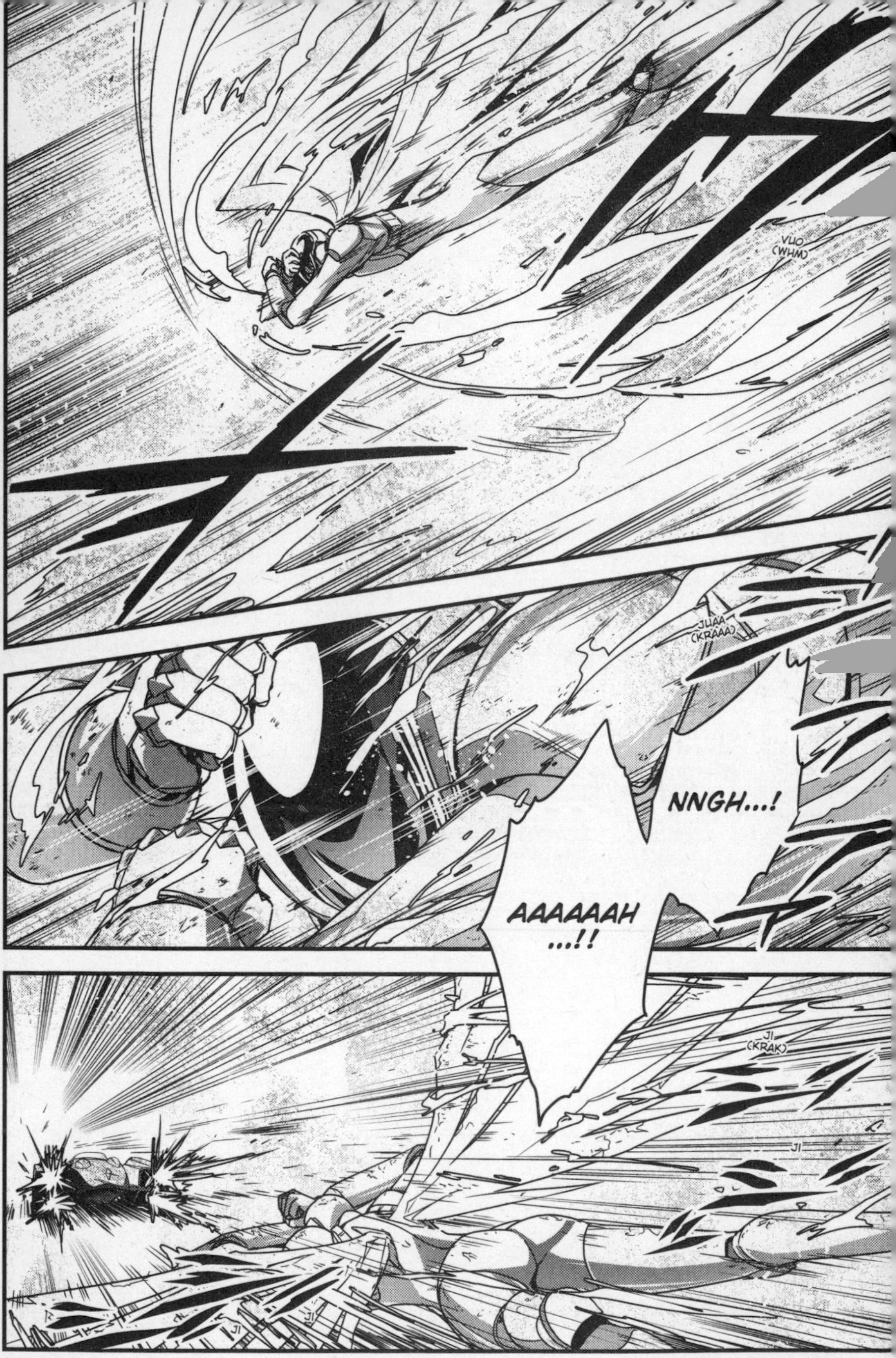
VUO
(WHM)
JUAA
(KRAAA)
NNGH...!
AAAAAAH
...!!
JI
(KRAK)
JI

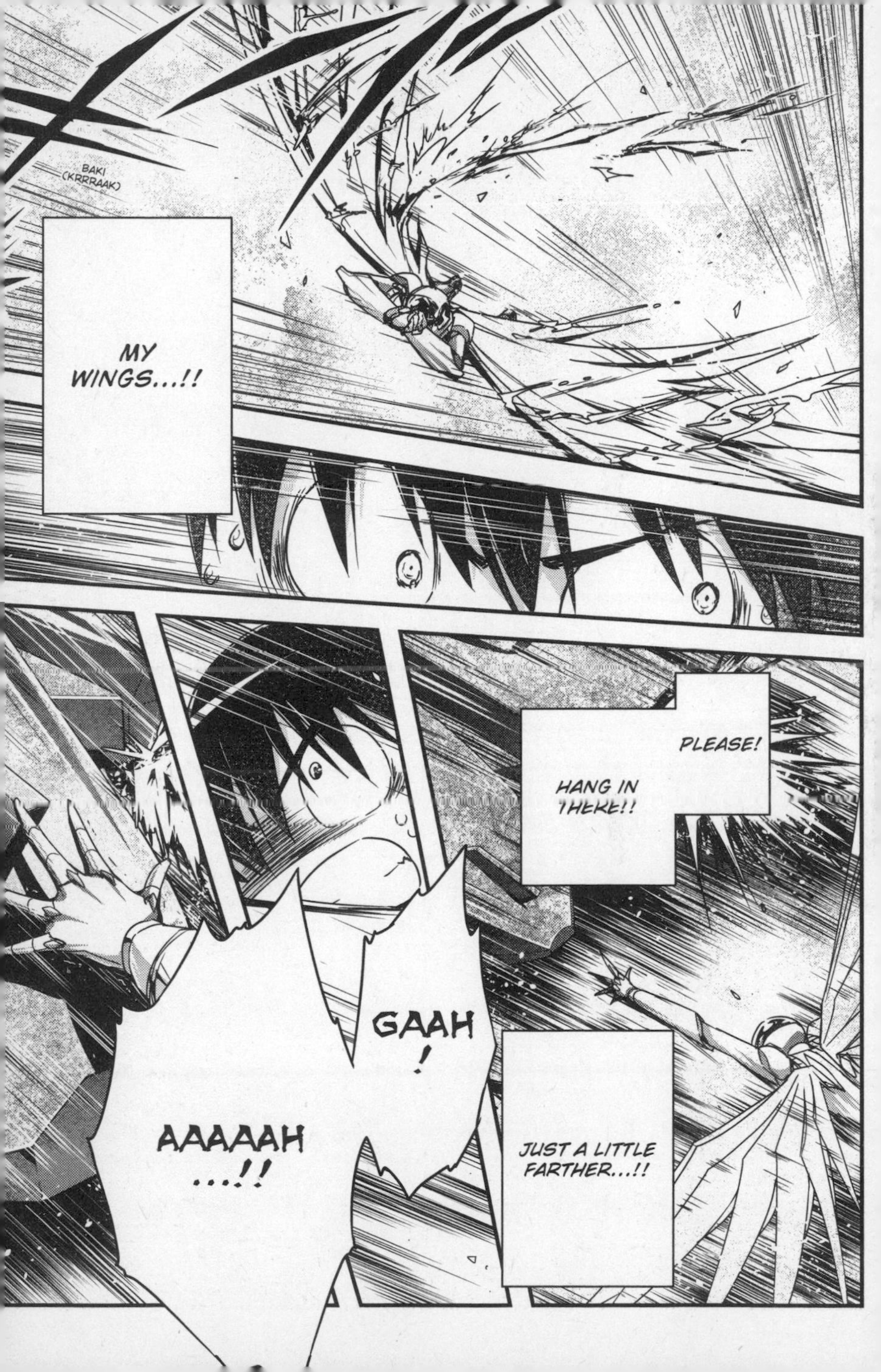
BAKI
(KRRRAAK)
MY WINGS...!!
PLEASE!
HANG IN THERE!!
JUST A LITTLE FARTHER...!!
GAAH!
AAAAAH...!!

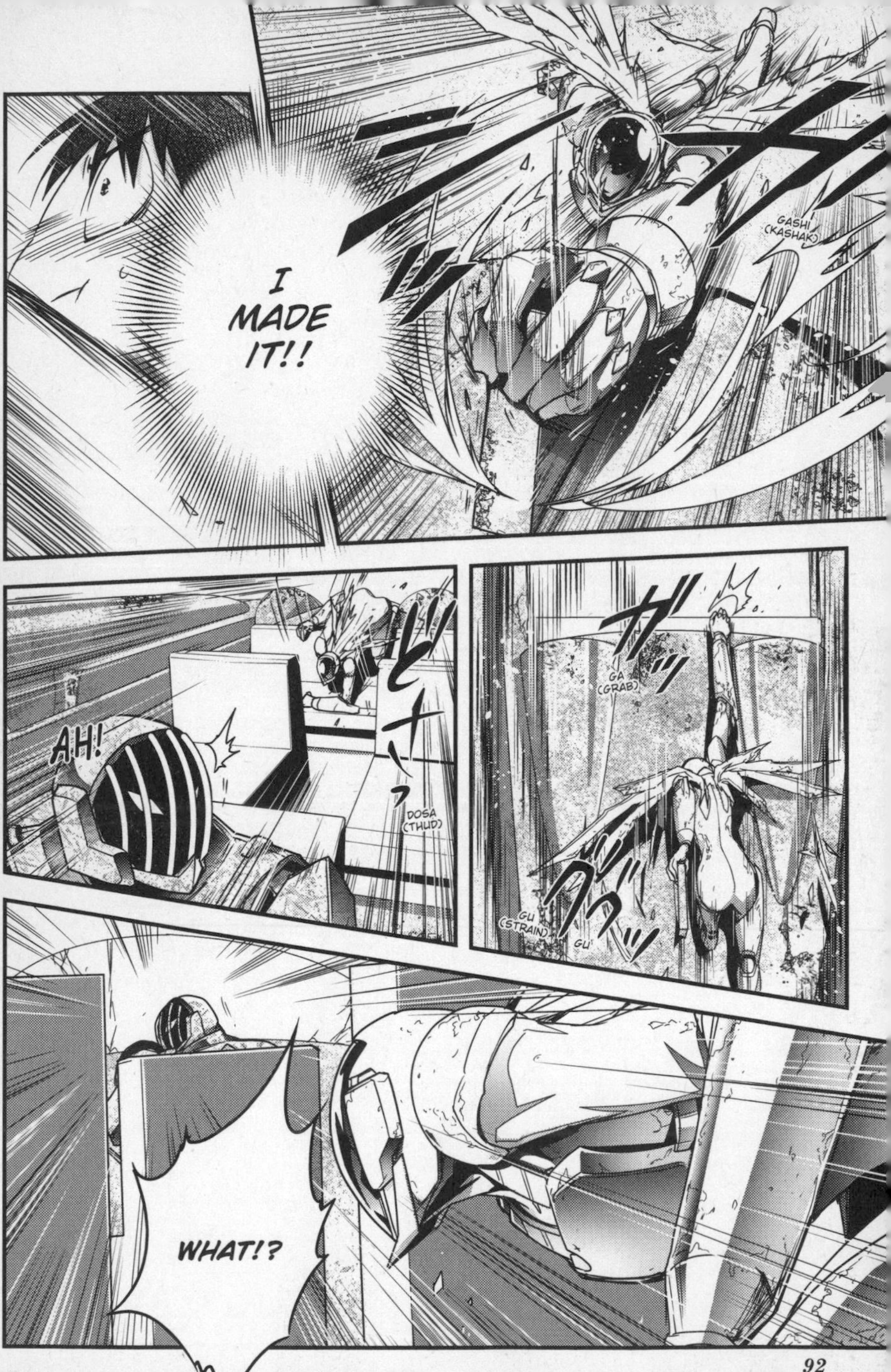
GASHI (KASHAK)
I MADE IT!!
GA (GRAB)
GU (STRAIN) GU
DOSA (THUD)
AH!
WHAT!?

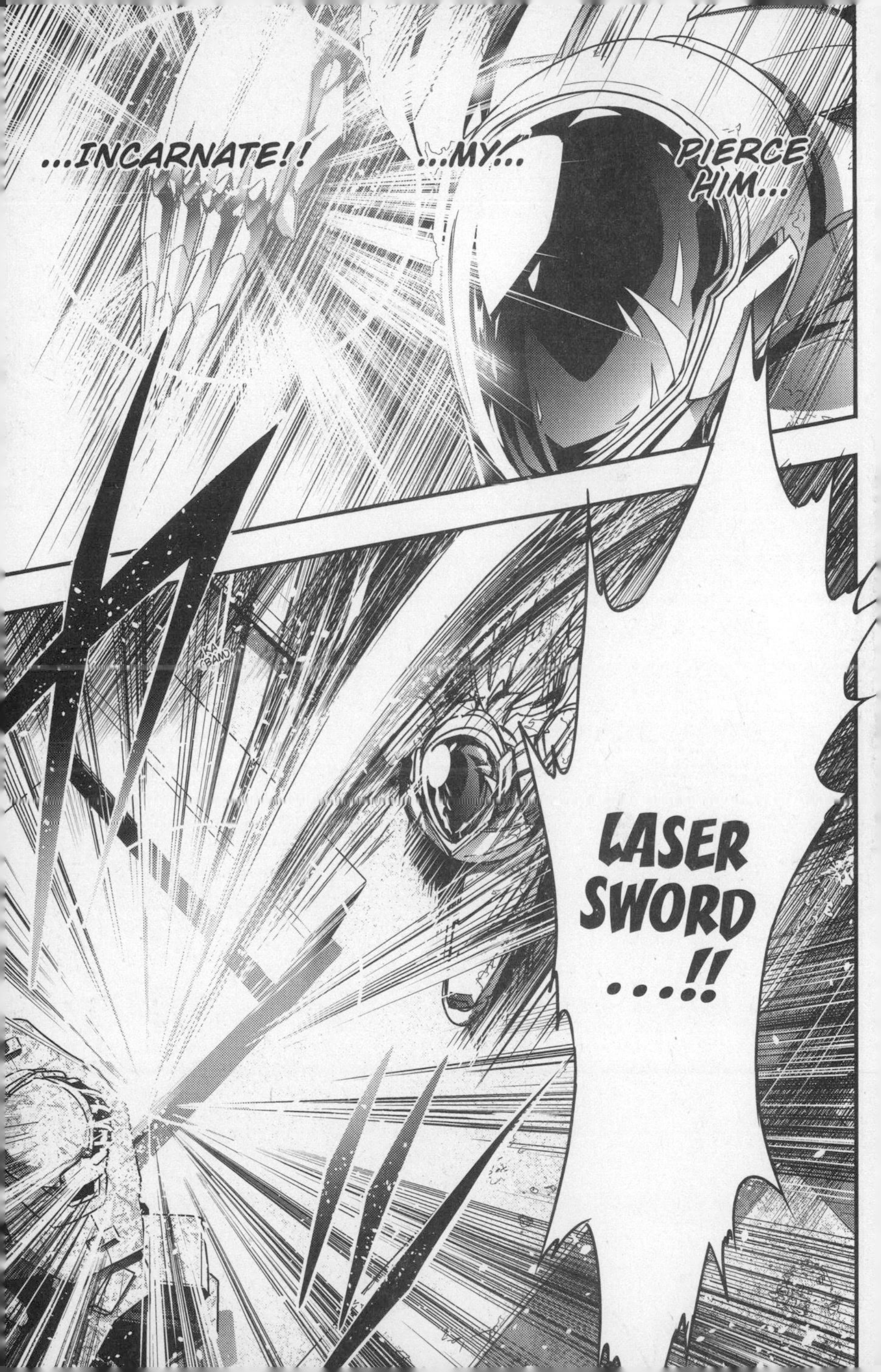
PIERCE HIM...
...MY...
...INCARNATE!!
LASER SWORD ...!!
KA BAM

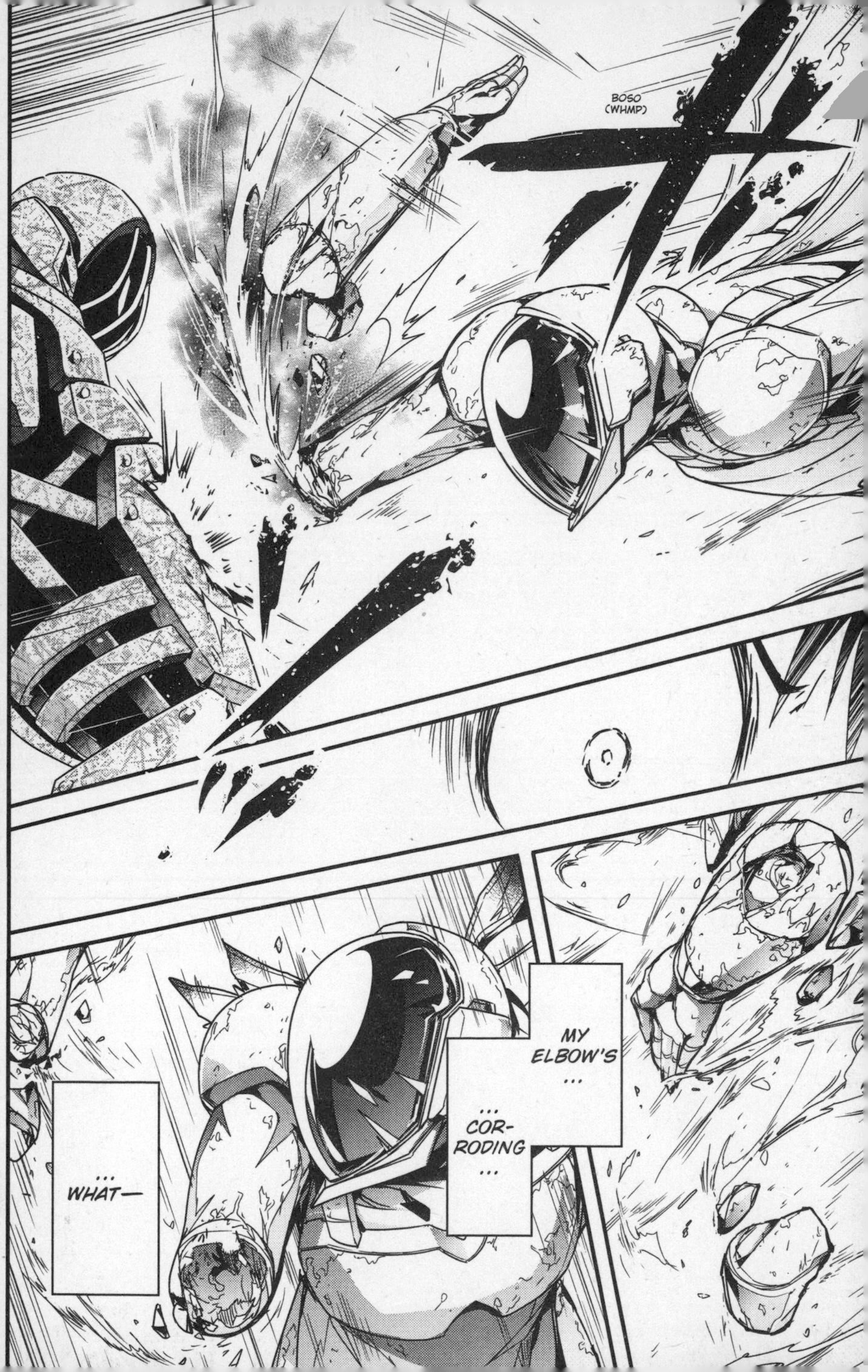
BOSO (WHMP)
MY ELBOW'S...
...COR-RODING...
...WHAT—

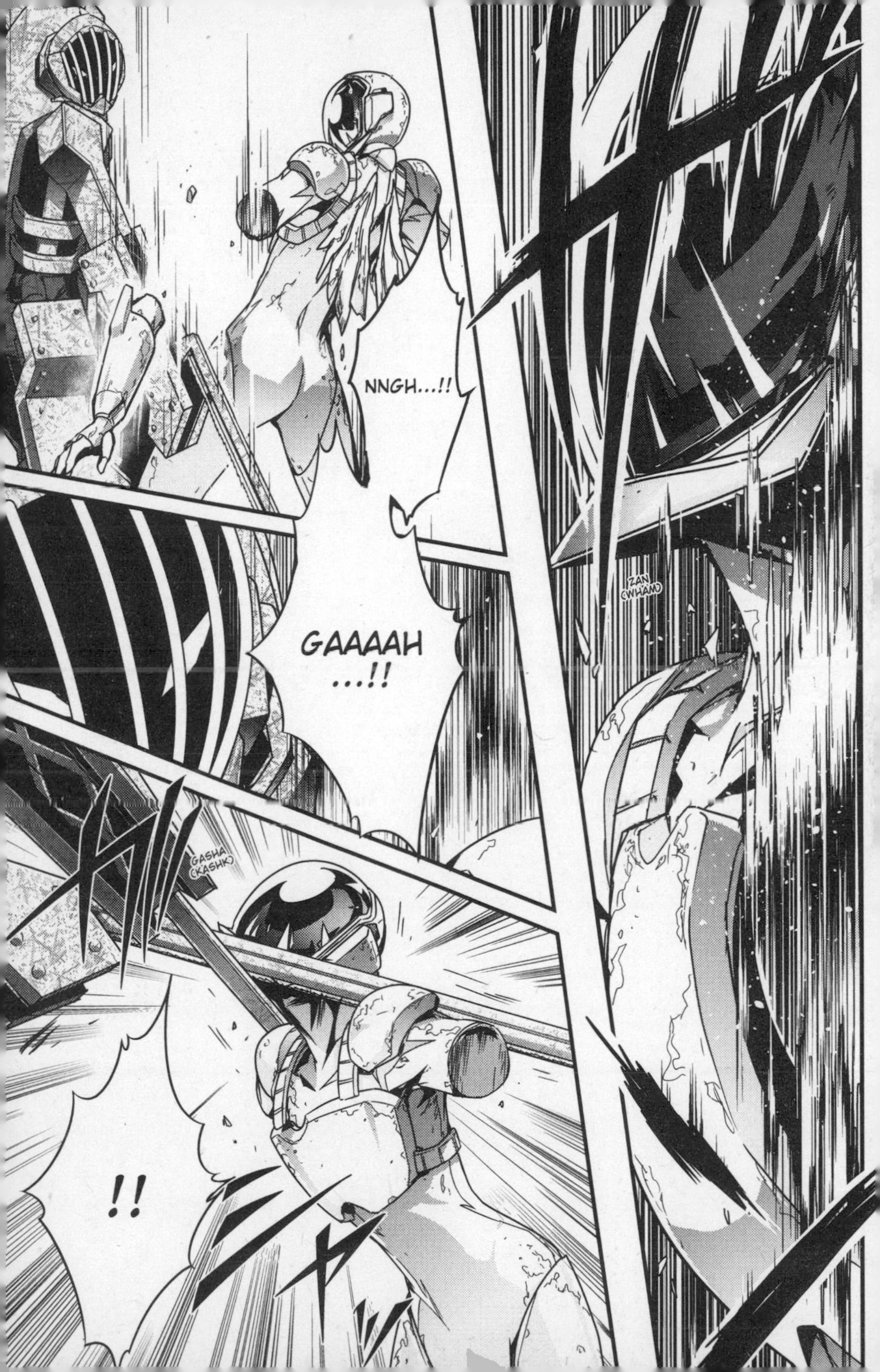
ZAN (WHAM)
NNGH...!!
GAAAH ...!!
GASHA (KASHK)
!!

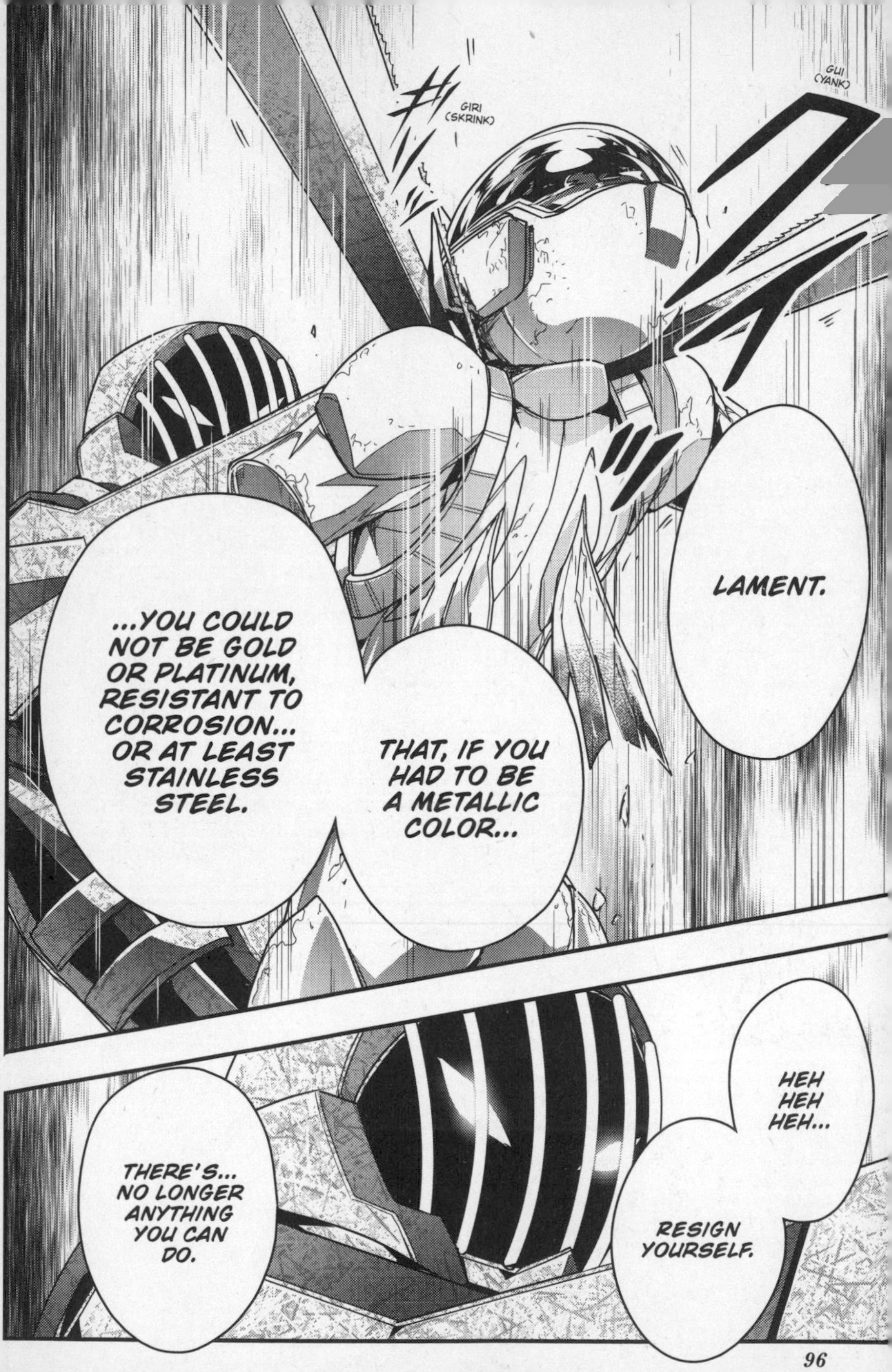
GUI (YANK)
GIRI (SKRINK)
LAMENT.
THAT, IF YOU HAD TO BE A METALLIC COLOR...
...YOU COULD NOT BE GOLD OR PLATINUM, RESISTANT TO CORROSION... OR AT LEAST STAINLESS STEEL.
HEH HEH HEH...
RESIGN YOURSELF.
THERE'S... NO LONGER ANYTHING YOU CAN DO.

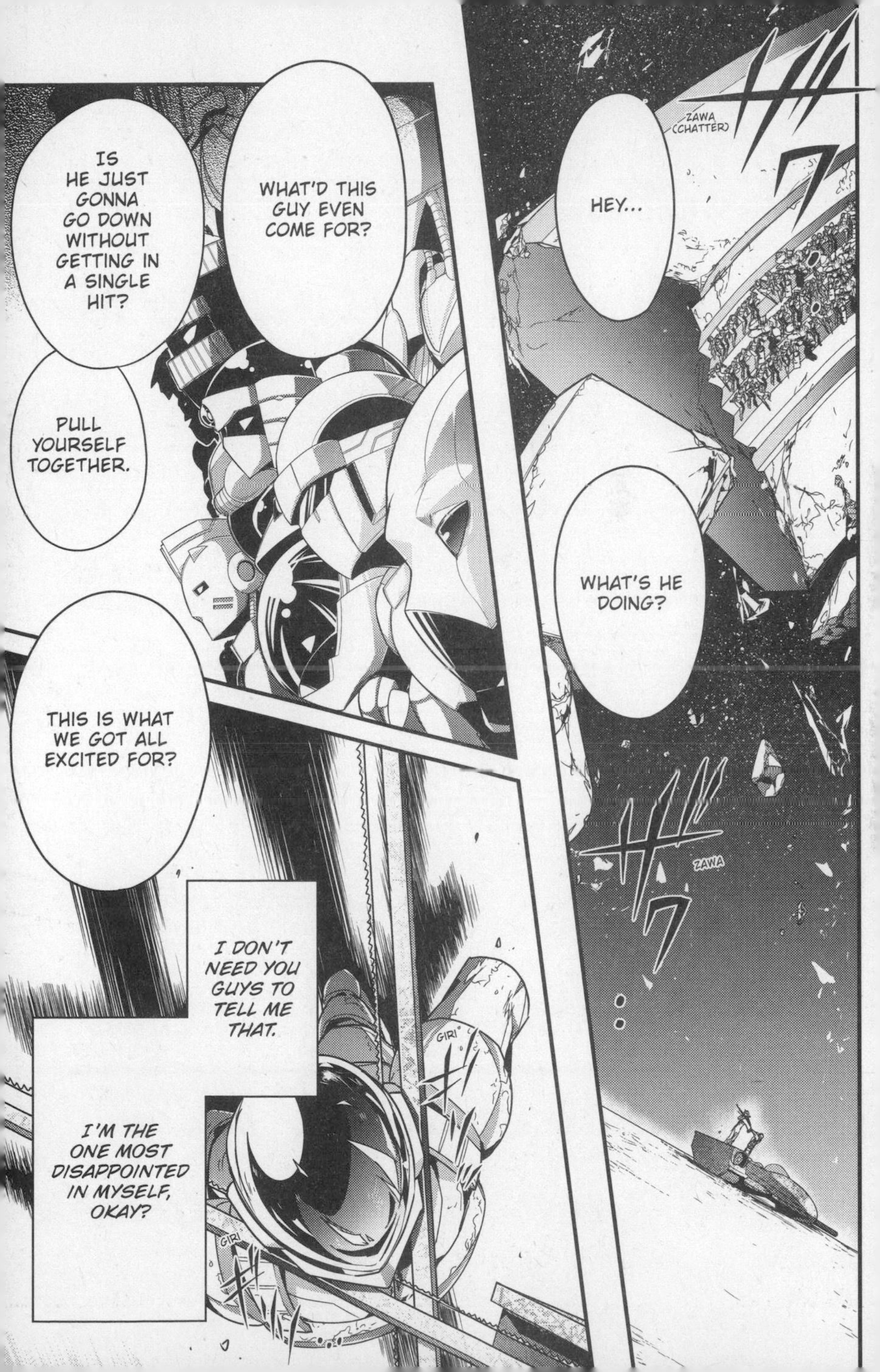
ZAWA (CHATTER)
HEY...
WHAT'S HE DOING?
ZAWA
WHAT'D THIS GUY EVEN COME FOR?
IS HE JUST GONNA GO DOWN WITHOUT GETTING IN A SINGLE HIT?
PULL YOURSELF TOGETHER.
THIS IS WHAT WE GOT ALL EXCITED FOR?
GIRI
I DON'T NEED YOU GUYS TO TELL ME THAT.
I'M THE ONE MOST DISAPPOINTED IN MYSELF, OKAY?
GIRI

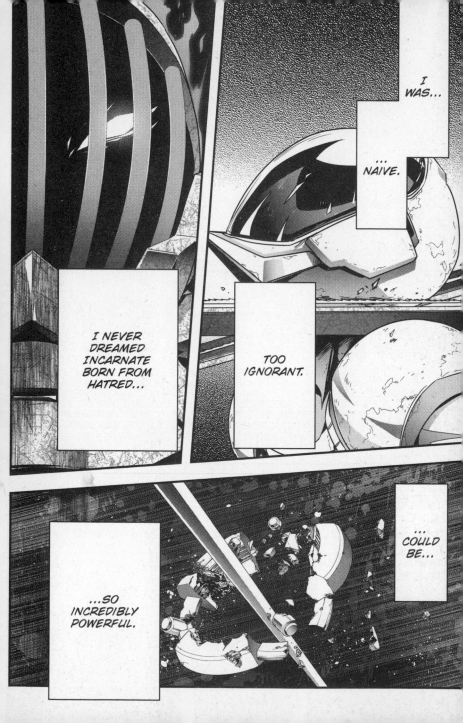

I WAS...

... NAÏVE.

I NEVER DREAMED INCARNATE BORN FROM HATRED...

TOO IGNORANT.

... COULD BE...

...SO INCREDIBLY POWERFUL.

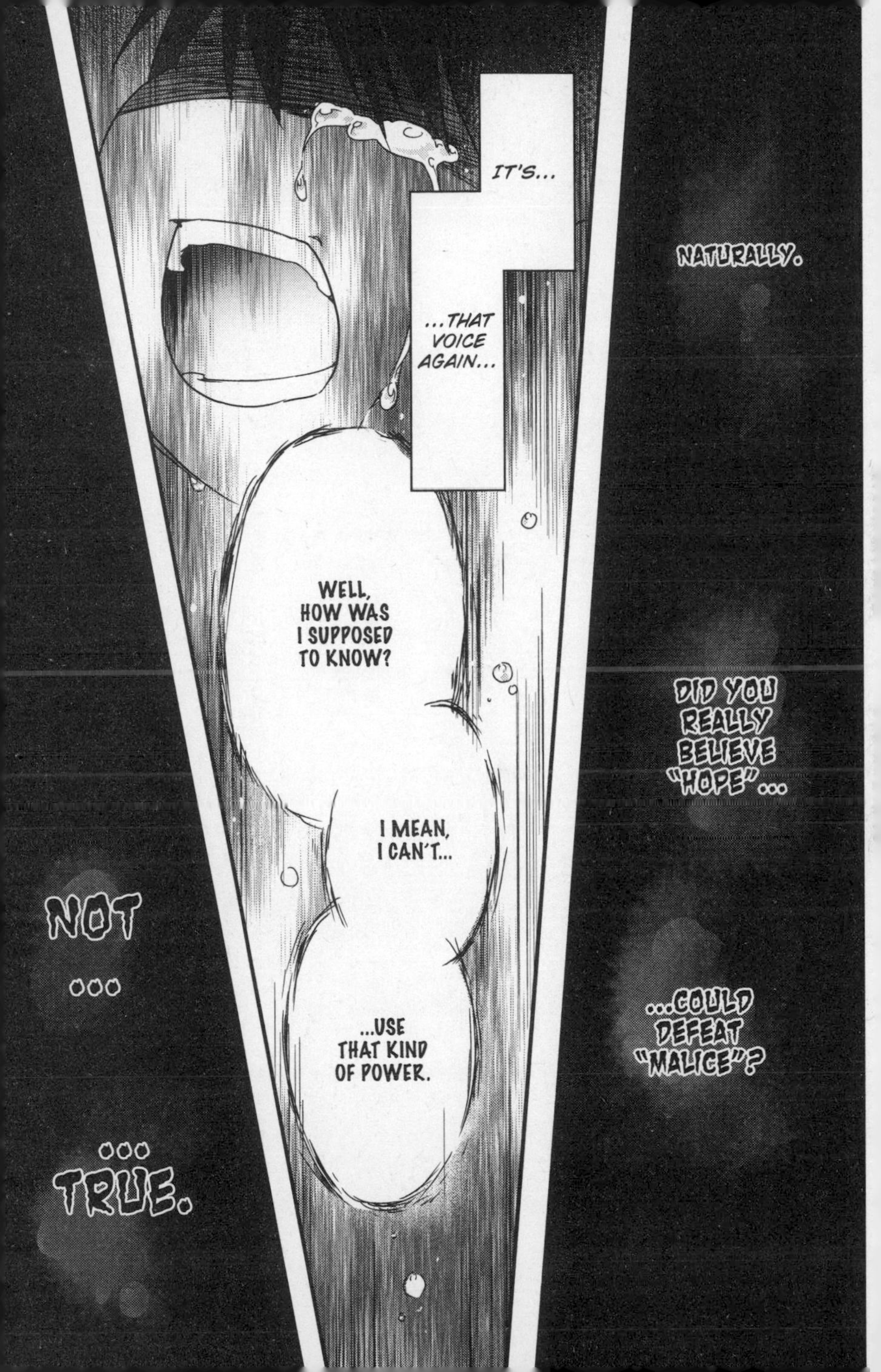
NATURALLY.
DID YOU REALLY BELIEVE "HOPE"...
...COULD DEFEAT "MALICE"?
IT'S...
...THAT VOICE AGAIN...
WELL, HOW WAS I SUPPOSED TO KNOW?
I MEAN, I CAN'T...
...USE THAT KIND OF POWER.
NOT ...
... TRUE.

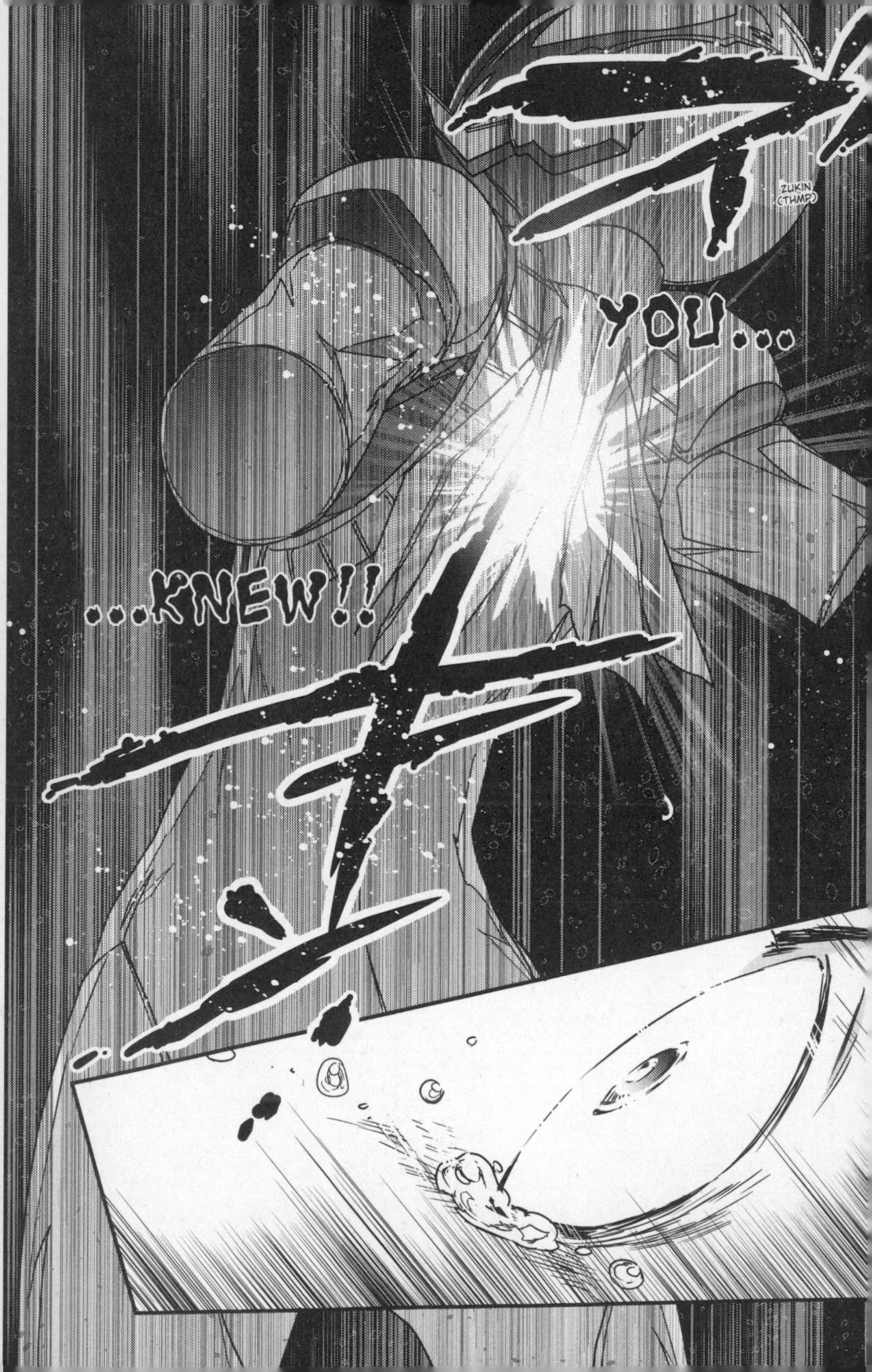
ZUKIN
(THMP)
YOU...
...KNEW!!

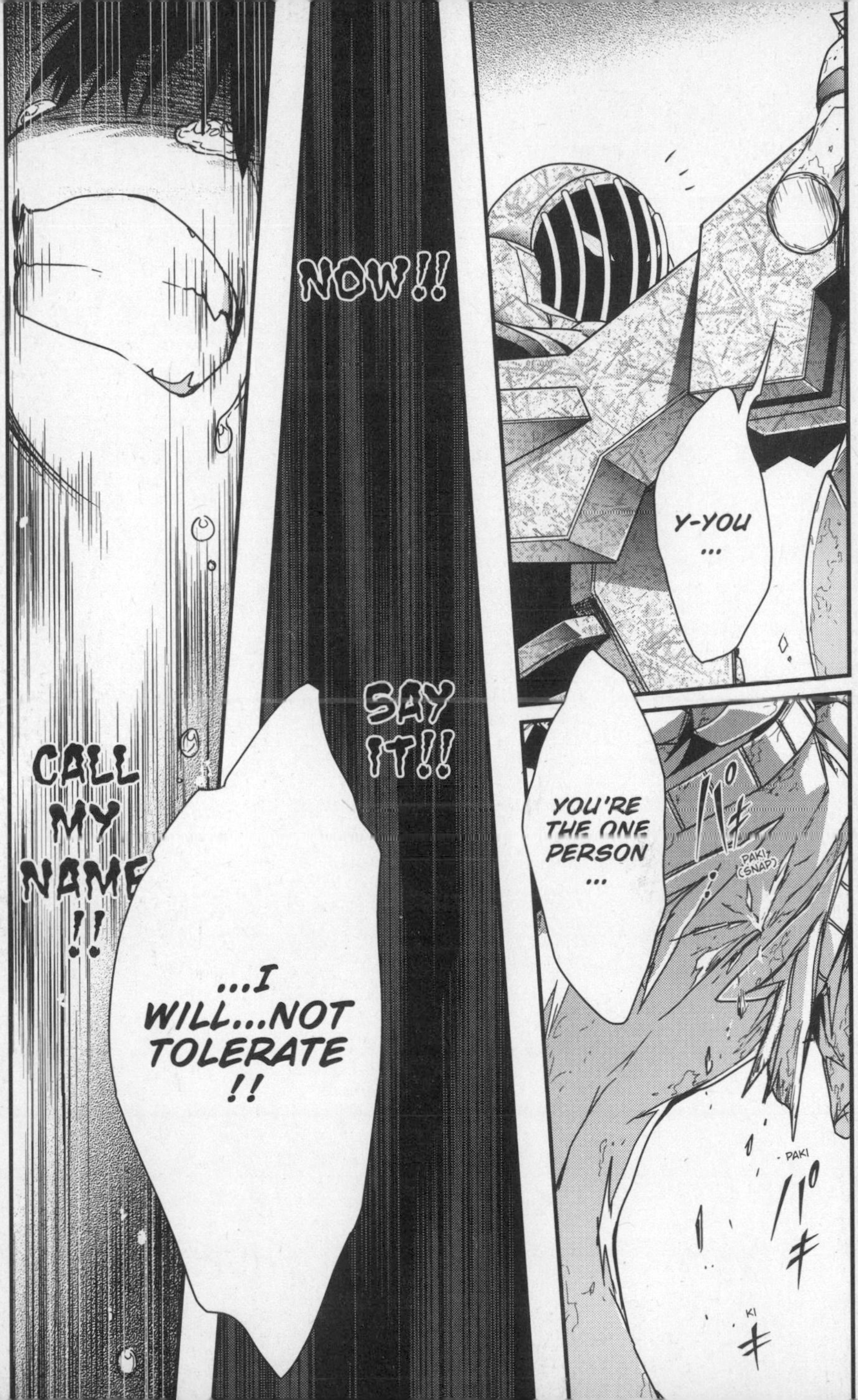
Y-YOU ...
YOU'RE THE ONE PERSON ...
PAKI (SNAP)
PAKI
KI
...I WILL...NOT TOLERATE !!
SAY IT!!
NOW!!
CALL MY NAME !!

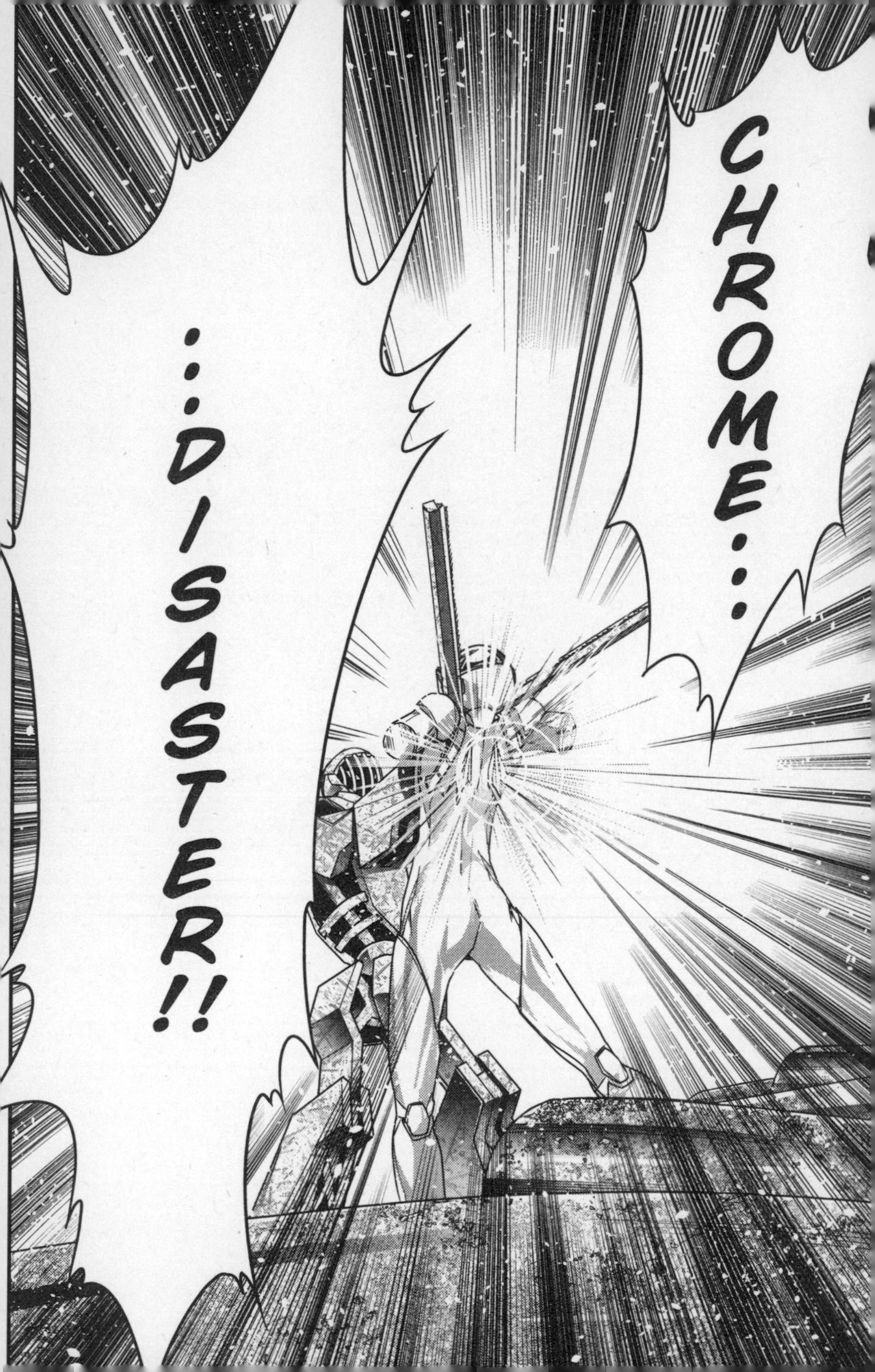
CHROME...
...DISASTER!!

CHAPTER #38

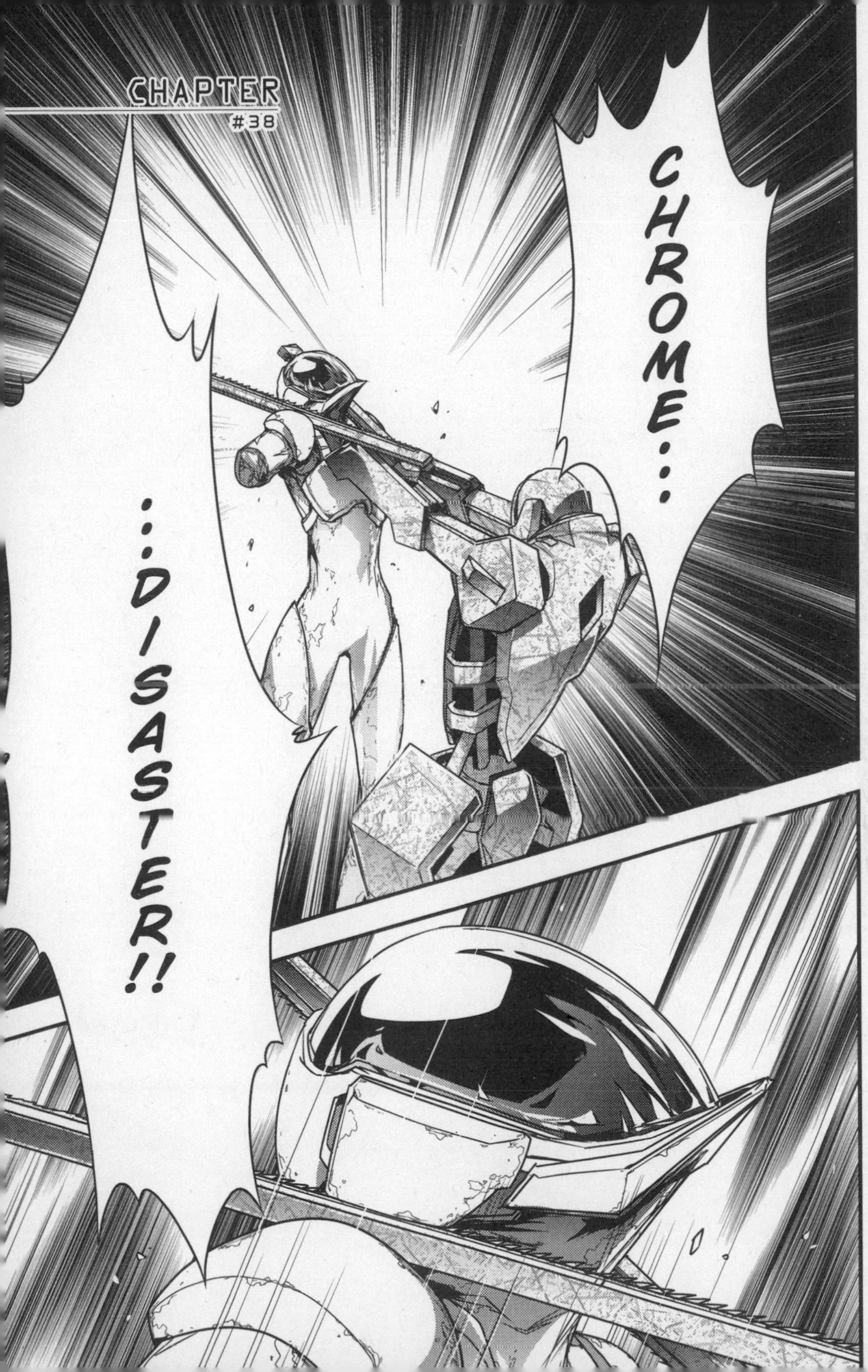
CHROME...
...DISASTER!!

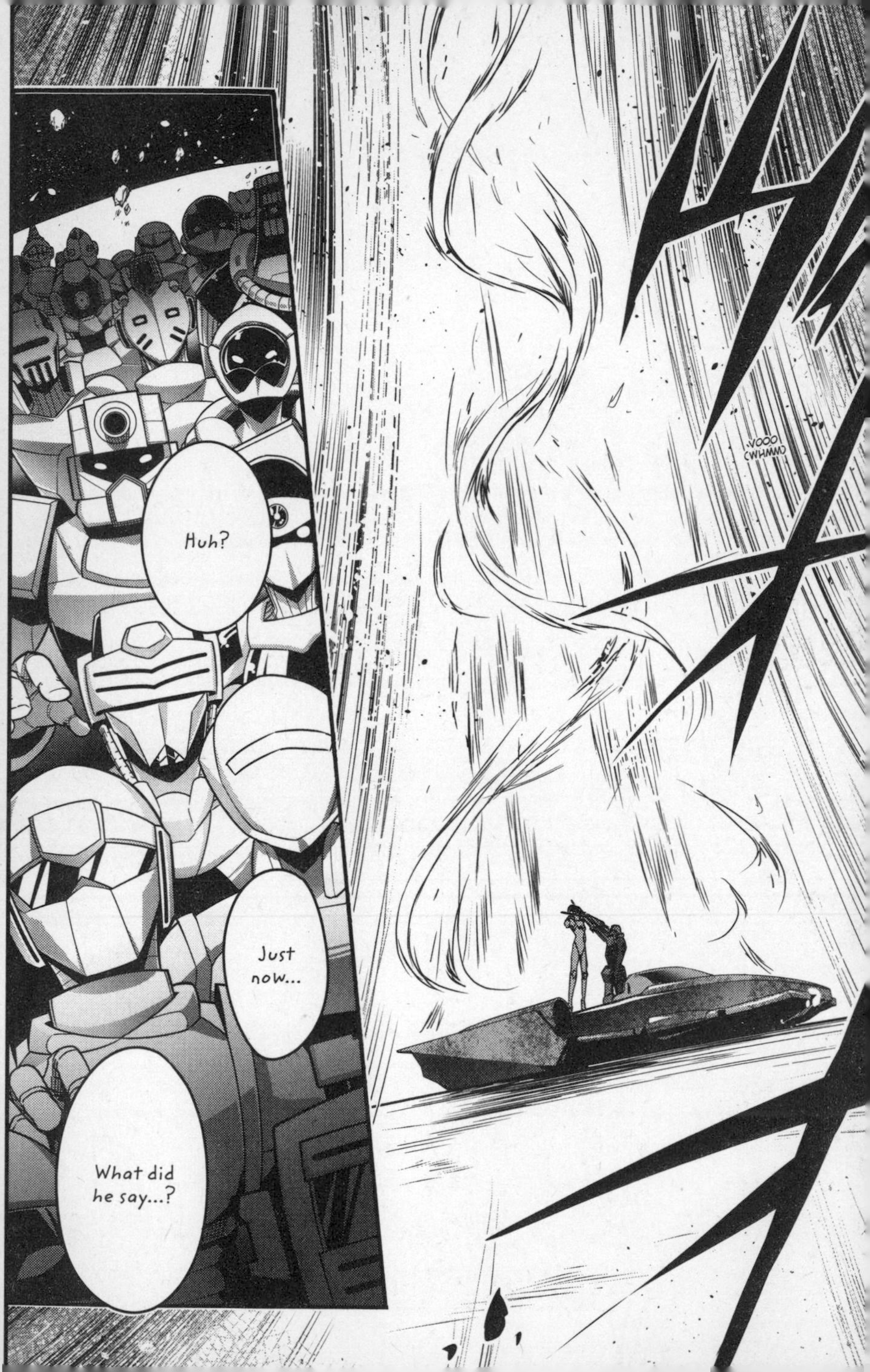
VOOO (WHMM)
Huh?
Just now...
What did he say...?

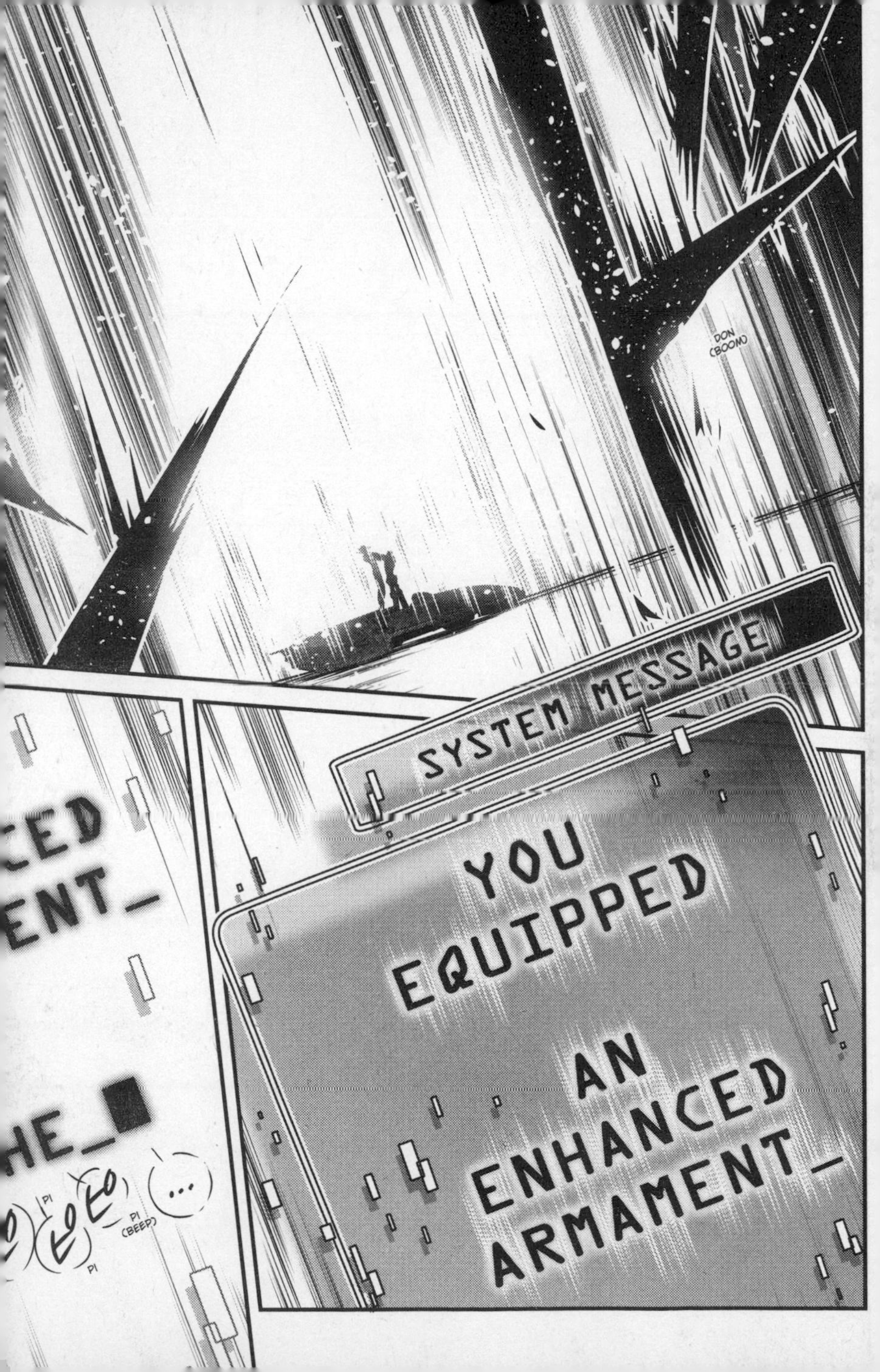
DON (BOOM)
SYSTEM MESSAGE
YOU EQUIPPED AN ENHANCED ARMAMENT_
CED
ENT_
HE_
PI
PI
PI (BEEP)
...

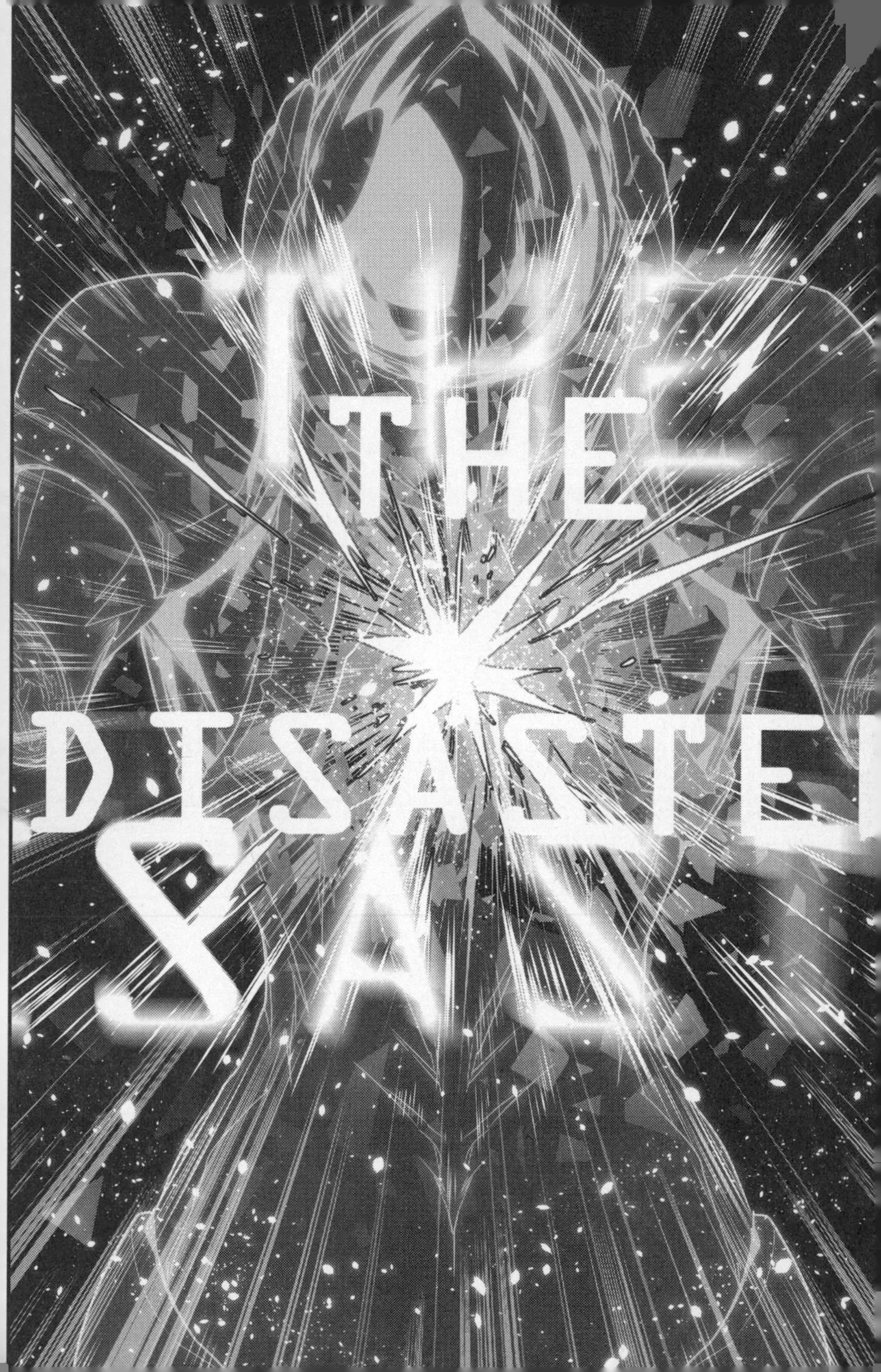
I THE
DISASTE

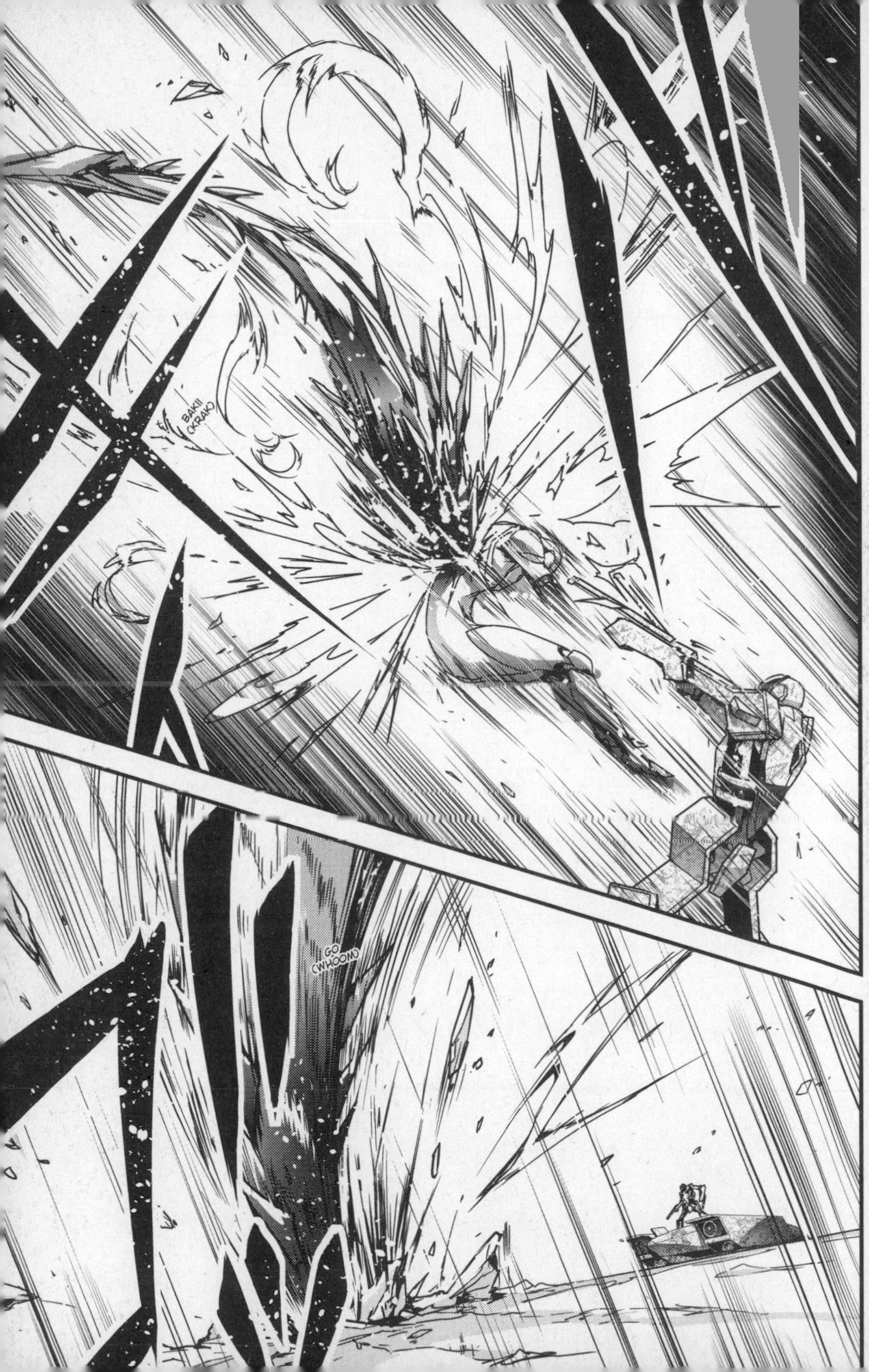
BAKI! (KRAK)
GO (WHOOM)

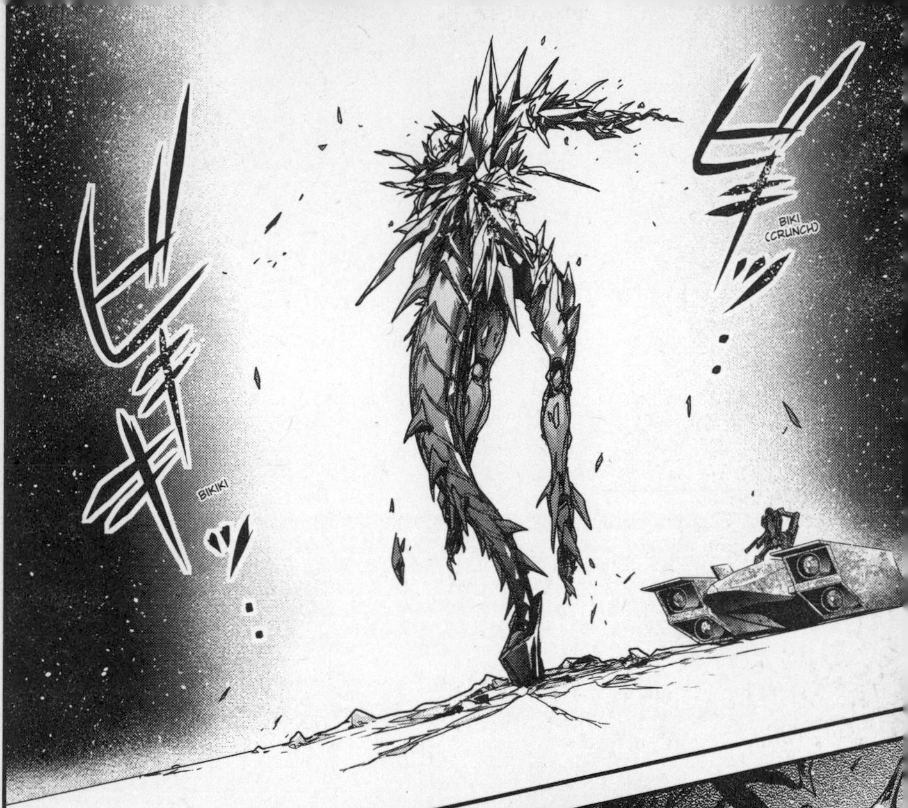
BIKI (CRUNCH)
BIKIKI
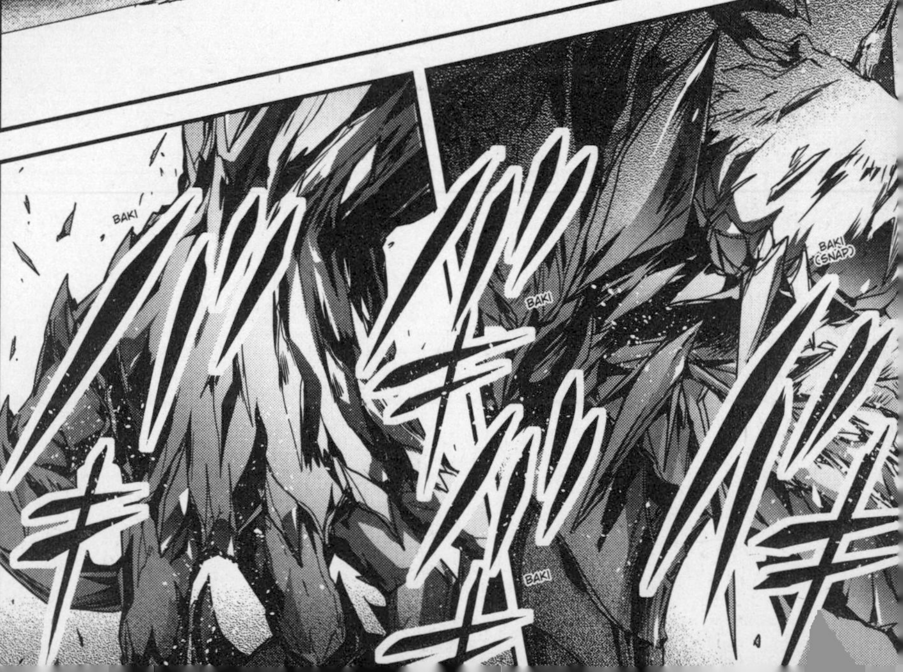
BAKI (SNAP)
BAKI
BAKI
BAKI

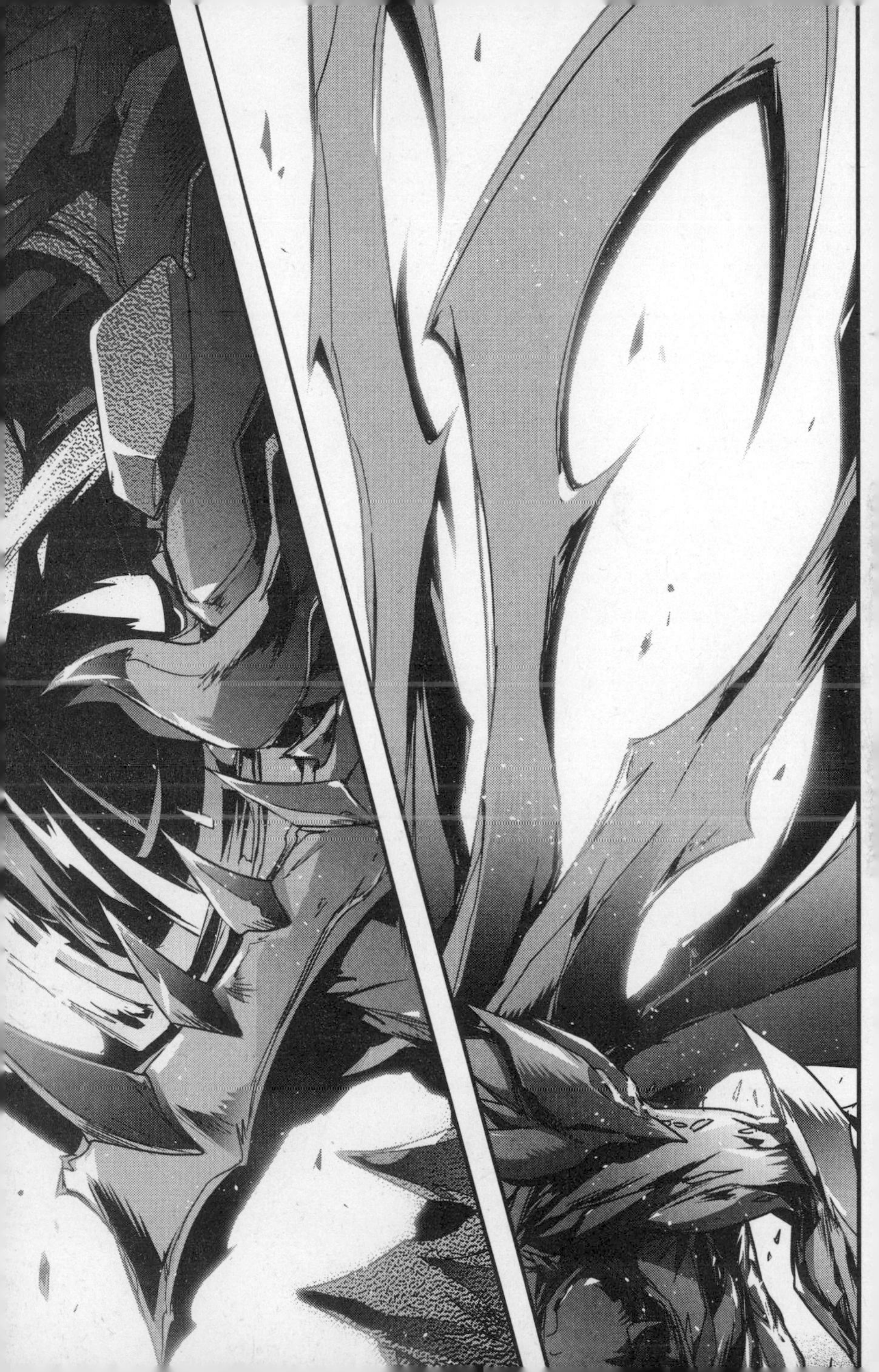

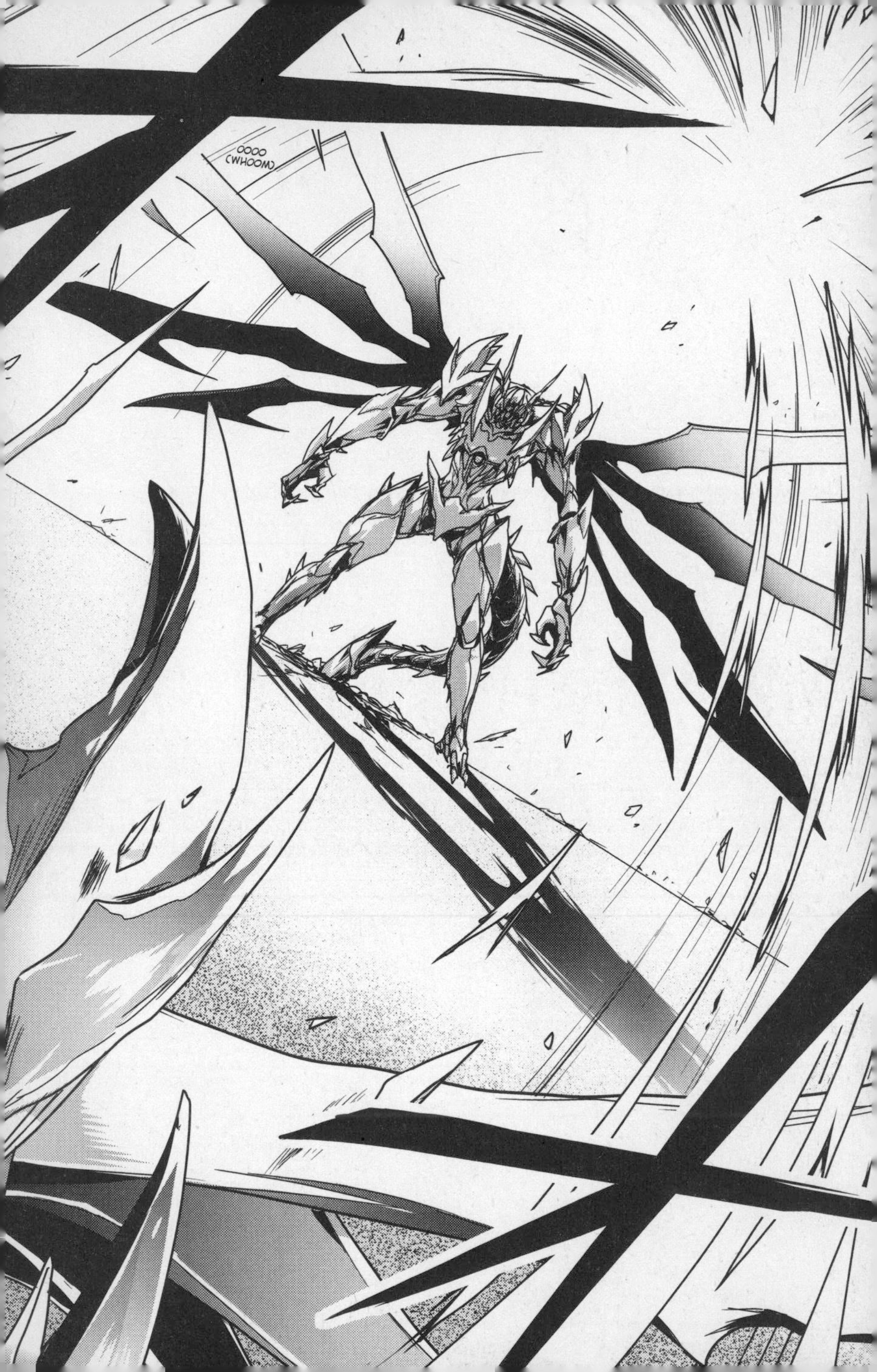
OOOO
(WHOOM)

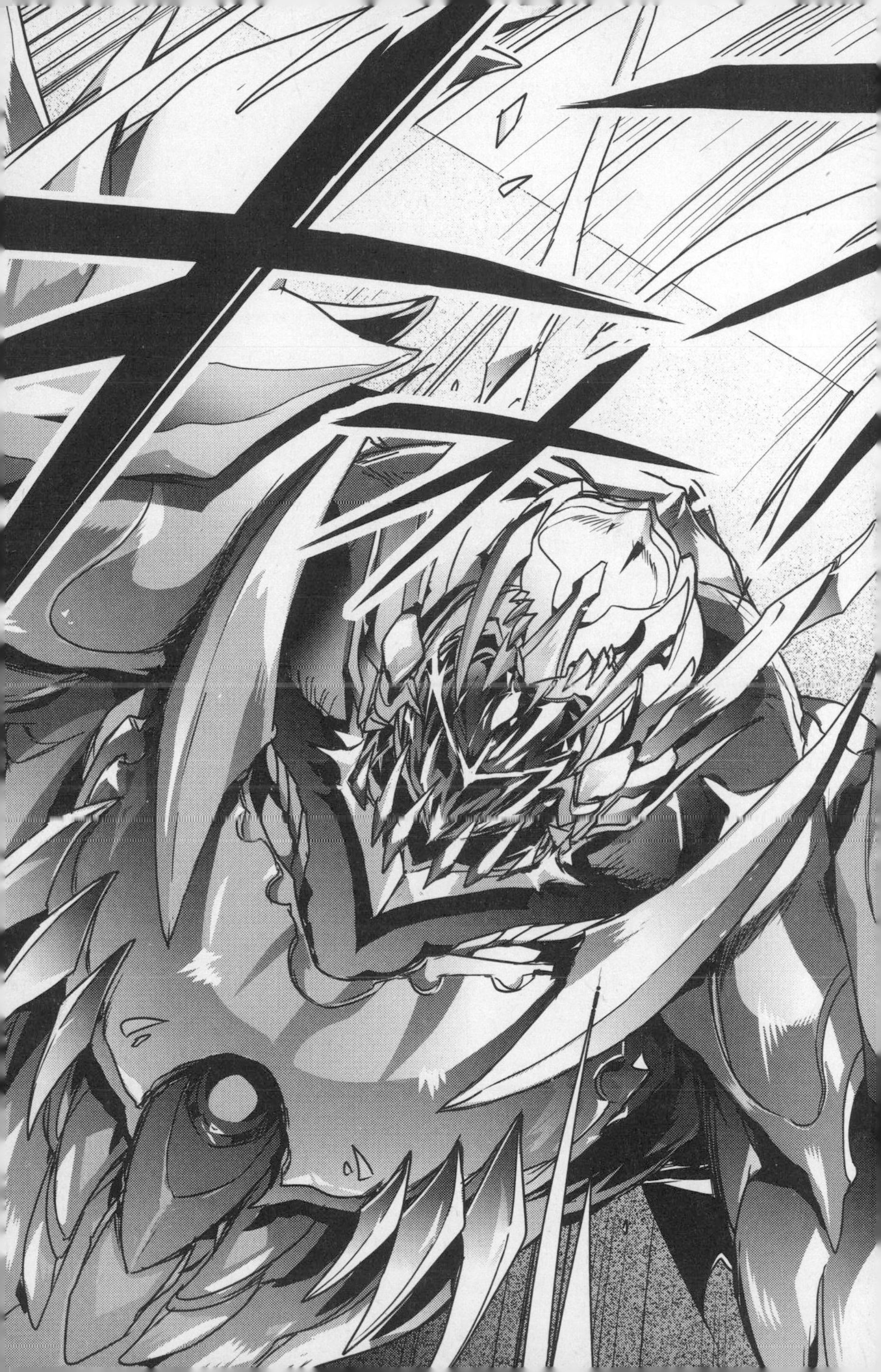

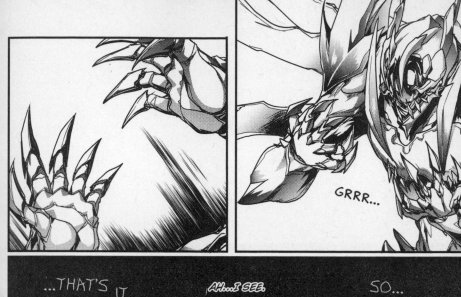

GRRR...
SO...
AH...I SEE.
...THAT'S IT...
I'M AL-READY... THE SIXTH...
...CHROME DISAS-TER.

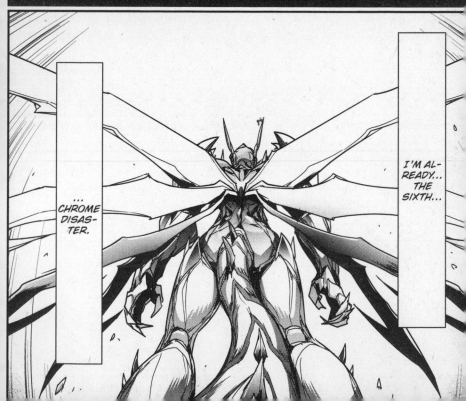

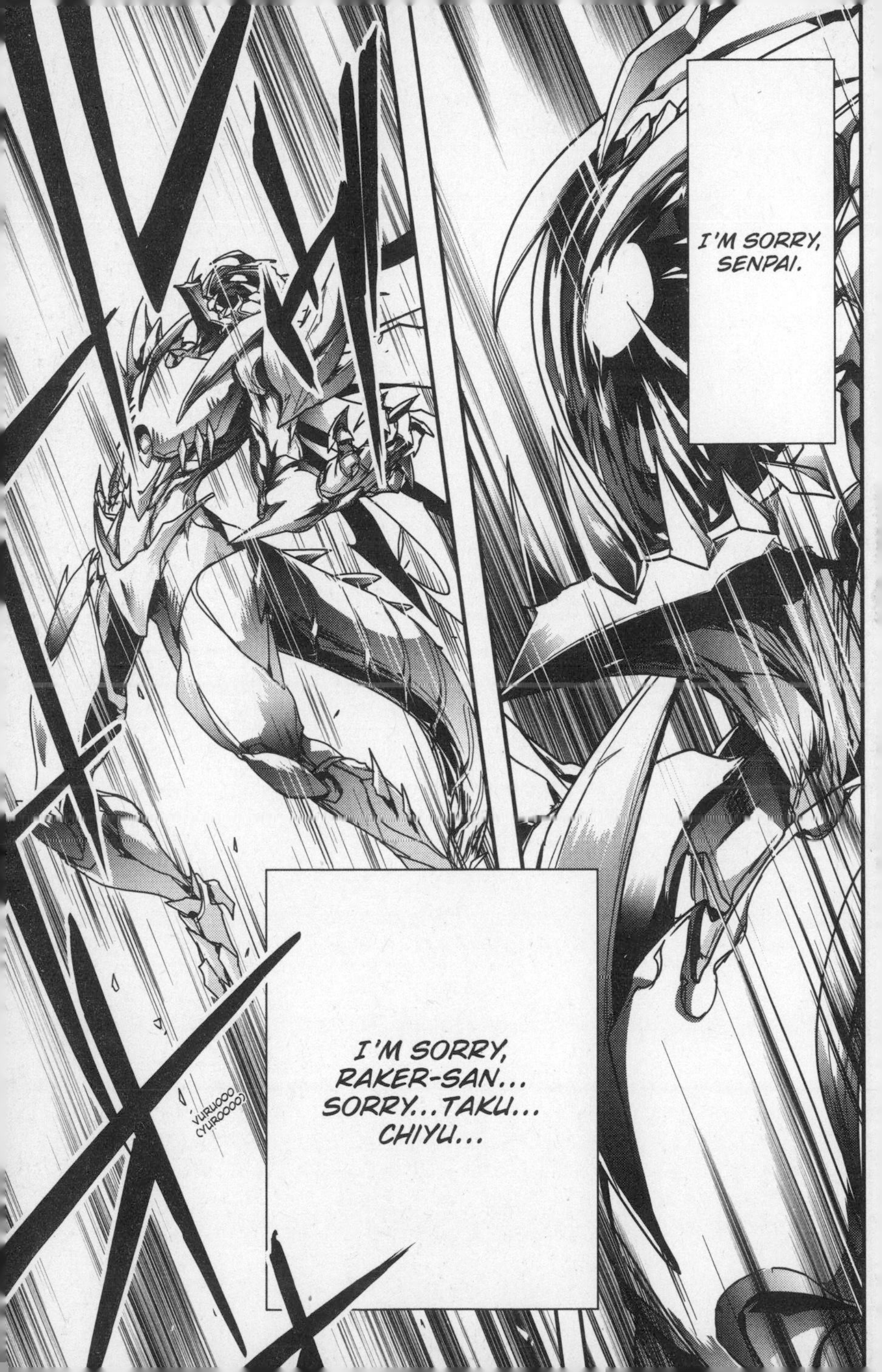
I'M SORRY, SENPAI.
I'M SORRY, RAKER-SAN... SORRY...TAKU... CHIYU...
YURUOOO (YUROOOO)

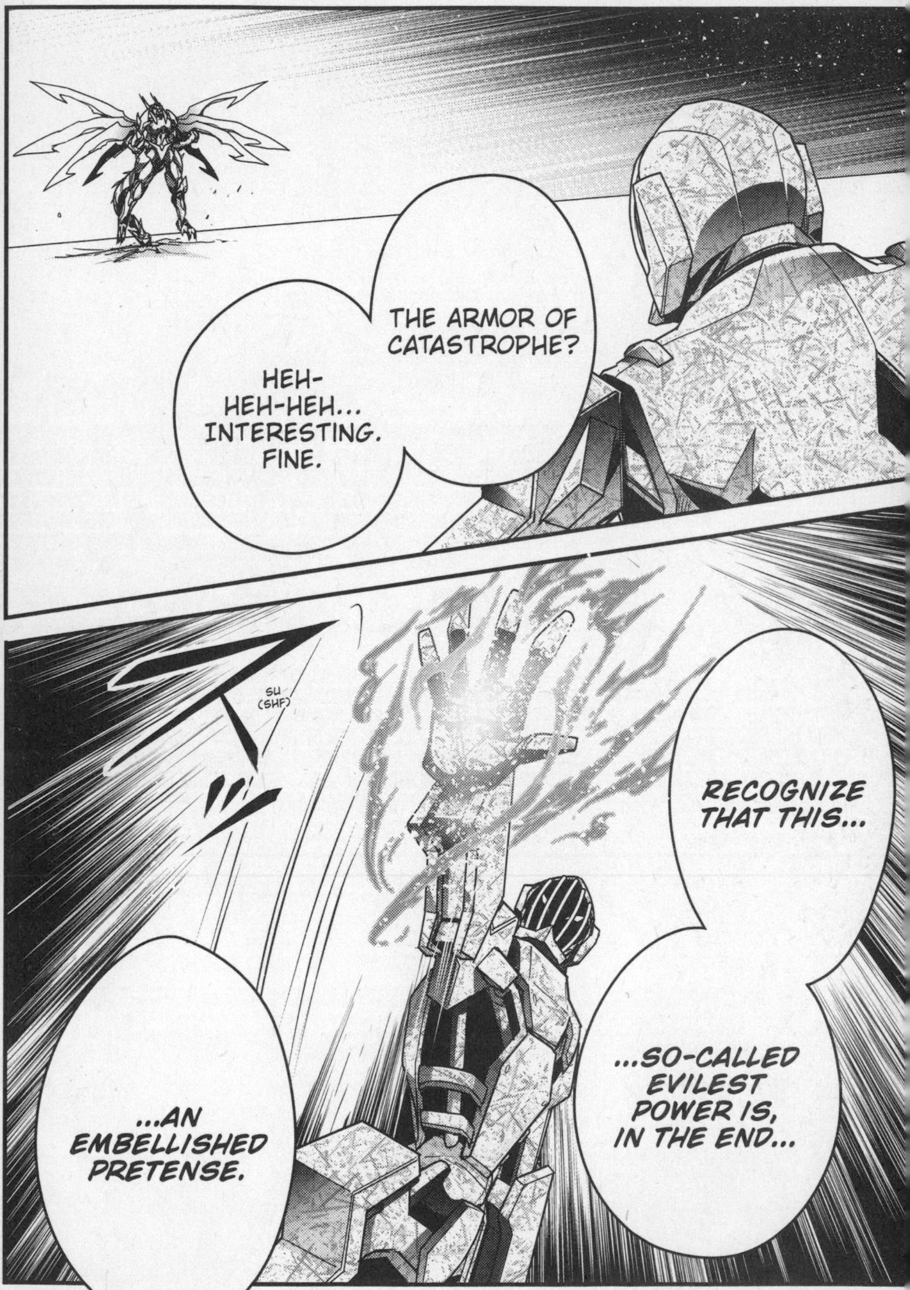
THE ARMOR OF CATASTROPHE?
HEH-HEH-HEH... INTERESTING. FINE.
RECOGNIZE THAT THIS...
SU (SHF)
...SO-CALLED EVILEST POWER IS, IN THE END...
...AN EMBELLISHED PRETENSE.

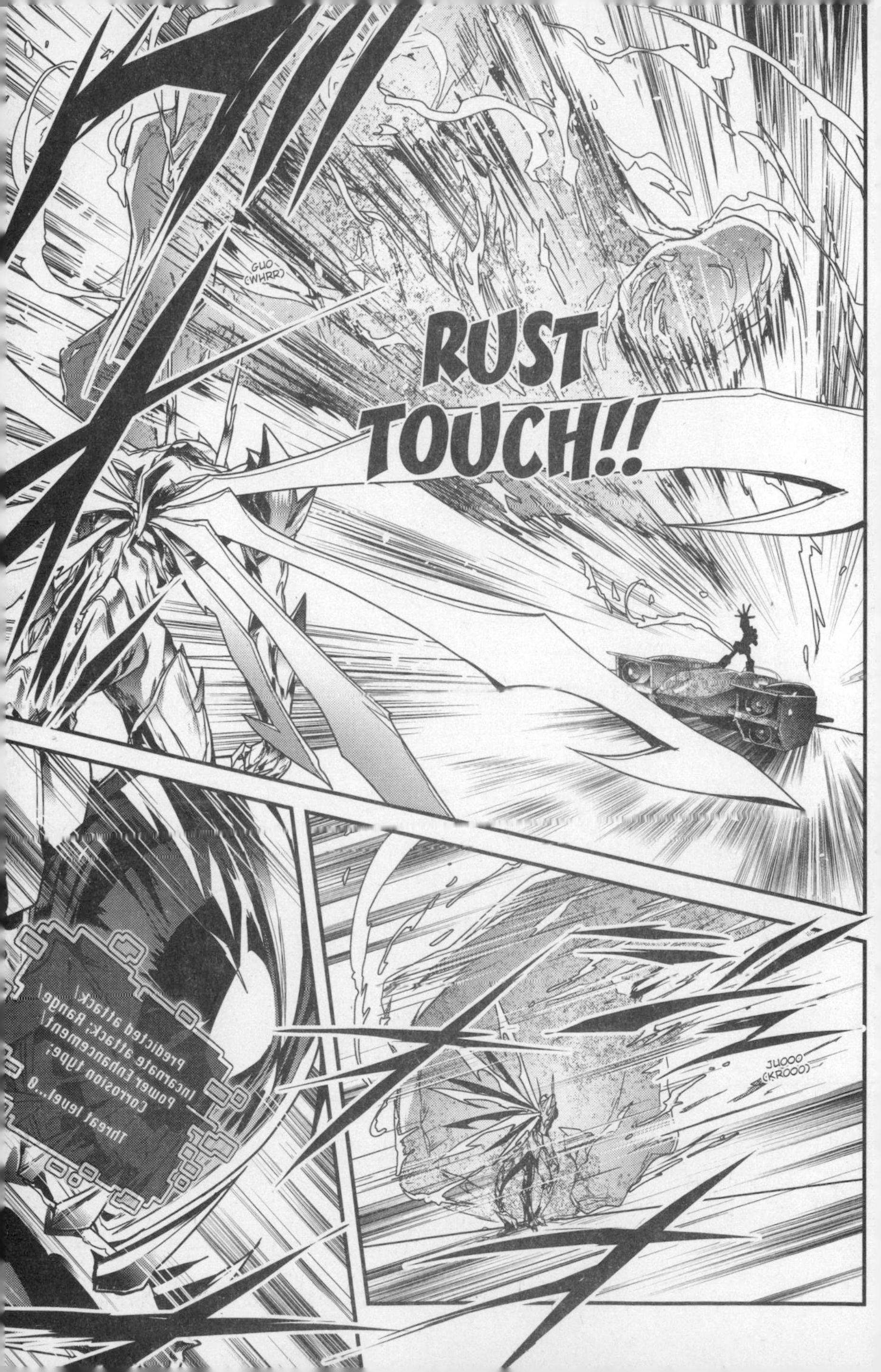
GUO
(WHRR)
RUST TOUCH!!
Predicted attack|
Incarnate attack; Range|
power Enhancement|
Corrosion type;
Threat level...0
JUOOO
(KROOO)

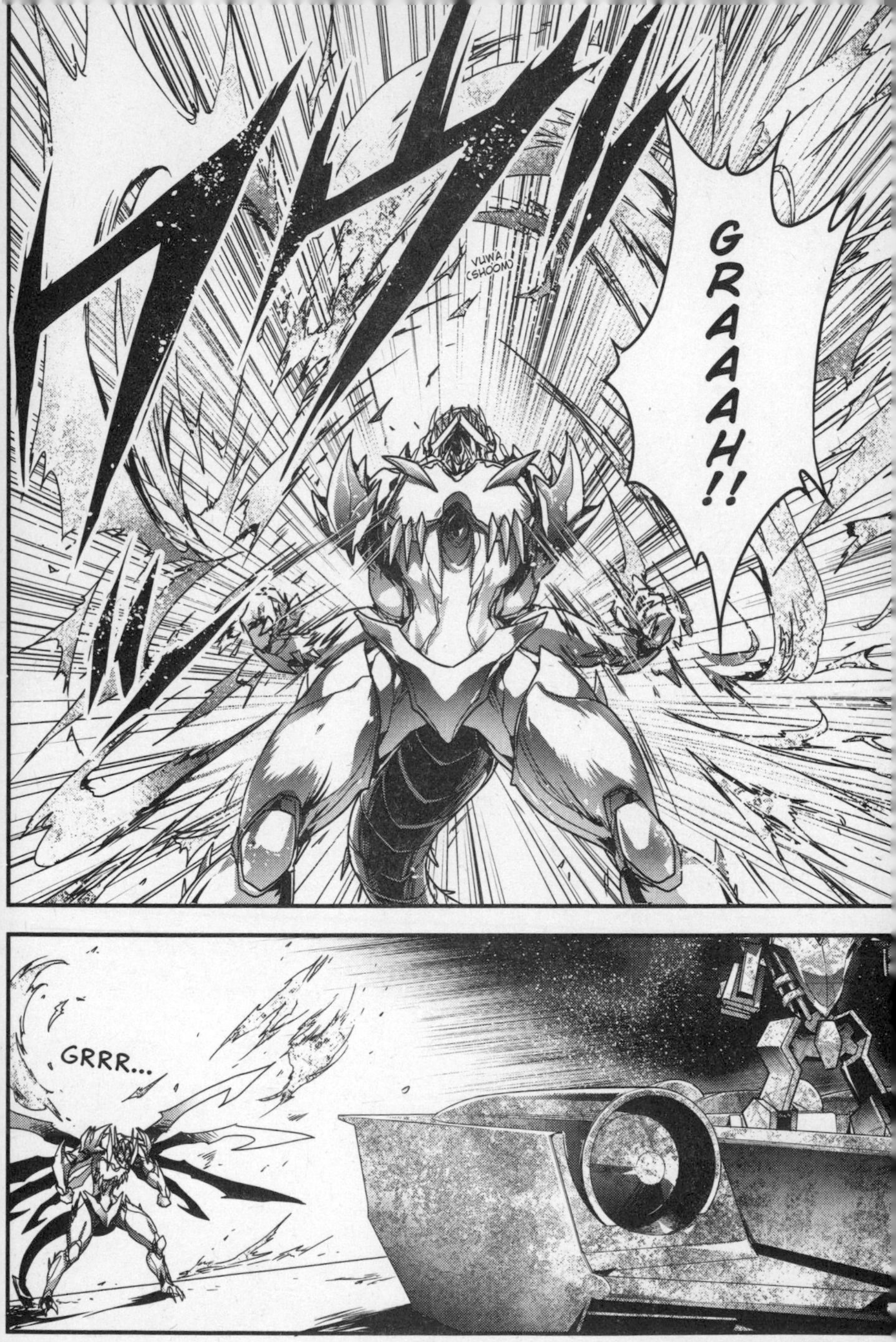
VUWA
(SHOOM)
GRAAAAH!!
GRRR...

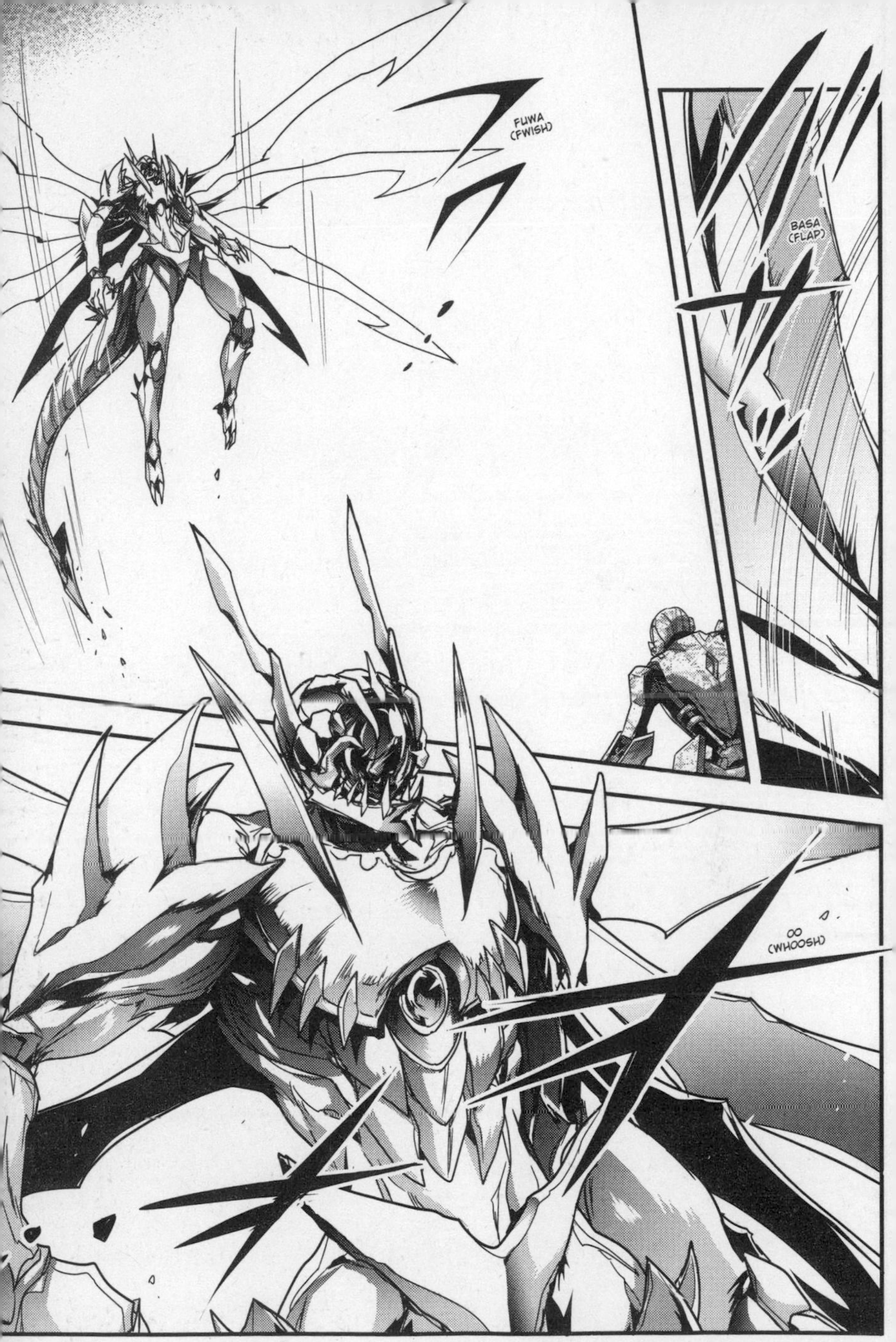
BASA
(FLAP)
FUWA
(FWISH)
OO
(WHOOSH)

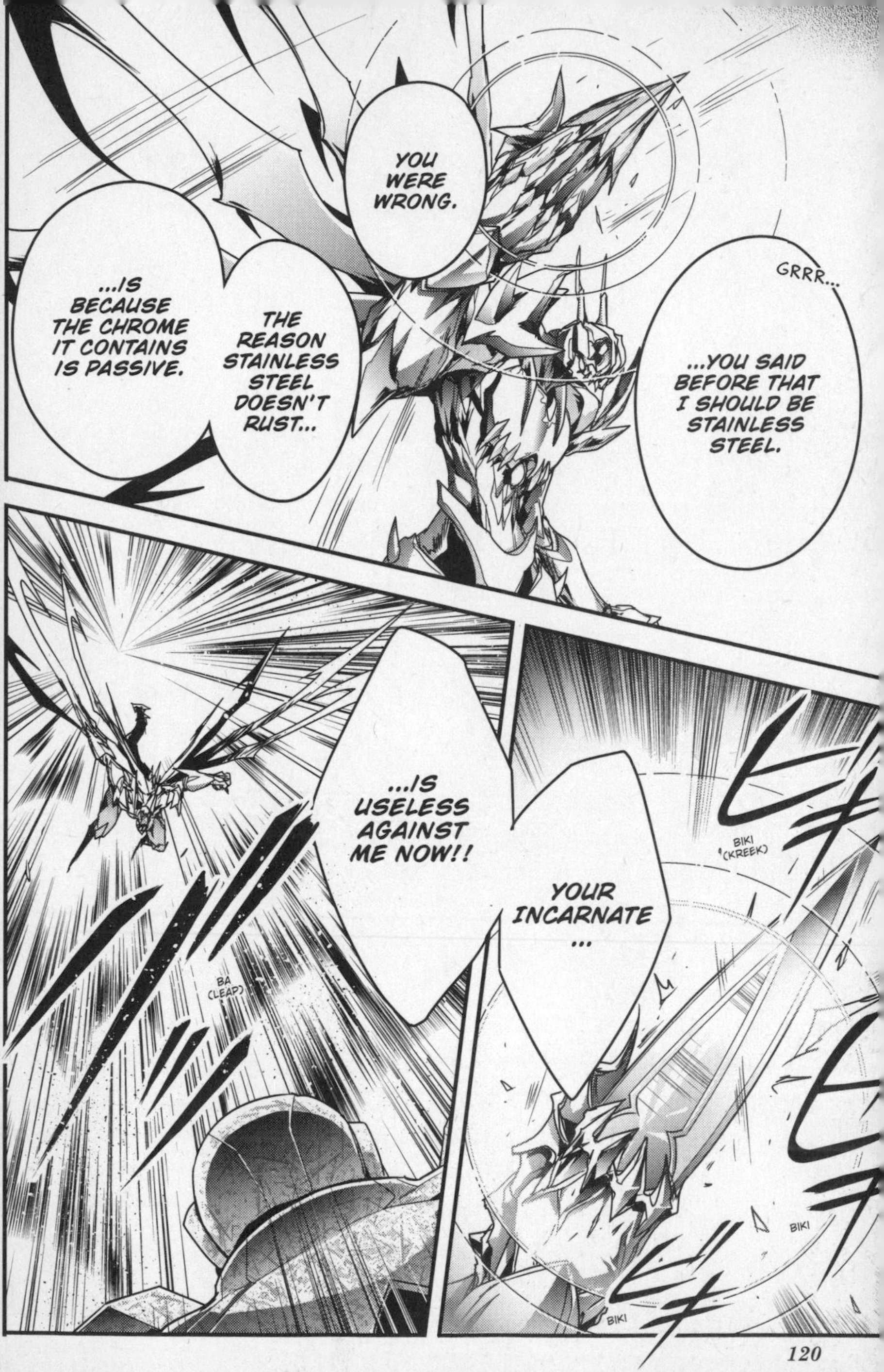
GRRR...
...YOU SAID BEFORE THAT I SHOULD BE STAINLESS STEEL.
YOU WERE WRONG.
THE REASON STAINLESS STEEL DOESN'T RUST...
...IS BECAUSE THE CHROME IT CONTAINS IS PASSIVE.
BIKI (KREEK)
BIKI
BIKI
YOUR INCARNATE ...
...IS USELESS AGAINST ME NOW!!
BA (LEAP)

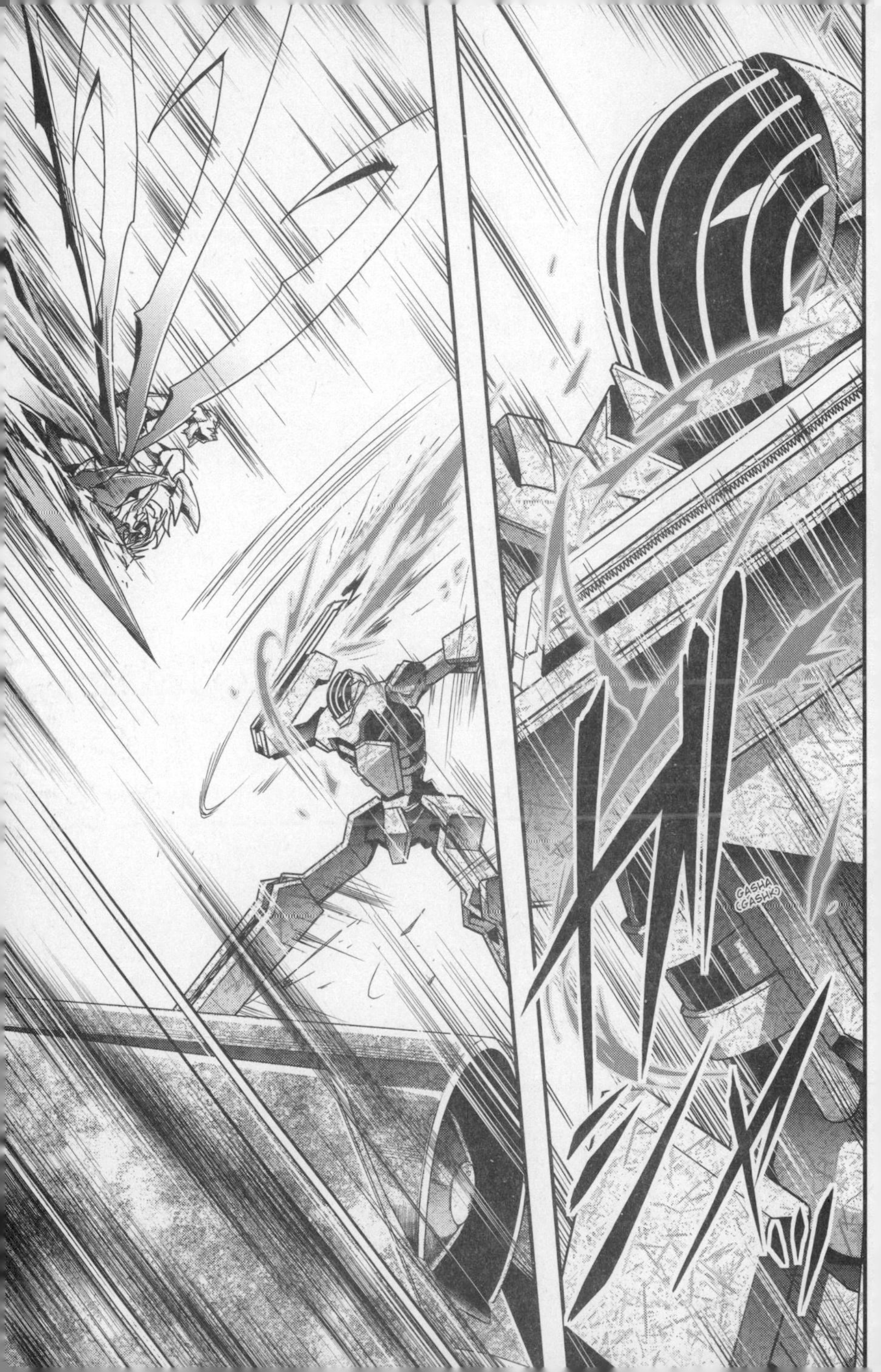
GASHA
(GASHK)

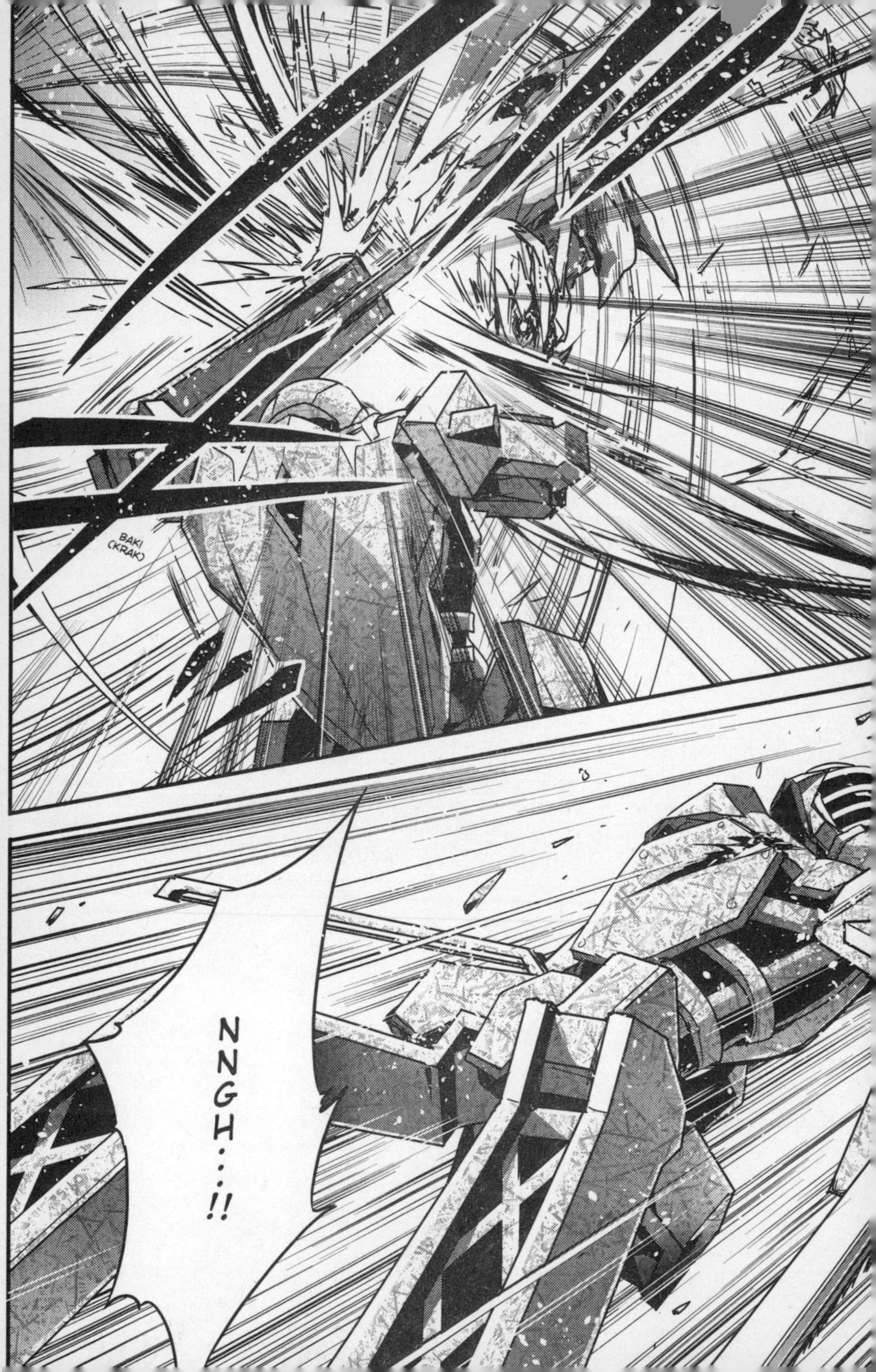
BAKI
(KRAK)
NNGH...!!

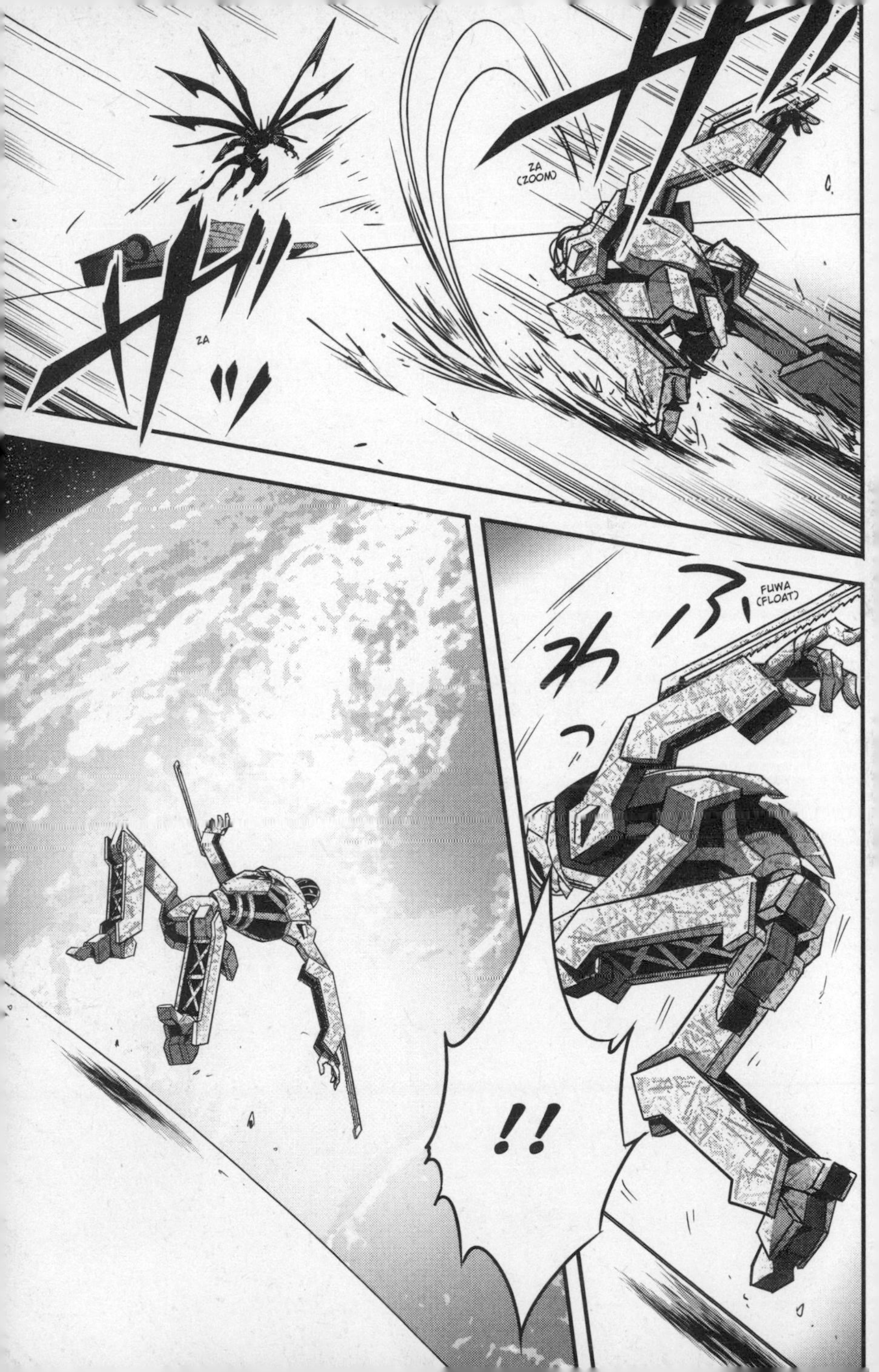
ZA
(ZOOM)
ZA
FUWA
(FLOAT)
!!

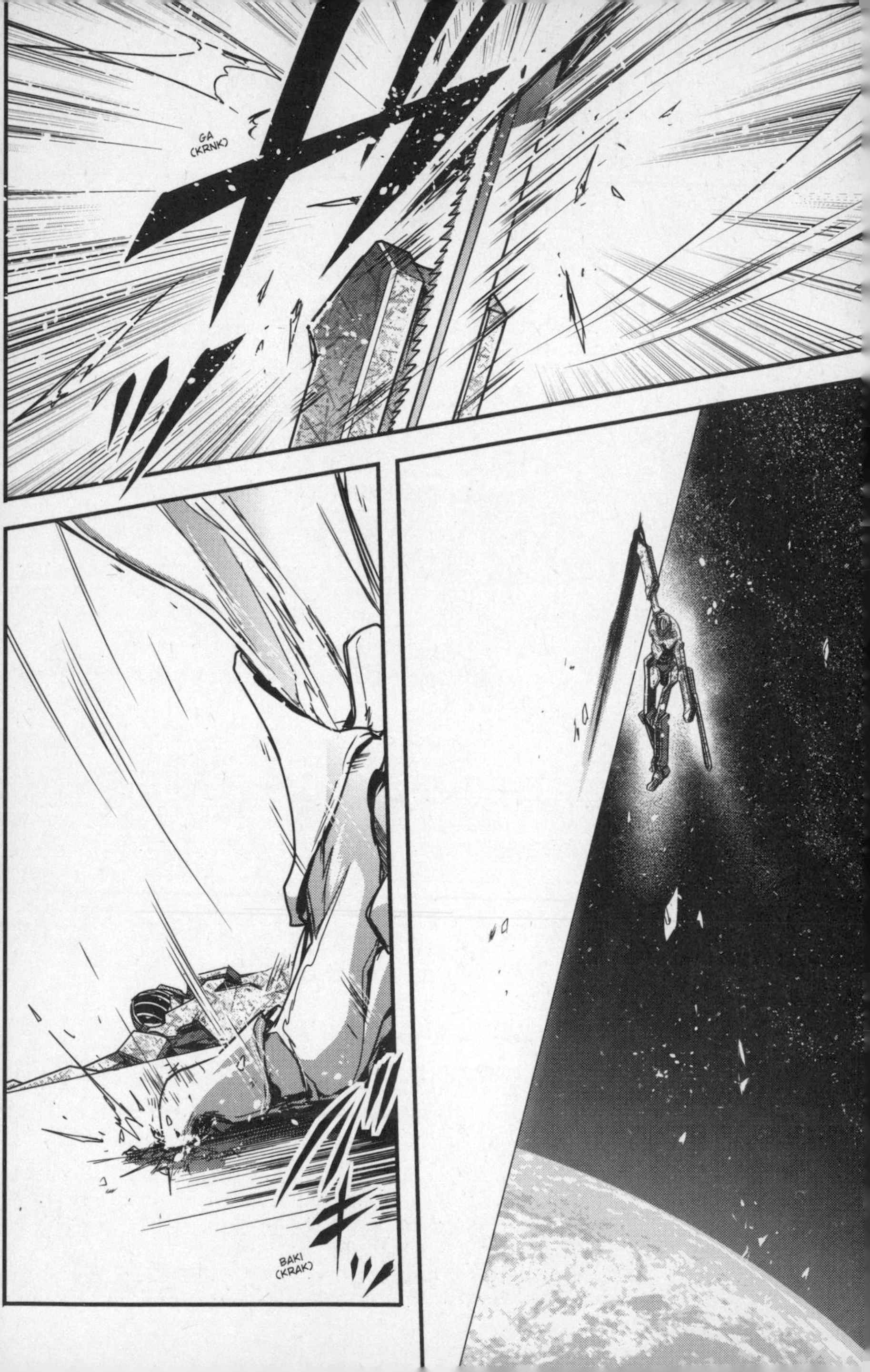
GA
(KRNK)
BAKI
(KRAK)

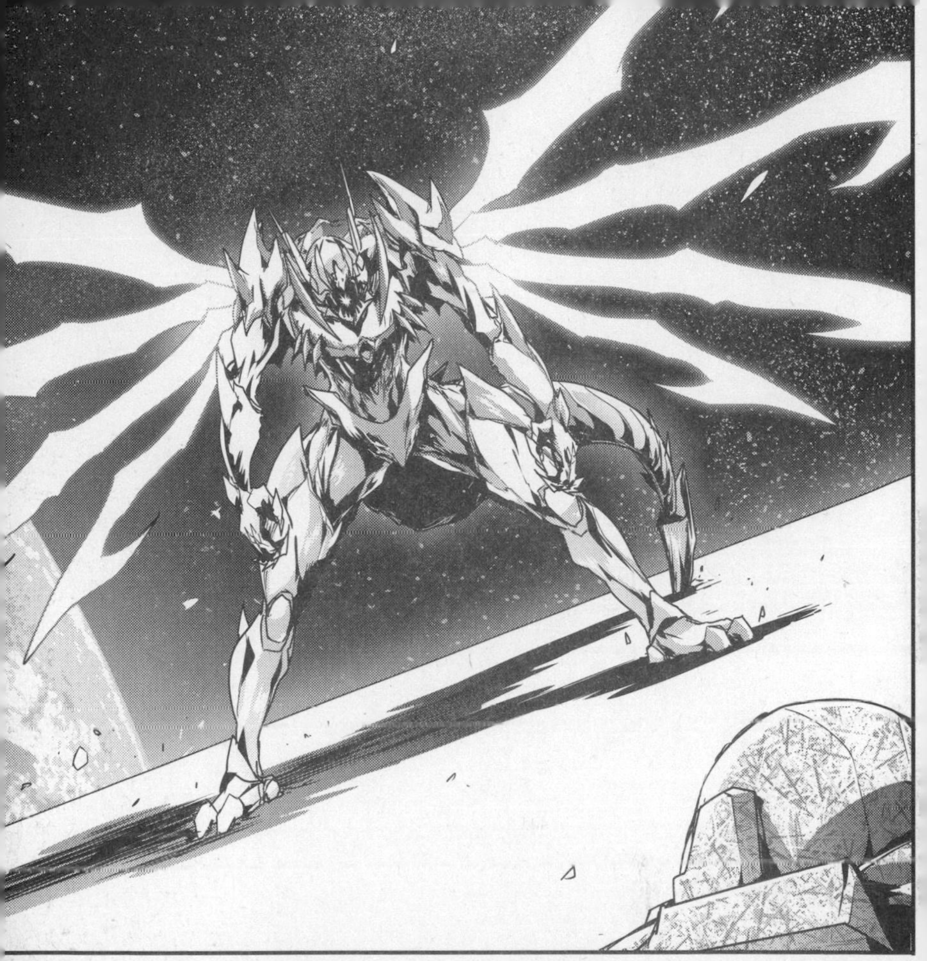
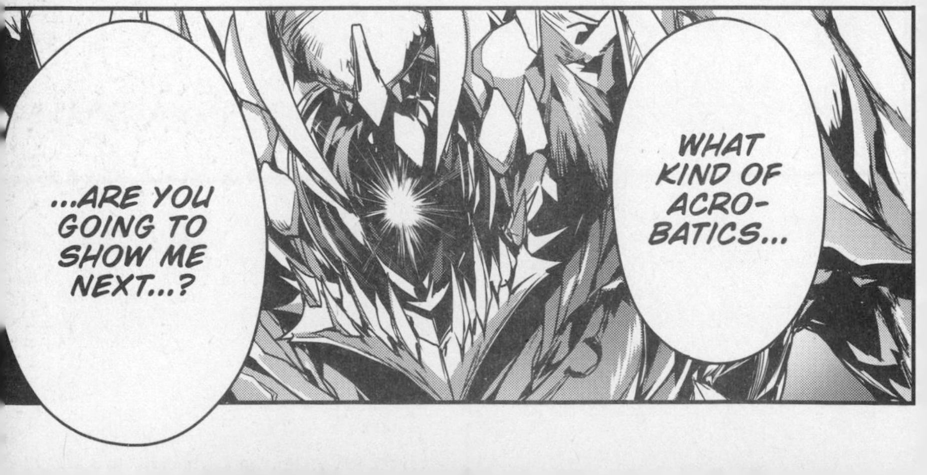
WHAT KIND OF ACRO-BATICS...
...ARE YOU GOING TO SHOW ME NEXT...?

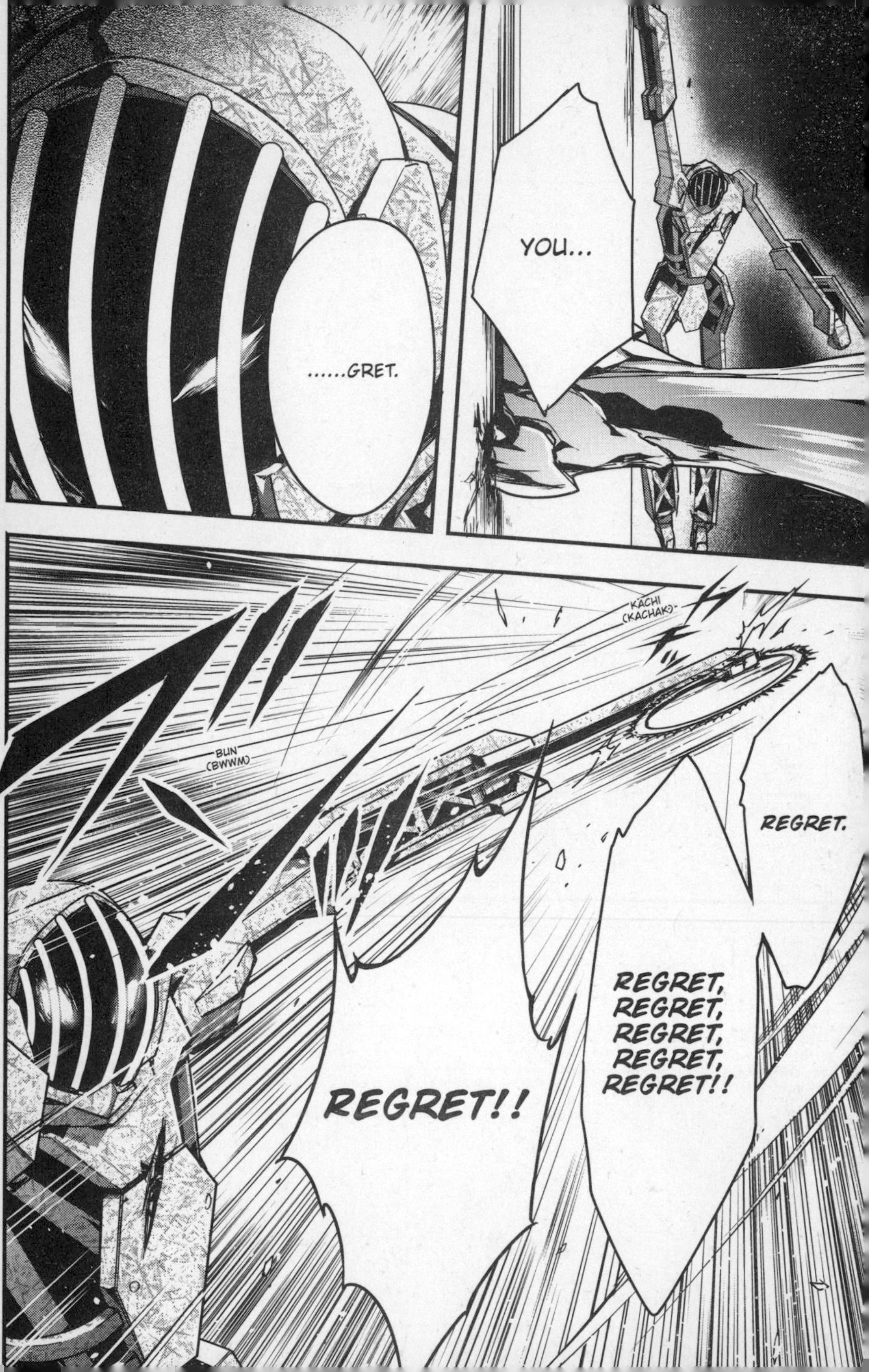
YOU...
......GRET.
KACHI (KACHAK)
BUN (BWWM)
REGRET.
REGRET, REGRET, REGRET, REGRET, REGRET!!
REGRET!!

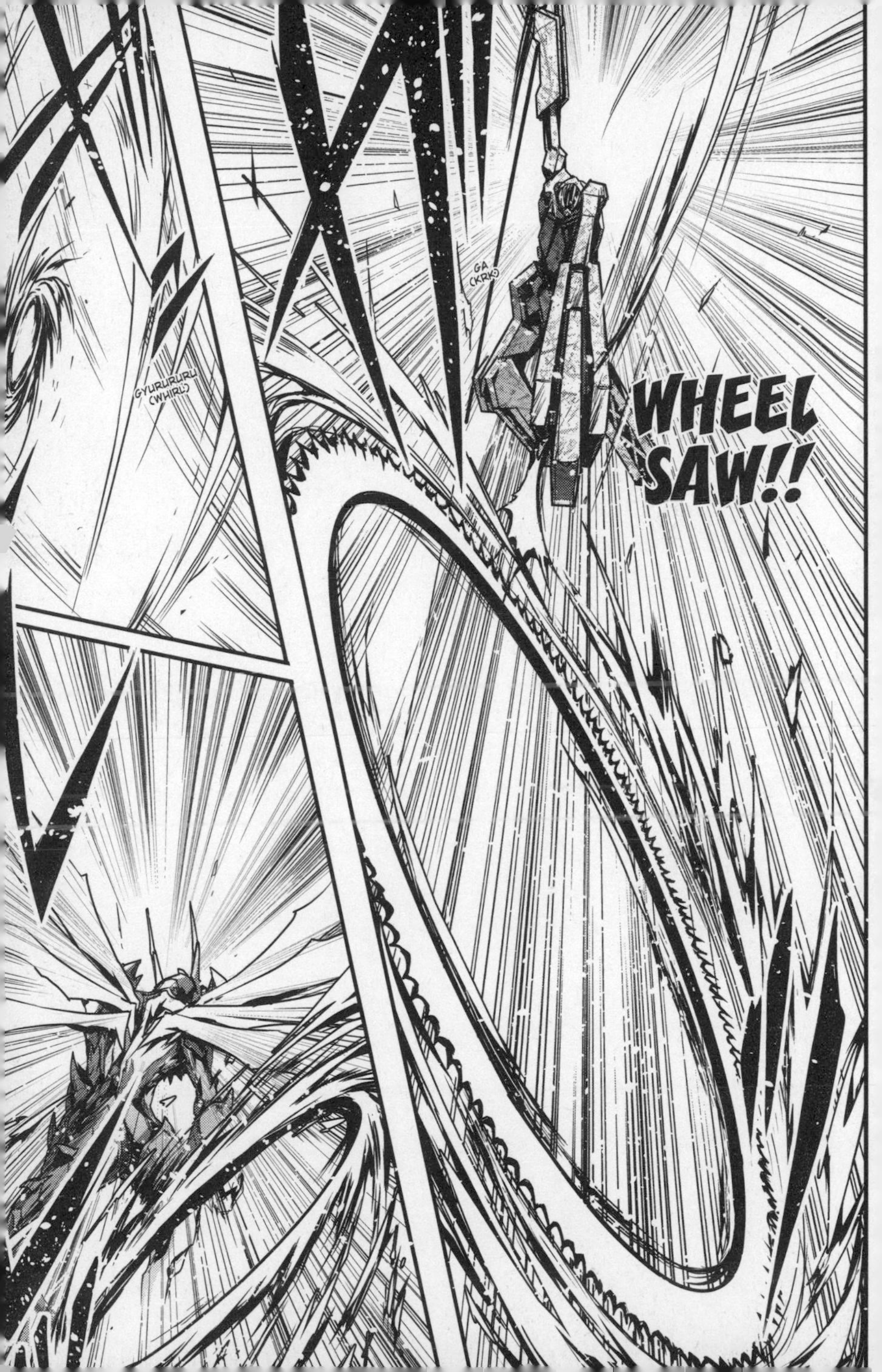
GA (KRK)
WHEEL SAW!!
GYURURURU (WHIRL)

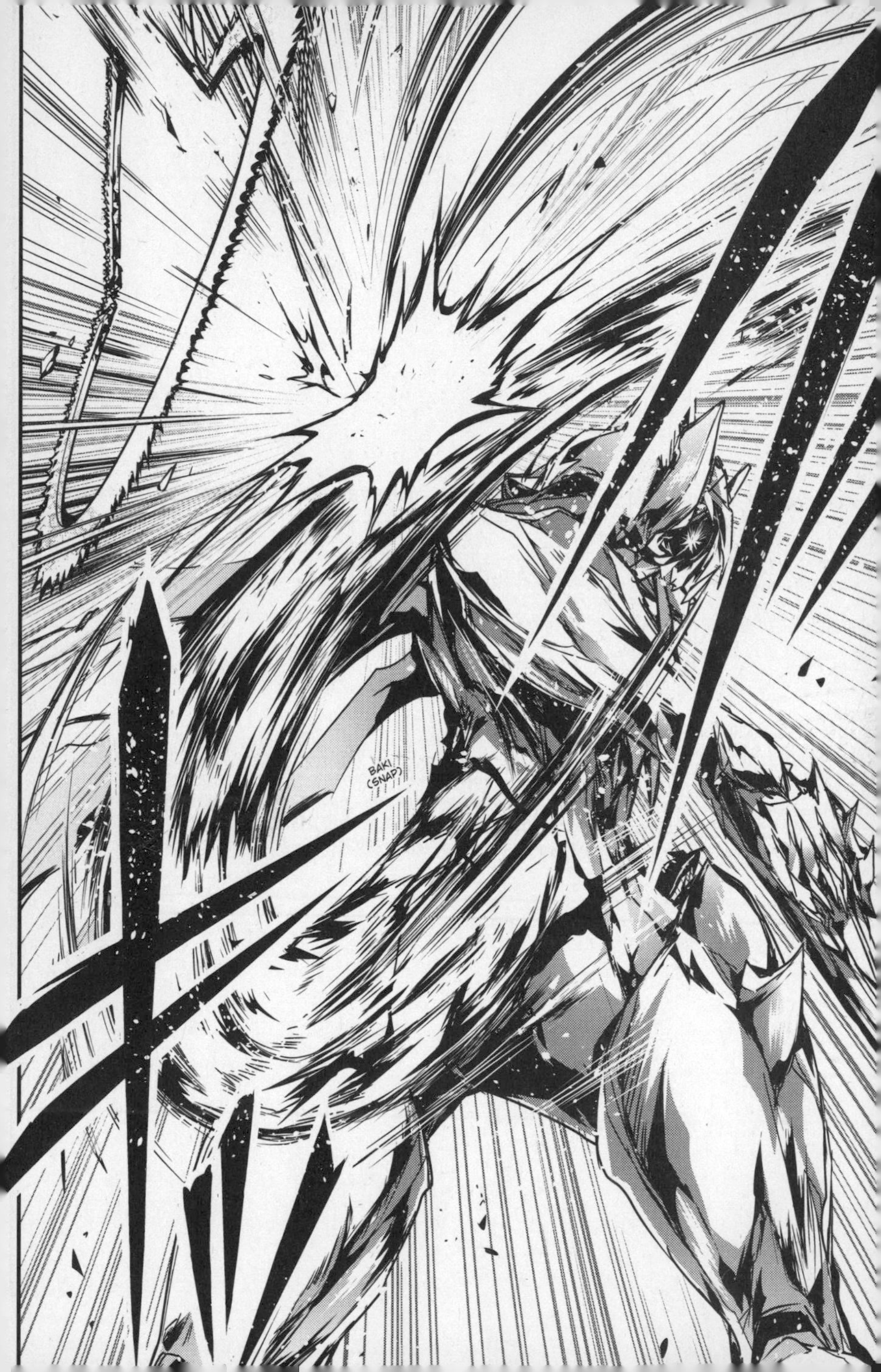
BAKI
(SNAP)

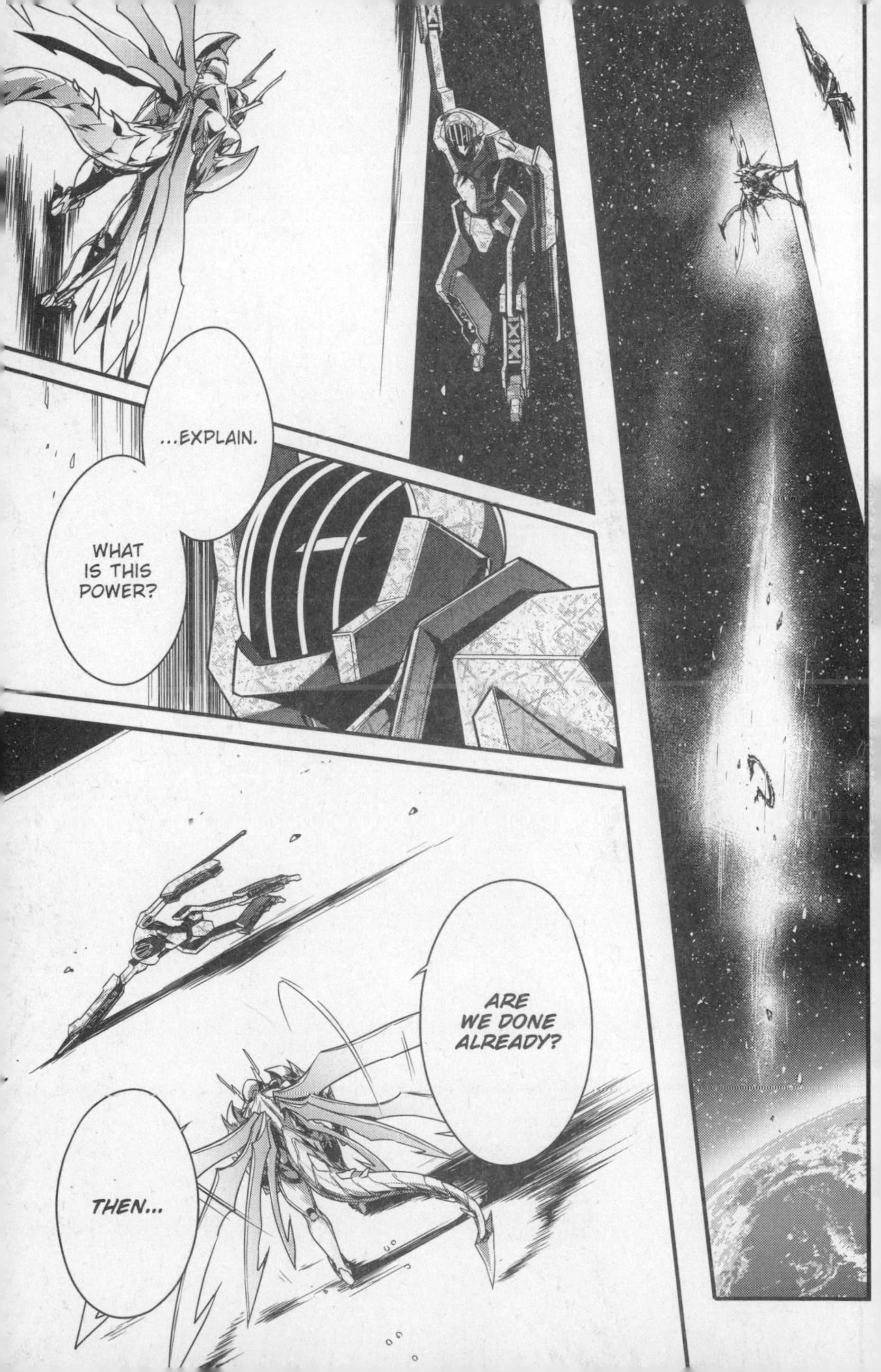
...EXPLAIN.
WHAT IS THIS POWER?
ARE WE DONE ALREADY?
THEN...

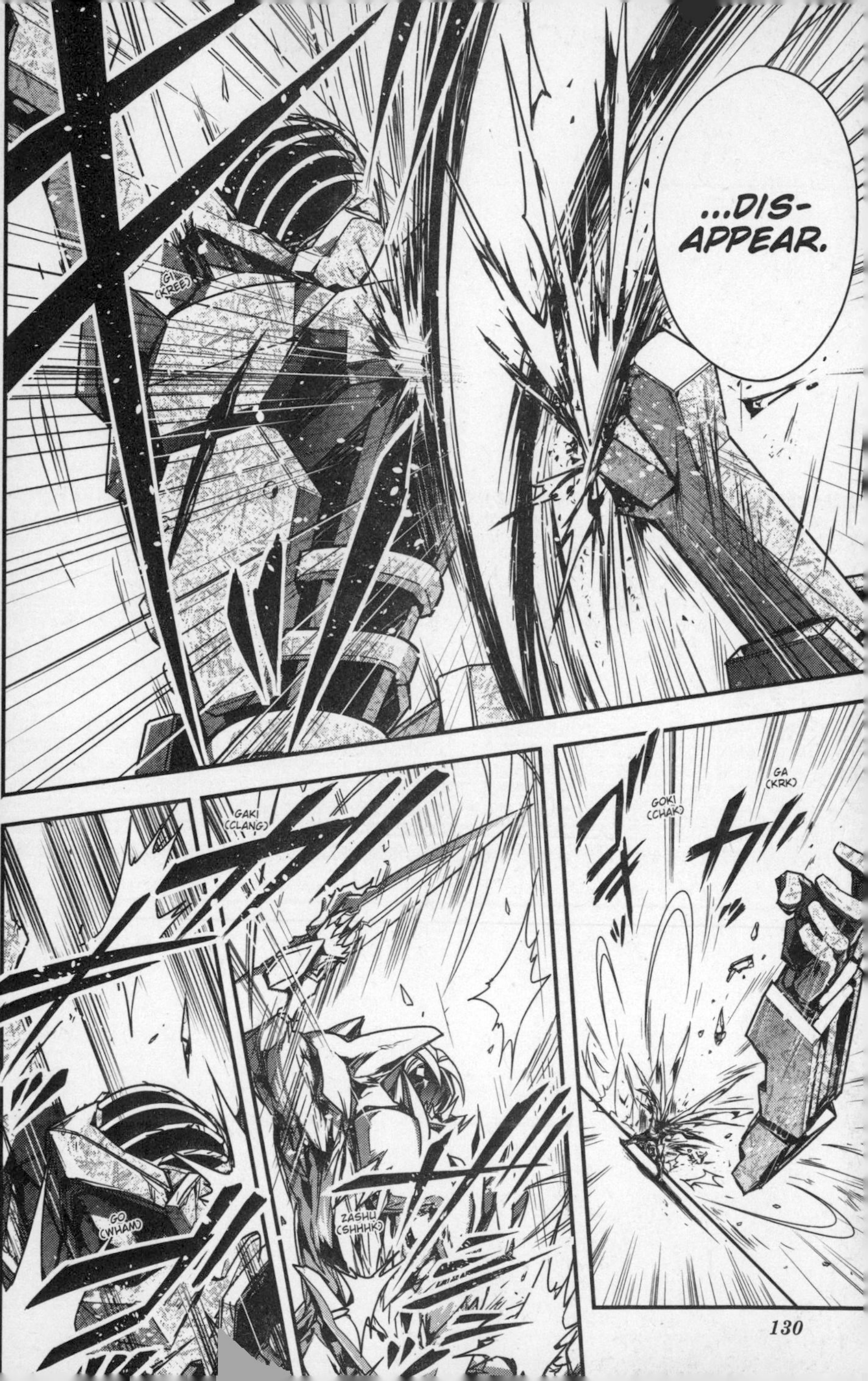
...DIS-
APPEAR.
GI
(KREE)
GA
(KRK)
GOKI
(CHAK)
GAKI
(CLANG)
ZASHU
(SHHHK)
GO
(WHAM)

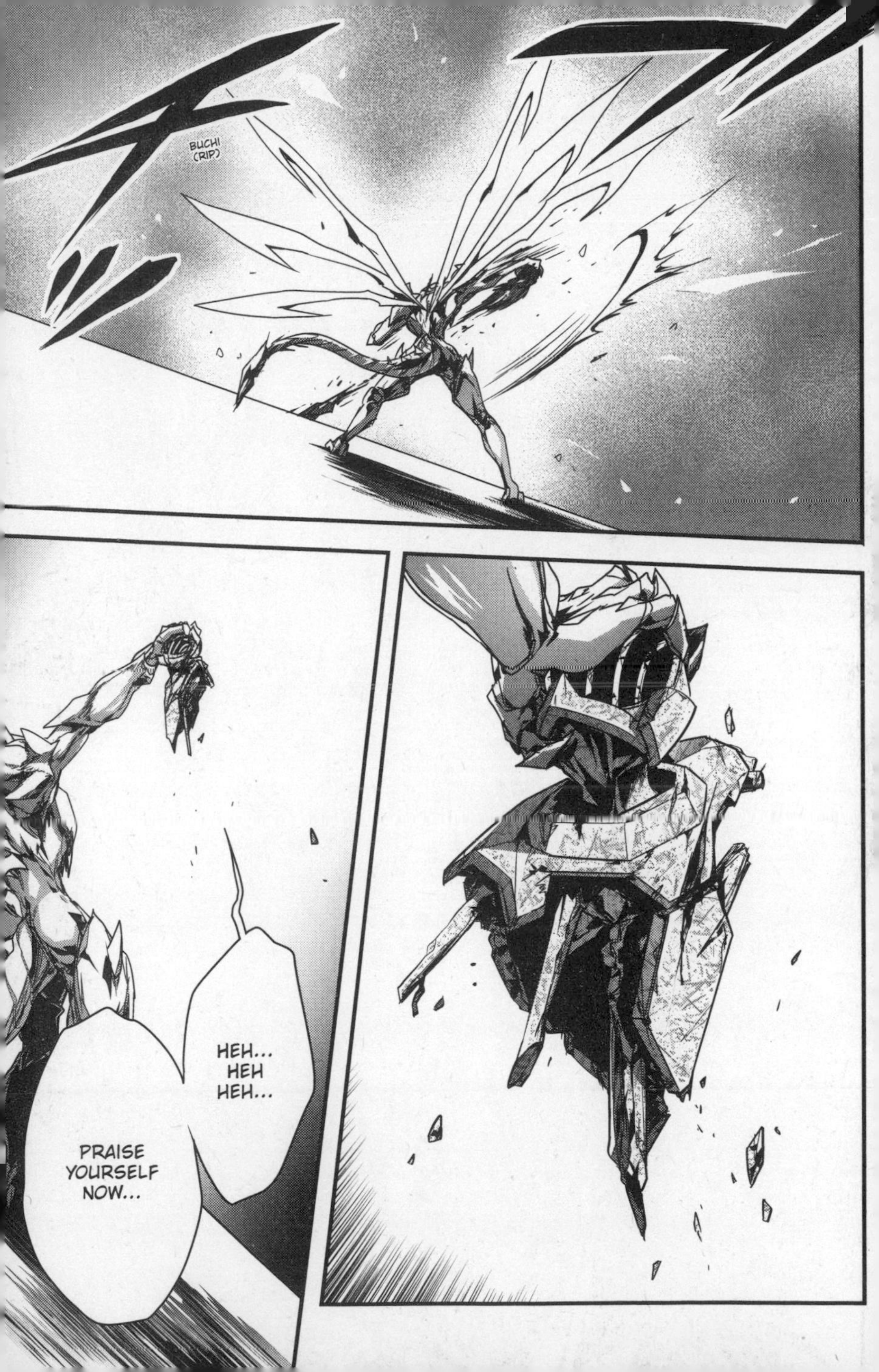
BUCHI (RIP)
HEH... HEH HEH...
PRAISE YOURSELF NOW...

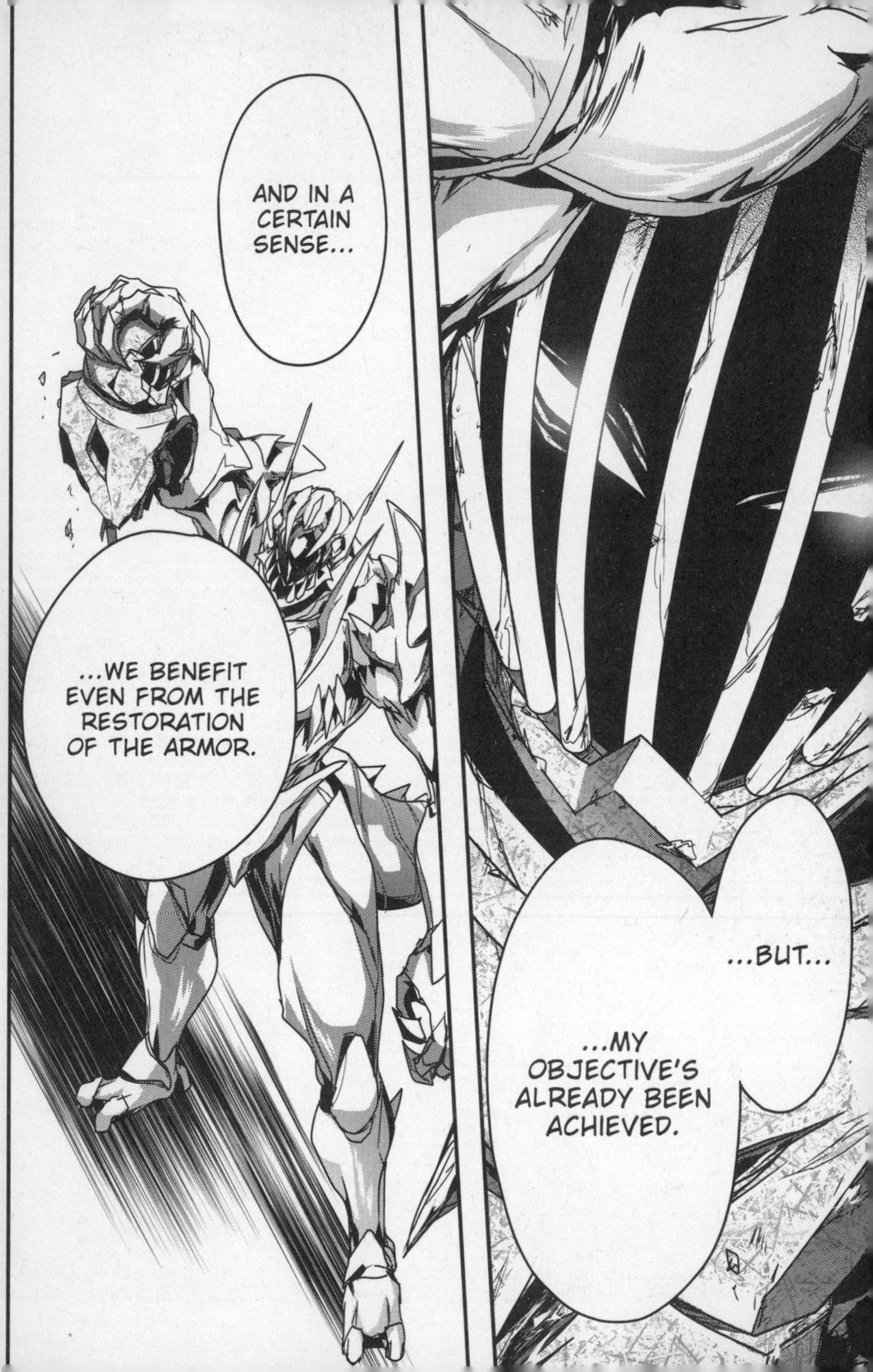
...BUT...
...MY OBJECTIVE'S ALREADY BEEN ACHIEVED.
AND IN A CERTAIN SENSE...
...WE BENEFIT EVEN FROM THE RESTORATION OF THE ARMOR.

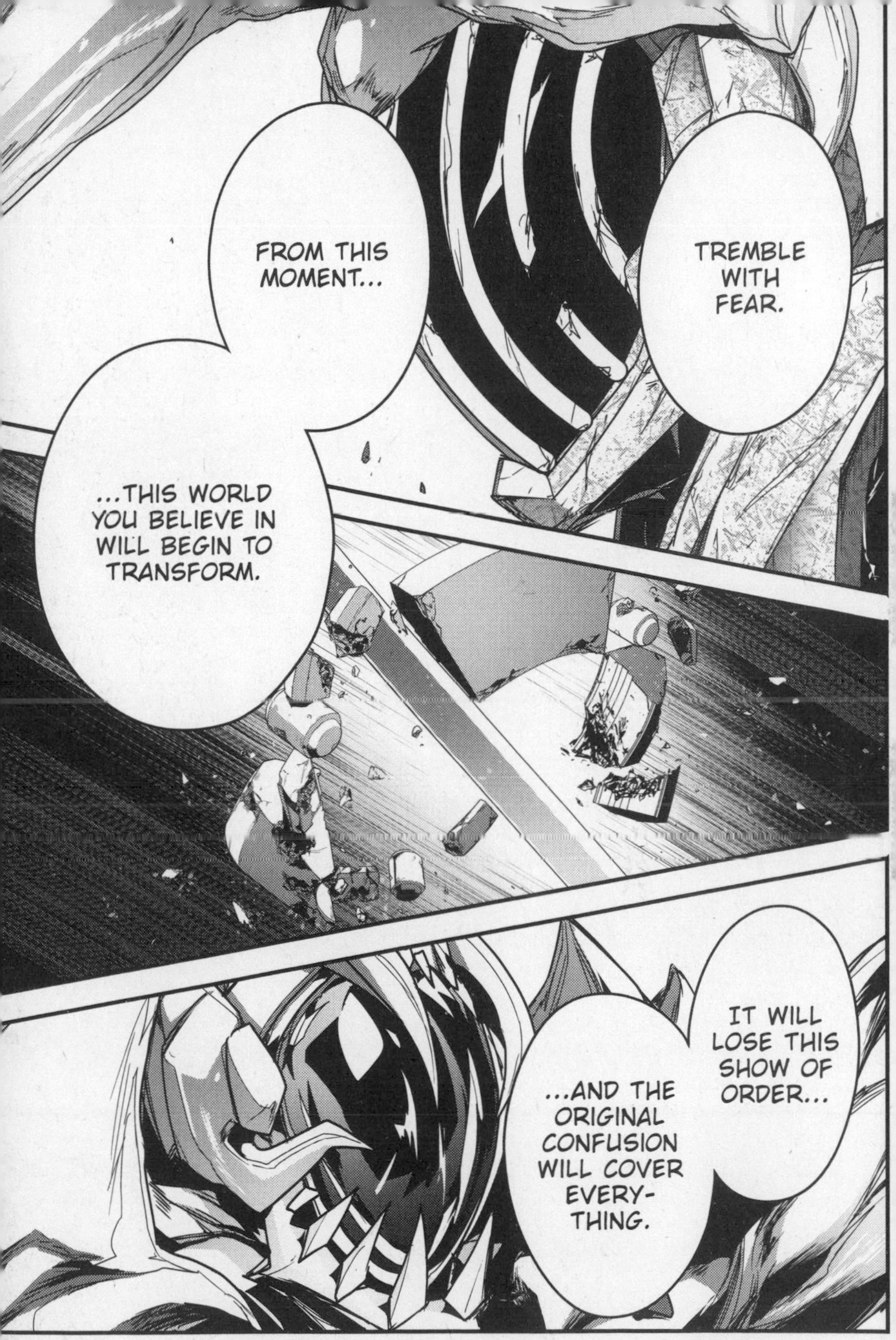
TREMBLE WITH FEAR.
FROM THIS MOMENT...
...THIS WORLD YOU BELIEVE IN WILL BEGIN TO TRANSFORM.
IT WILL LOSE THIS SHOW OF ORDER...
...AND THE ORIGINAL CONFUSION WILL COVER EVERY-THING.

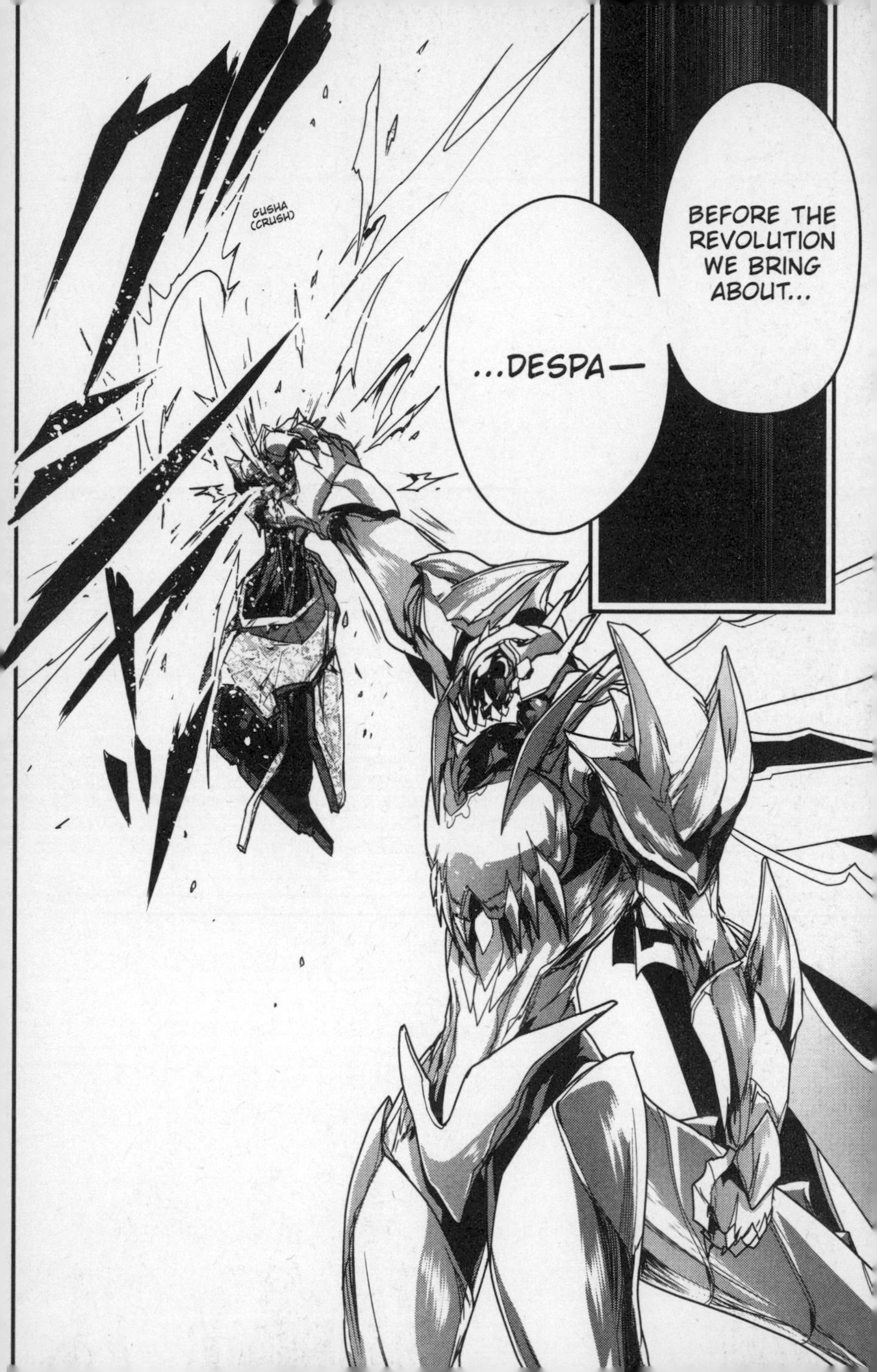
BEFORE THE REVOLUTION WE BRING ABOUT...
...DESPA—
GUSHA (CRUSH)

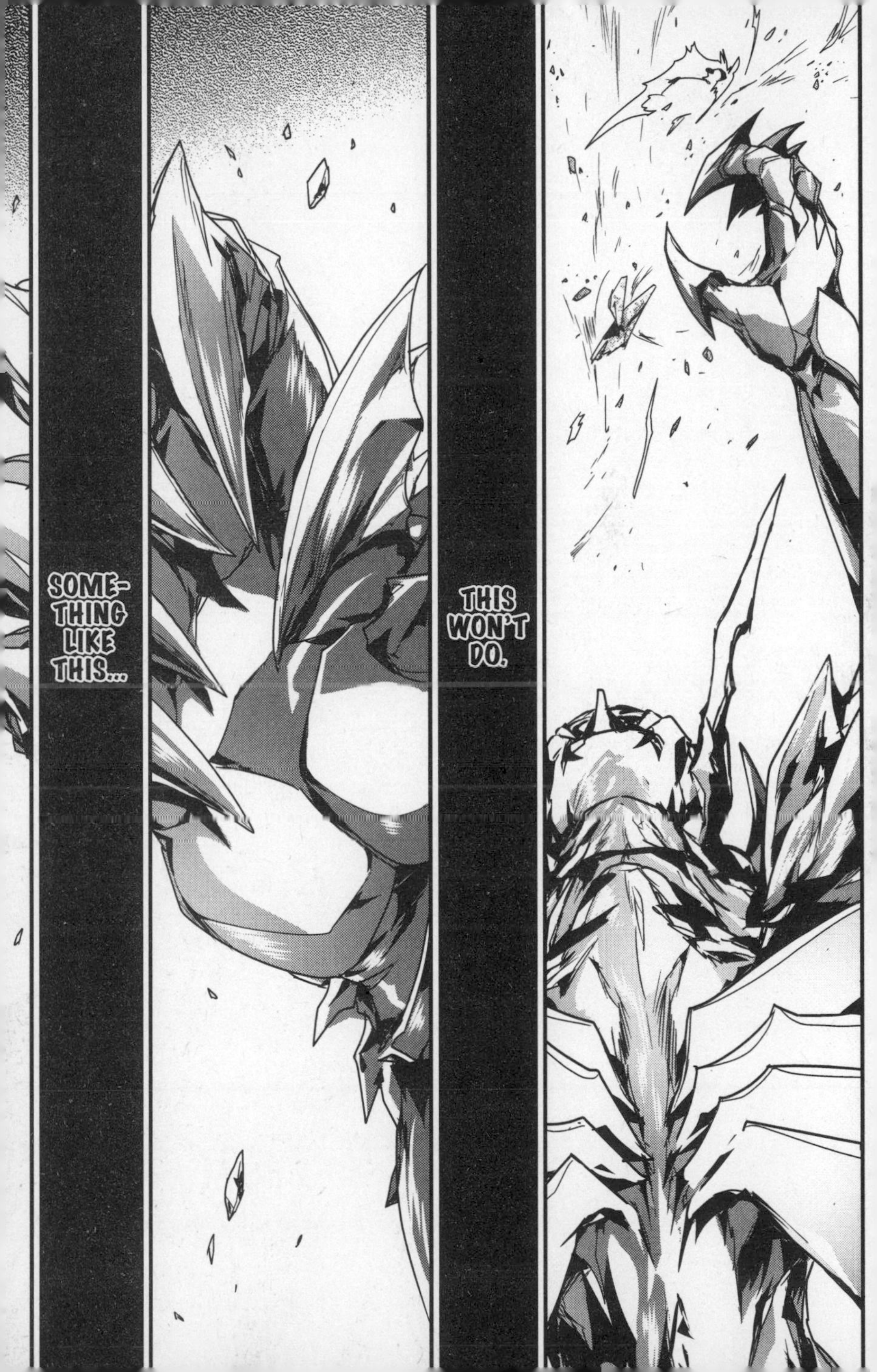
THIS WON'T DO.
SOME-THING LIKE THIS...

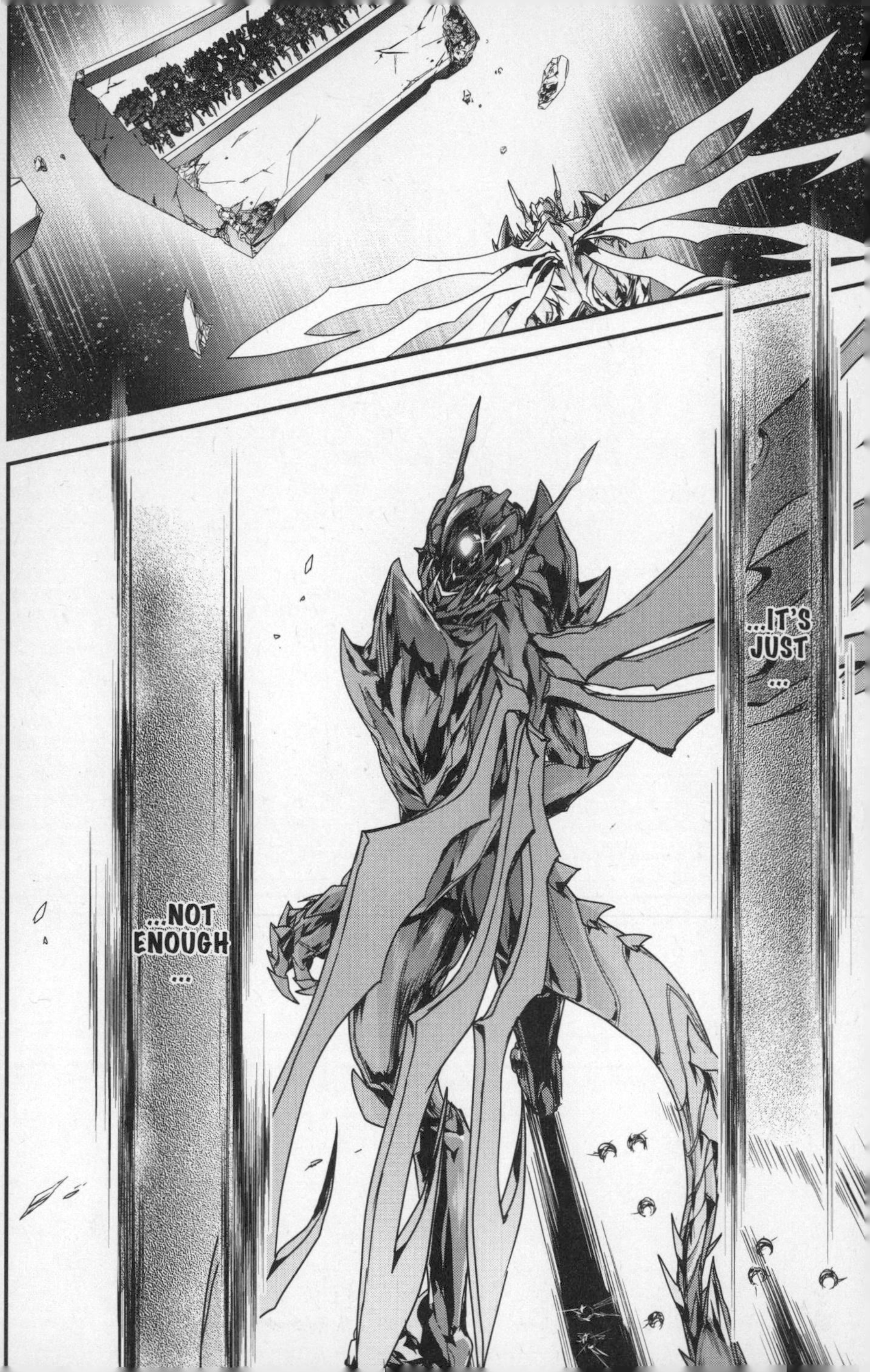
...IT'S JUST ...
...NOT ENOUGH ...

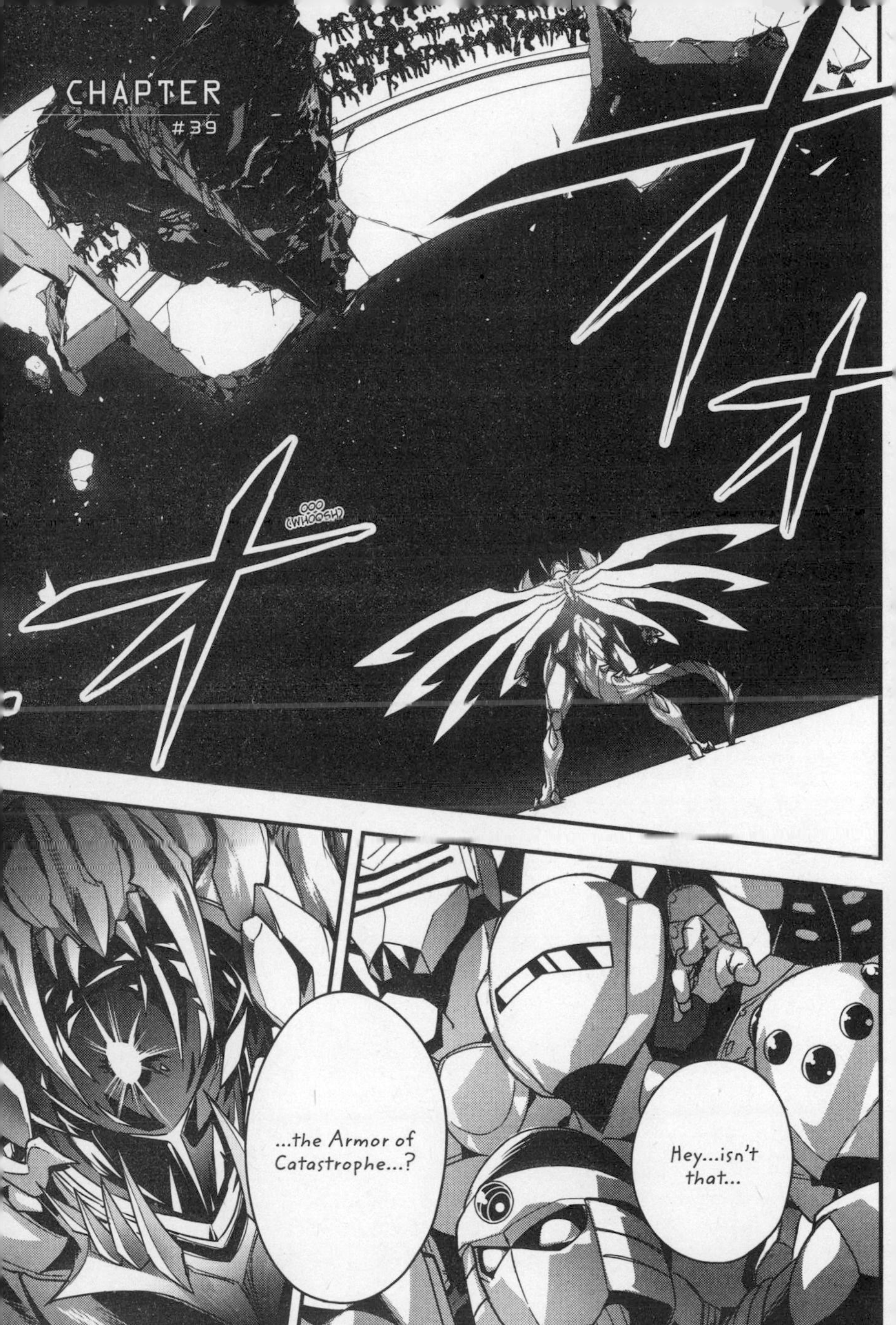
CHAPTER
#39
OOO (WHOOSH)
Hey...isn't that...
...the Armor of Catastrophe...?

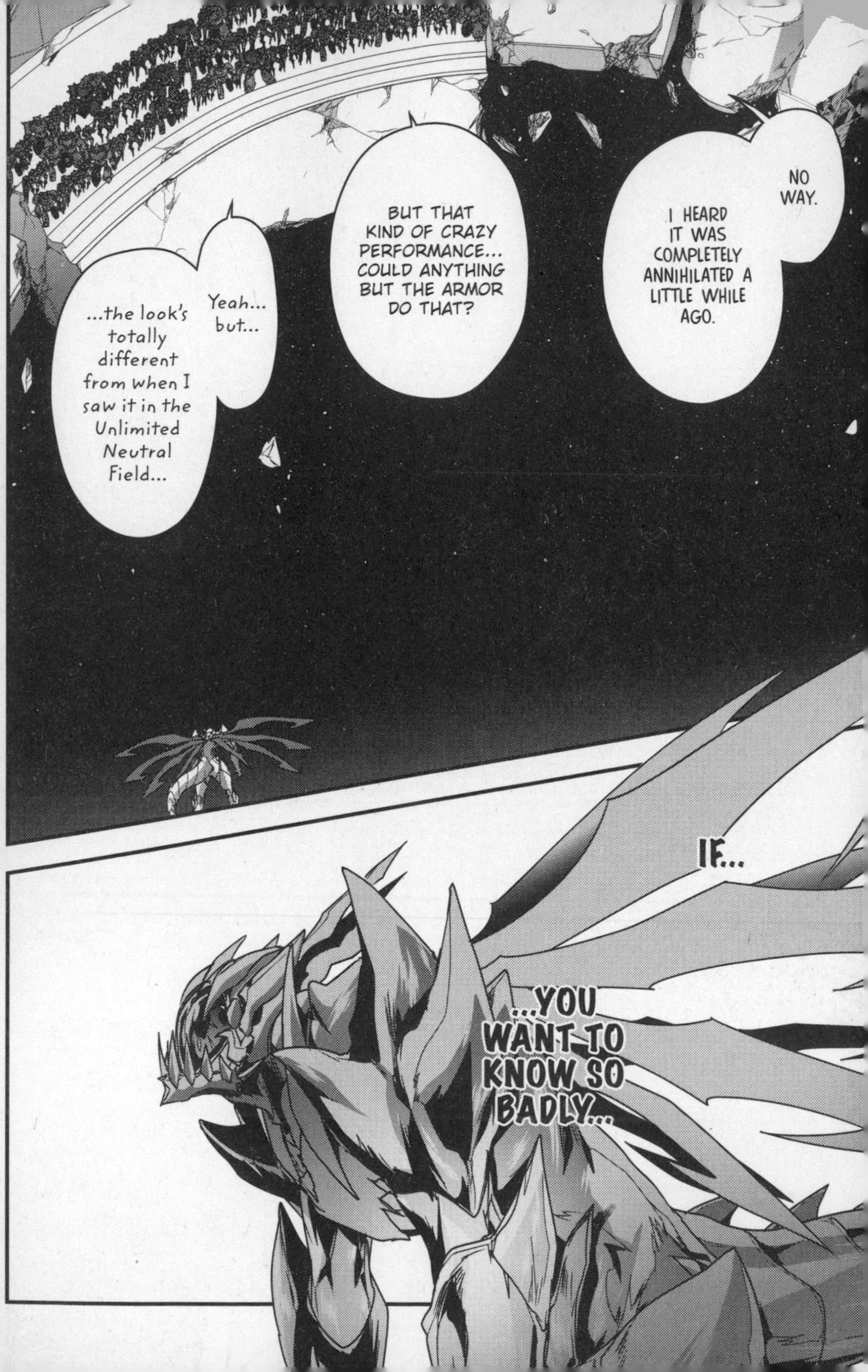
NO WAY.
I HEARD IT WAS COMPLETELY ANNIHILATED A LITTLE WHILE AGO.
BUT THAT KIND OF CRAZY PERFORMANCE... COULD ANYTHING BUT THE ARMOR DO THAT?
Yeah... but...
...the look's totally different from when I saw it in the Unlimited Neutral Field...
IF...
...YOU WANT TO KNOW SO BADLY...

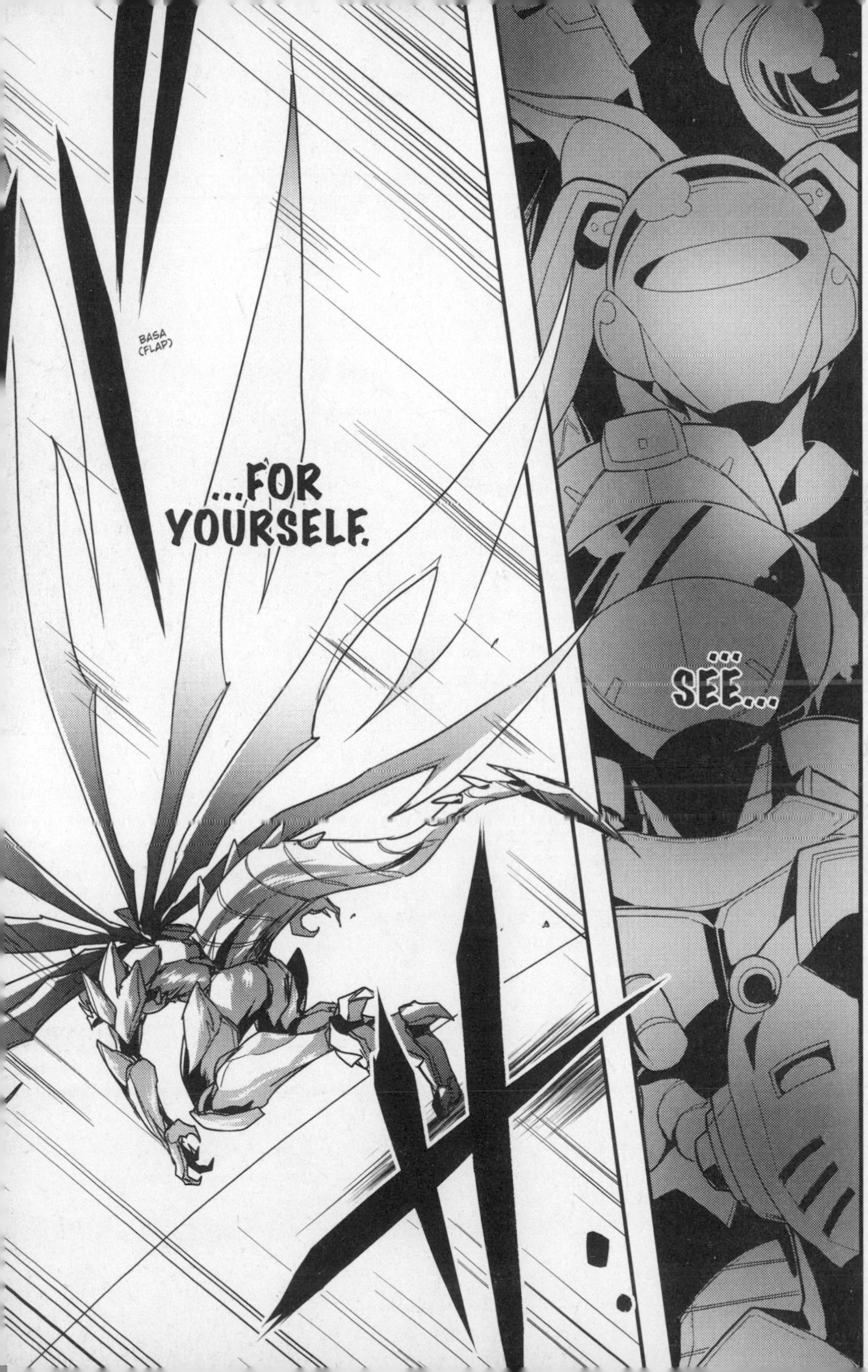
...SEE...
BASA (FLAP)
...FOR YOURSELF.

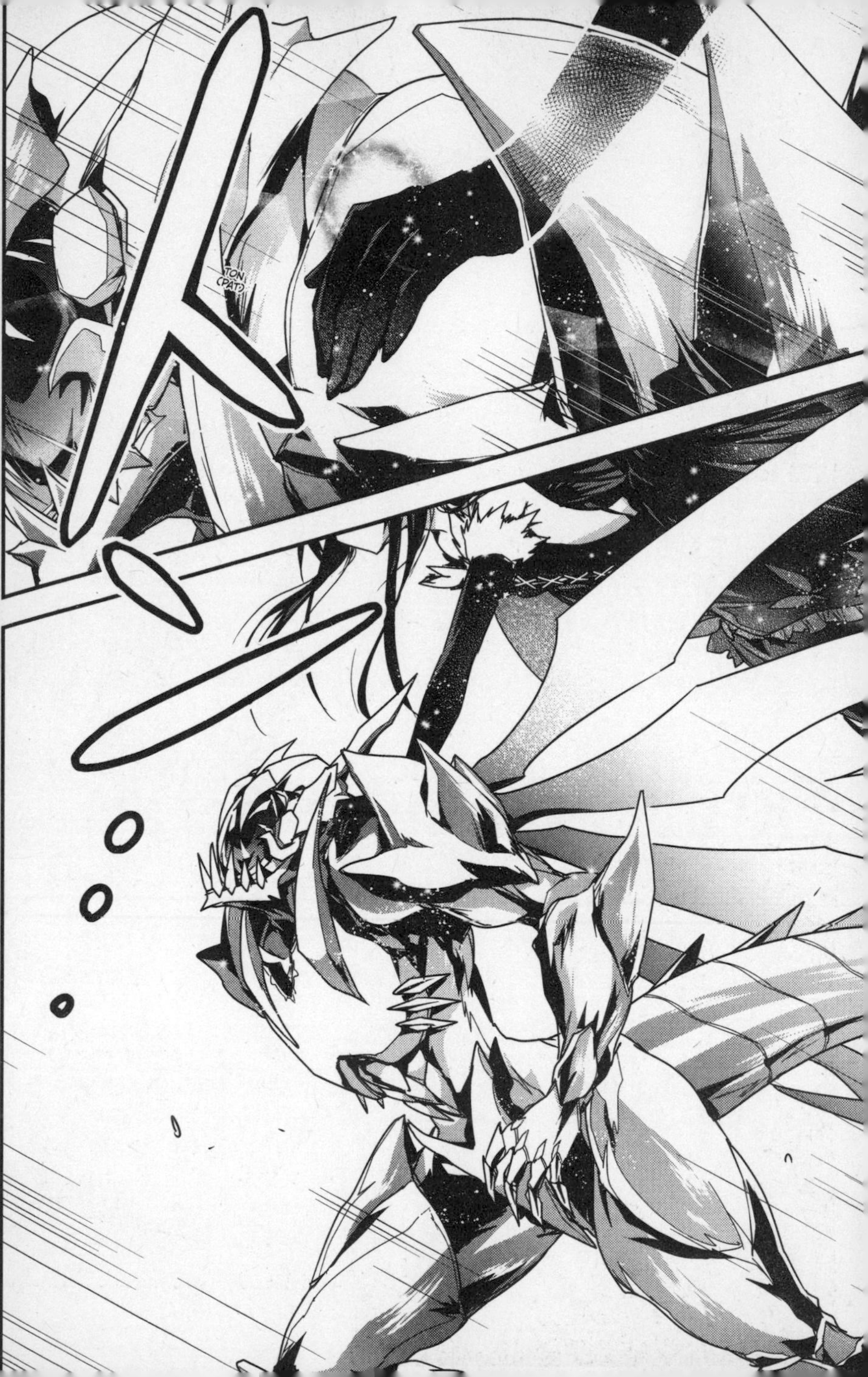
TON
(PAT)

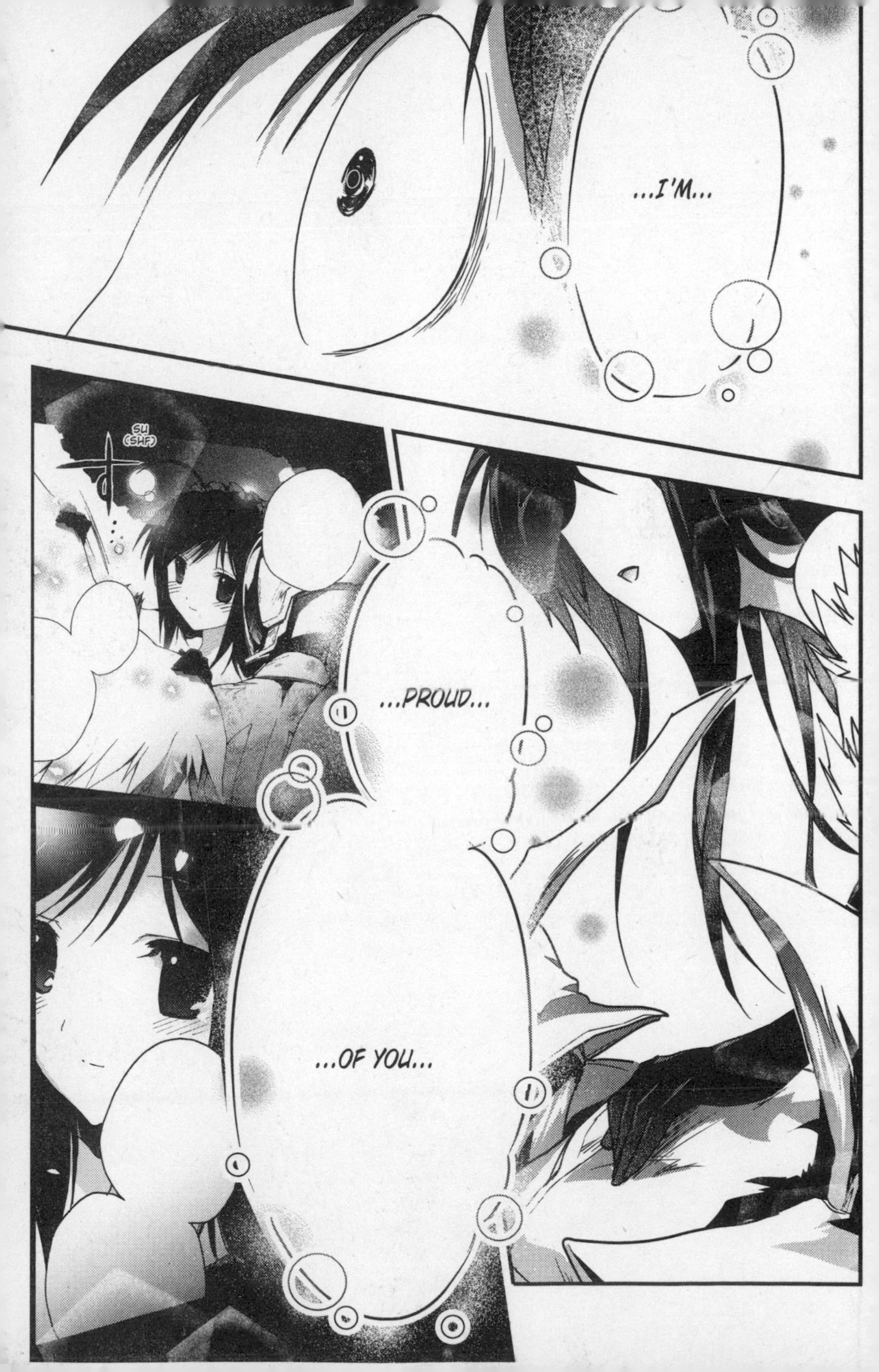
...I'M...
...PROUD...
SU (SHF)
...OF YOU...

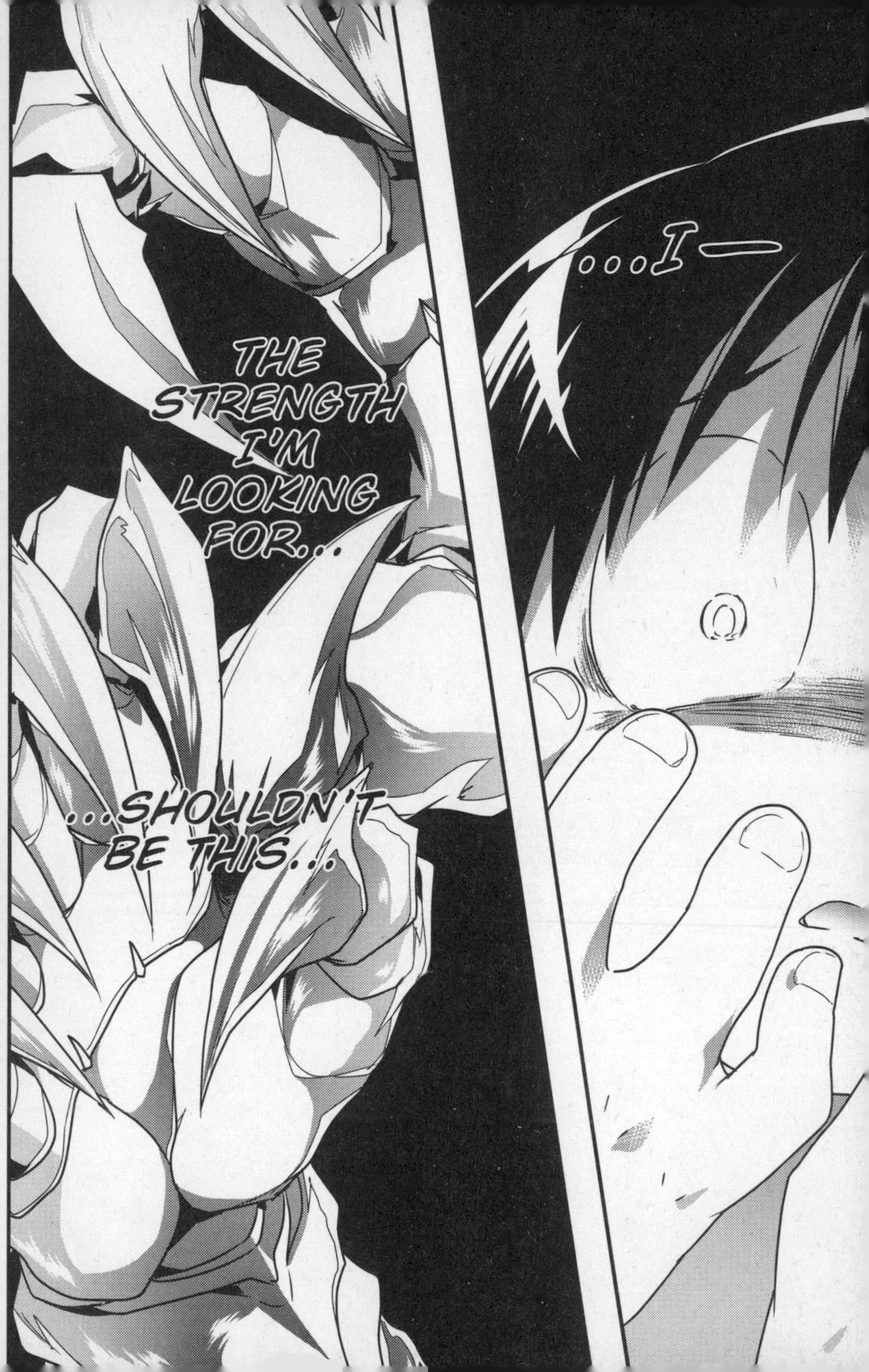
...I—
THE STRENGTH I'M LOOKING FOR...
...SHOULDN'T BE THIS...

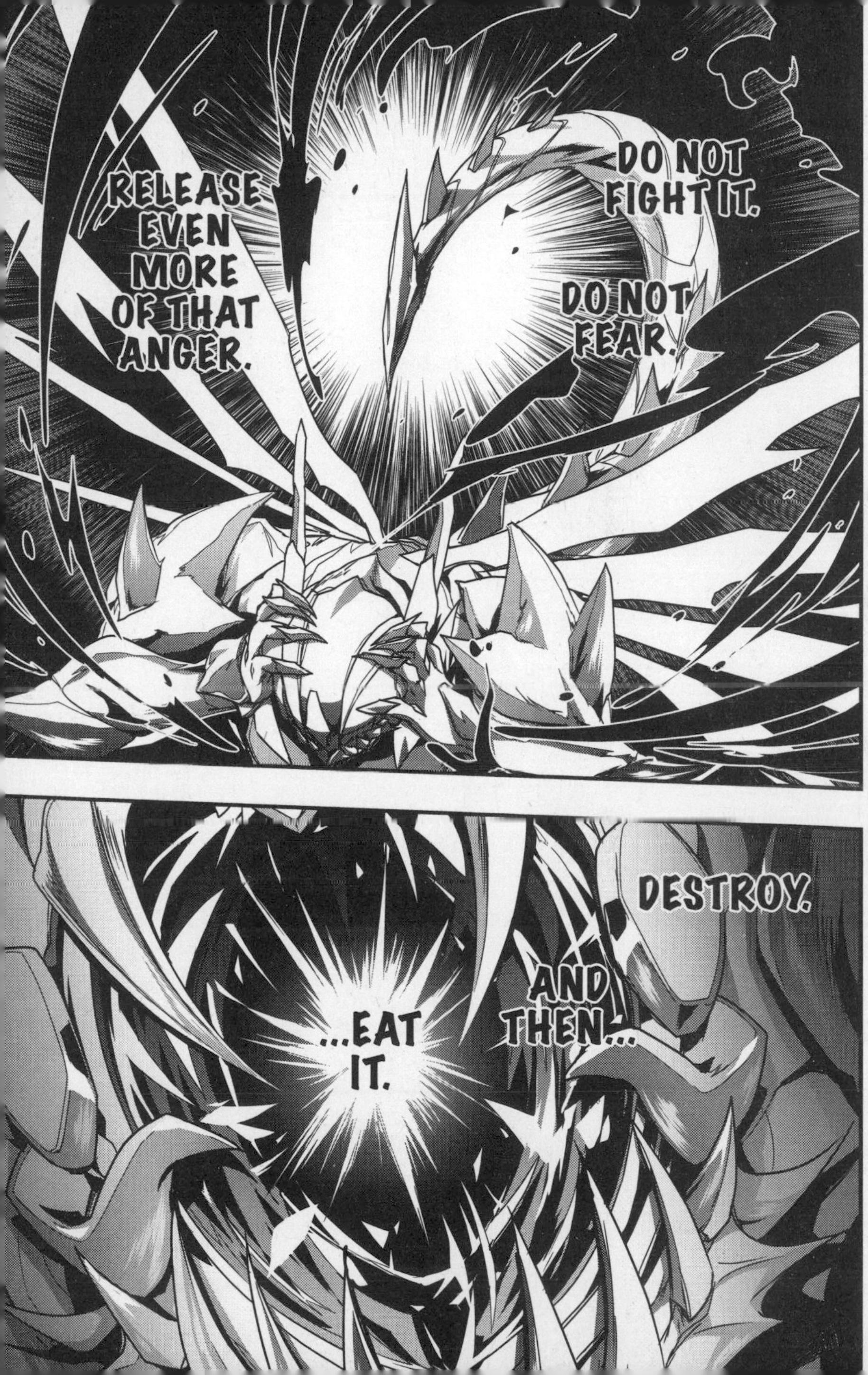
DO NOT FIGHT IT.
DO NOT FEAR.
RELEASE EVEN MORE OF THAT ANGER.
DESTROY.
AND THEN...
...EAT IT.

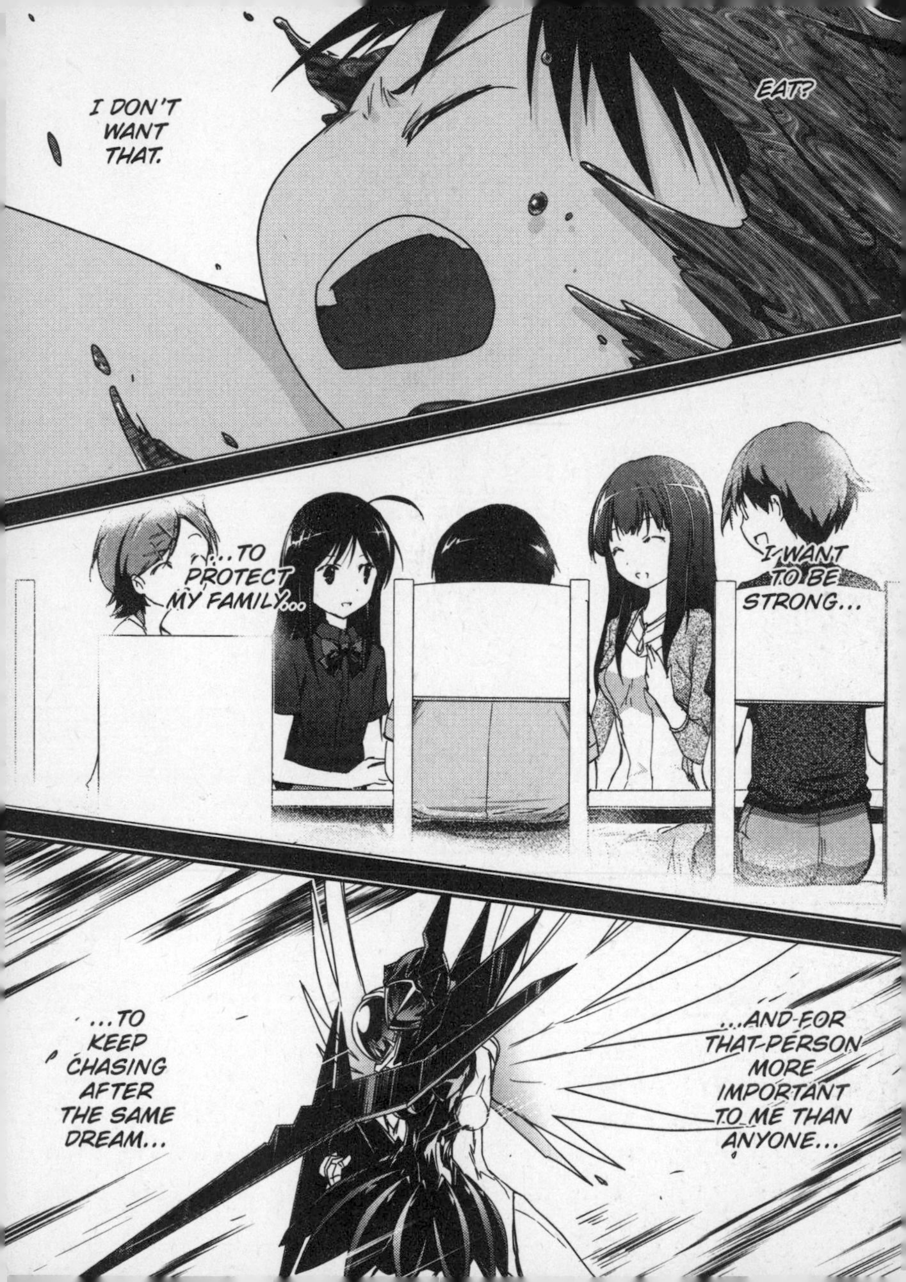
EAT?
I DON'T WANT THAT.
I WANT TO BE STRONG...
...TO PROTECT MY FAMILY...
...AND FOR THAT PERSON MORE IMPORTANT TO ME THAN ANYONE...
...TO KEEP CHASING AFTER THE SAME DREAM...

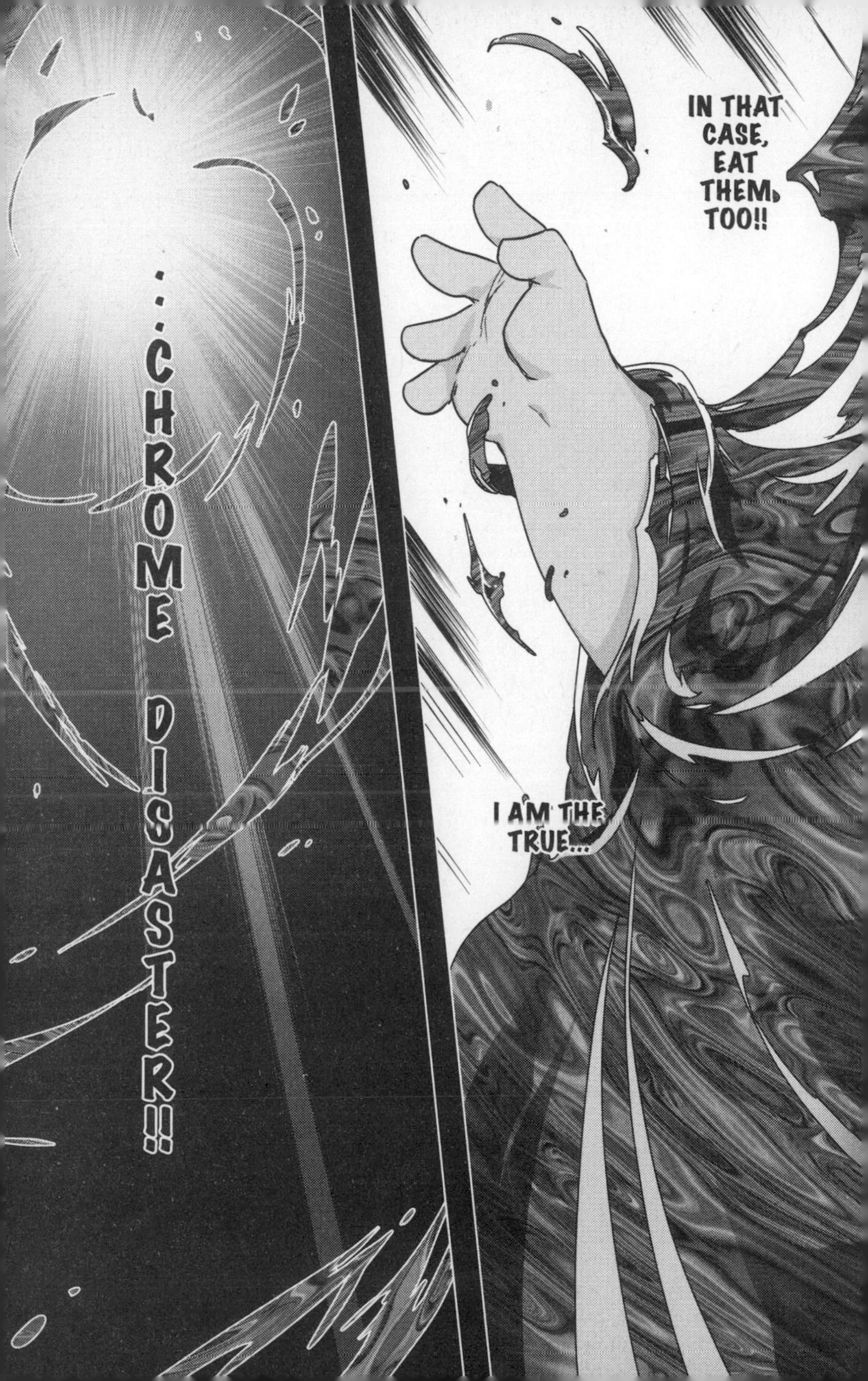
IN THAT CASE, EAT THEM, TOO!!
I AM THE TRUE...
...CHROME DISASTER!!

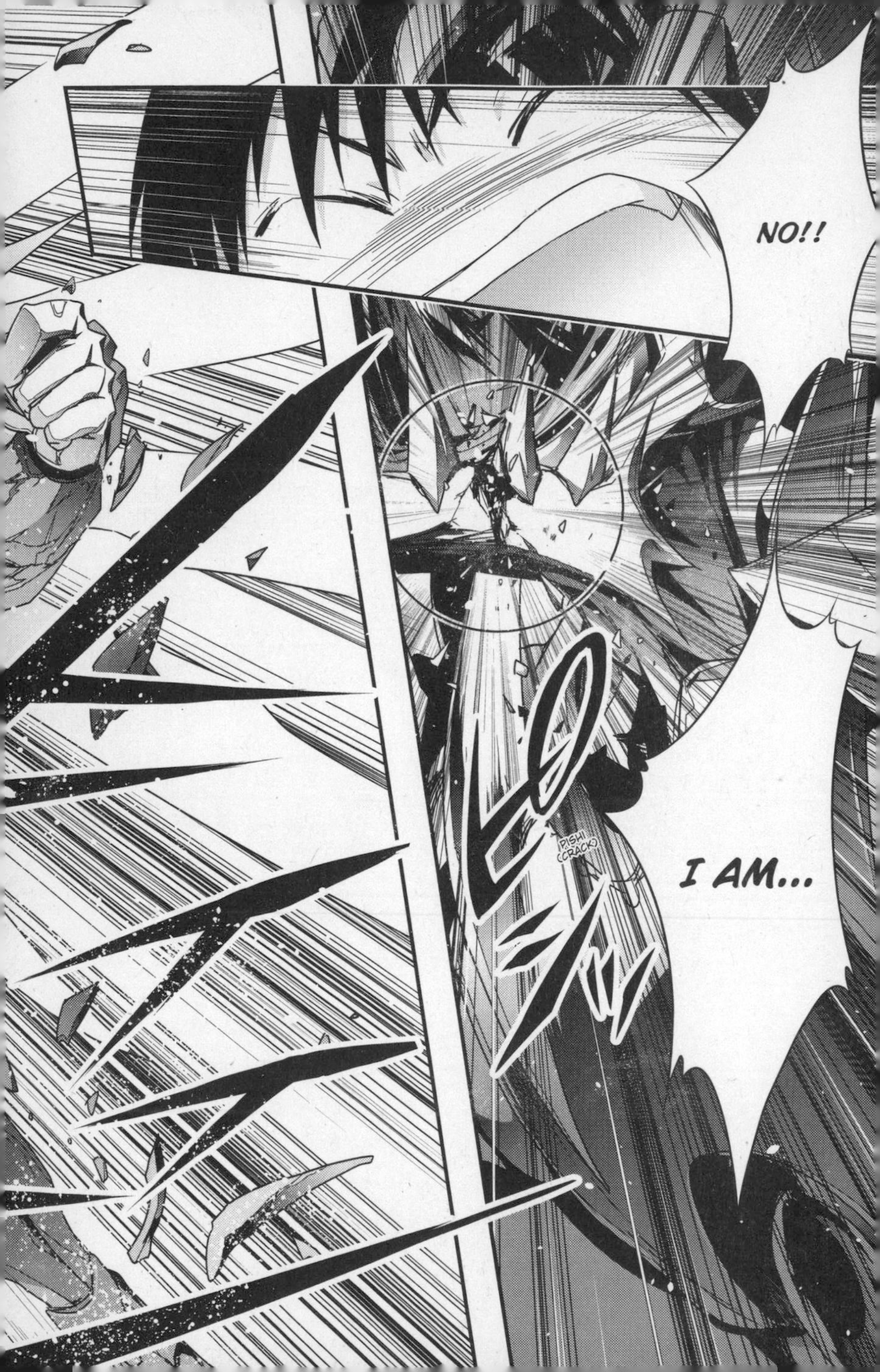
NO!!
I AM...
PISHI (CRACK)

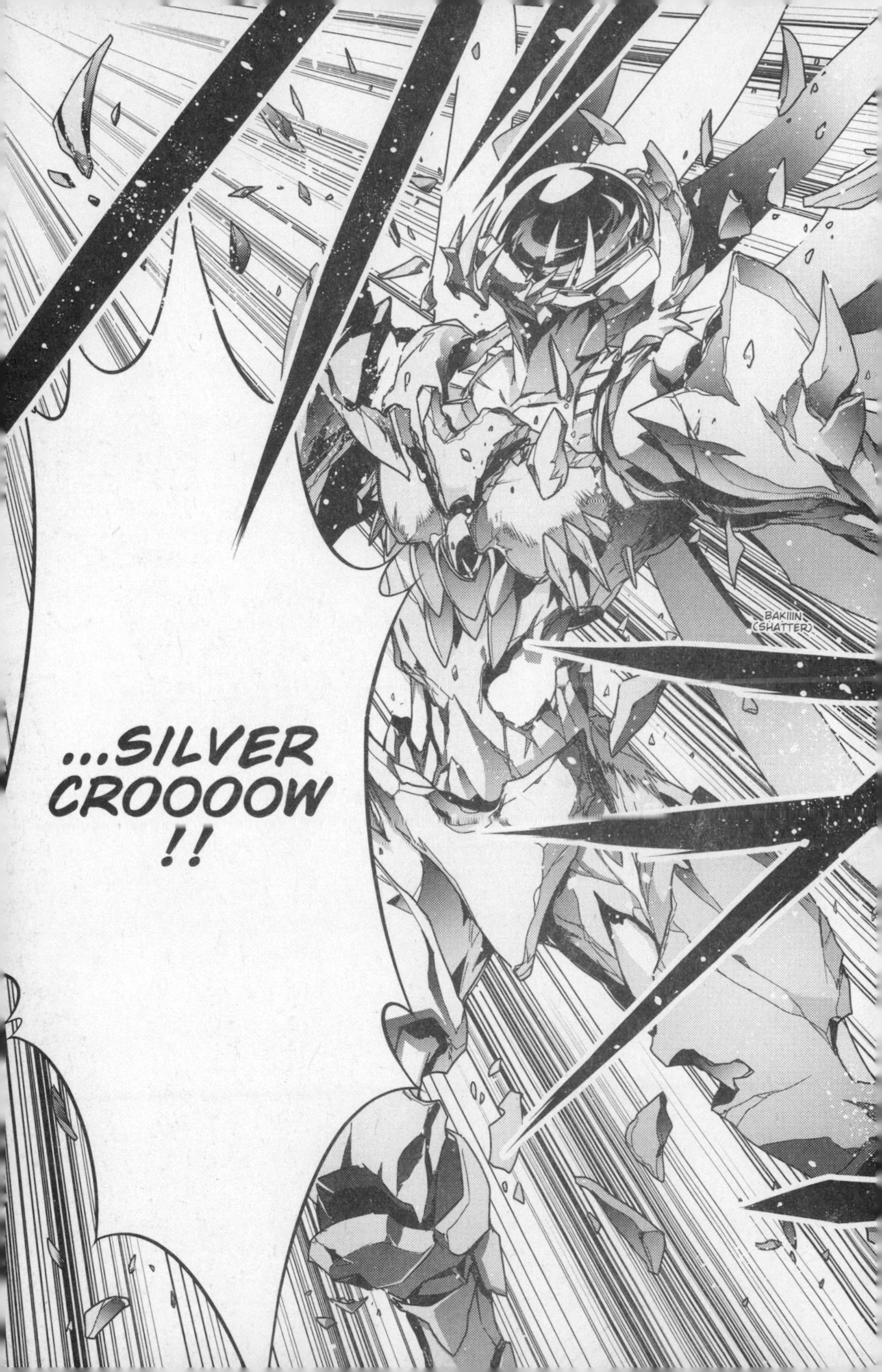
BAKIIIN (SHATTER)
...SILVER CROOOOW !!

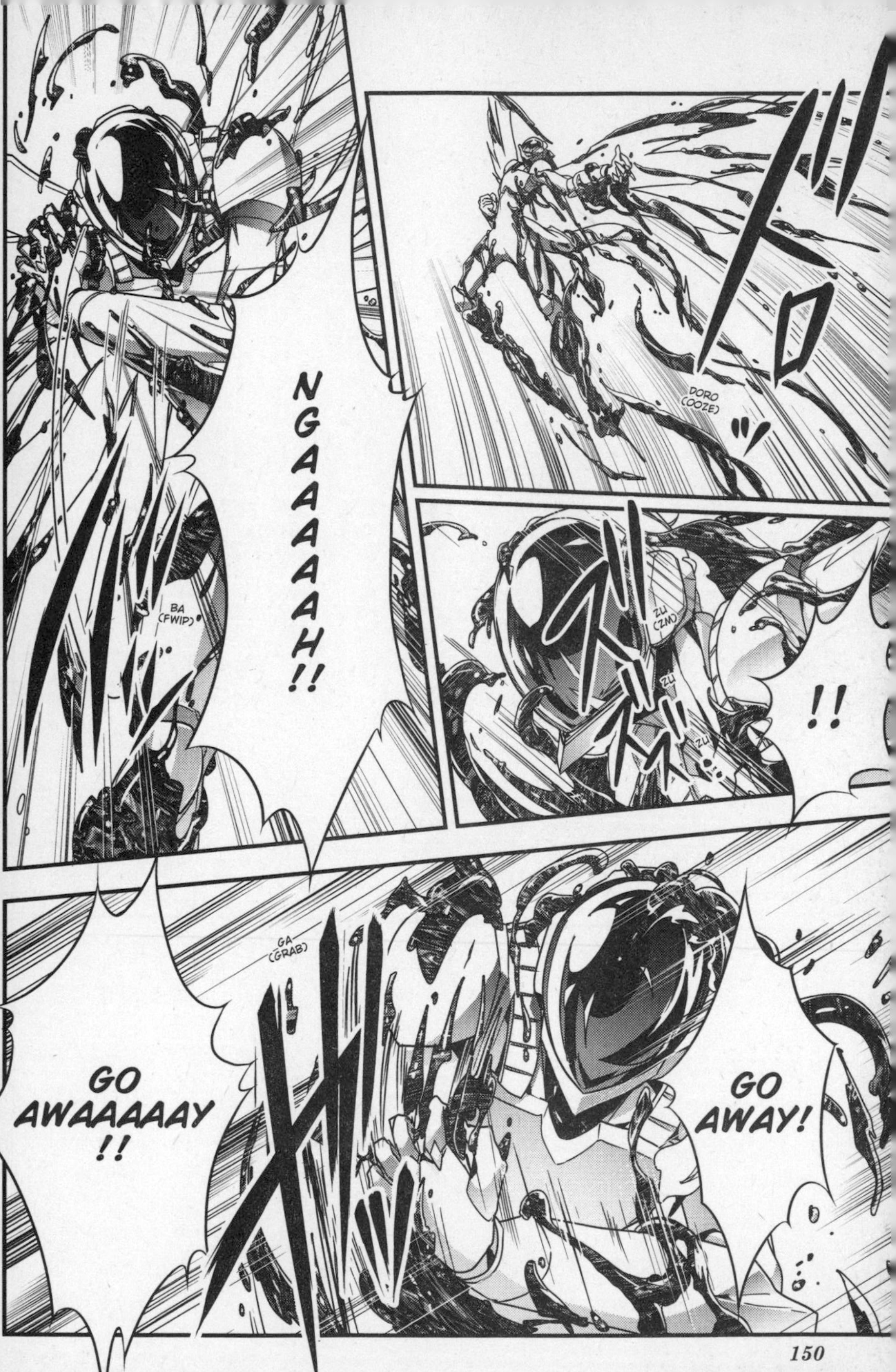
DORO (OOZE)
ZU (ZM)
ZU
ZU
!!
NGAAAAAAAH!!
BA (FWIP)
GO AWAY!
GA (GRAB)
GO AWAAAAAY!!

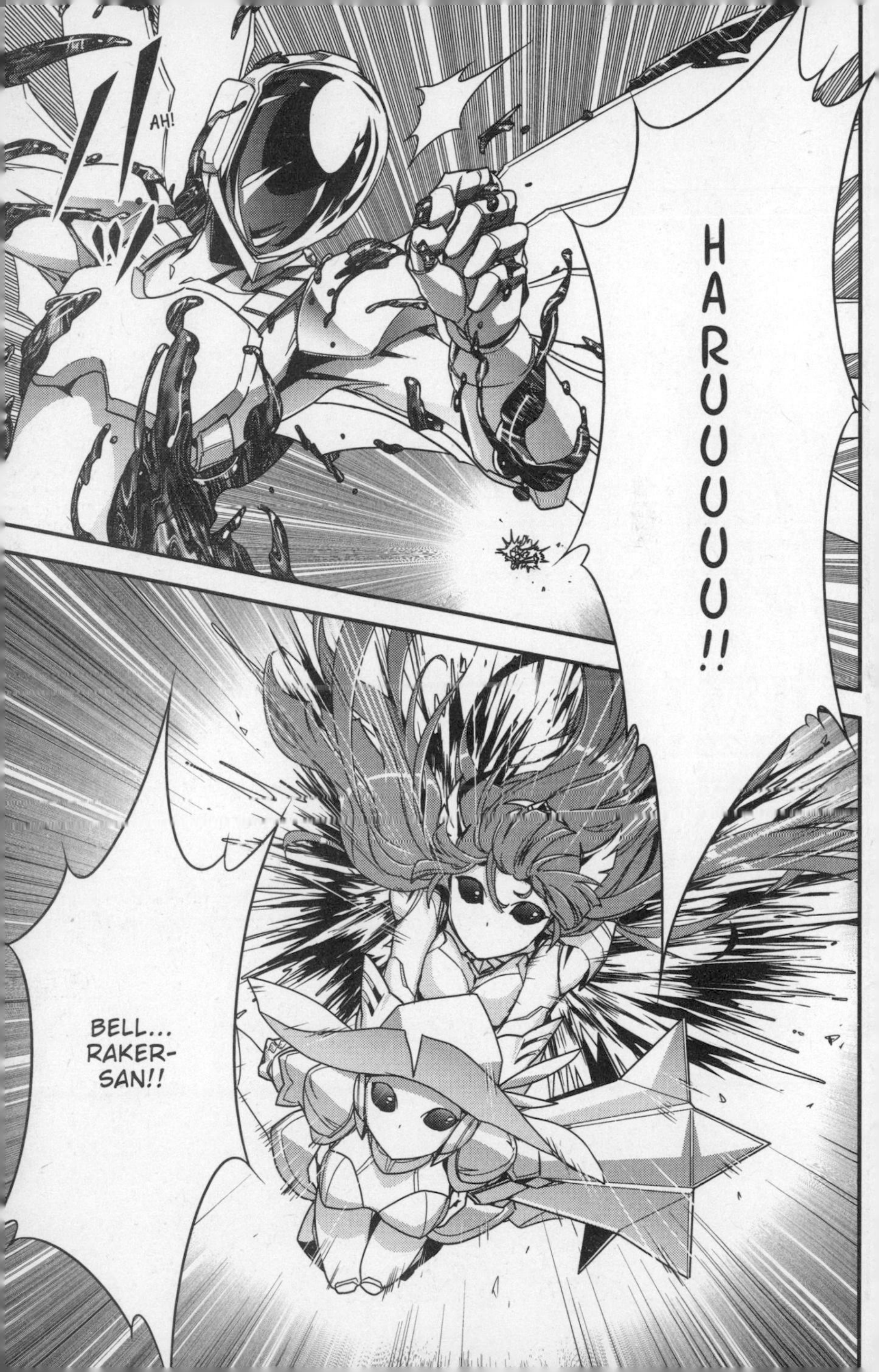
HARUUUUU!!
AH!
BELL... RAKER-SAN!!

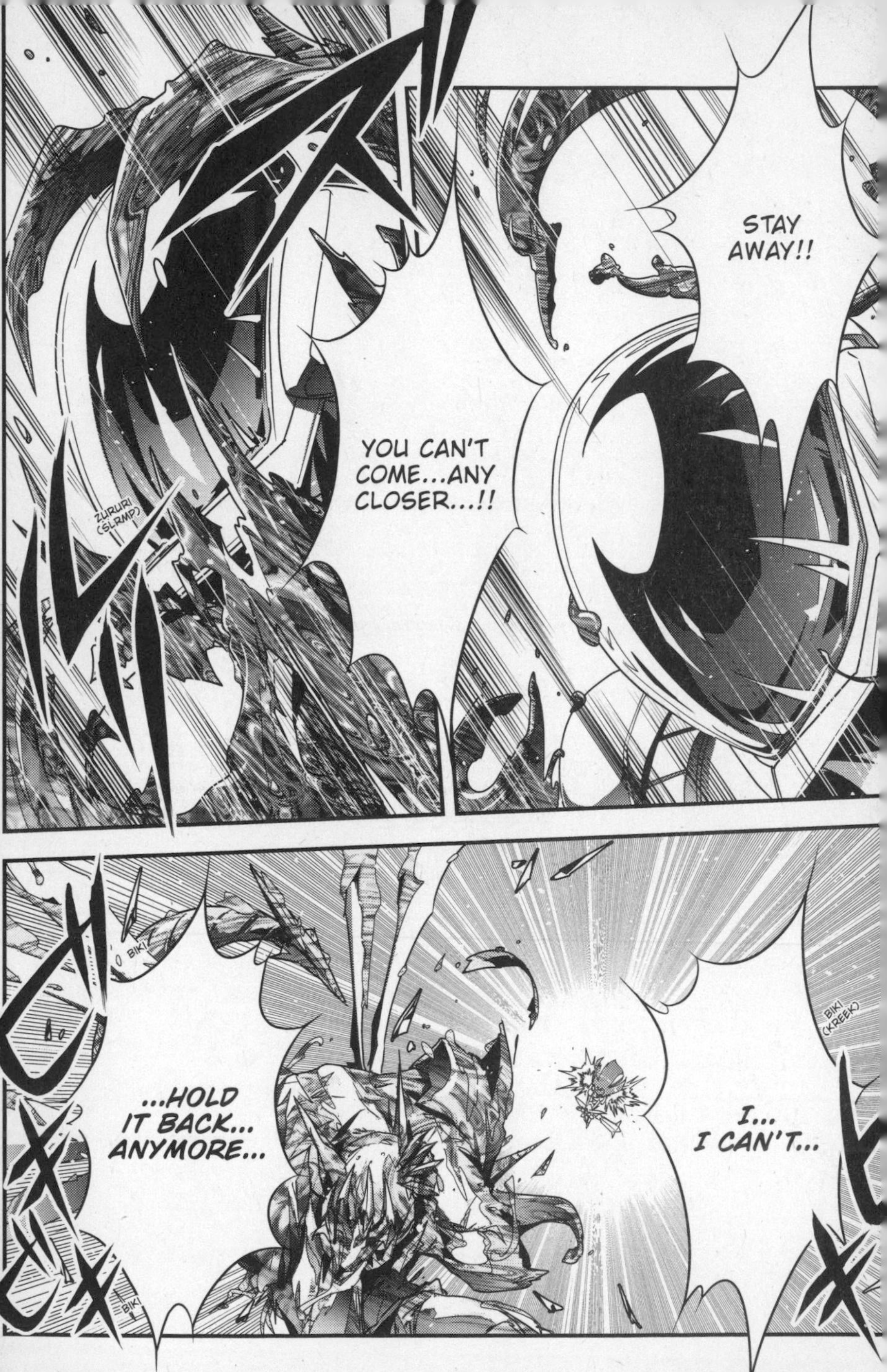
STAY AWAY!!
YOU CAN'T COME...ANY CLOSER...!!
ZURURI (SLRMP)
BIKI (KREEK)
I... I CAN'T...
...HOLD IT BACK... ANYMORE...
BIKI
BIKI

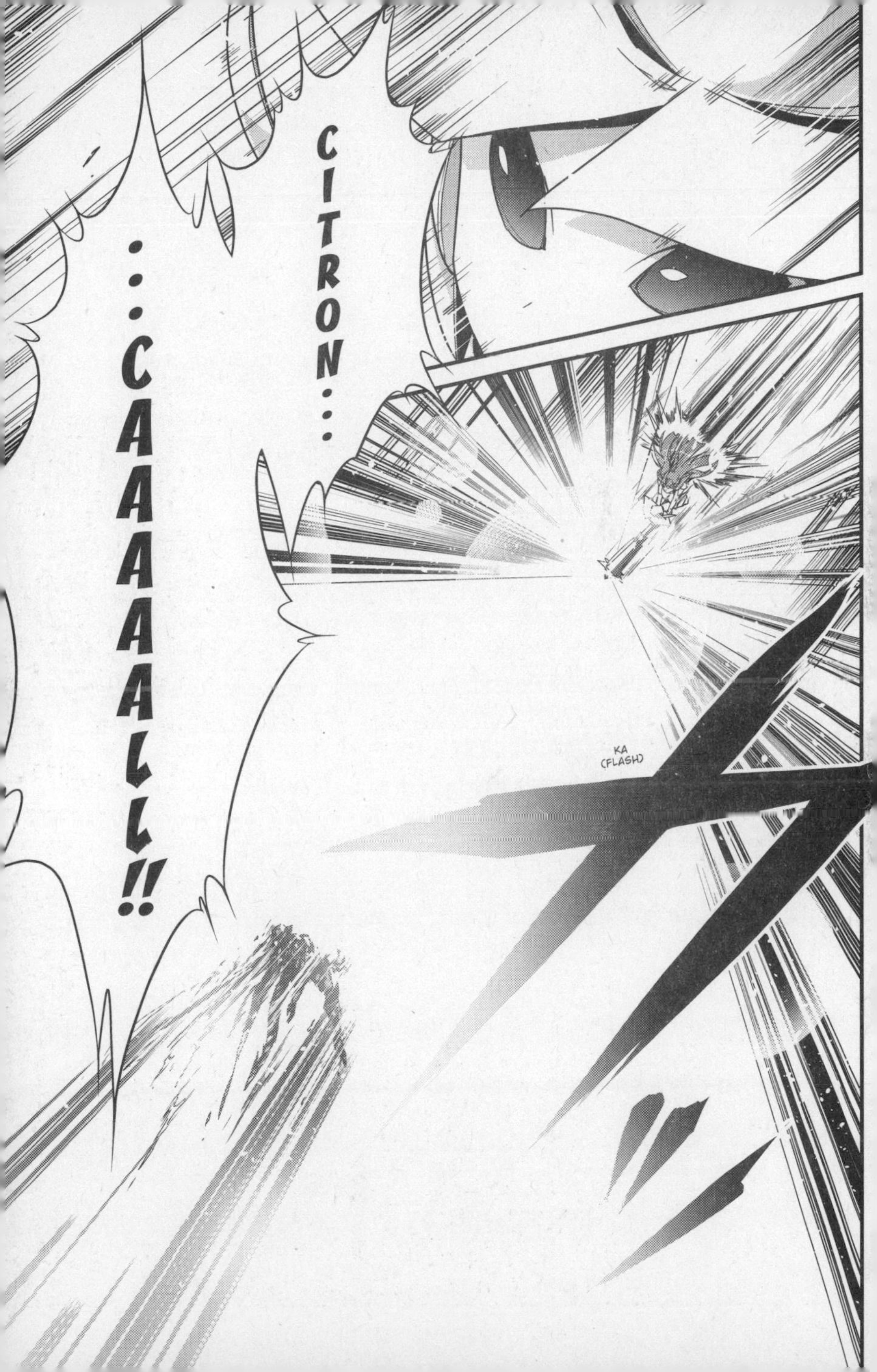
CITRON...
...CAAAAALL!!
KA
(FLASH)

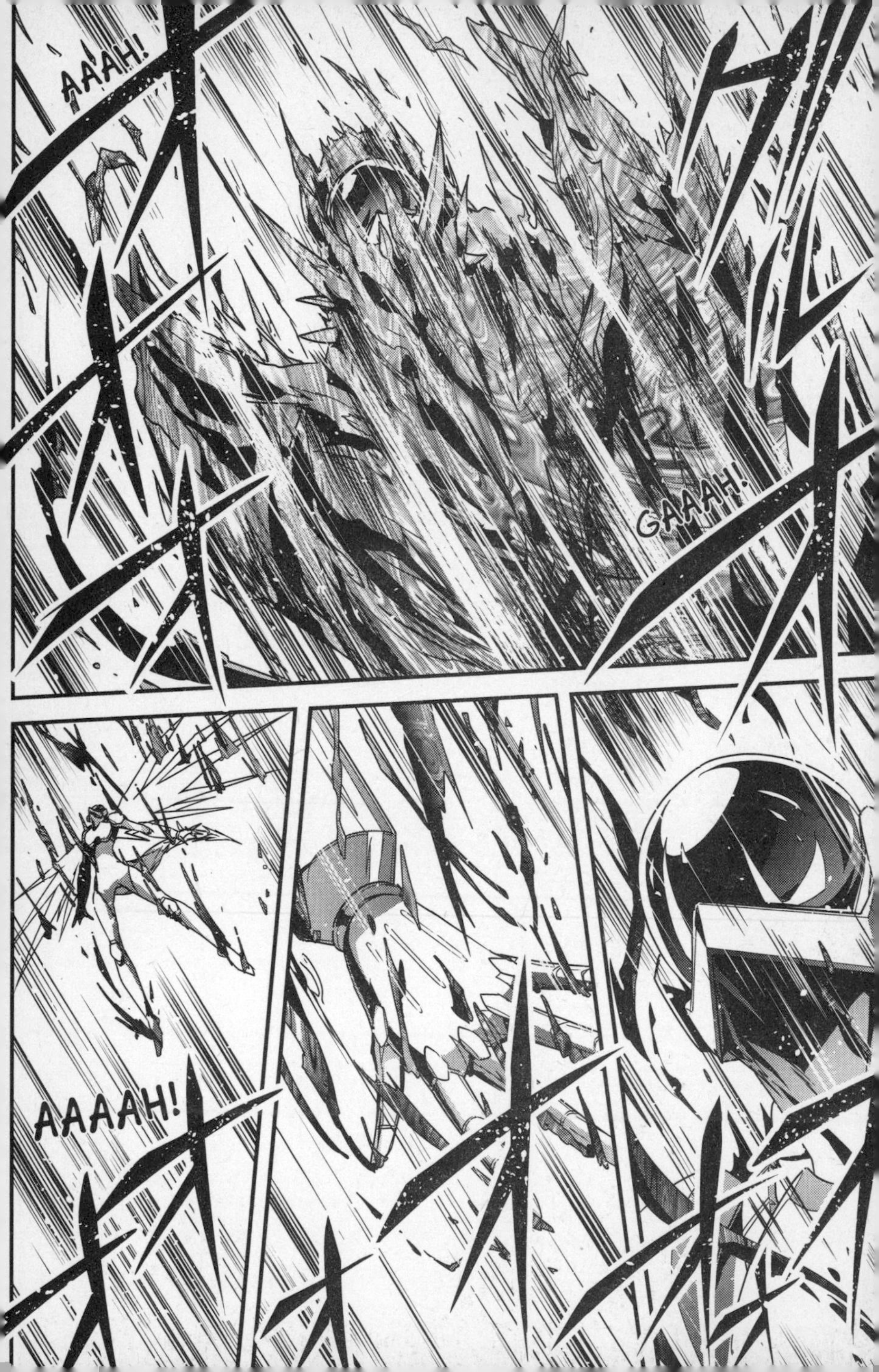
AAAH!
GAAAH!
AAAAH!

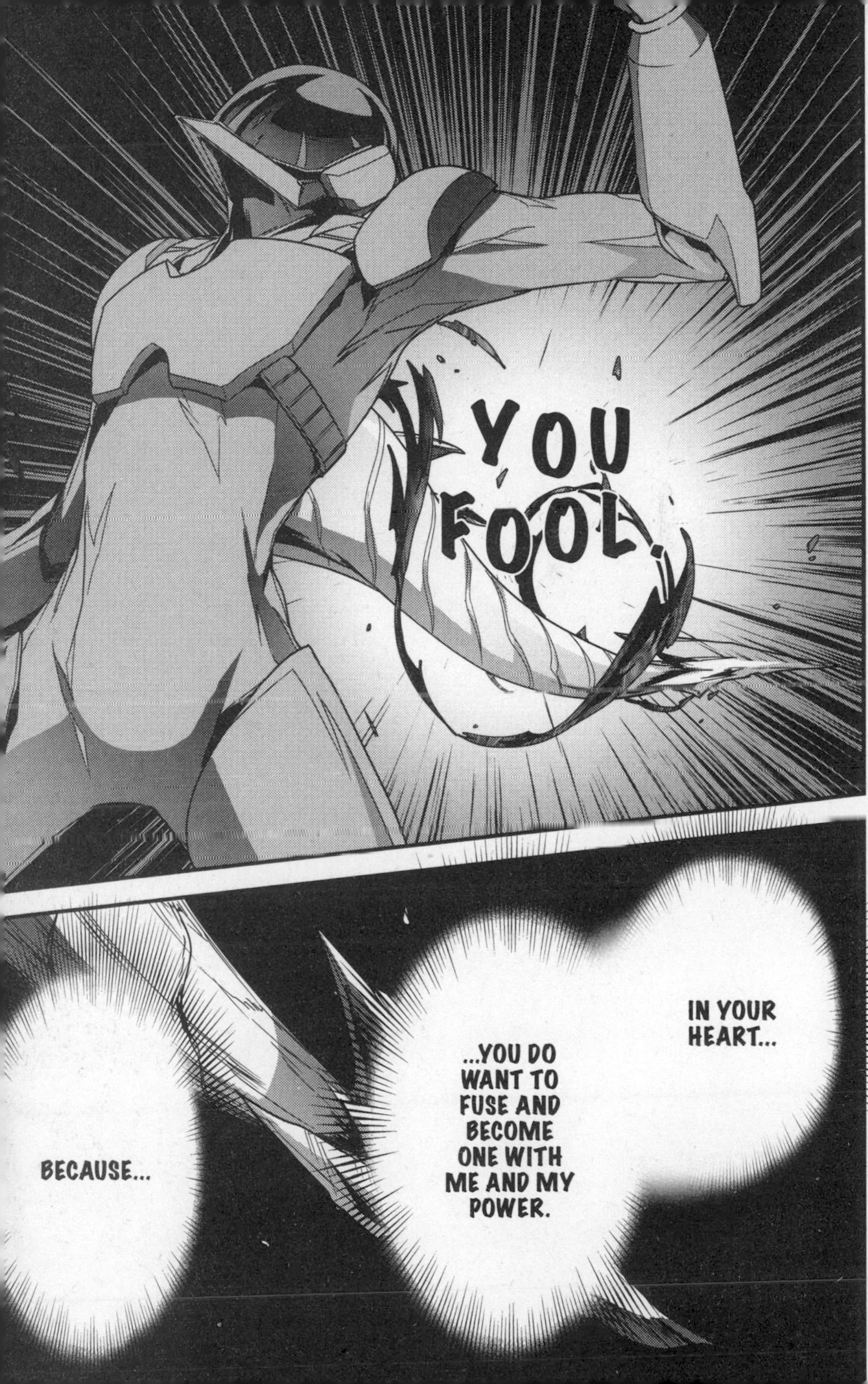
YOU FOOL.
IN YOUR HEART...
...YOU DO WANT TO FUSE AND BECOME ONE WITH ME AND MY POWER.
BECAUSE...

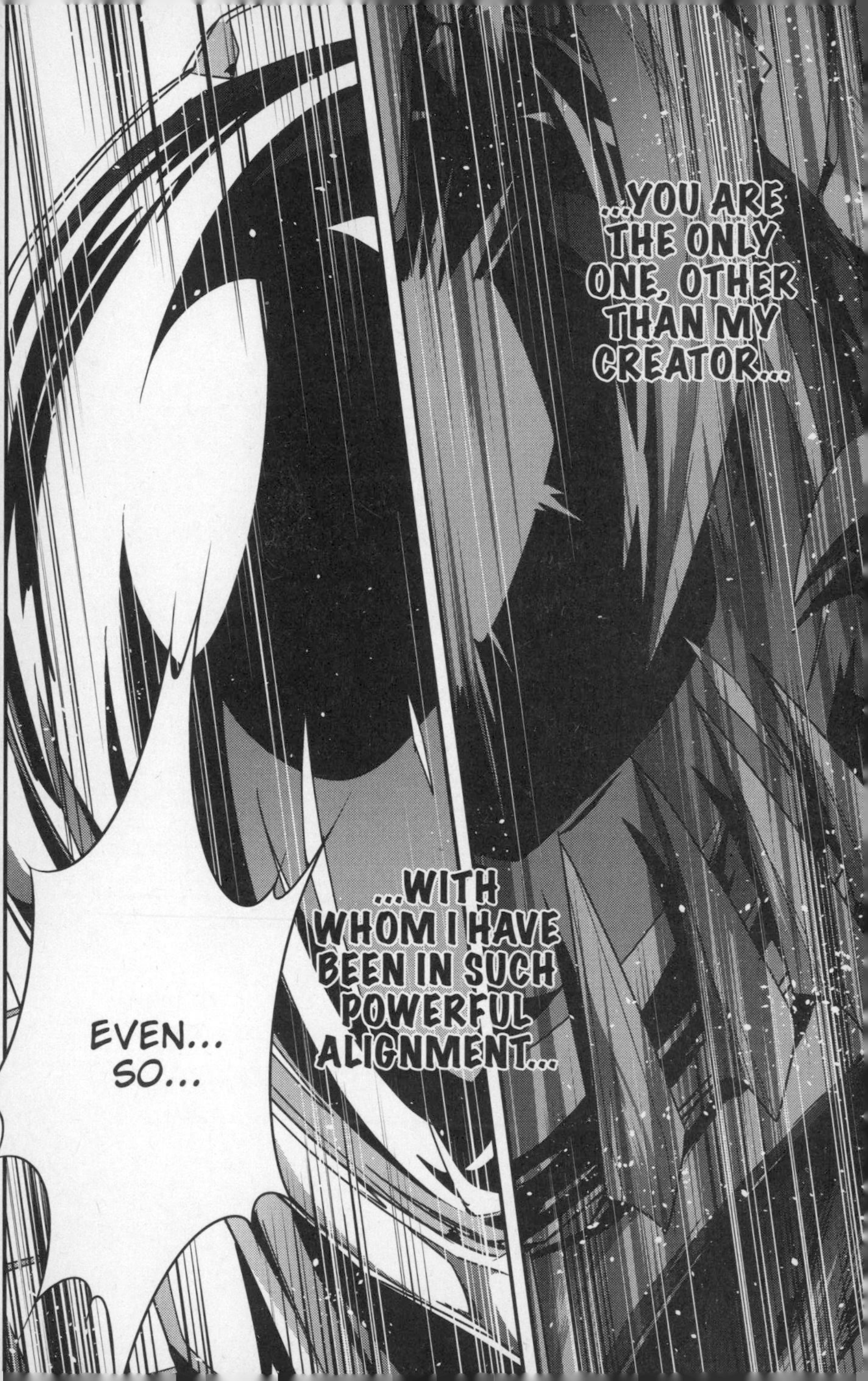
...YOU ARE THE ONLY ONE, OTHER THAN MY CREATOR...
...WITH WHOM I HAVE BEEN IN SUCH POWERFUL ALIGNMENT...
EVEN... SO...

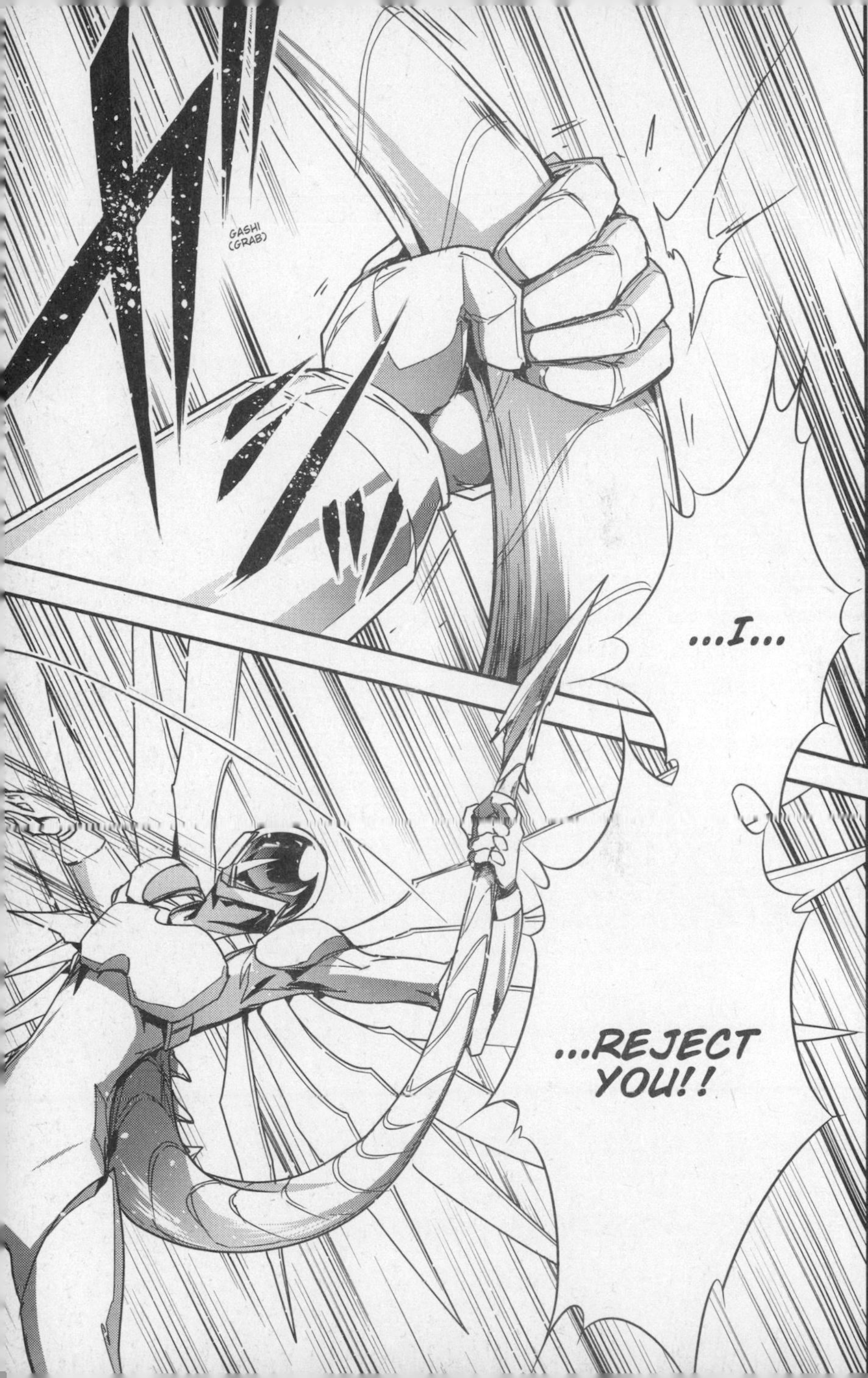
GASHI (GRAB)
...I...
...REJECT YOU!!

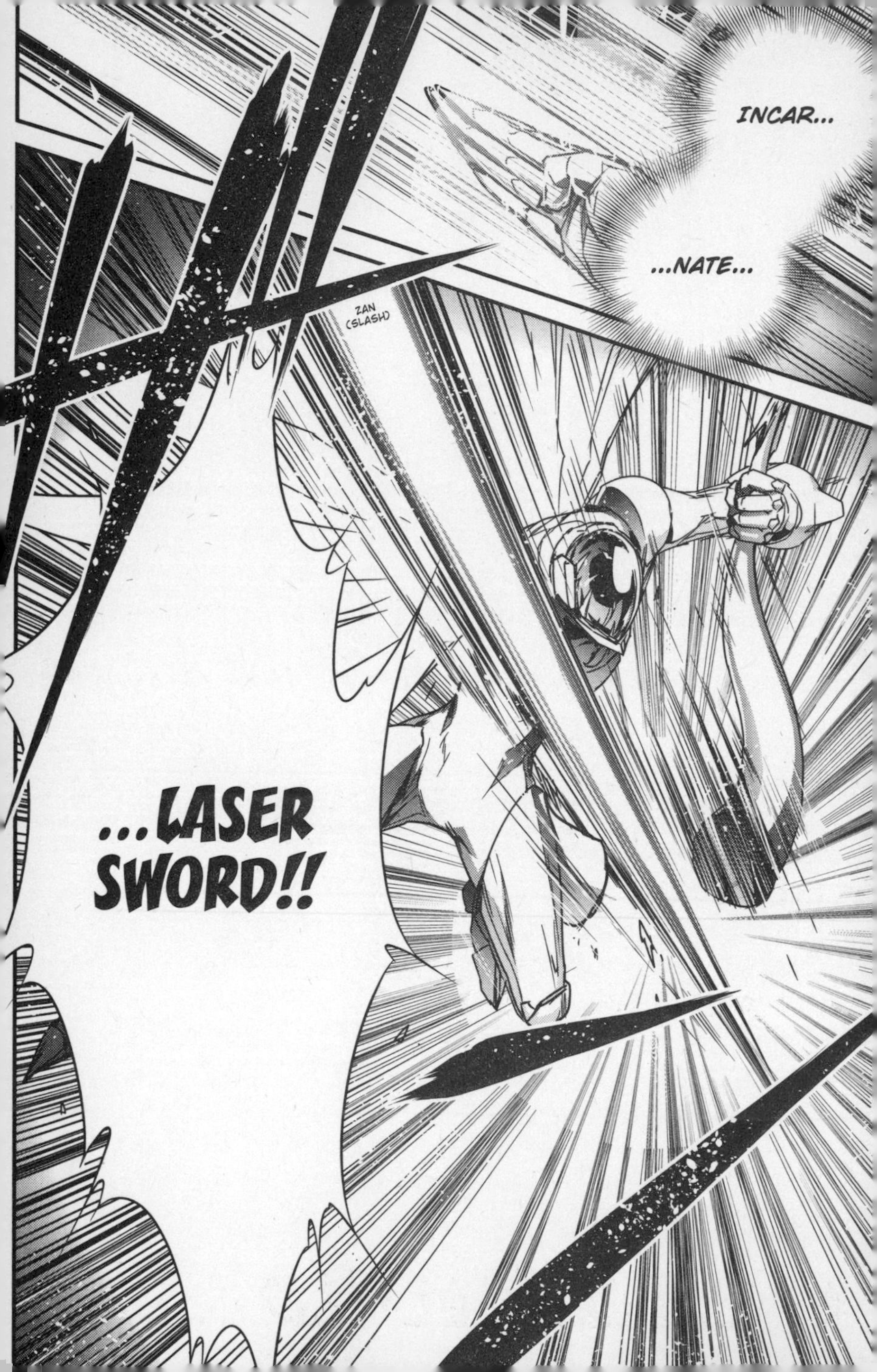
INCAR...
...NATE...
ZAN (SLASH)
...LASER SWORD!!

ACCEL • WORLD

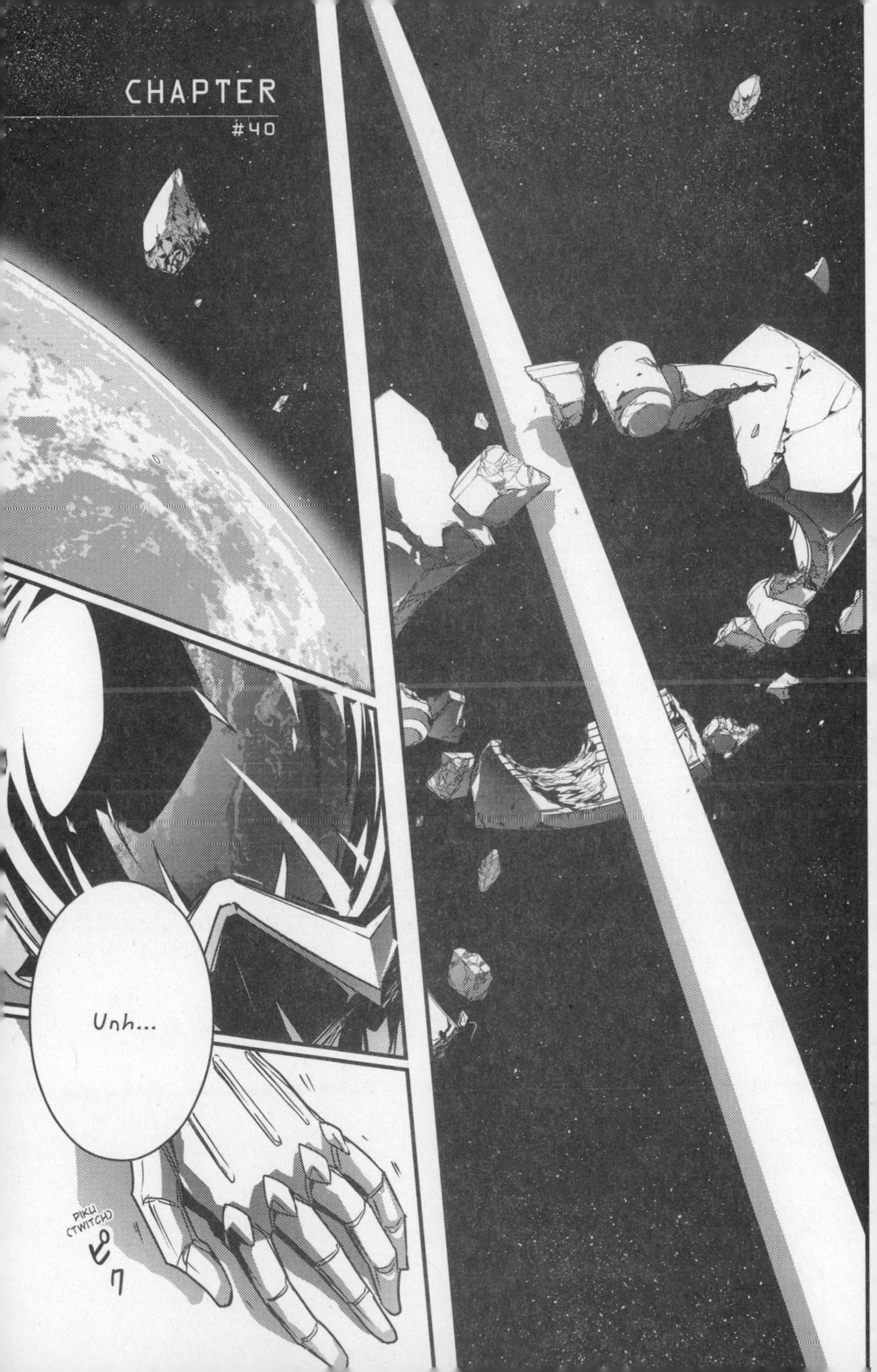
CHAPTER
#40
Unh...
PIKU (TWITCH)
ピク

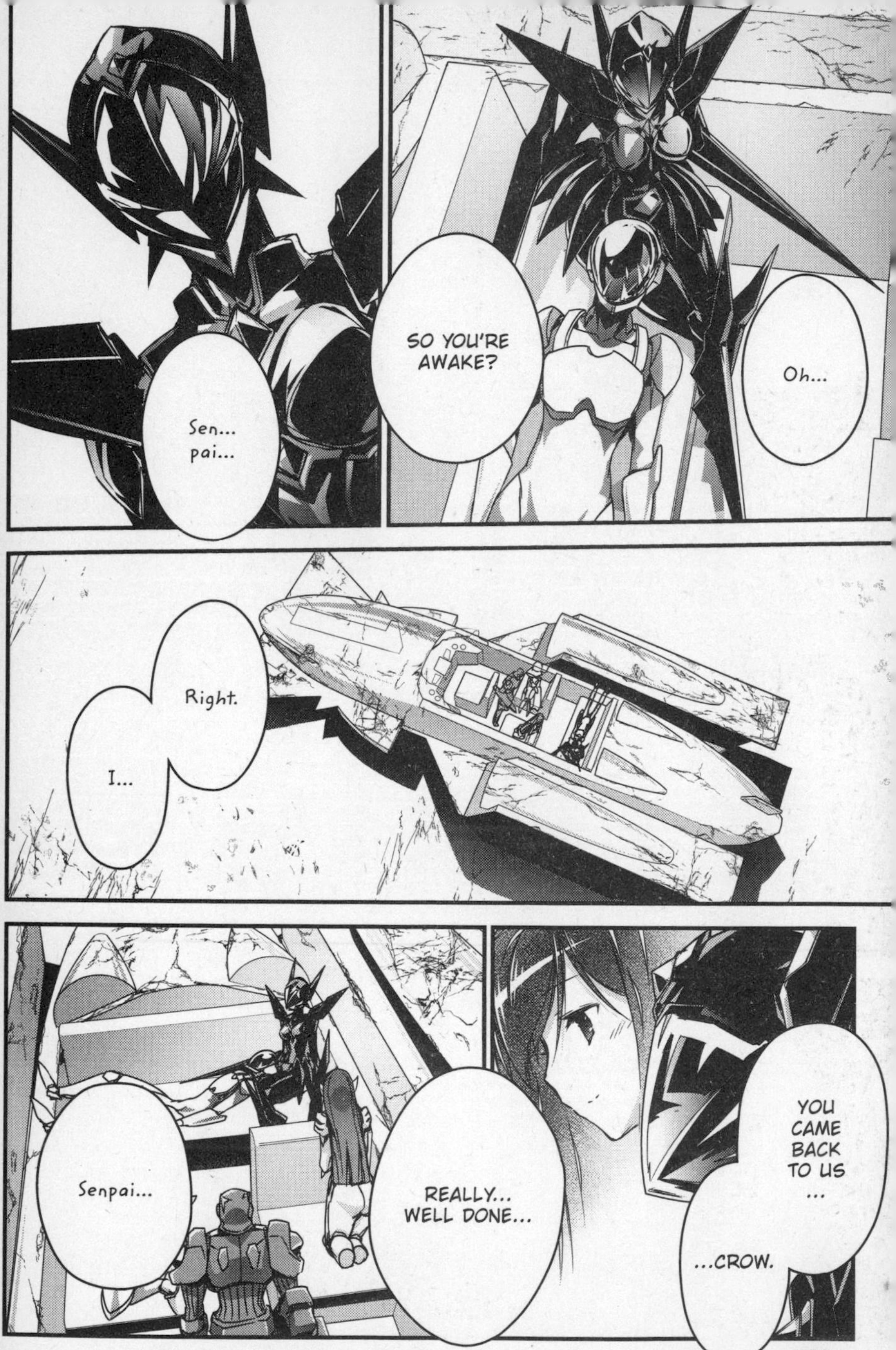
Oh...
SO YOU'RE AWAKE?
Sen... pai...
Right. I...
YOU CAME BACK TO US ... ...CROW.
REALLY... WELL DONE...
Senpai...

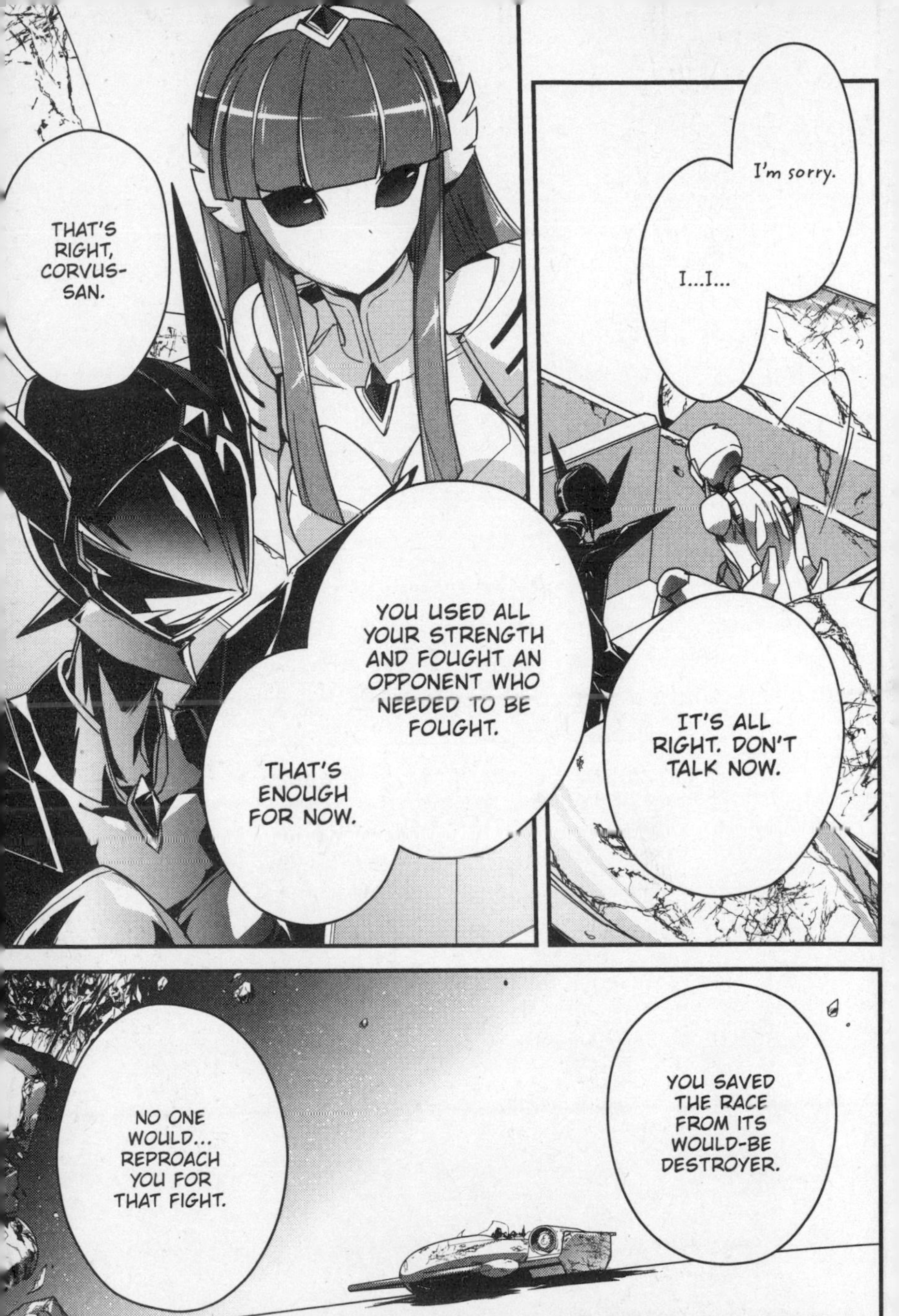
I'm sorry.
I...I...
IT'S ALL RIGHT. DON'T TALK NOW.
THAT'S RIGHT, CORVUS-SAN.
YOU USED ALL YOUR STRENGTH AND FOUGHT AN OPPONENT WHO NEEDED TO BE FOUGHT.
THAT'S ENOUGH FOR NOW.
YOU SAVED THE RACE FROM ITS WOULD-BE DESTROYER.
NO ONE WOULD... REPROACH YOU FOR THAT FIGHT.

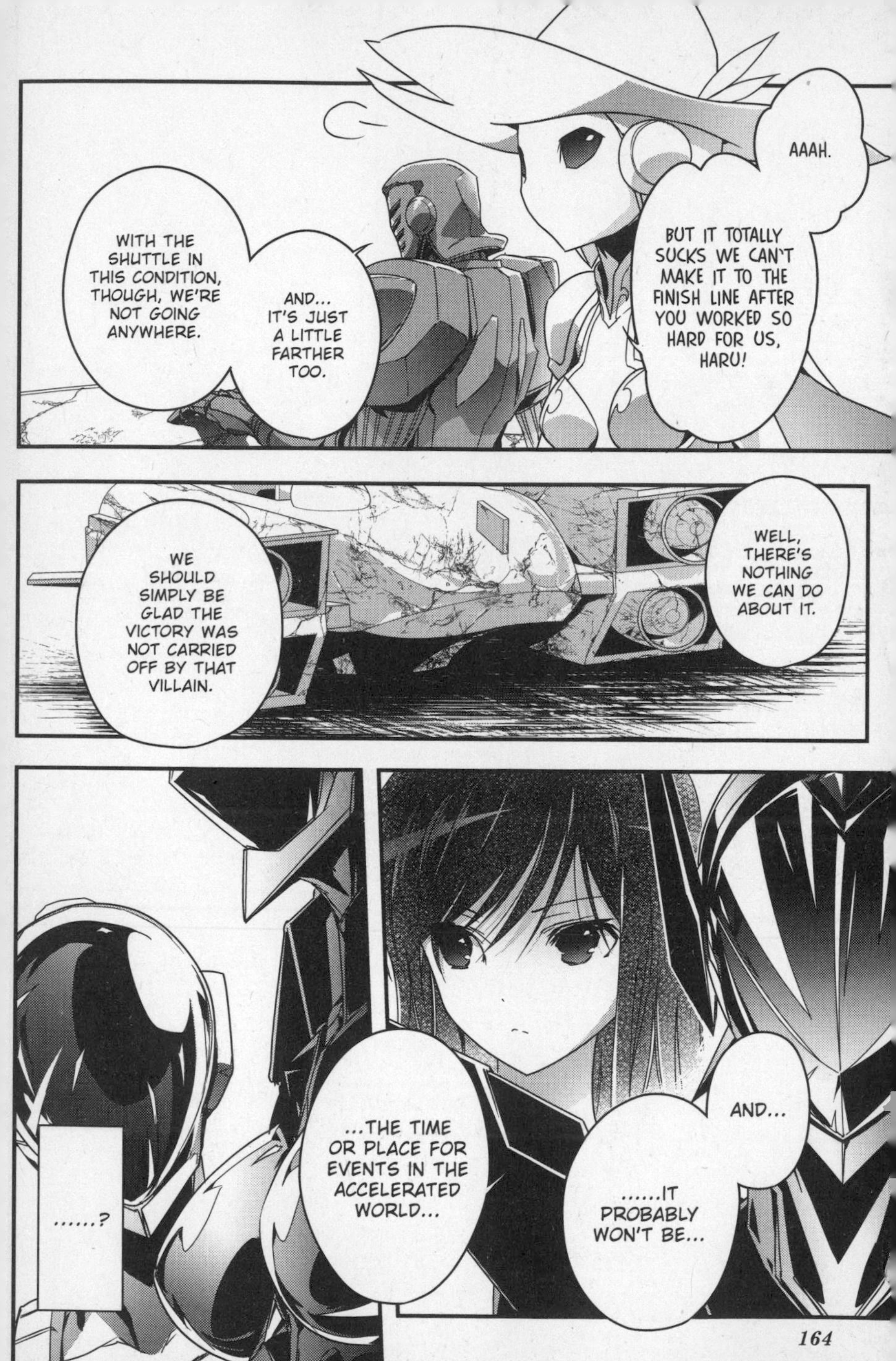
AAAH.
BUT IT TOTALLY SUCKS WE CAN'T MAKE IT TO THE FINISH LINE AFTER YOU WORKED SO HARD FOR US, HARU!
AND... IT'S JUST A LITTLE FARTHER TOO.
WITH THE SHUTTLE IN THIS CONDITION, THOUGH, WE'RE NOT GOING ANYWHERE.
WELL, THERE'S NOTHING WE CAN DO ABOUT IT.
WE SHOULD SIMPLY BE GLAD THE VICTORY WAS NOT CARRIED OFF BY THAT VILLAIN.
AND...
......IT PROBABLY WON'T BE...
...THE TIME OR PLACE FOR EVENTS IN THE ACCELERATED WORLD...
......?

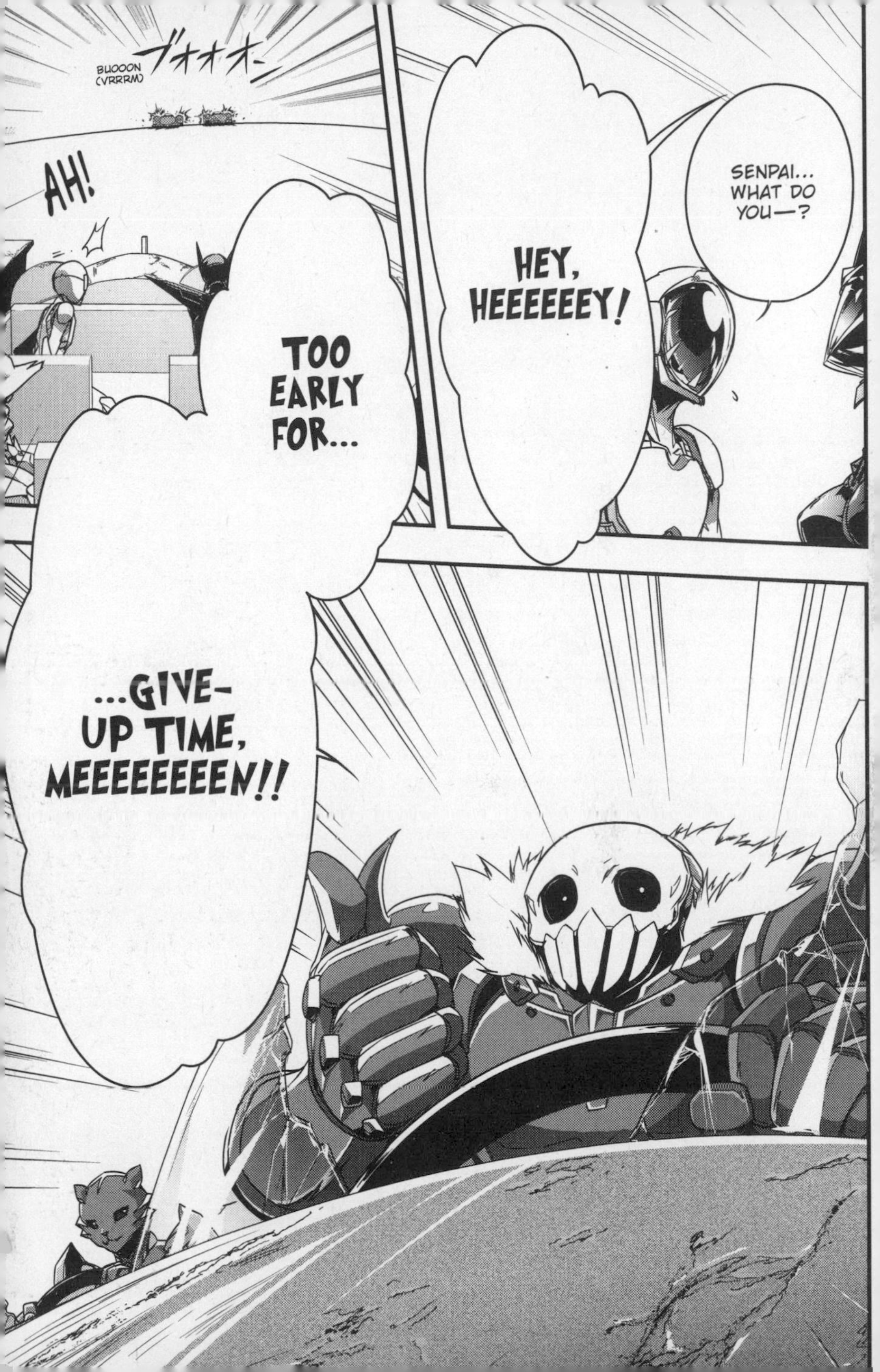
SENPAI... WHAT DO YOU—?
HEY, HEEEEEEY!
ブオオオン
BUOOON (VRRRM)
AH!
TOO EARLY FOR...
...GIVE-UP TIME, MEEEEEEEEN!!

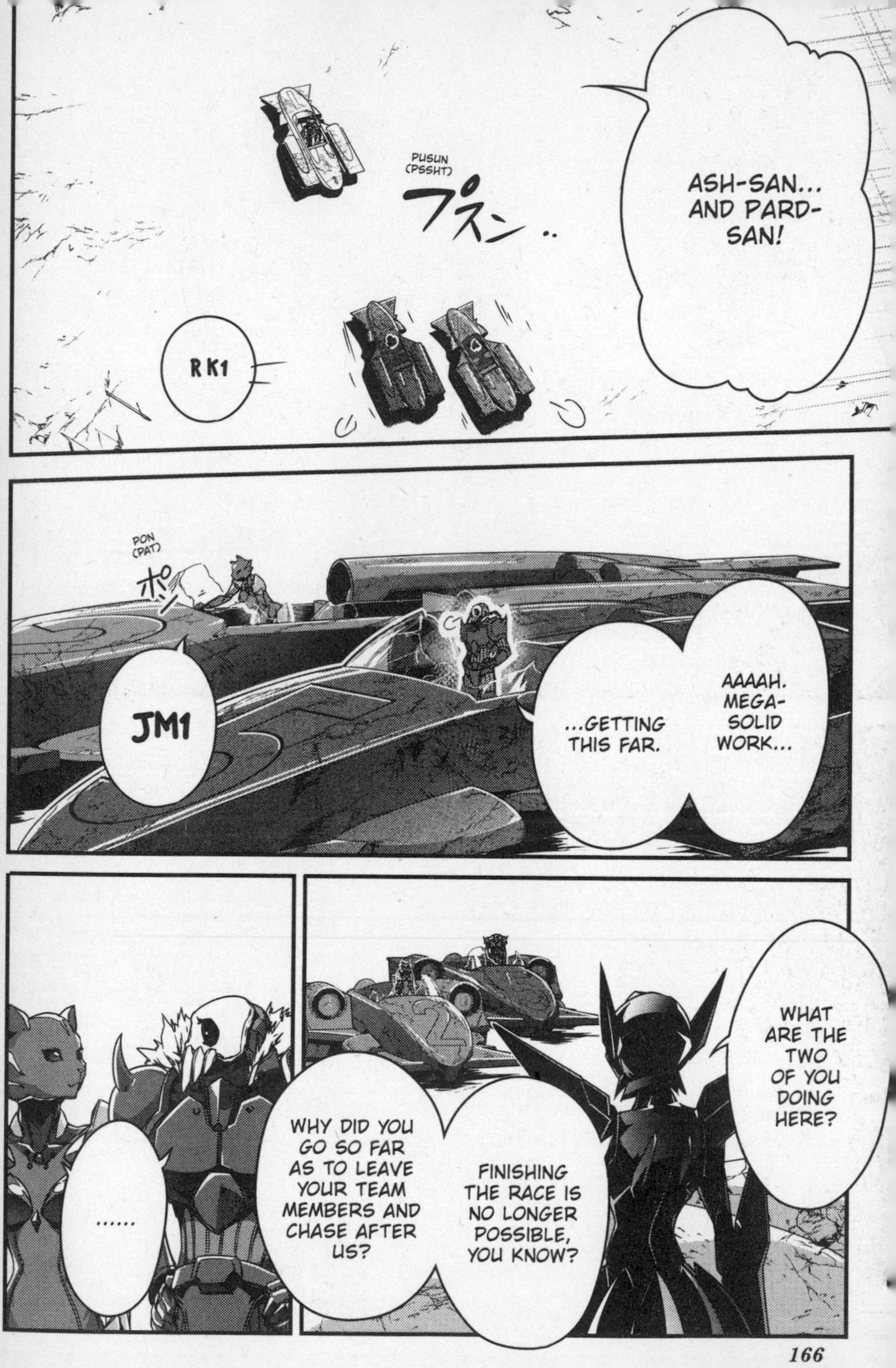
ASH-SAN... AND PARD-SAN!
PUSUN (PSSHT)
プスン..
RK1
AAAAH. MEGA-SOLID WORK...
...GETTING THIS FAR.
PON (PAT)
ポン
JM1
WHAT ARE THE TWO OF YOU DOING HERE?
FINISHING THE RACE IS NO LONGER POSSIBLE, YOU KNOW?
WHY DID YOU GO SO FAR AS TO LEAVE YOUR TEAM MEMBERS AND CHASE AFTER US?
......

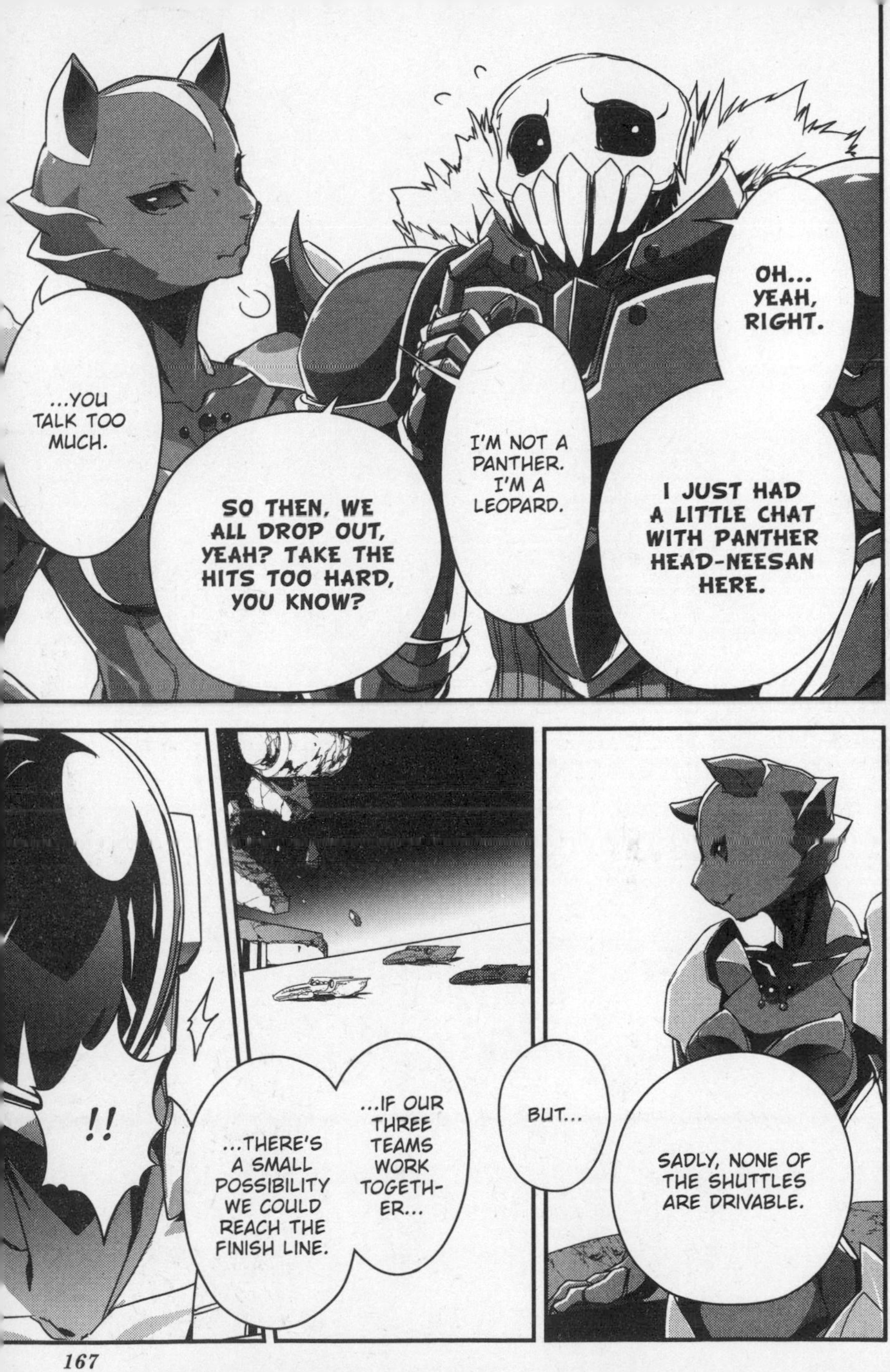

OH... YEAH, RIGHT.
I JUST HAD A LITTLE CHAT WITH PANTHER HEAD-NEESAN HERE.
I'M NOT A PANTHER. I'M A LEOPARD.
SO THEN, WE ALL DROP OUT, YEAH? TAKE THE HITS TOO HARD, YOU KNOW?
...YOU TALK TOO MUCH.
SADLY, NONE OF THE SHUTTLES ARE DRIVABLE.
BUT...
...IF OUR THREE TEAMS WORK TOGETH-ER...
...THERE'S A SMALL POSSIBILITY WE COULD REACH THE FINISH LINE.
!!

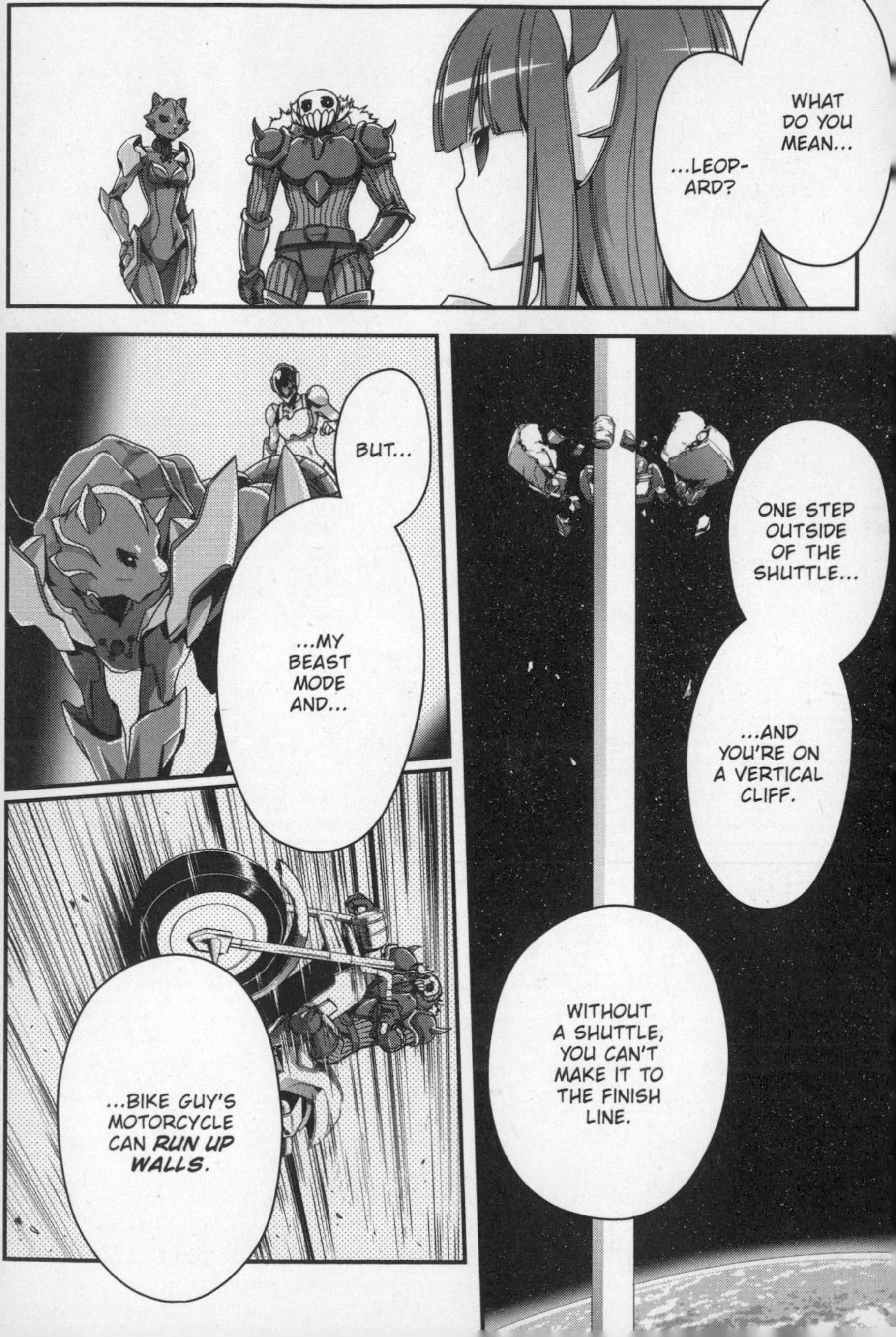
WHAT DO YOU MEAN...
...LEOP-ARD?
ONE STEP OUTSIDE OF THE SHUTTLE...
...AND YOU'RE ON A VERTICAL CLIFF.
WITHOUT A SHUTTLE, YOU CAN'T MAKE IT TO THE FINISH LINE.
BUT...
...MY BEAST MODE AND...
...BIKE GUY'S MOTORCYCLE CAN ***RUN UP WALLS***.

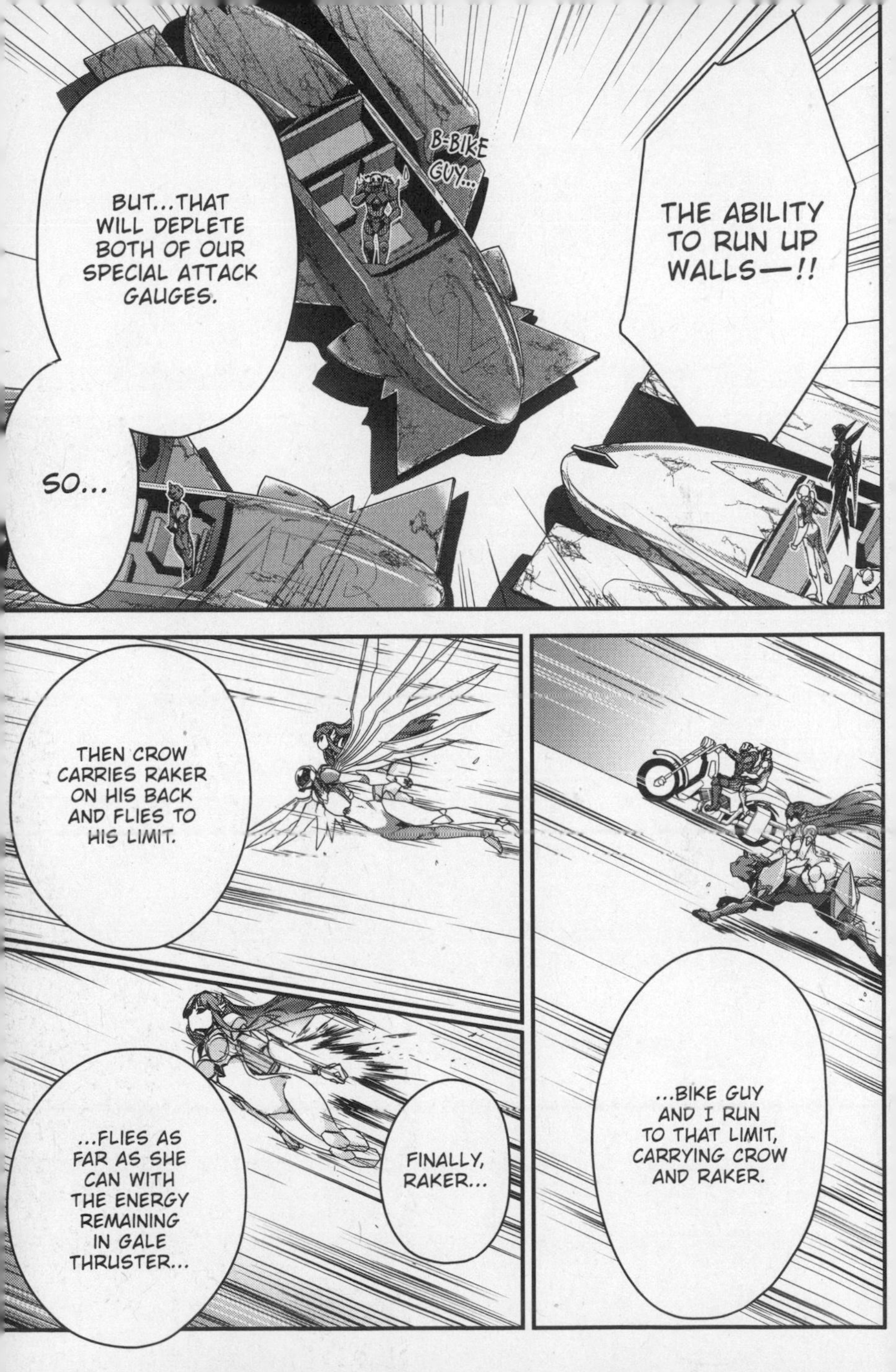
THE ABILITY TO RUN UP WALLS—!!
B-BIKE GUY...
BUT...THAT WILL DEPLETE BOTH OF OUR SPECIAL ATTACK GAUGES.
SO...
...BIKE GUY AND I RUN TO THAT LIMIT, CARRYING CROW AND RAKER.
THEN CROW CARRIES RAKER ON HIS BACK AND FLIES TO HIS LIMIT.
FINALLY, RAKER...
...FLIES AS FAR AS SHE CAN WITH THE ENERGY REMAINING IN GALE THRUSTER...

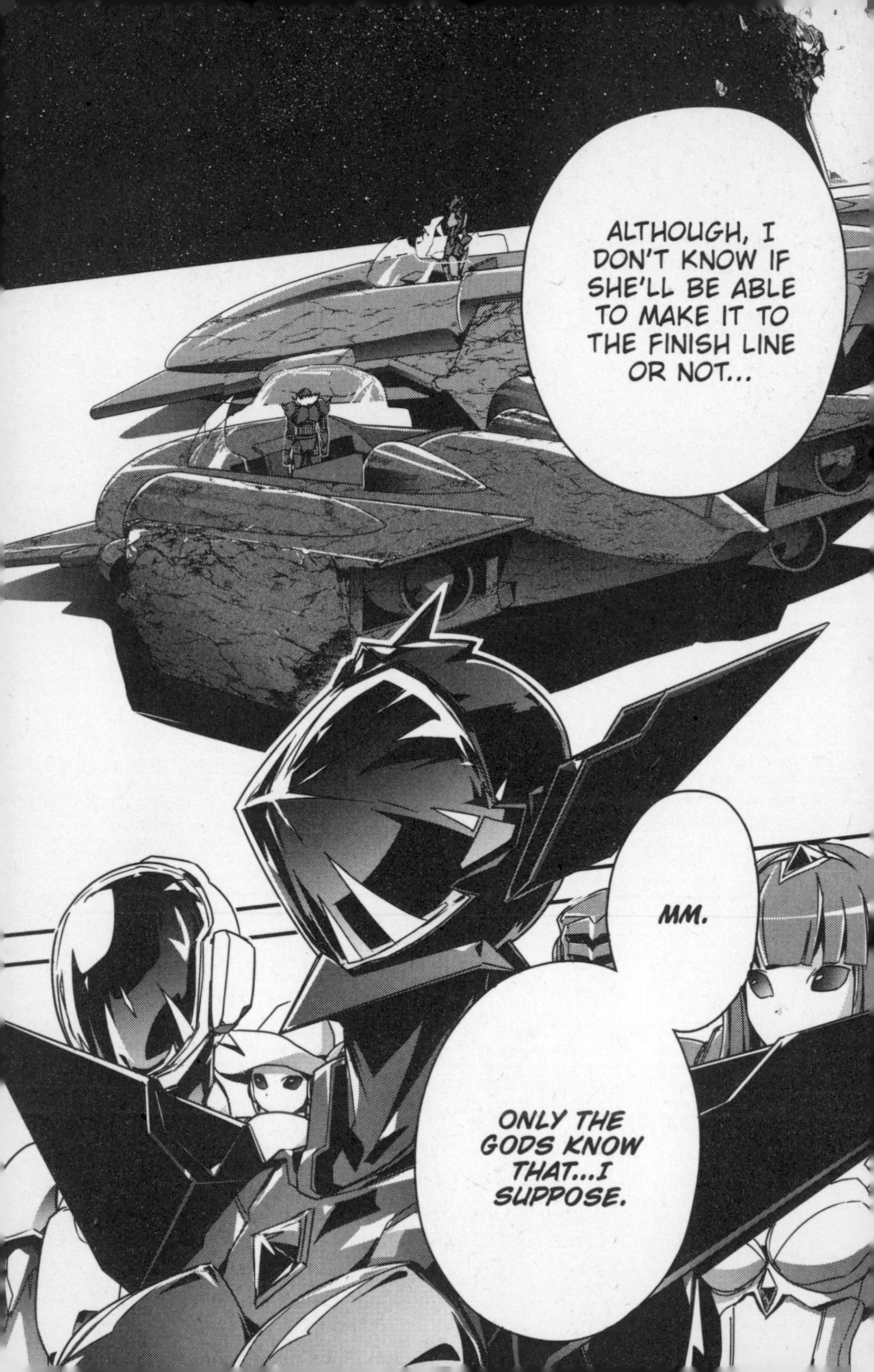
ALTHOUGH, I DON'T KNOW IF SHE'LL BE ABLE TO MAKE IT TO THE FINISH LINE OR NOT...
MM.
ONLY THE GODS KNOW THAT...I SUPPOSE.

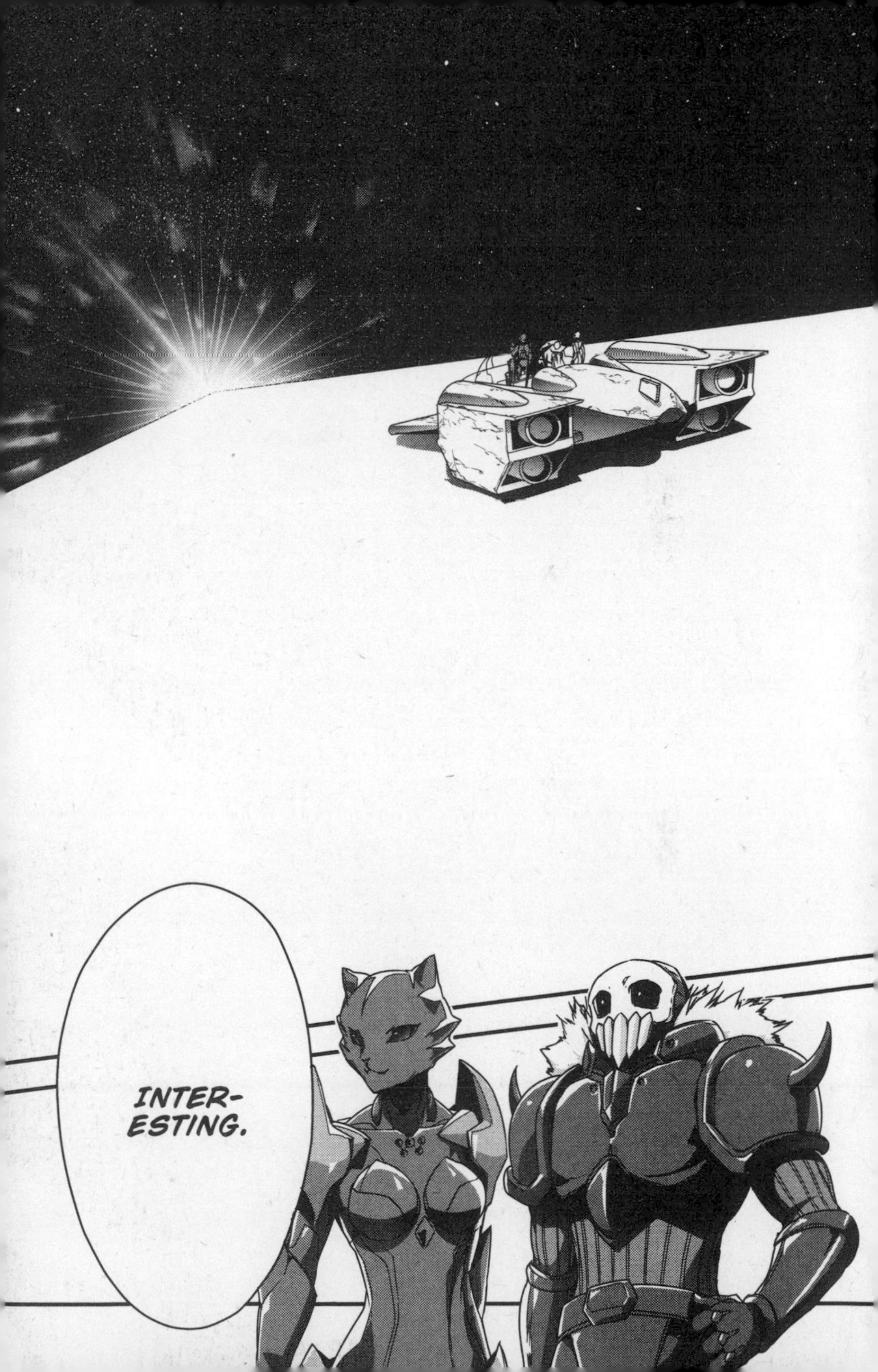
INTER-
ESTING.

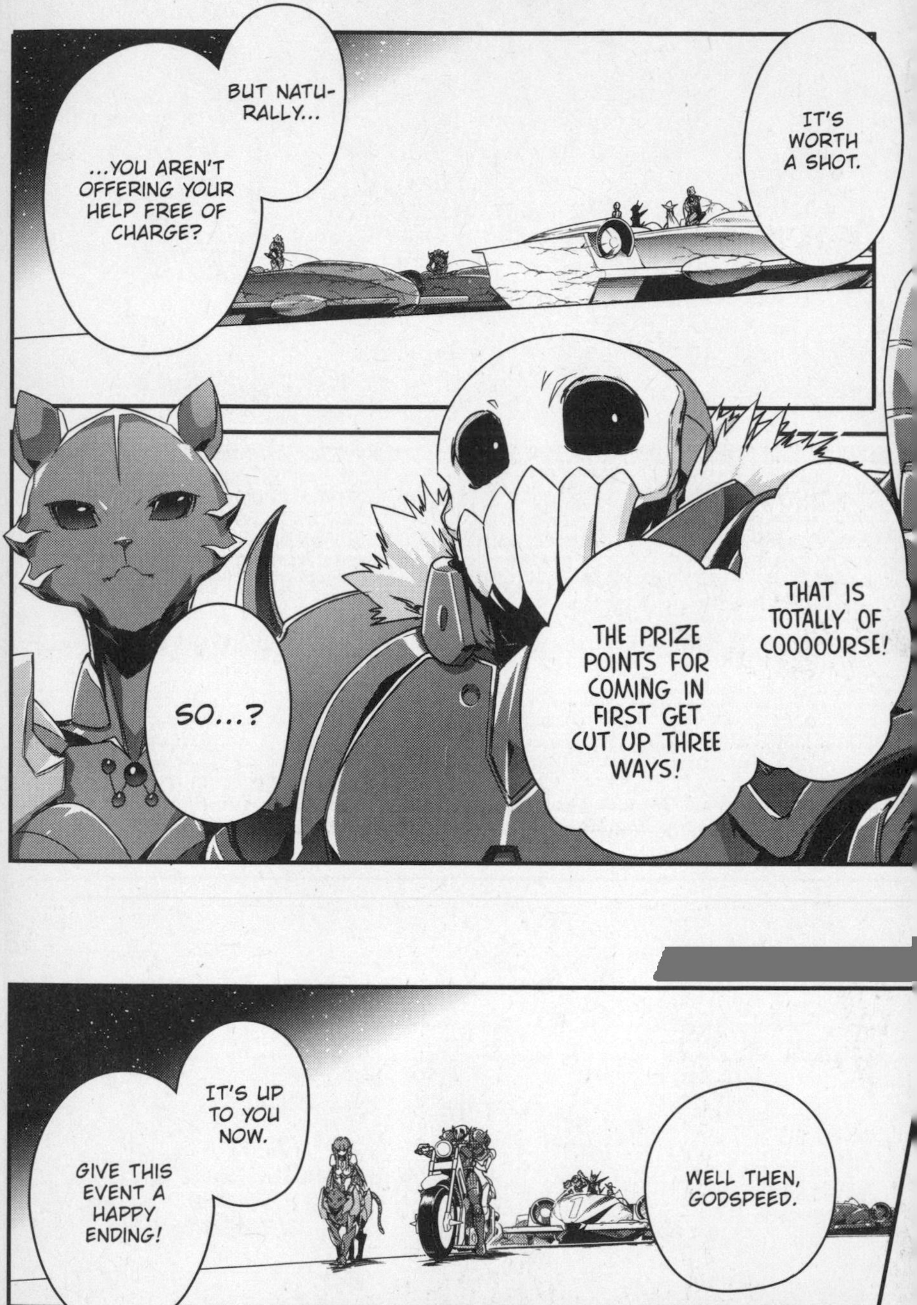
IT'S WORTH A SHOT.
BUT NATU-RALLY...
...YOU AREN'T OFFERING YOUR HELP FREE OF CHARGE?
THAT IS TOTALLY OF COOOOURSE!
THE PRIZE POINTS FOR COMING IN FIRST GET CUT UP THREE WAYS!
SO...?
WELL THEN, GODSPEED.
IT'S UP TO YOU NOW.
GIVE THIS EVENT A HAPPY ENDING!

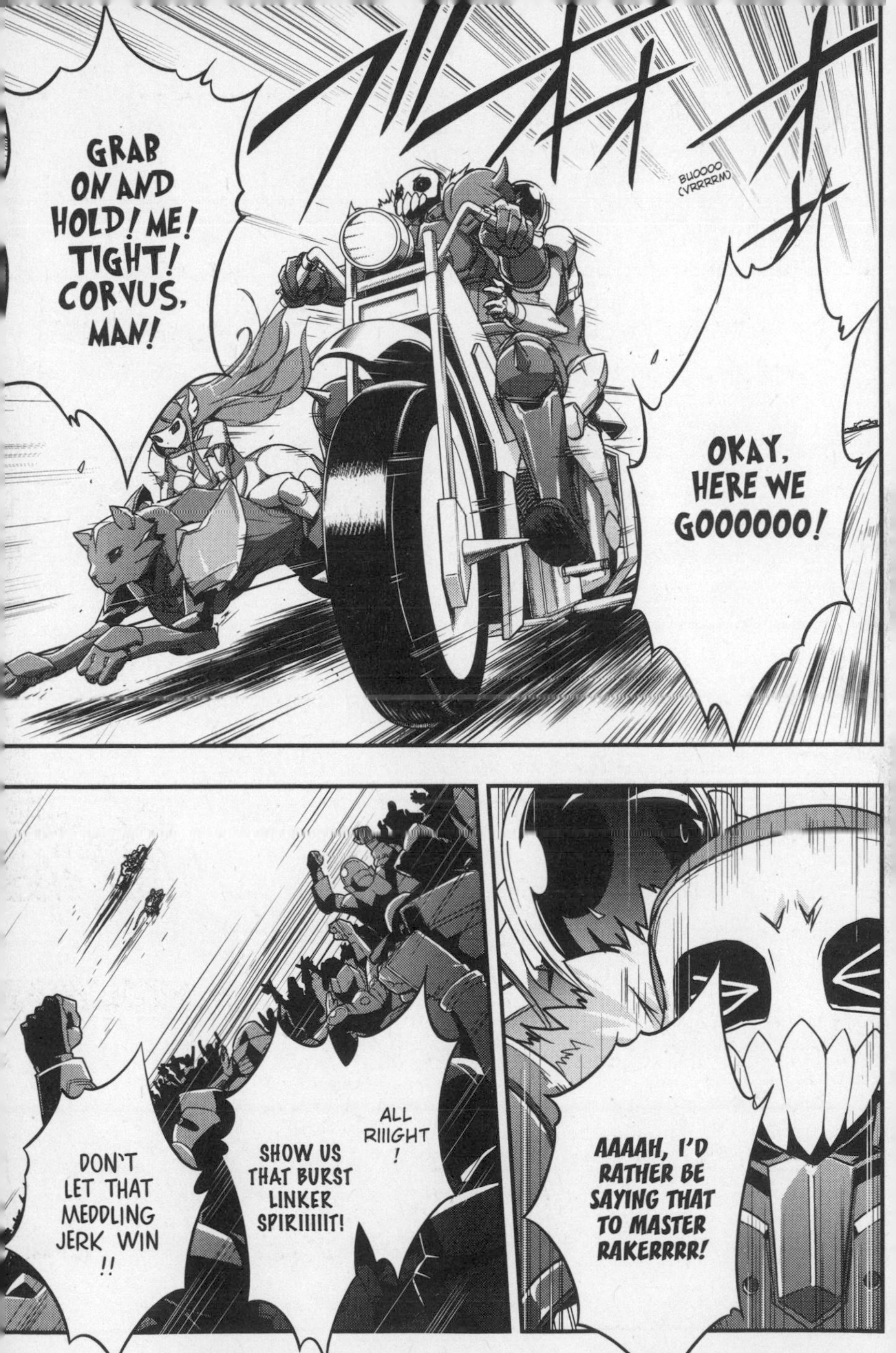
BUOOOO (VRRRRM)
GRAB ON AND HOLD! ME! TIGHT! CORVUS, MAN!
OKAY, HERE WE GOOOOOO!
AAAAH, I'D RATHER BE SAYING THAT TO MASTER RAKERRRR!
ALL RIIIGHT!
SHOW US THAT BURST LINKER SPIRIIIIIT!
DON'T LET THAT MEDDLING JERK WIN!!

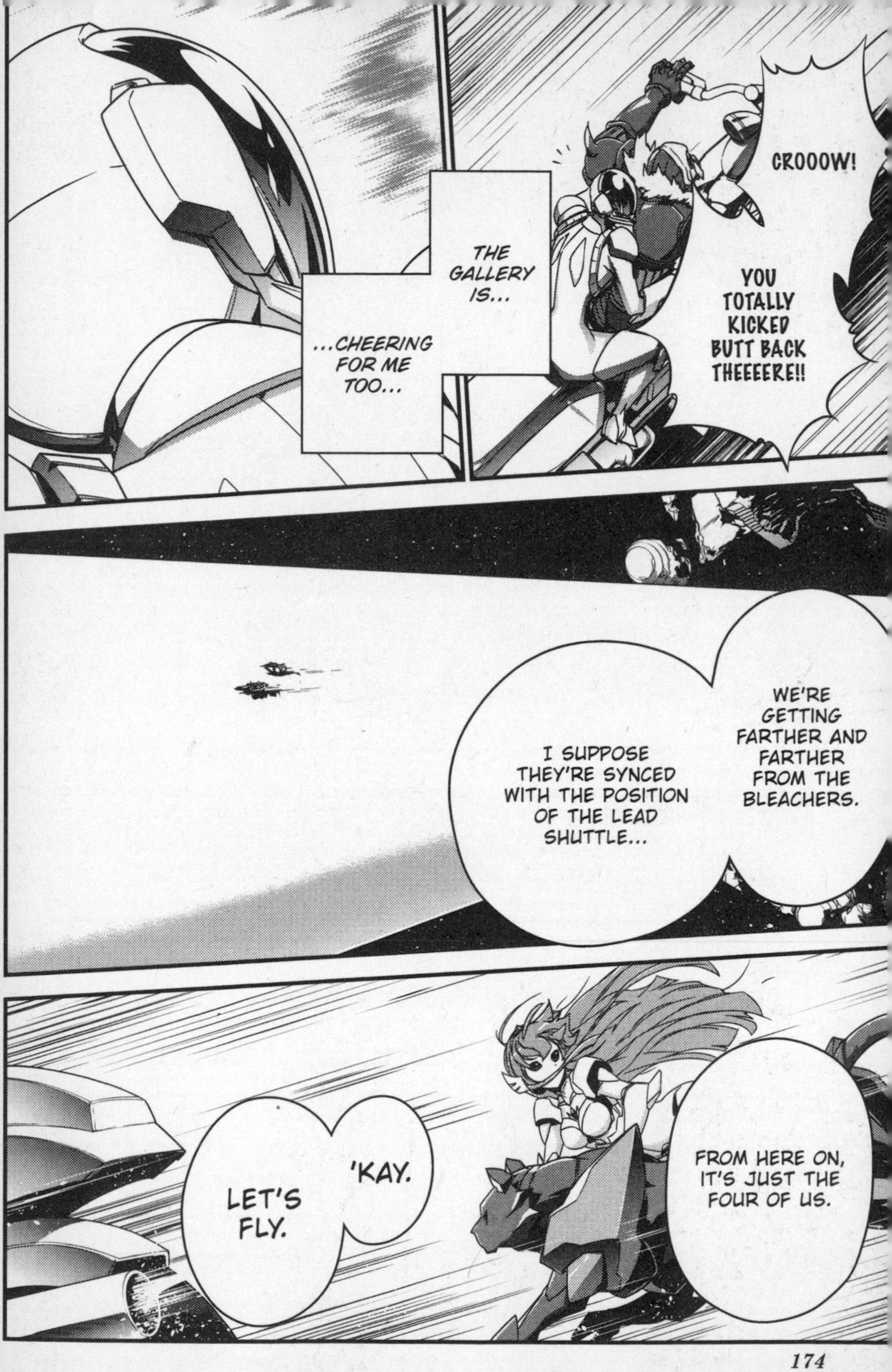
CROOOW!
YOU TOTALLY KICKED BUTT BACK THEEEERE!!
THE GALLERY IS...
...CHEERING FOR ME TOO...
WE'RE GETTING FARTHER AND FARTHER FROM THE BLEACHERS.
I SUPPOSE THEY'RE SYNCED WITH THE POSITION OF THE LEAD SHUTTLE...
FROM HERE ON, IT'S JUST THE FOUR OF US.
'KAY.
LET'S FLY.

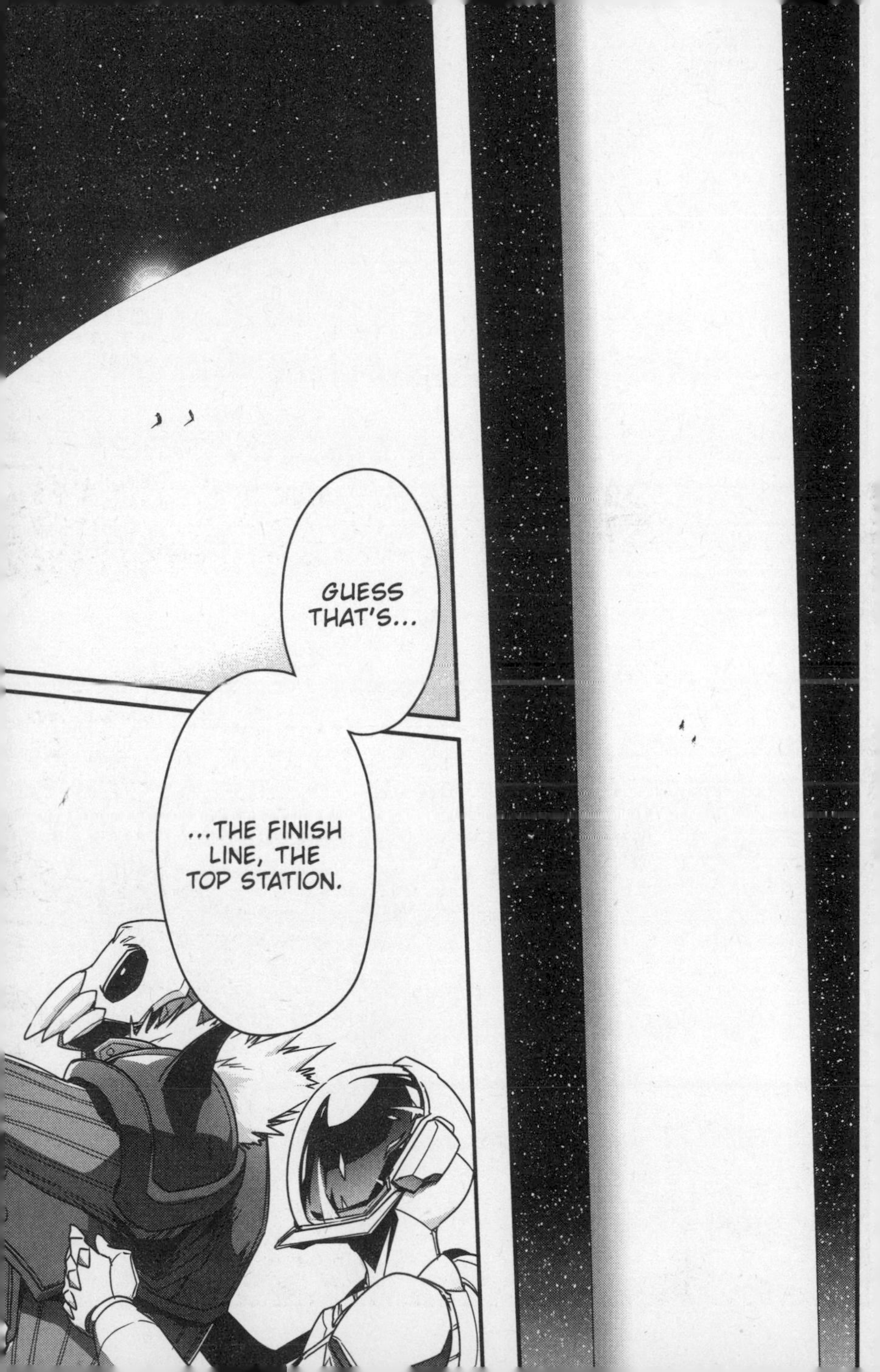
GUESS THAT'S...
...THE FINISH LINE, THE TOP STATION.

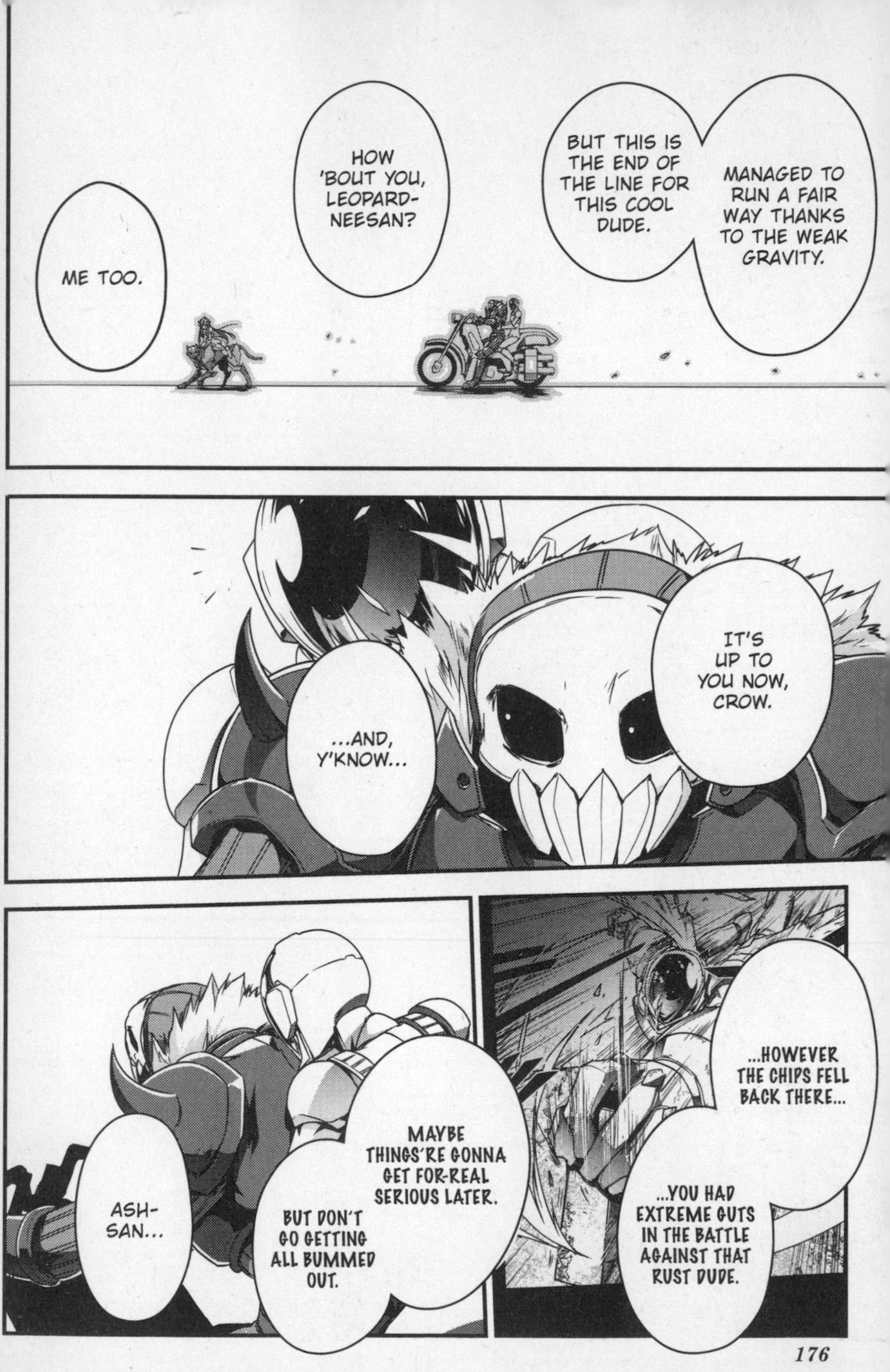
MANAGED TO RUN A FAIR WAY THANKS TO THE WEAK GRAVITY.
BUT THIS IS THE END OF THE LINE FOR THIS COOL DUDE.
HOW 'BOUT YOU, LEOPARD-NEESAN?
ME TOO.
IT'S UP TO YOU NOW, CROW.
...AND, Y'KNOW...
...HOWEVER THE CHIPS FELL BACK THERE...
...YOU HAD EXTREME GUTS IN THE BATTLE AGAINST THAT RUST DUDE.
MAYBE THINGS'RE GONNA GET FOR-REAL SERIOUS LATER.
BUT DON'T GO GETTING ALL BUMMED OUT.
ASH-SAN...

RAKER.

THANK YOU...!!

WELCOME BACK...

ONE THING.

AND YOU BETTER NOT FORGET OUR SHARE!!

YUP.

...ICBM.

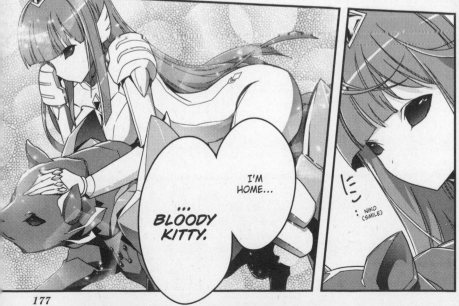

I'M HOME...

...BLOODY KITTY.

NIKO (SMILE)

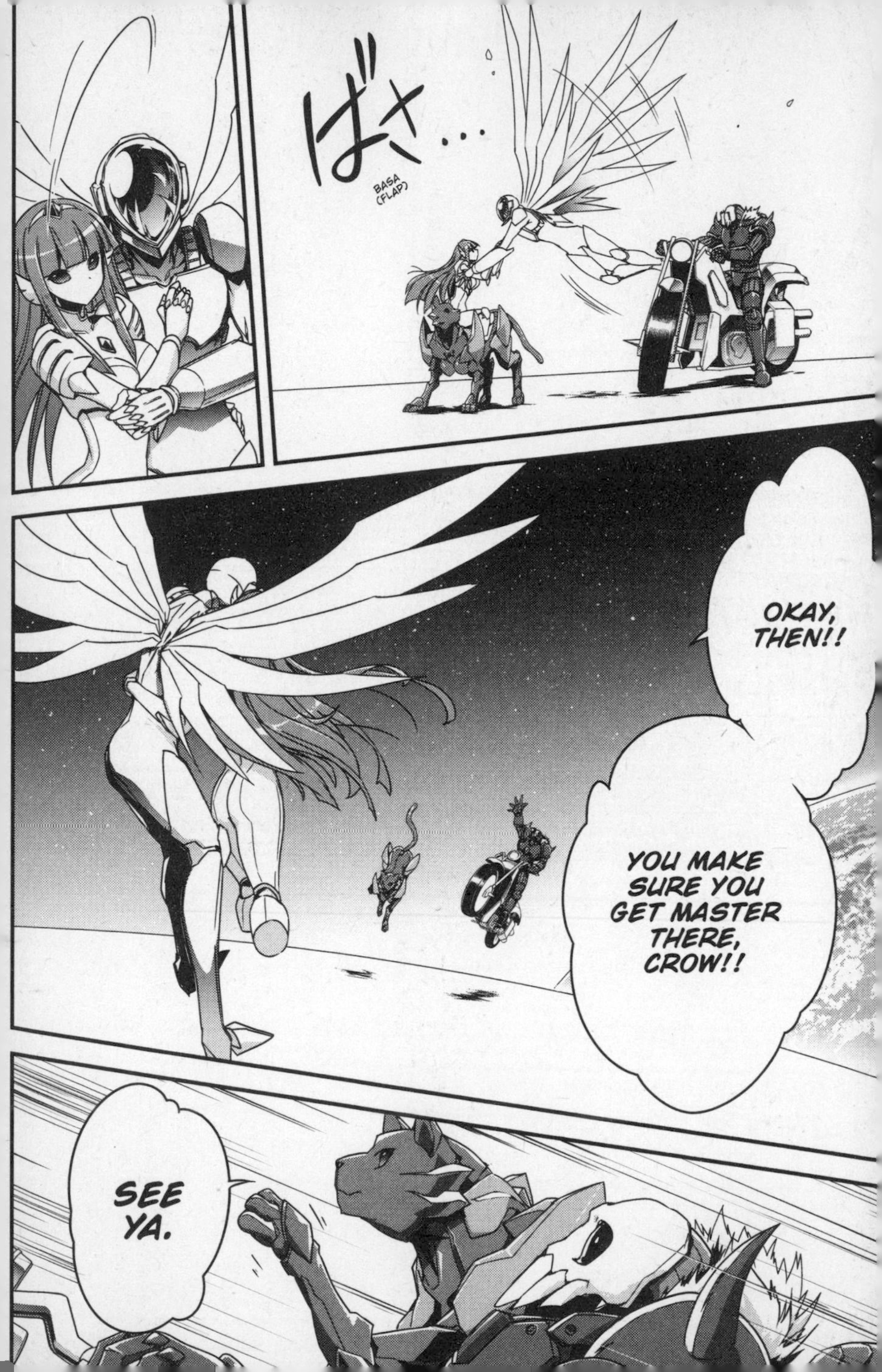
ばさ…
BASA (FLAP)
OKAY, THEN!!
YOU MAKE SURE YOU GET MASTER THERE, CROW!!
SEE YA.

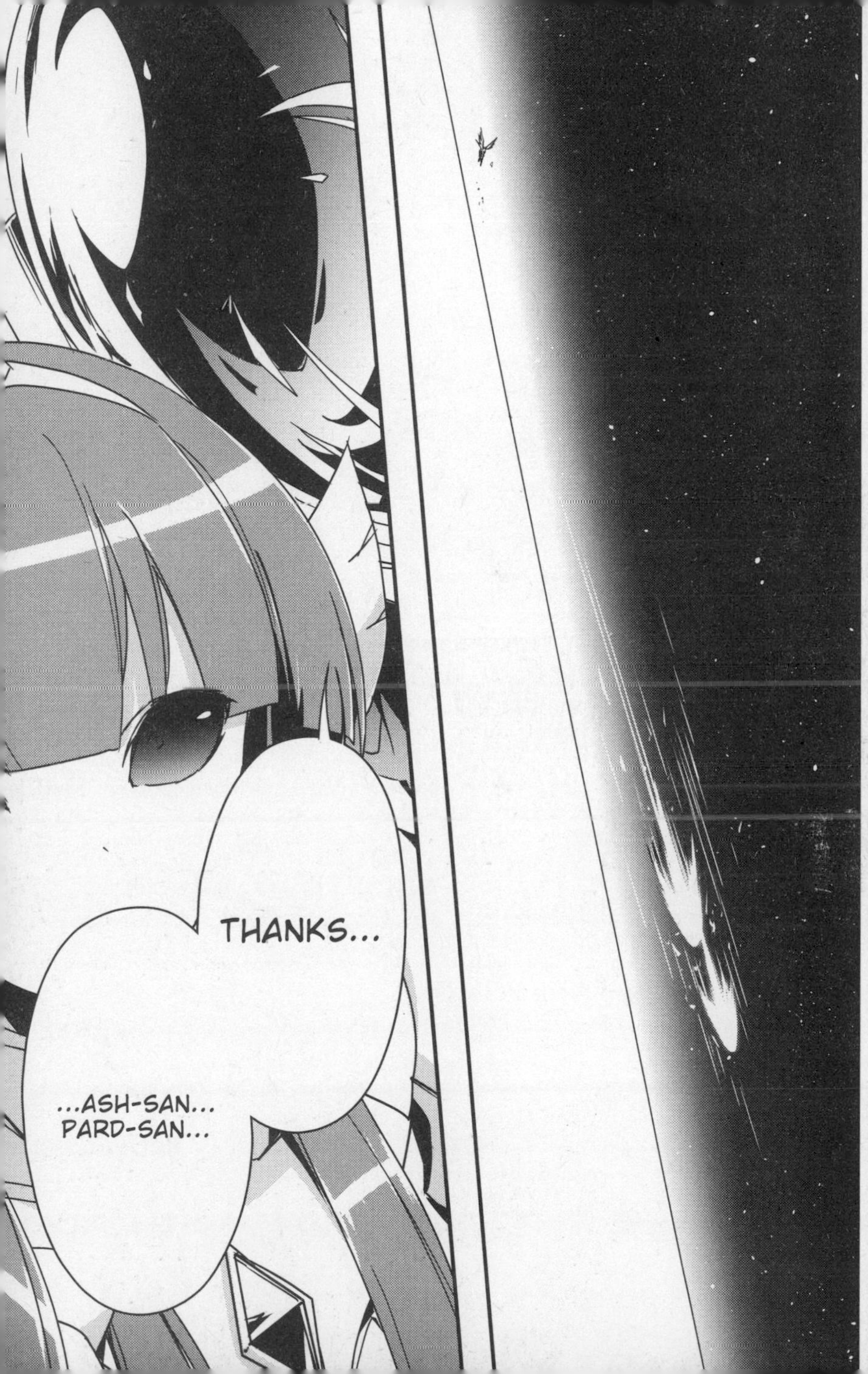
THANKS...
...ASH-SAN... PARD-SAN...

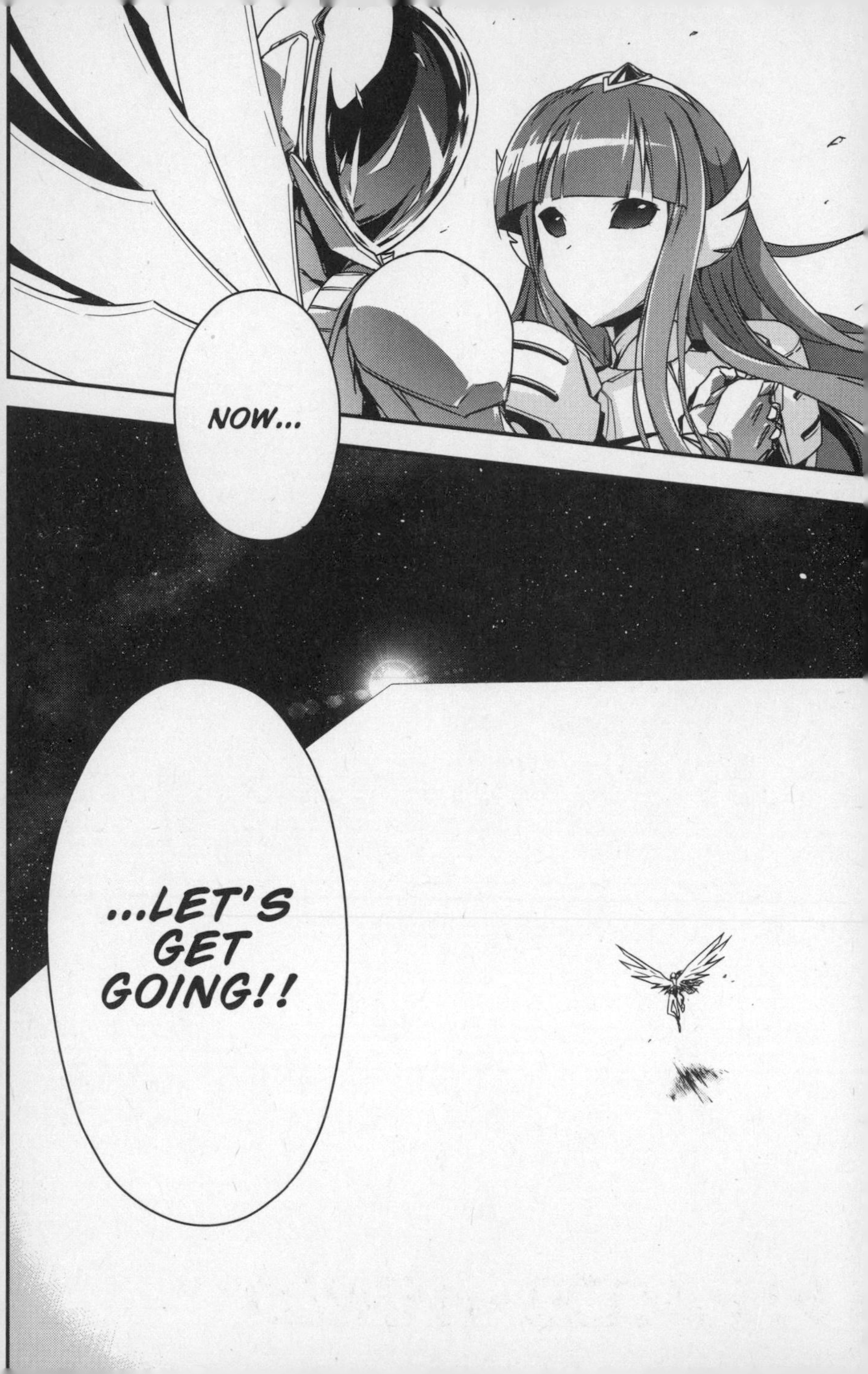
NOW...
...LET'S GET GOING!!

►►► ACCEL·WORLD

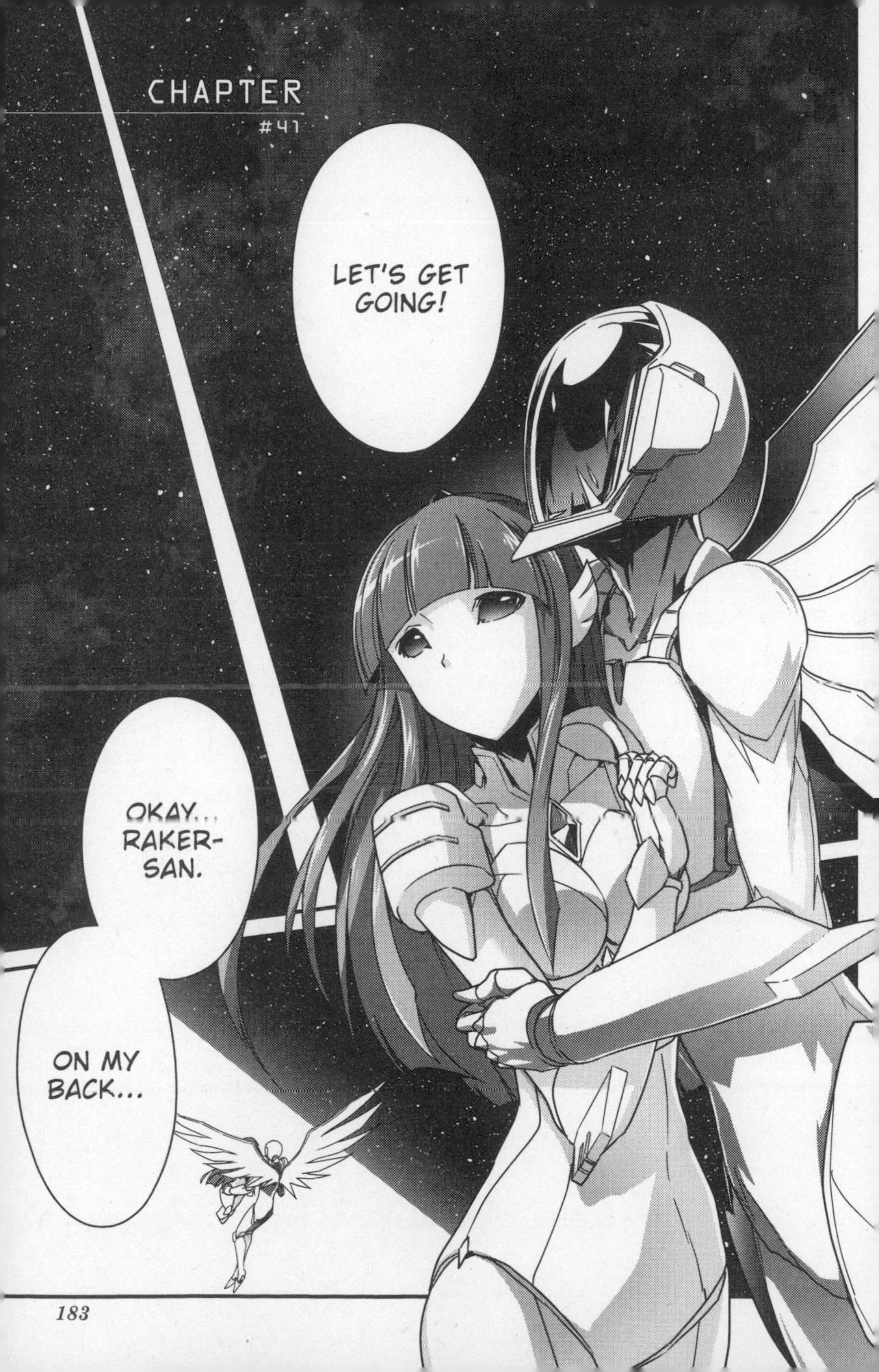
CHAPTER
#41
LET'S GET GOING!
OKAY... RAKER-SAN.
ON MY BACK...

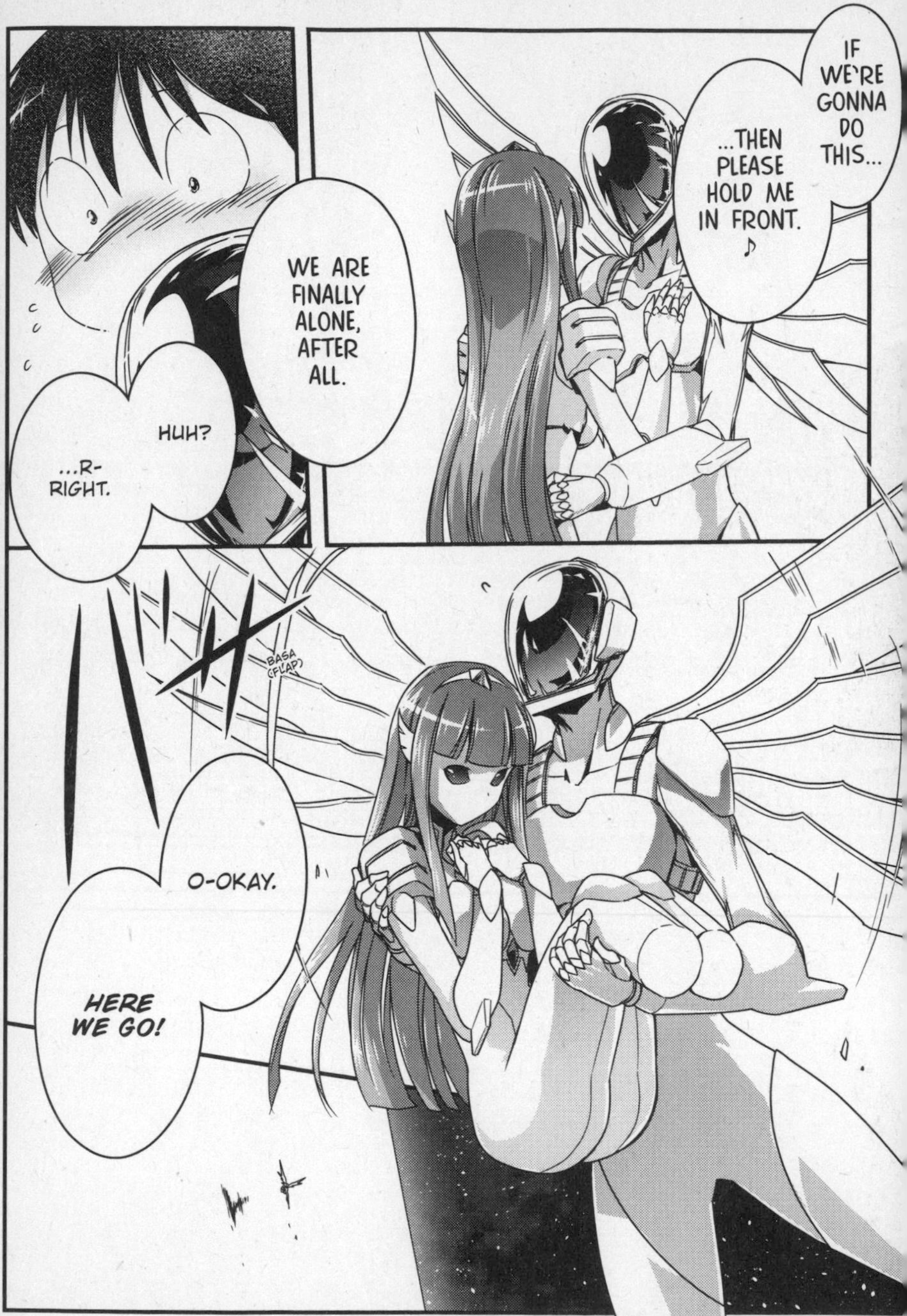
IF WE'RE GONNA DO THIS...
...THEN PLEASE HOLD ME IN FRONT. ♪
WE ARE FINALLY ALONE, AFTER ALL.
HUH? ...R-RIGHT.
BASA (FLAP)
O-OKAY. HERE WE GO!

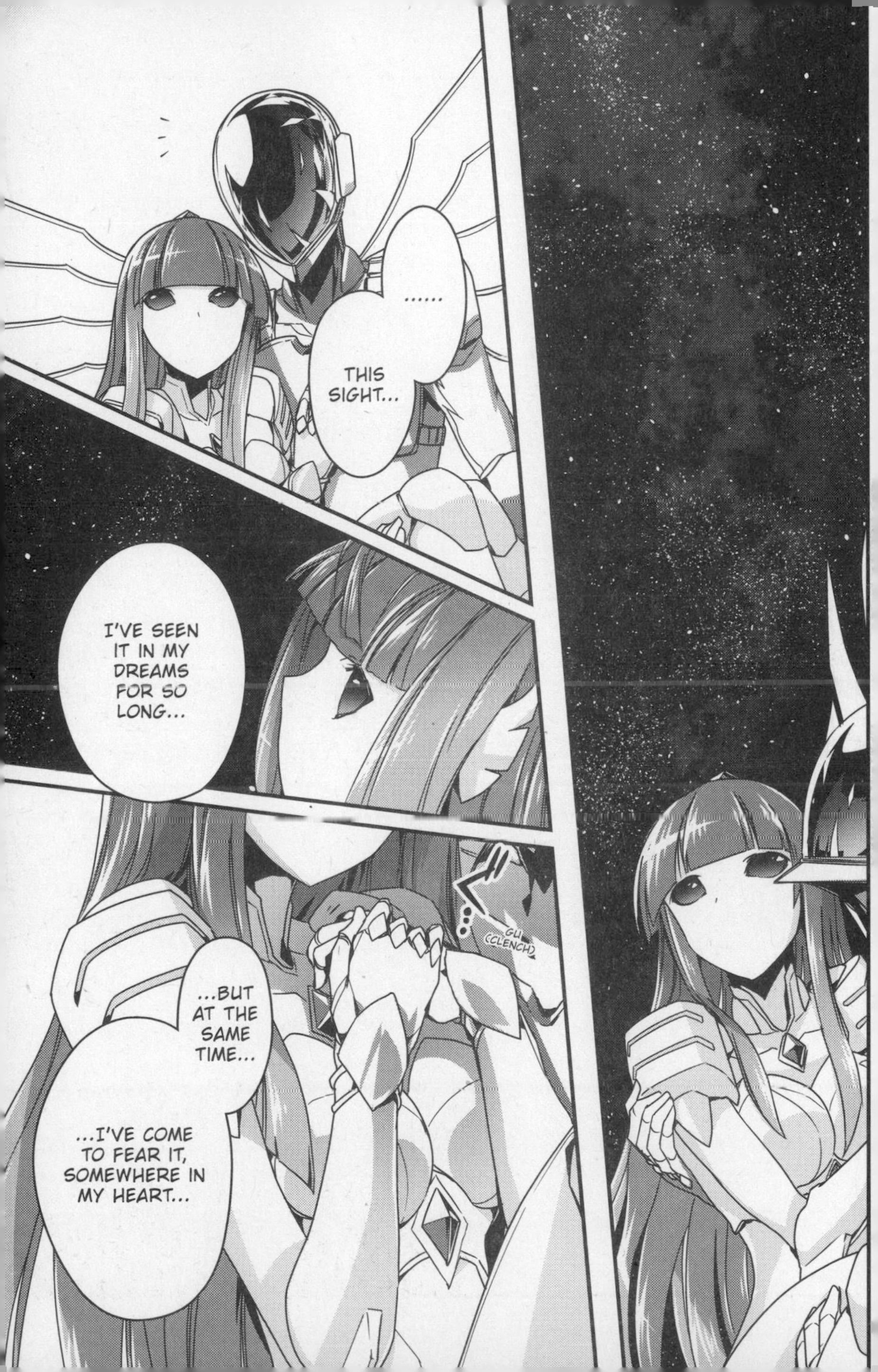

......
THIS SIGHT...
I'VE SEEN IT IN MY DREAMS FOR SO LONG...
GU (CLENCH)
...BUT AT THE SAME TIME...
...I'VE COME TO FEAR IT, SOMEWHERE IN MY HEART...

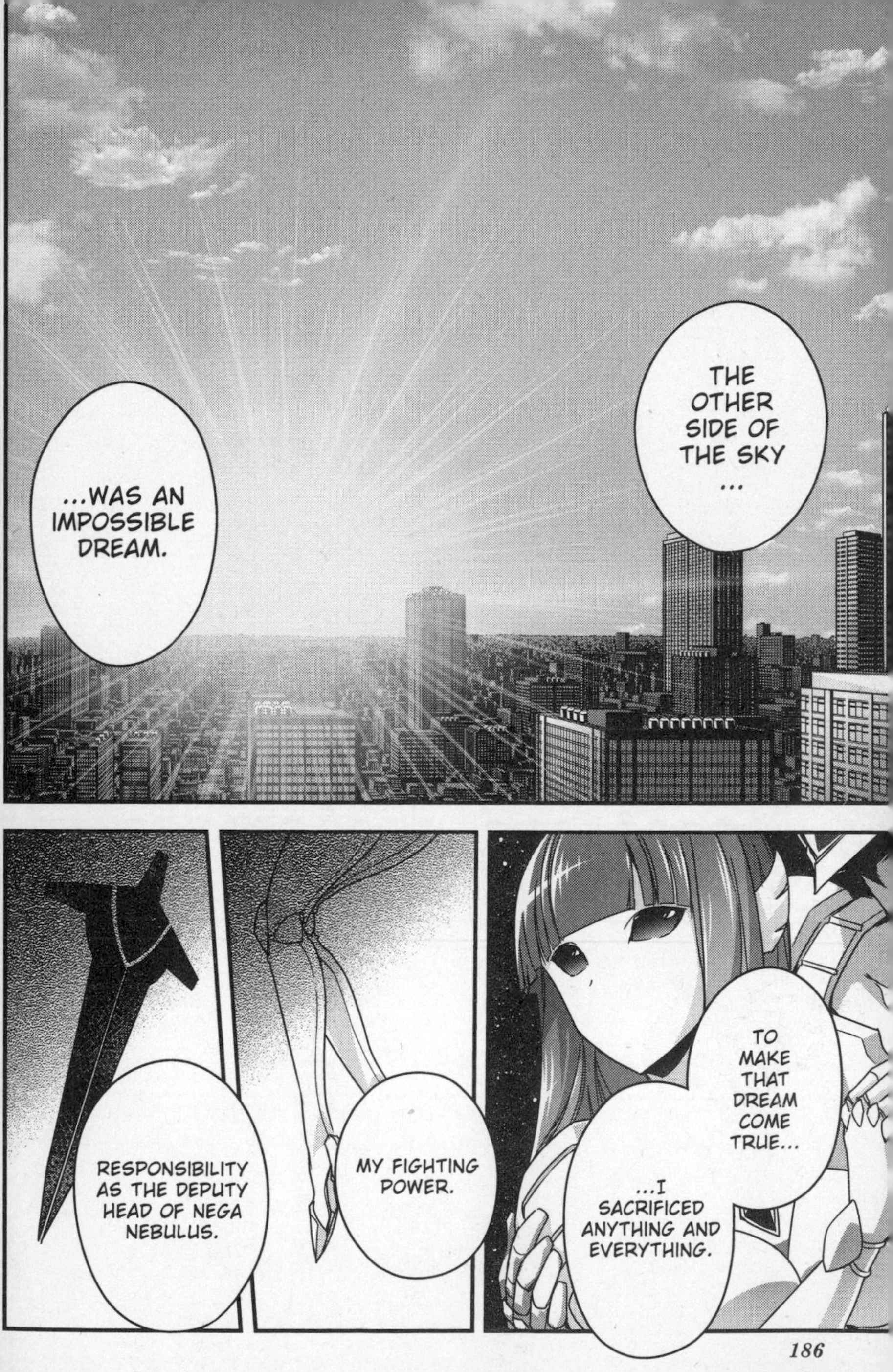
THE OTHER SIDE OF THE SKY...
...WAS AN IMPOSSIBLE DREAM.
TO MAKE THAT DREAM COME TRUE...
...I SACRIFICED ANYTHING AND EVERYTHING.
MY FIGHTING POWER.
RESPONSIBILITY AS THE DEPUTY HEAD OF NEGA NEBULUS.

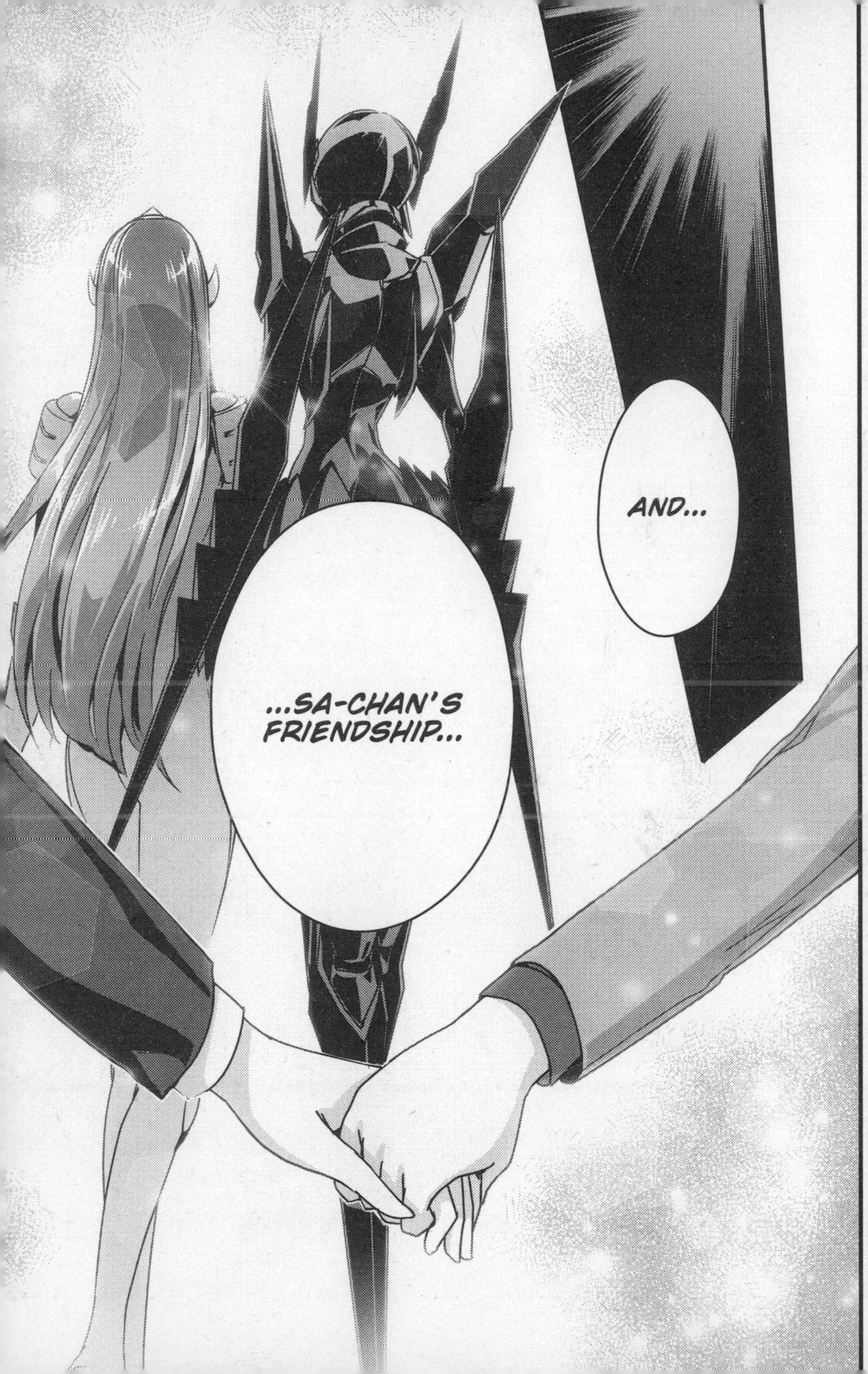
AND...
...SA-CHAN'S FRIENDSHIP...

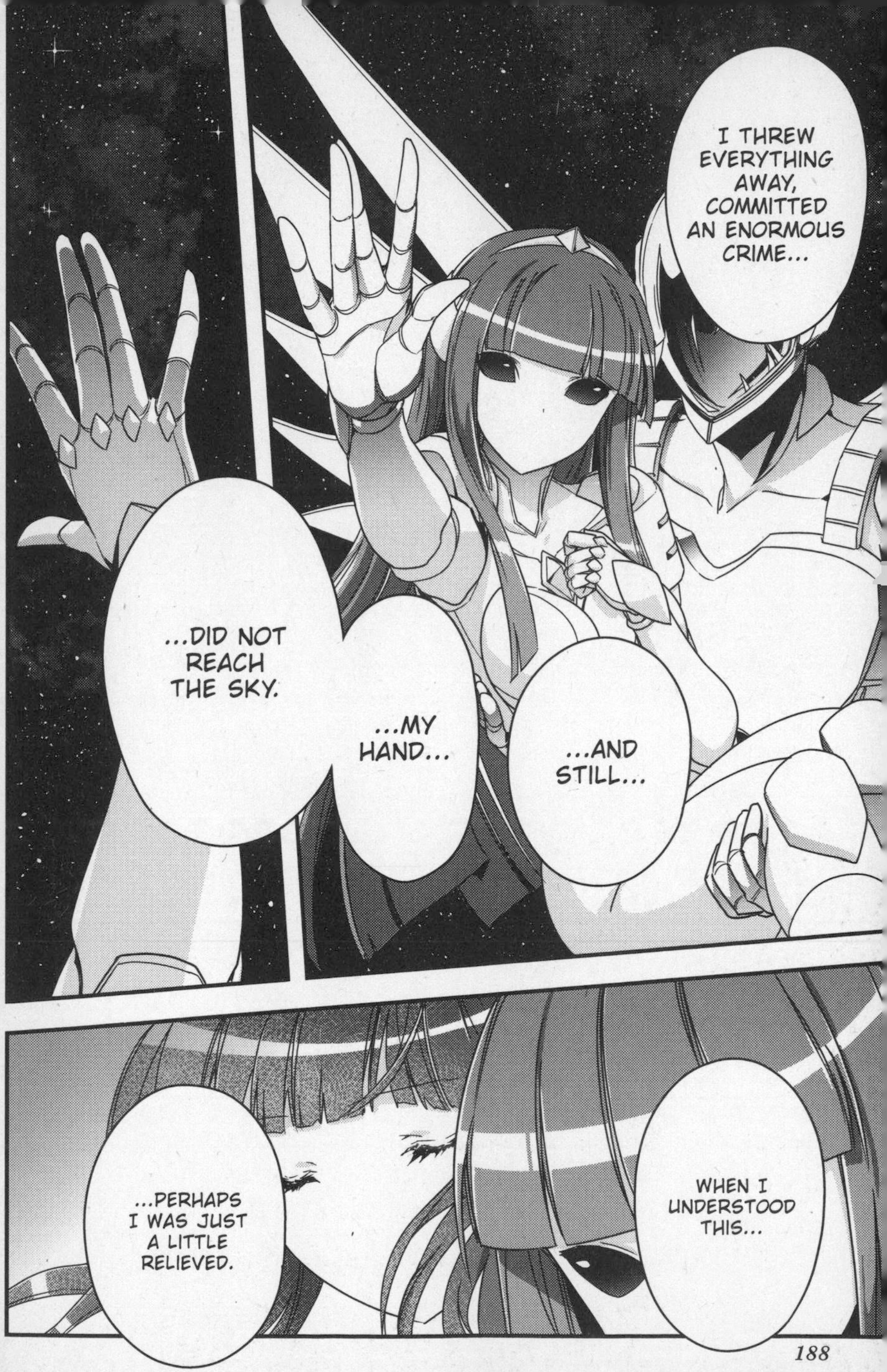
I THREW EVERYTHING AWAY, COMMITTED AN ENORMOUS CRIME...
...AND STILL...
...MY HAND...
...DID NOT REACH THE SKY.
WHEN I UNDERSTOOD THIS...
...PERHAPS I WAS JUST A LITTLE RELIEVED.

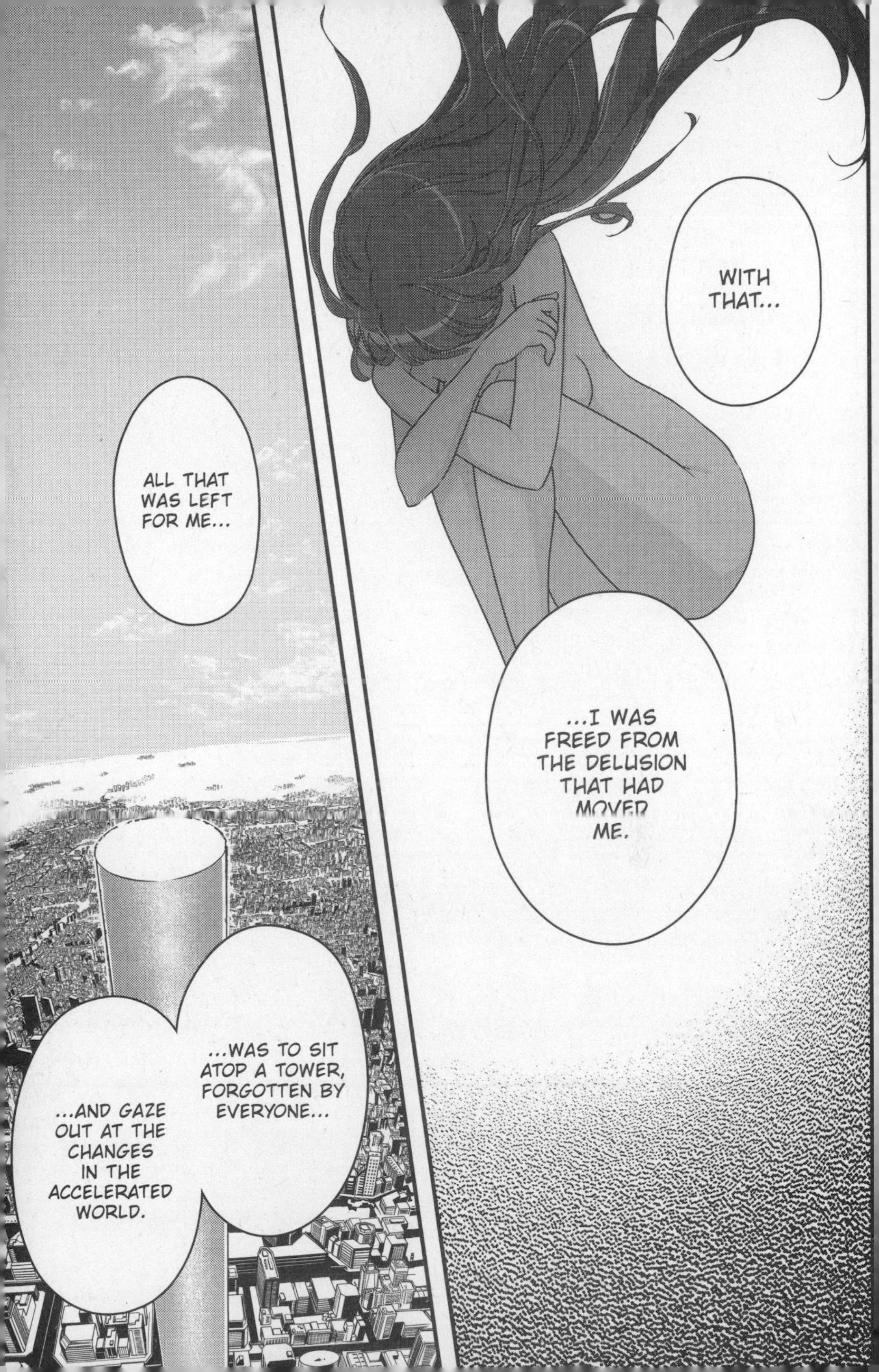
WITH THAT...
...I WAS FREED FROM THE DELUSION THAT HAD MOVED ME.
ALL THAT WAS LEFT FOR ME...
...WAS TO SIT ATOP A TOWER, FORGOTTEN BY EVERYONE...
...AND GAZE OUT AT THE CHANGES IN THE ACCELERATED WORLD.

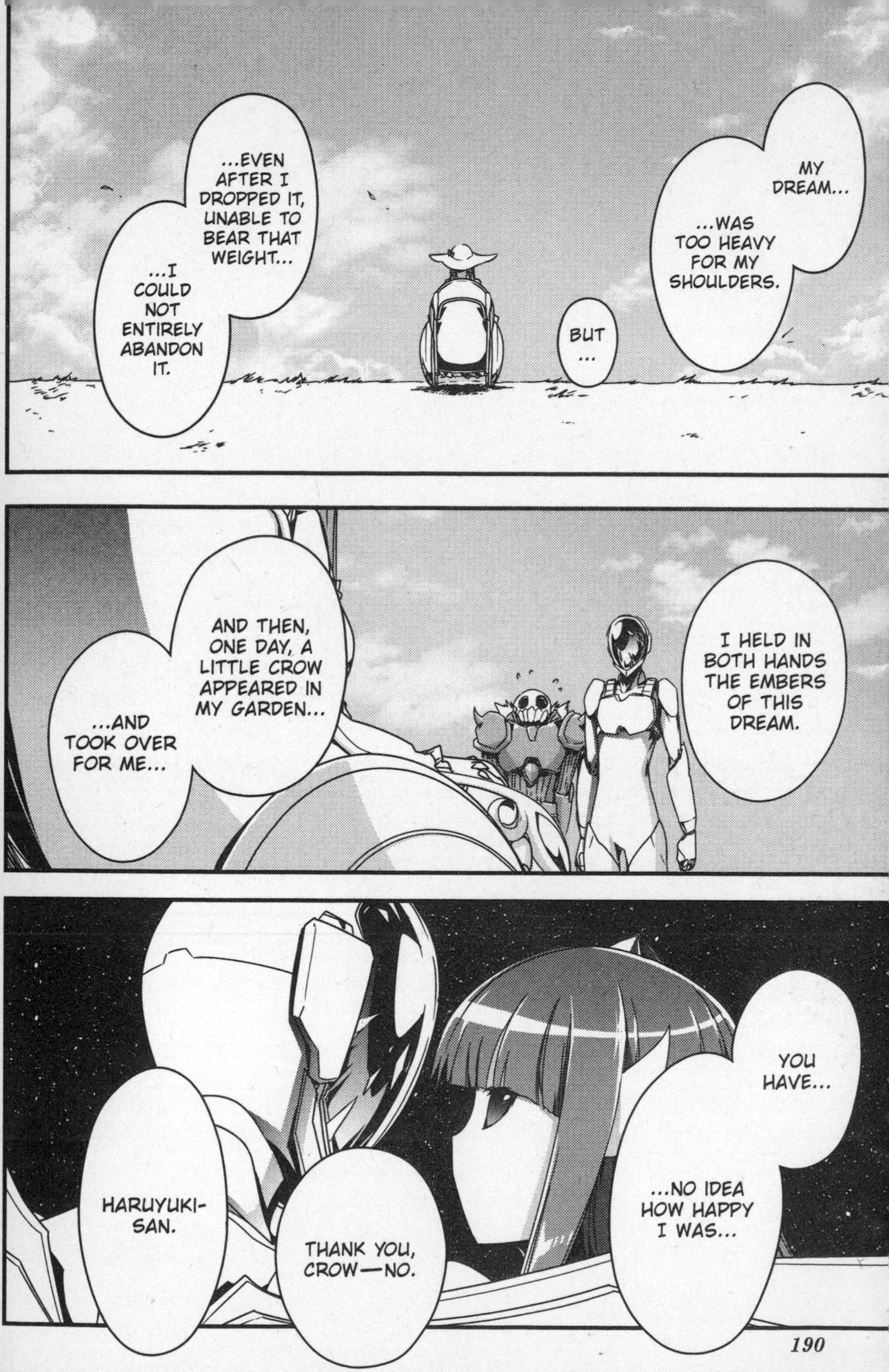
MY DREAM...
...WAS TOO HEAVY FOR MY SHOULDERS.
BUT ...
...EVEN AFTER I DROPPED IT, UNABLE TO BEAR THAT WEIGHT...
...I COULD NOT ENTIRELY ABANDON IT.
I HELD IN BOTH HANDS THE EMBERS OF THIS DREAM.
AND THEN, ONE DAY, A LITTLE CROW APPEARED IN MY GARDEN...
...AND TOOK OVER FOR ME...
YOU HAVE...
...NO IDEA HOW HAPPY I WAS...
THANK YOU, CROW—NO.
HARUYUKI-SAN.

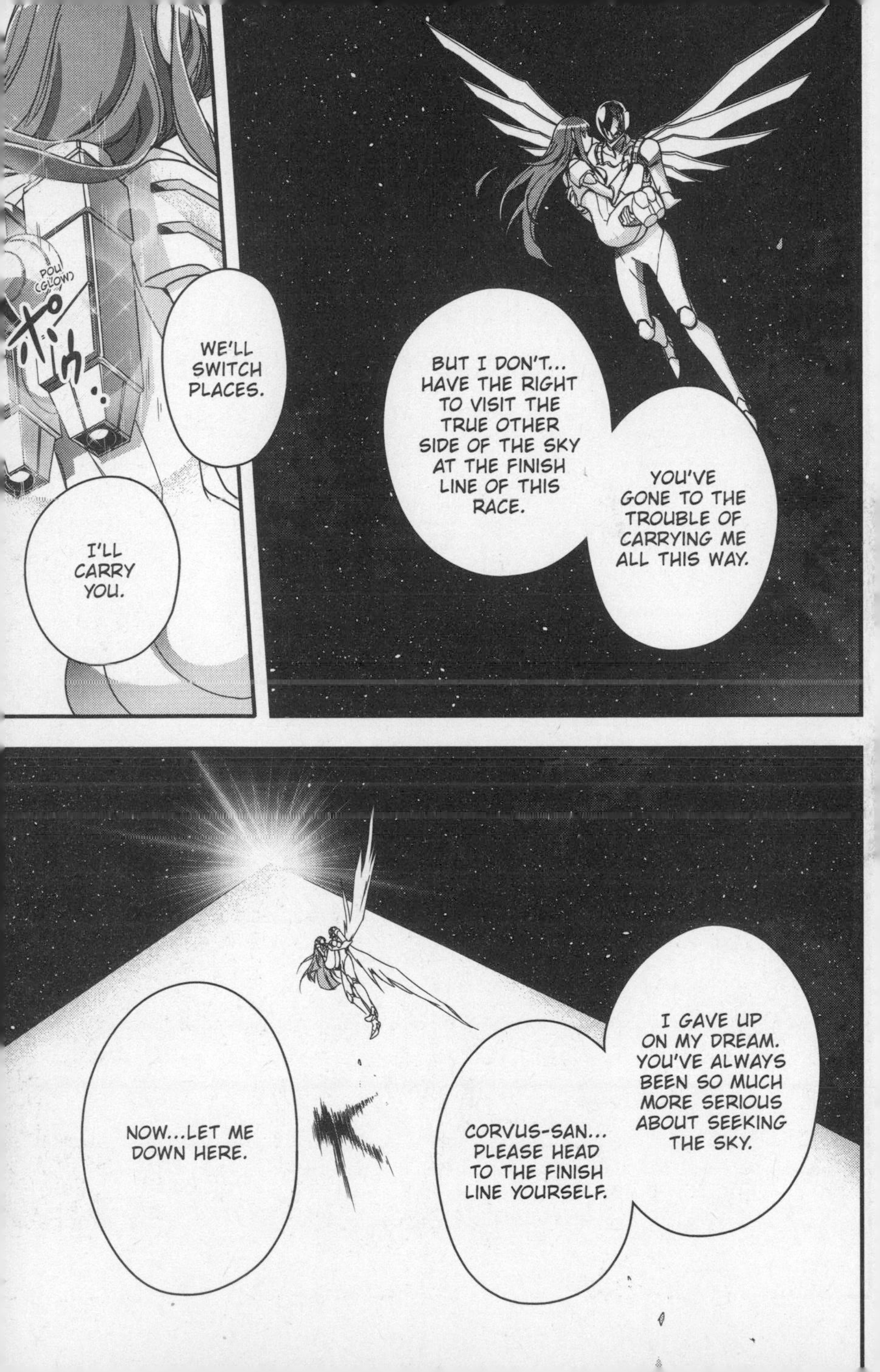
YOU'VE GONE TO THE TROUBLE OF CARRYING ME ALL THIS WAY.
BUT I DON'T... HAVE THE RIGHT TO VISIT THE TRUE OTHER SIDE OF THE SKY AT THE FINISH LINE OF THIS RACE.
WE'LL SWITCH PLACES.
POU (GLOW)
I'LL CARRY YOU.
I GAVE UP ON MY DREAM. YOU'VE ALWAYS BEEN SO MUCH MORE SERIOUS ABOUT SEEKING THE SKY.
CORVUS-SAN... PLEASE HEAD TO THE FINISH LINE YOURSELF.
NOW...LET ME DOWN HERE.

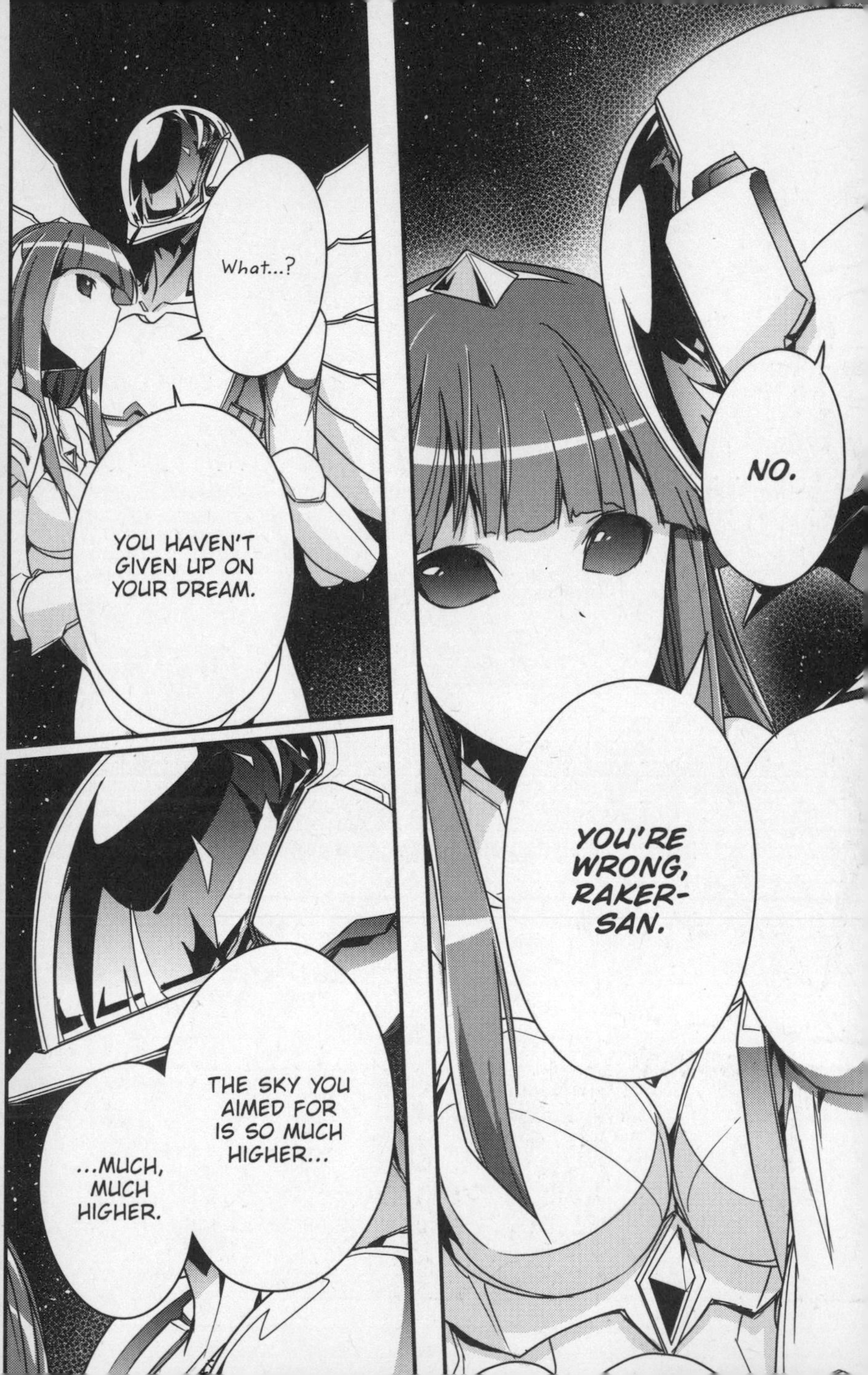
NO.
YOU'RE WRONG, RAKER-SAN.
What...?
YOU HAVEN'T GIVEN UP ON YOUR DREAM.
THE SKY YOU AIMED FOR IS SO MUCH HIGHER...
...MUCH, MUCH HIGHER.

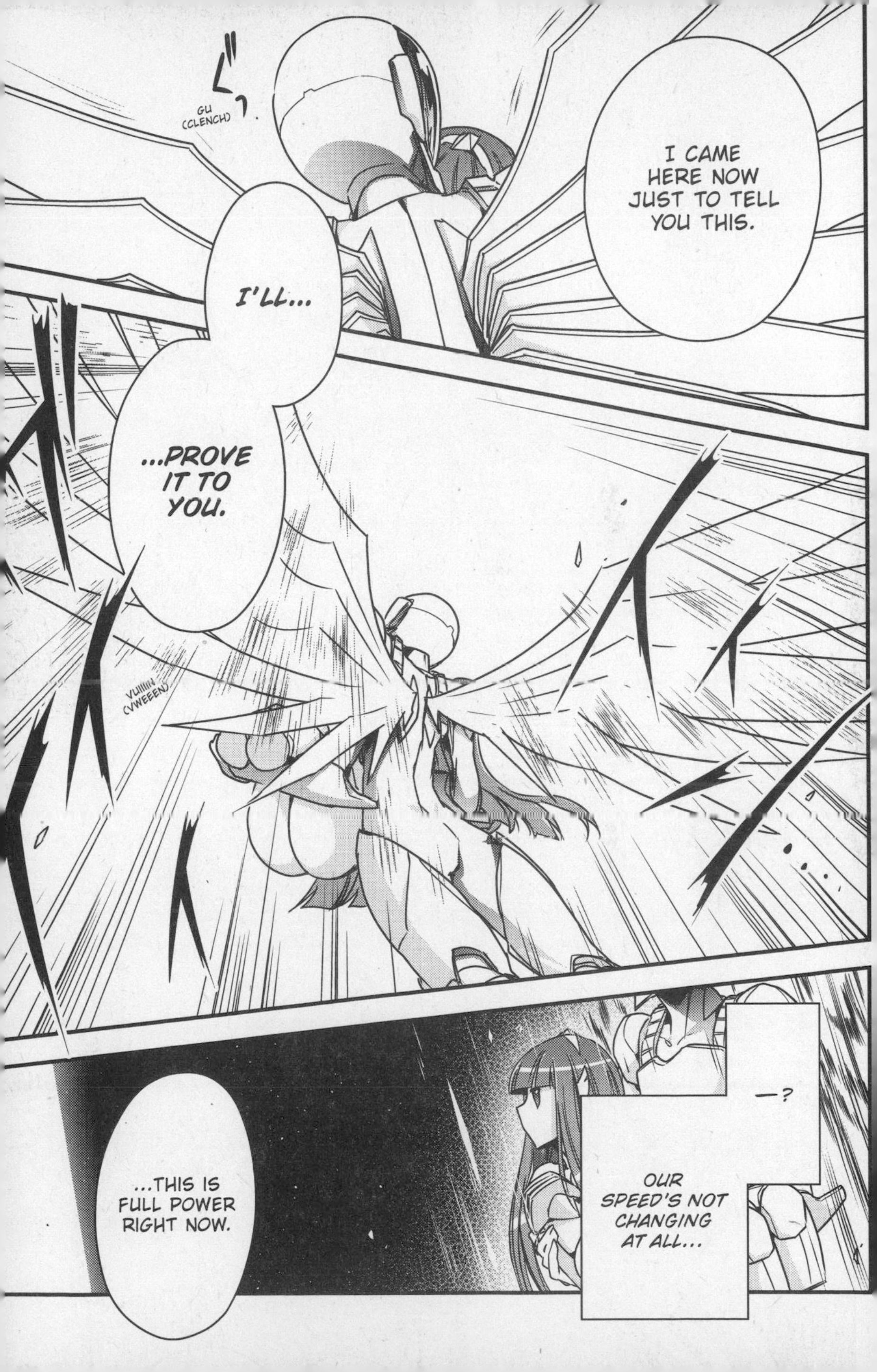
I CAME HERE NOW JUST TO TELL YOU THIS.
GU (CLENCH)
I'LL...
...PROVE IT TO YOU.
VUIIIIN (VWEEEN)
...
—?
OUR SPEED'S NOT CHANGING AT ALL...
...THIS IS FULL POWER RIGHT NOW.

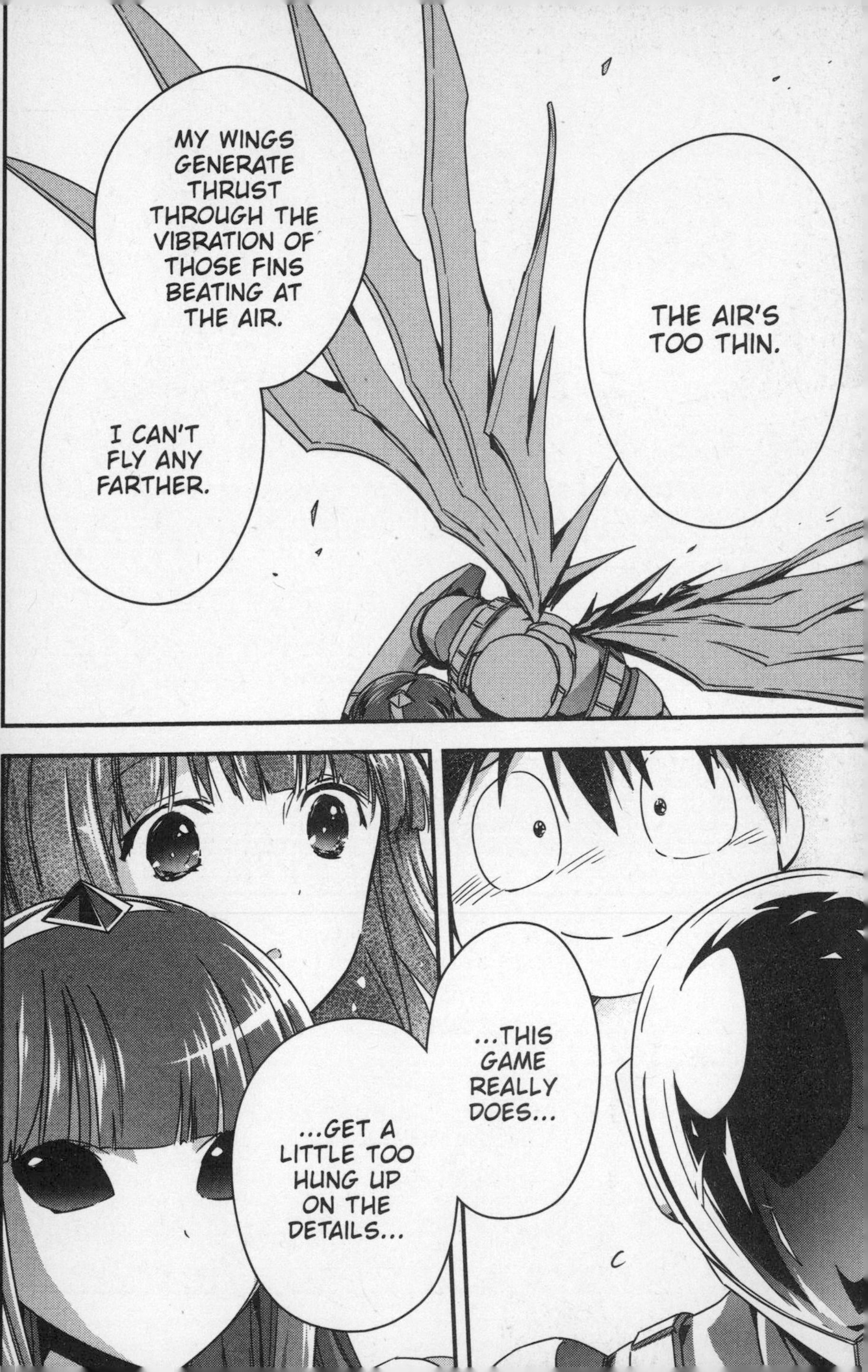
THE AIR'S TOO THIN.
MY WINGS GENERATE THRUST THROUGH THE VIBRATION OF THOSE FINS BEATING AT THE AIR.
I CAN'T FLY ANY FARTHER.
...THIS GAME REALLY DOES...
...GET A LITTLE TOO HUNG UP ON THE DETAILS...

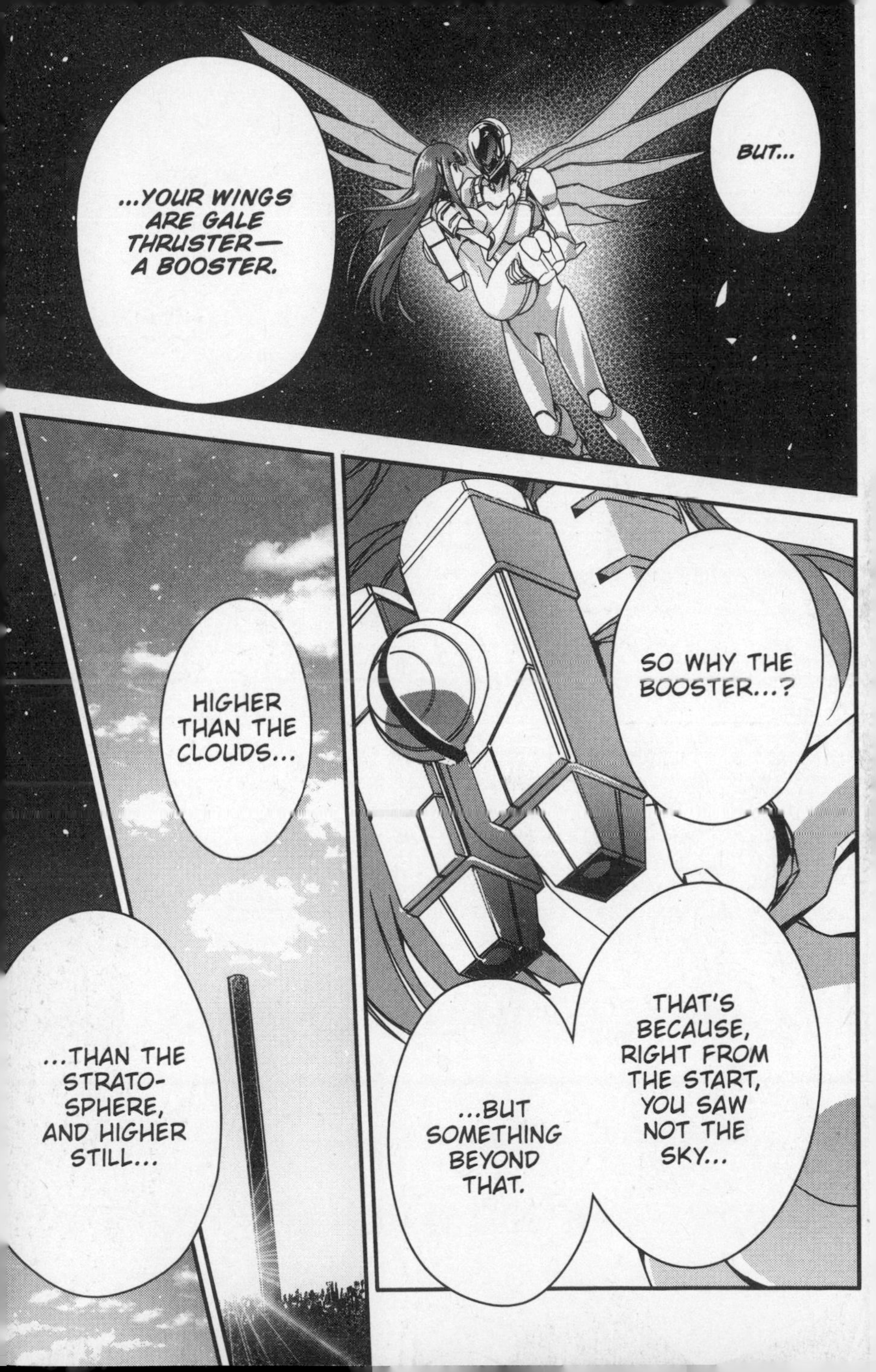
BUT...
...YOUR WINGS ARE GALE THRUSTER— A BOOSTER.
SO WHY THE BOOSTER...?
THAT'S BECAUSE, RIGHT FROM THE START, YOU SAW NOT THE SKY...
...BUT SOMETHING BEYOND THAT.
HIGHER THAN THE CLOUDS...
...THAN THE STRATO-SPHERE, AND HIGHER STILL...

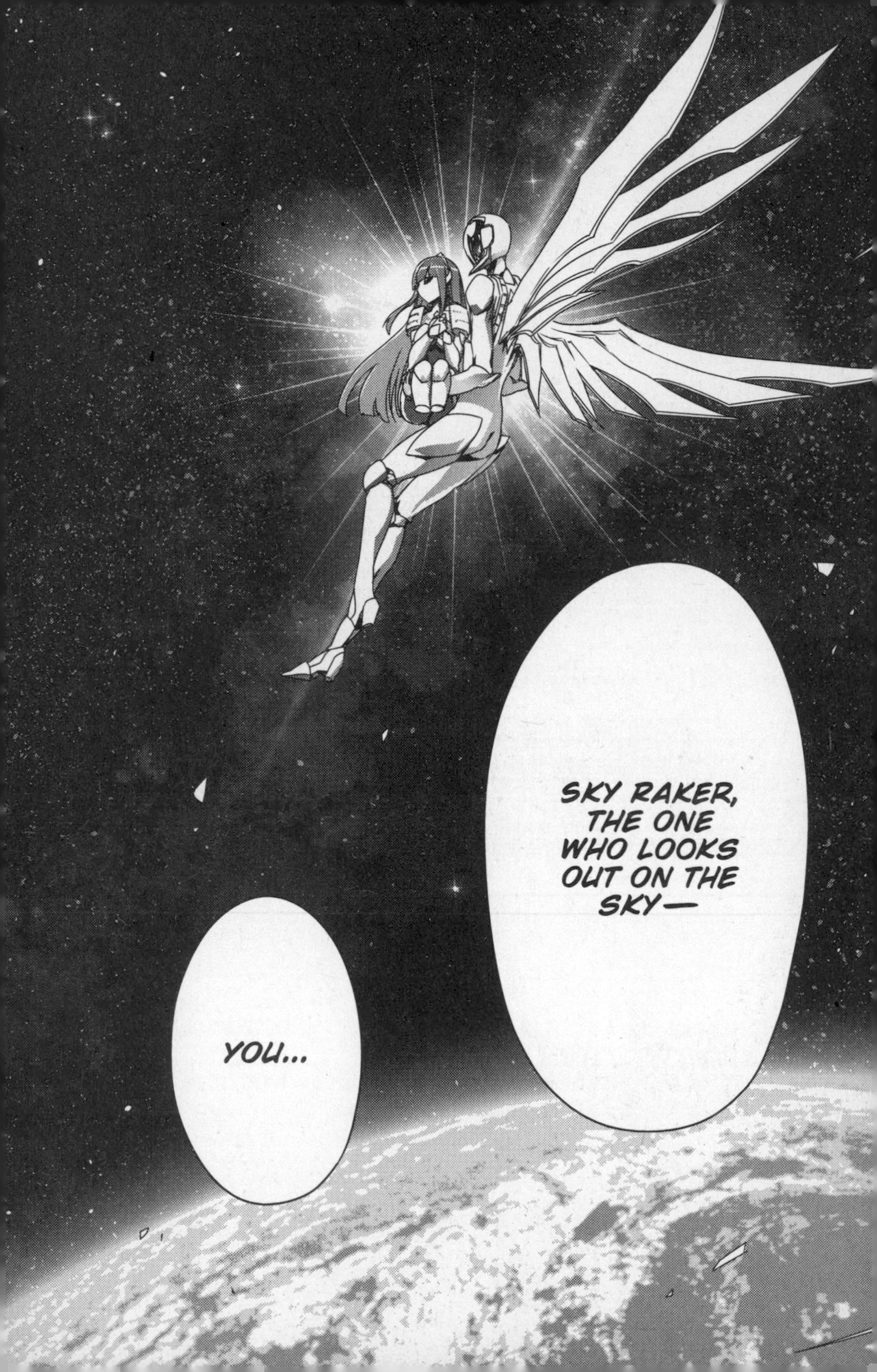
SKY RAKER, THE ONE WHO LOOKS OUT ON THE SKY—
YOU...

YOU'RE A DUEL AVATAR FOR FIGHTING IN SPACE.
...WERE BORN TO FLY IN THIS SKY.

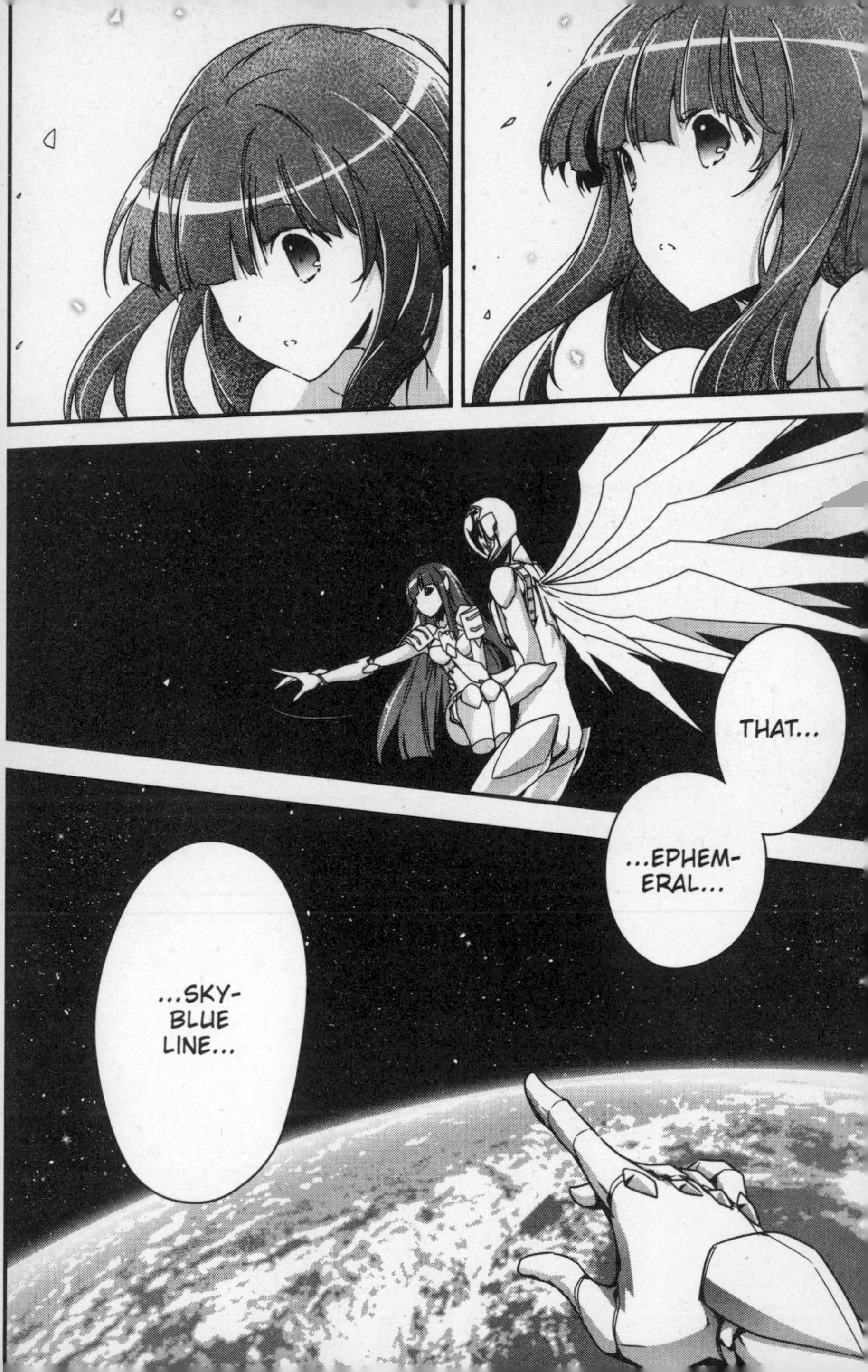
THAT...
...EPHEM-ERAL...
...SKY-BLUE LINE...

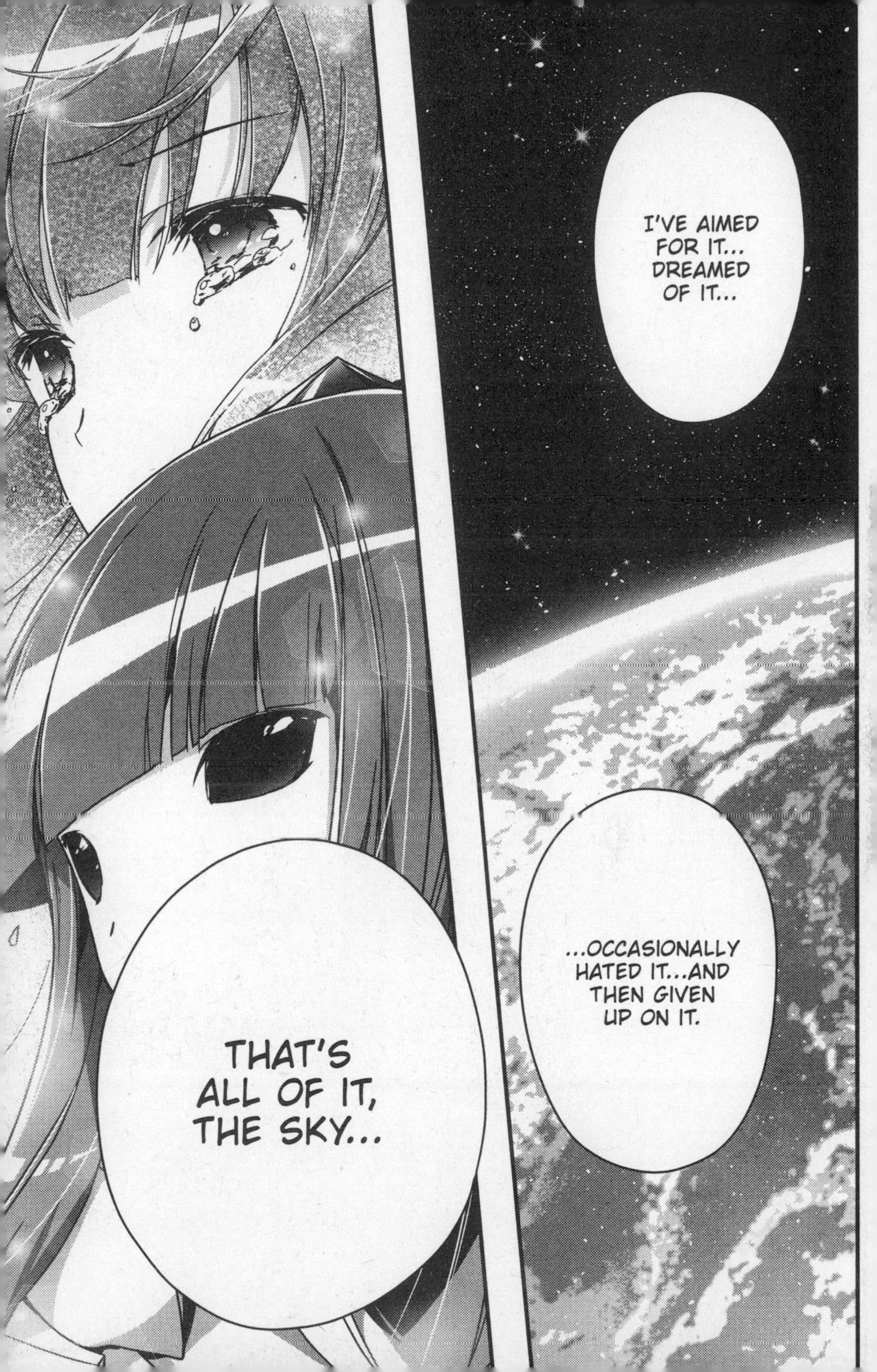
I'VE AIMED FOR IT... DREAMED OF IT...
...OCCASIONALLY HATED IT...AND THEN GIVEN UP ON IT.
THAT'S ALL OF IT, THE SKY...

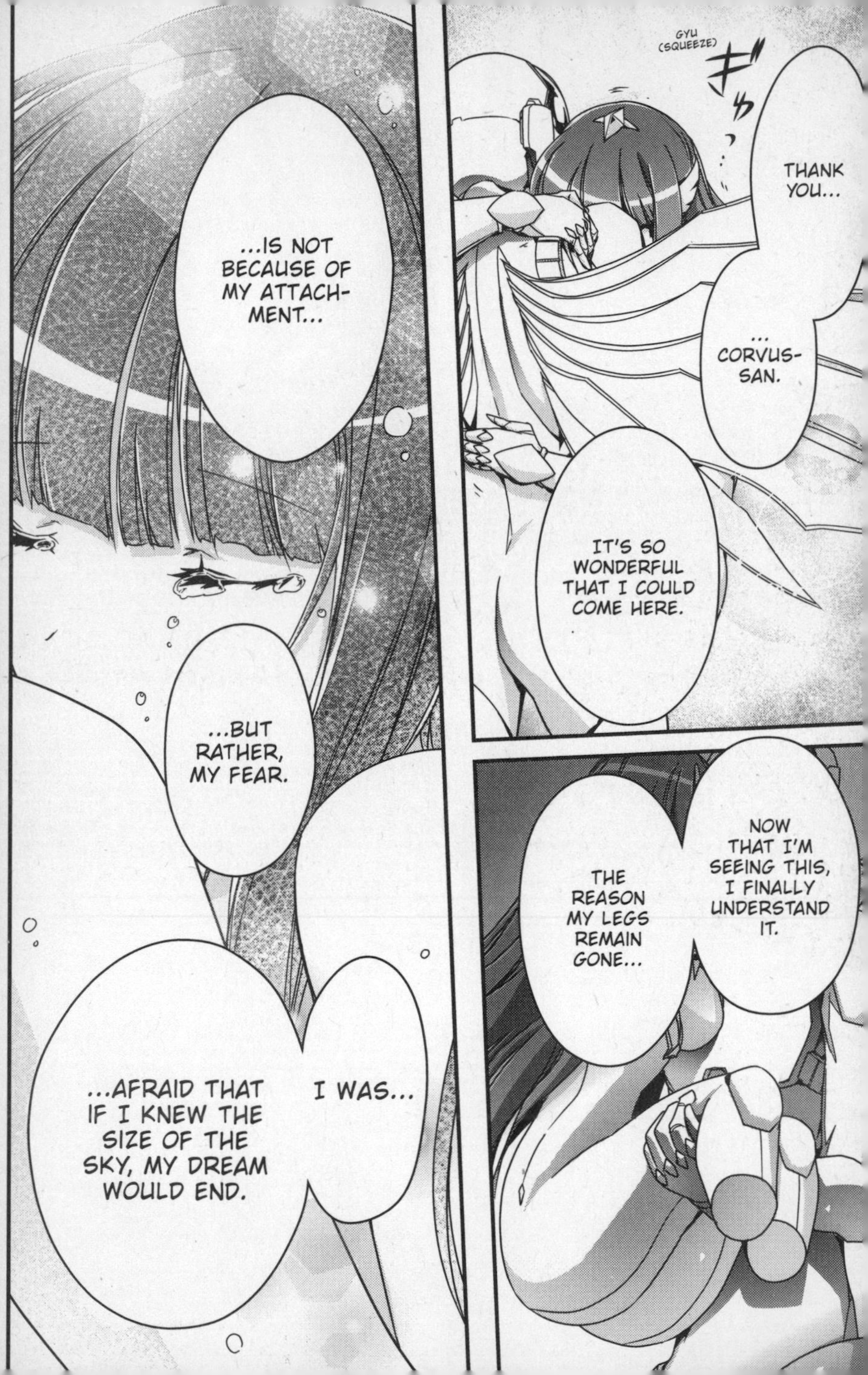
GYU (SQUEEZE)
THANK YOU...
...CORVUS-SAN.
IT'S SO WONDERFUL THAT I COULD COME HERE.
NOW THAT I'M SEEING THIS, I FINALLY UNDERSTAND IT.
THE REASON MY LEGS REMAIN GONE...
...IS NOT BECAUSE OF MY ATTACHMENT...
...BUT RATHER, MY FEAR.
I WAS...
...AFRAID THAT IF I KNEW THE SIZE OF THE SKY, MY DREAM WOULD END.

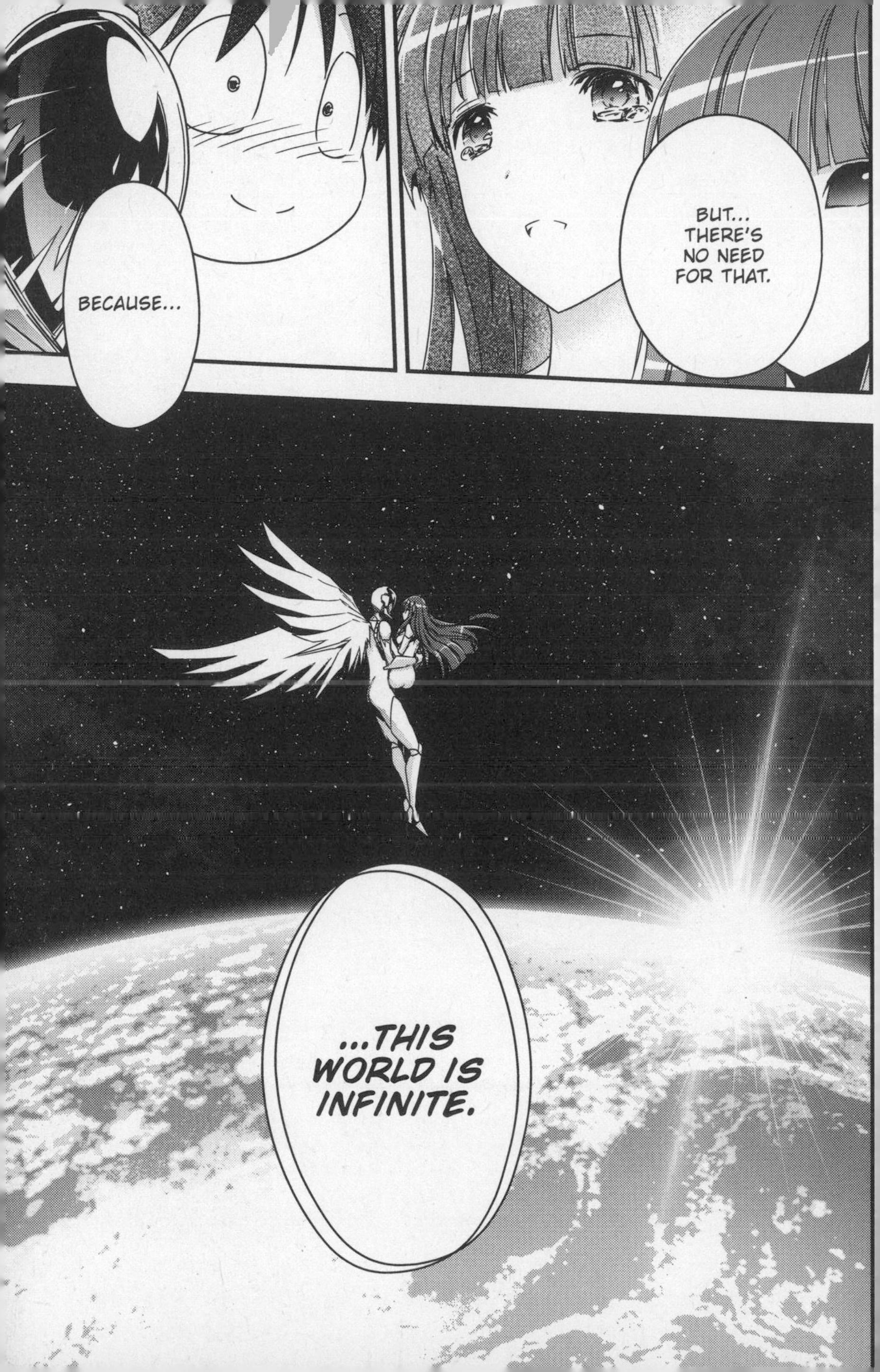
BUT... THERE'S NO NEED FOR THAT.
BECAUSE...
...THIS WORLD IS INFINITE.

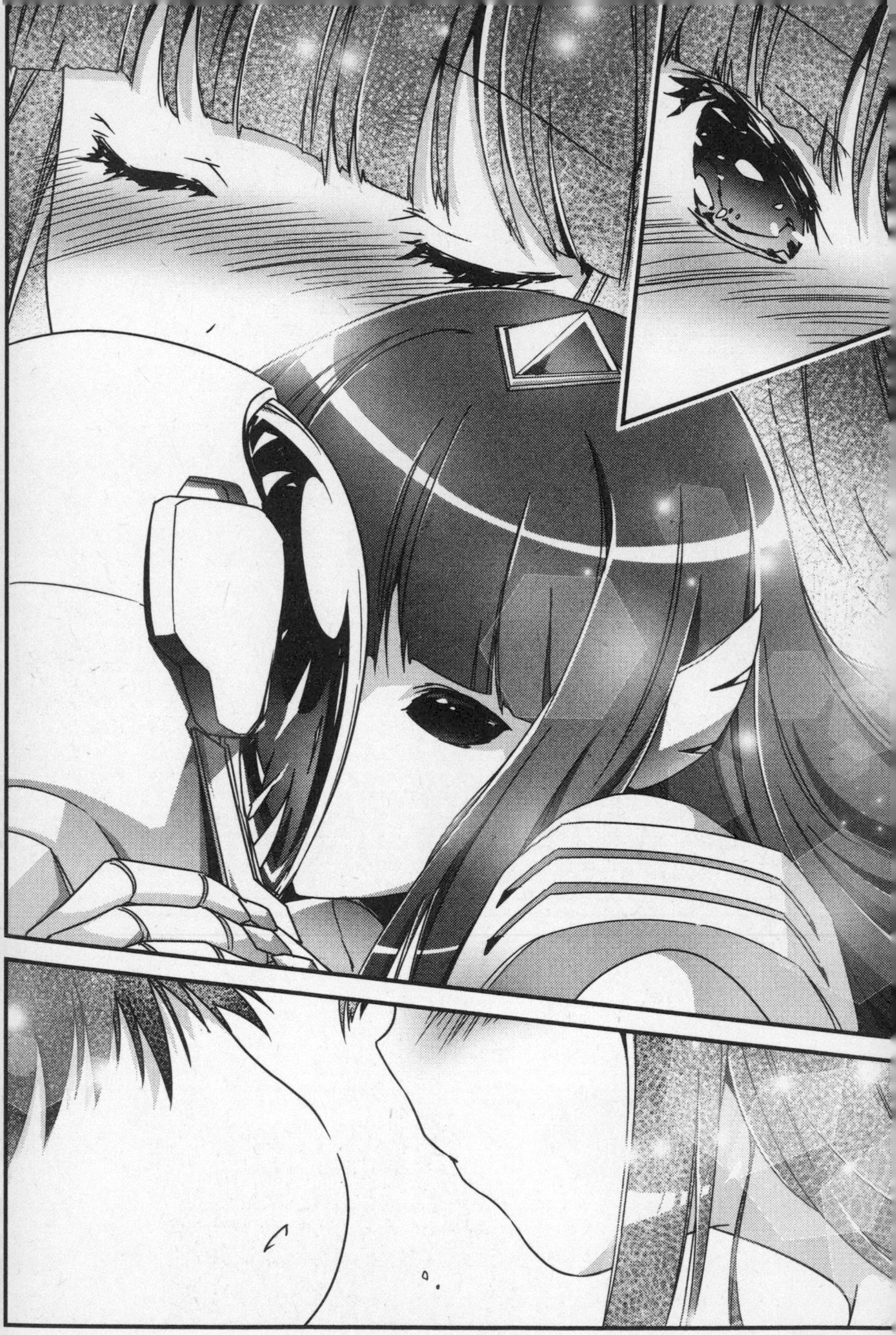

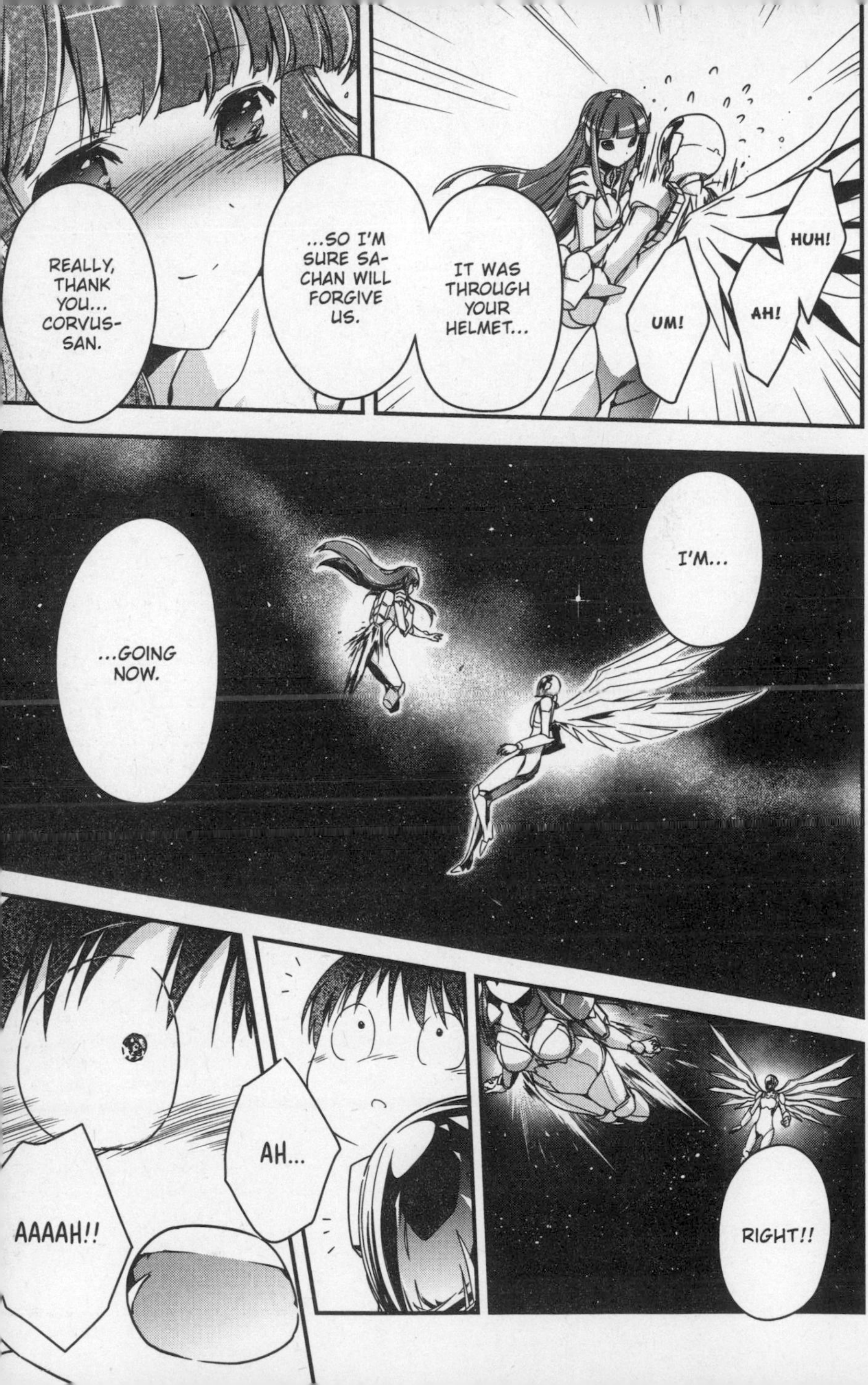
HUH!
AH!
UM!
IT WAS THROUGH YOUR HELMET...
...SO I'M SURE SA-CHAN WILL FORGIVE US.
REALLY, THANK YOU... CORVUS-SAN.
I'M...
...GOING NOW.
RIGHT!!
AH...
AAAAH!!

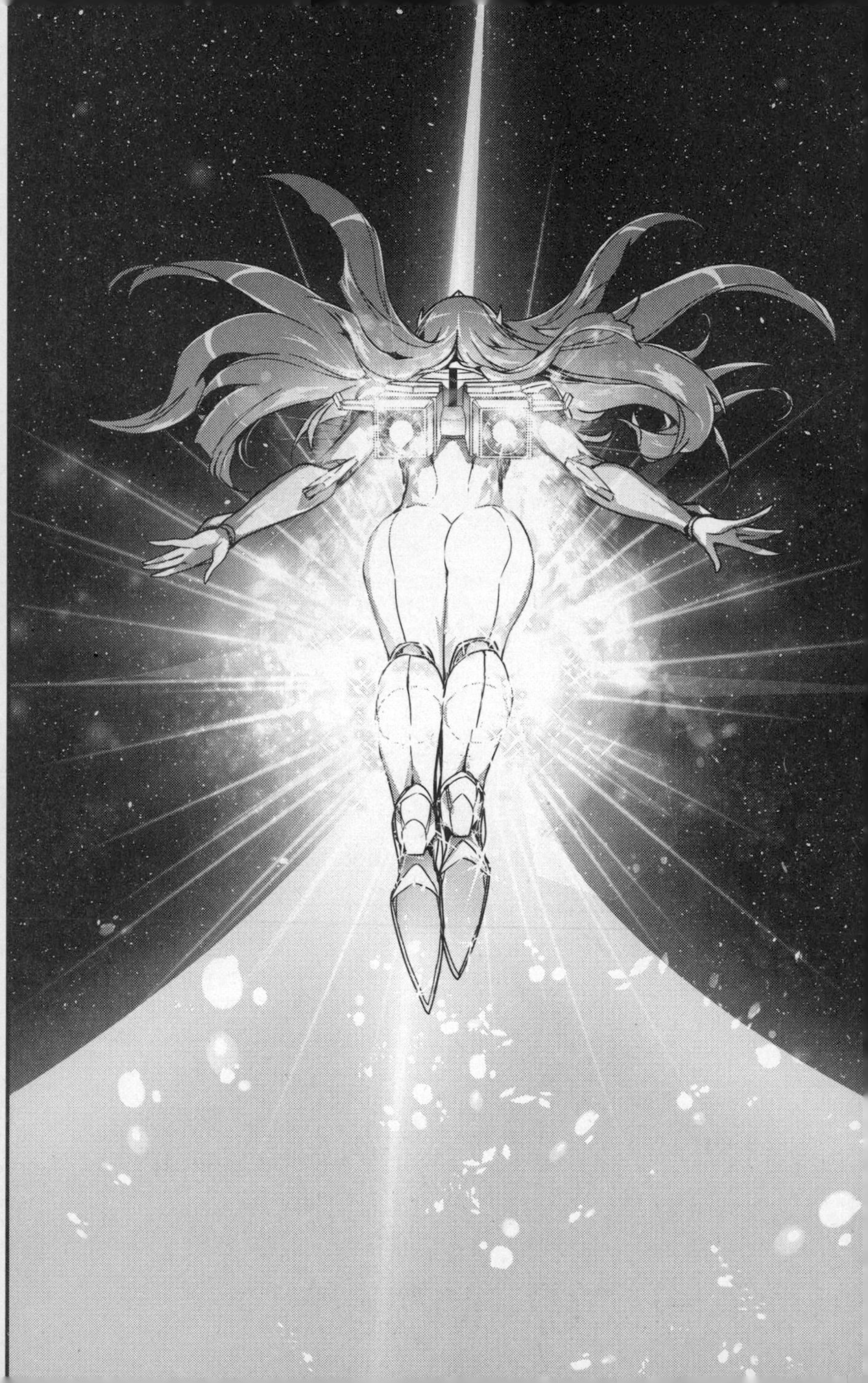

▶▶▶*ACCEL·WORLD*

CHAPTER
#42

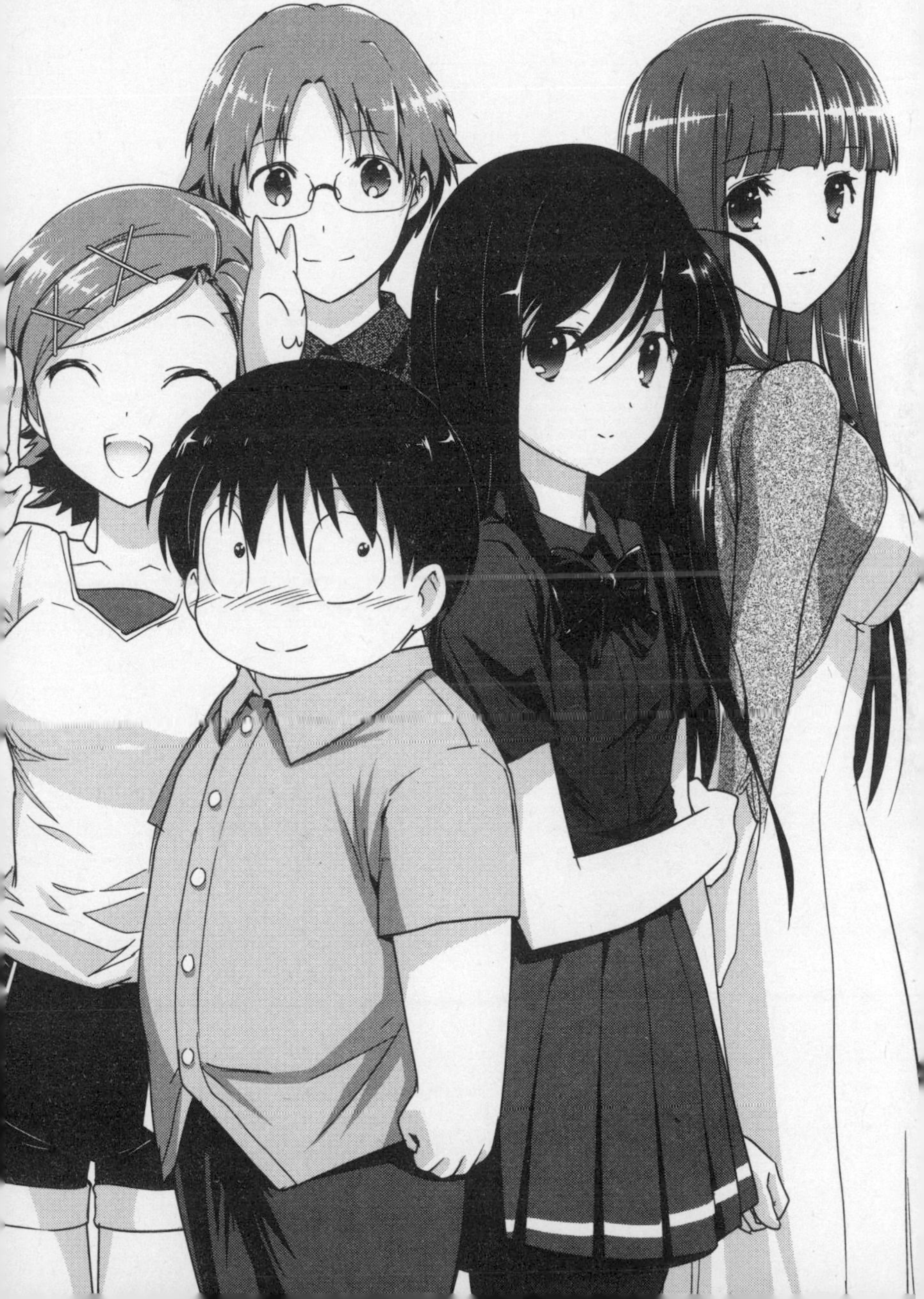

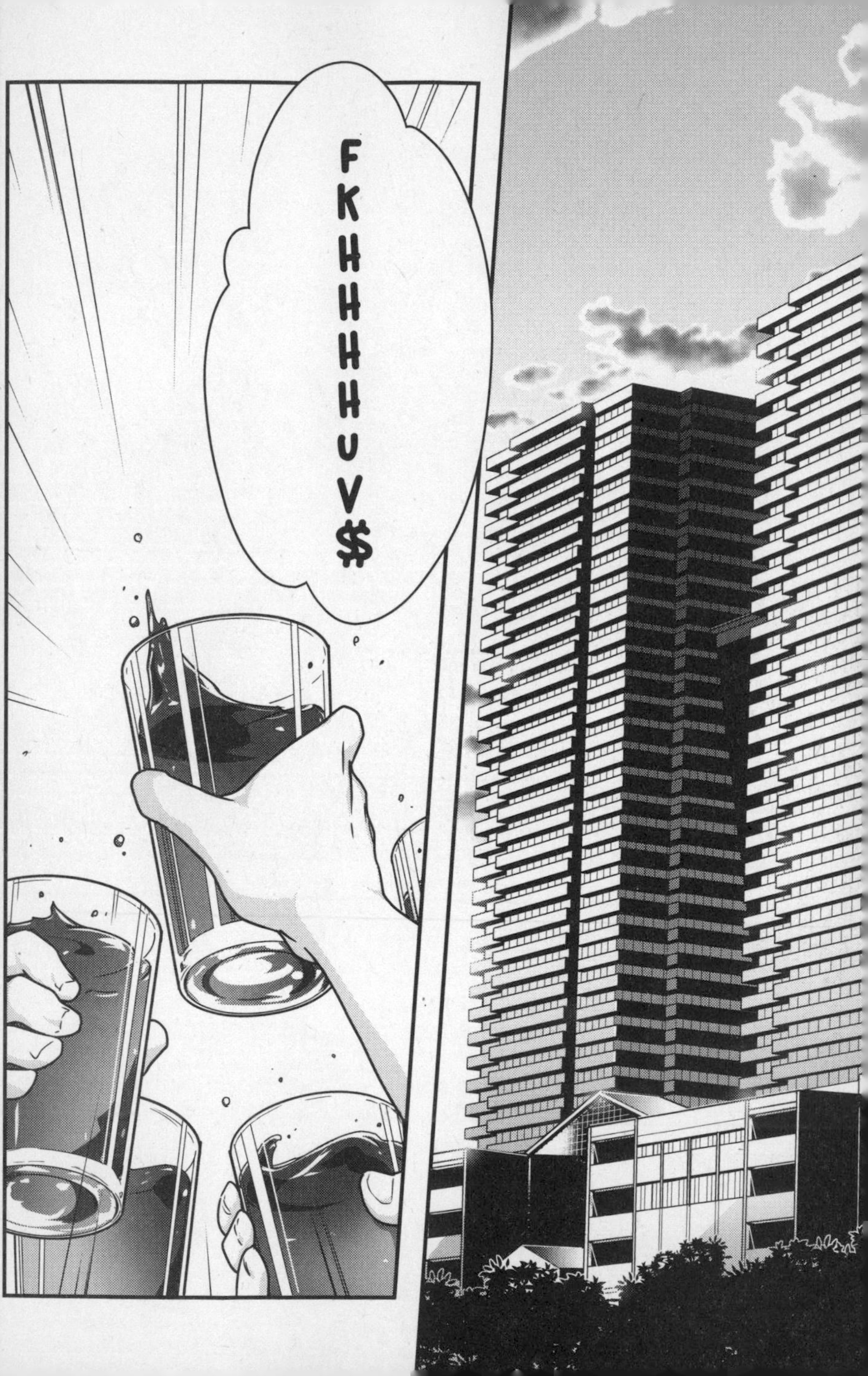
FKHHHHUV$

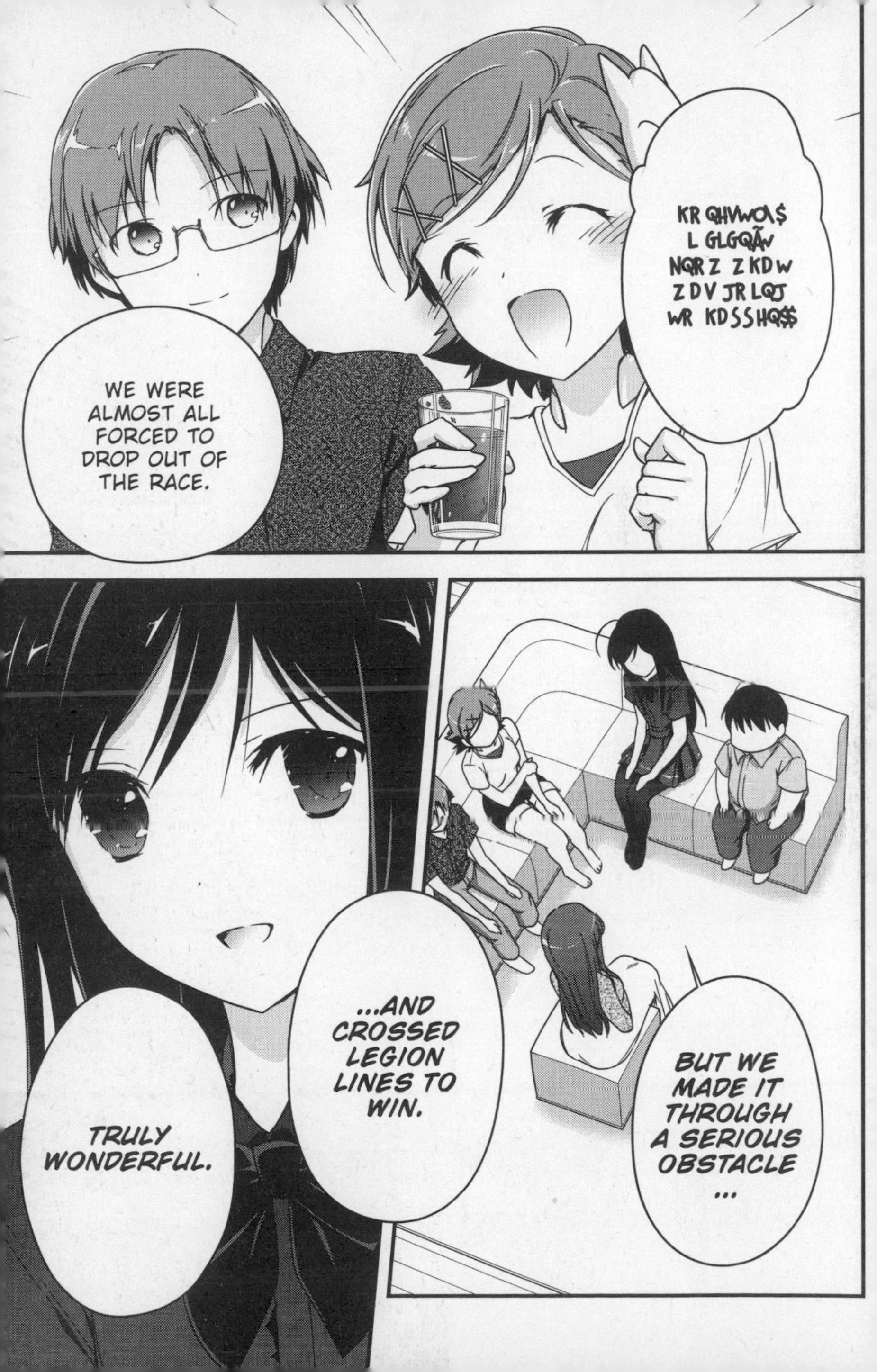
KR QHVWO\$ L GLGQÃW NQRZ ZKDW ZDV JR LQJ WR KDSSHQ$$
WE WERE ALMOST ALL FORCED TO DROP OUT OF THE RACE.
BUT WE MADE IT THROUGH A SERIOUS OBSTACLE...
...AND CROSSED LEGION LINES TO WIN.
TRULY WONDERFUL.

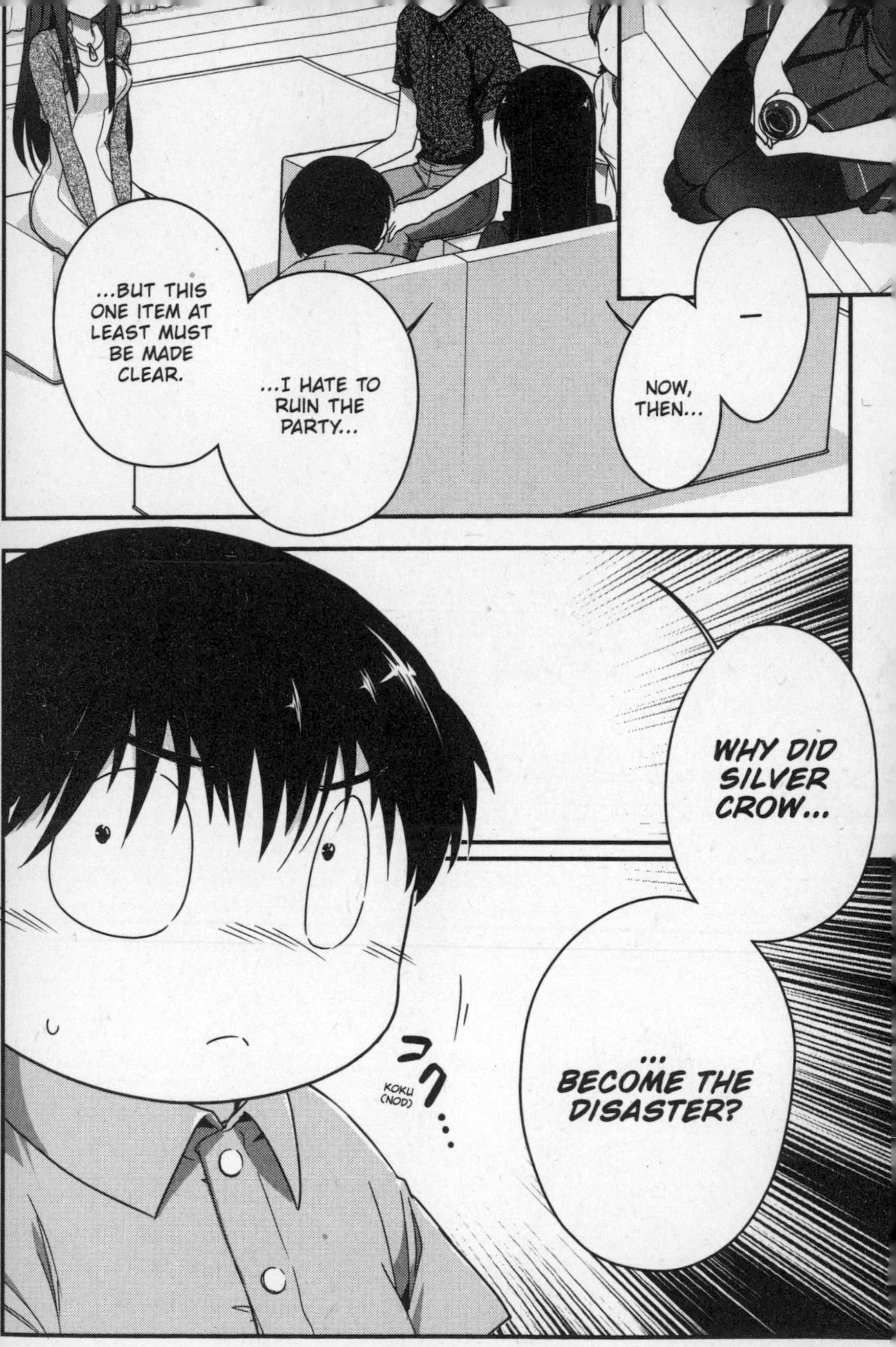
—
NOW, THEN...
...I HATE TO RUIN THE PARTY...
...BUT THIS ONE ITEM AT LEAST MUST BE MADE CLEAR.
WHY DID SILVER CROW...
...BECOME THE DISASTER?
KOKU (NOD)

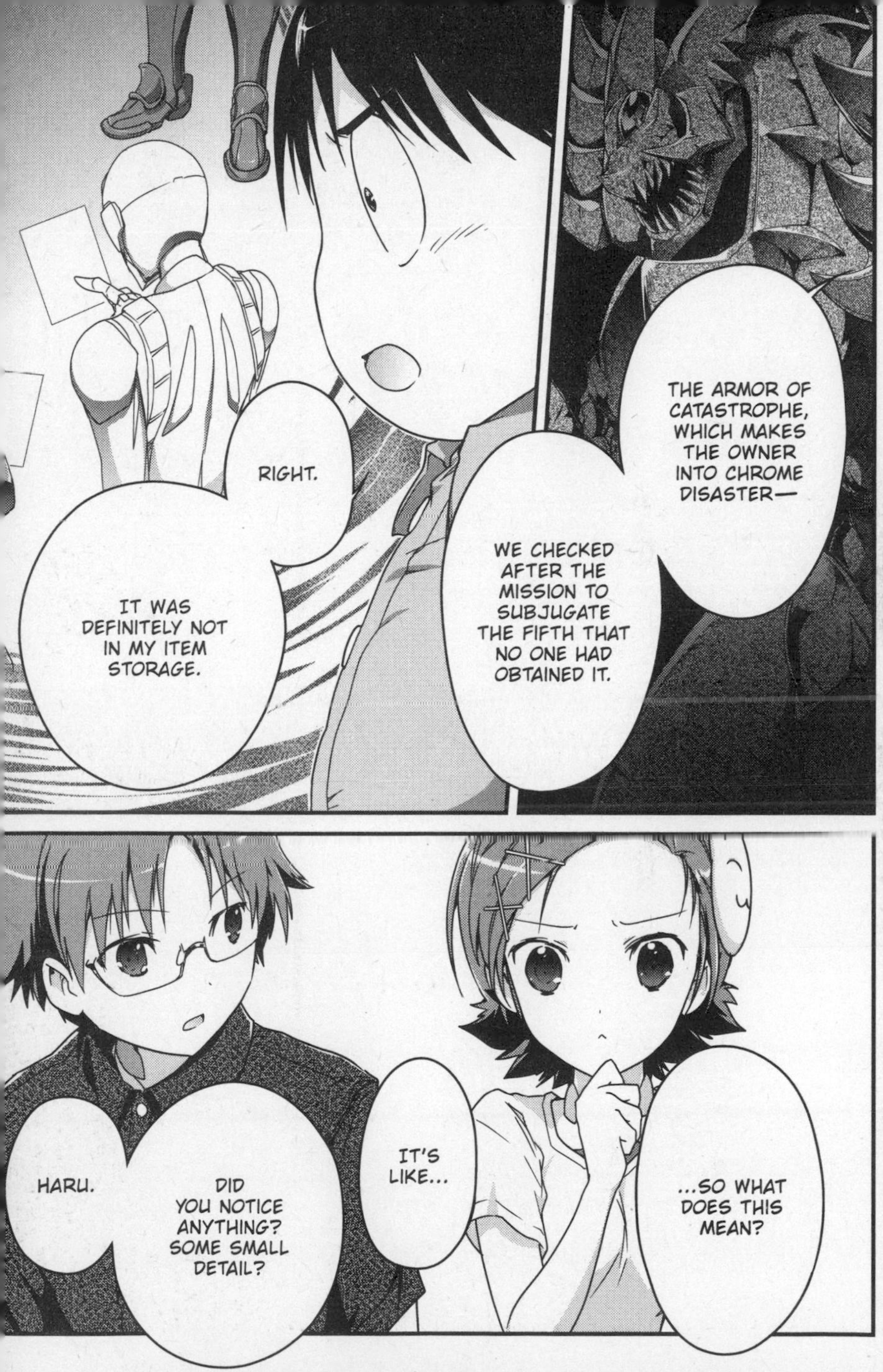
THE ARMOR OF CATASTROPHE, WHICH MAKES THE OWNER INTO CHROME DISASTER—
WE CHECKED AFTER THE MISSION TO SUBJUGATE THE FIFTH THAT NO ONE HAD OBTAINED IT.
RIGHT.
IT WAS DEFINITELY NOT IN MY ITEM STORAGE.
...SO WHAT DOES THIS MEAN?
IT'S LIKE...
HARU.
DID YOU NOTICE ANYTHING? SOME SMALL DETAIL?

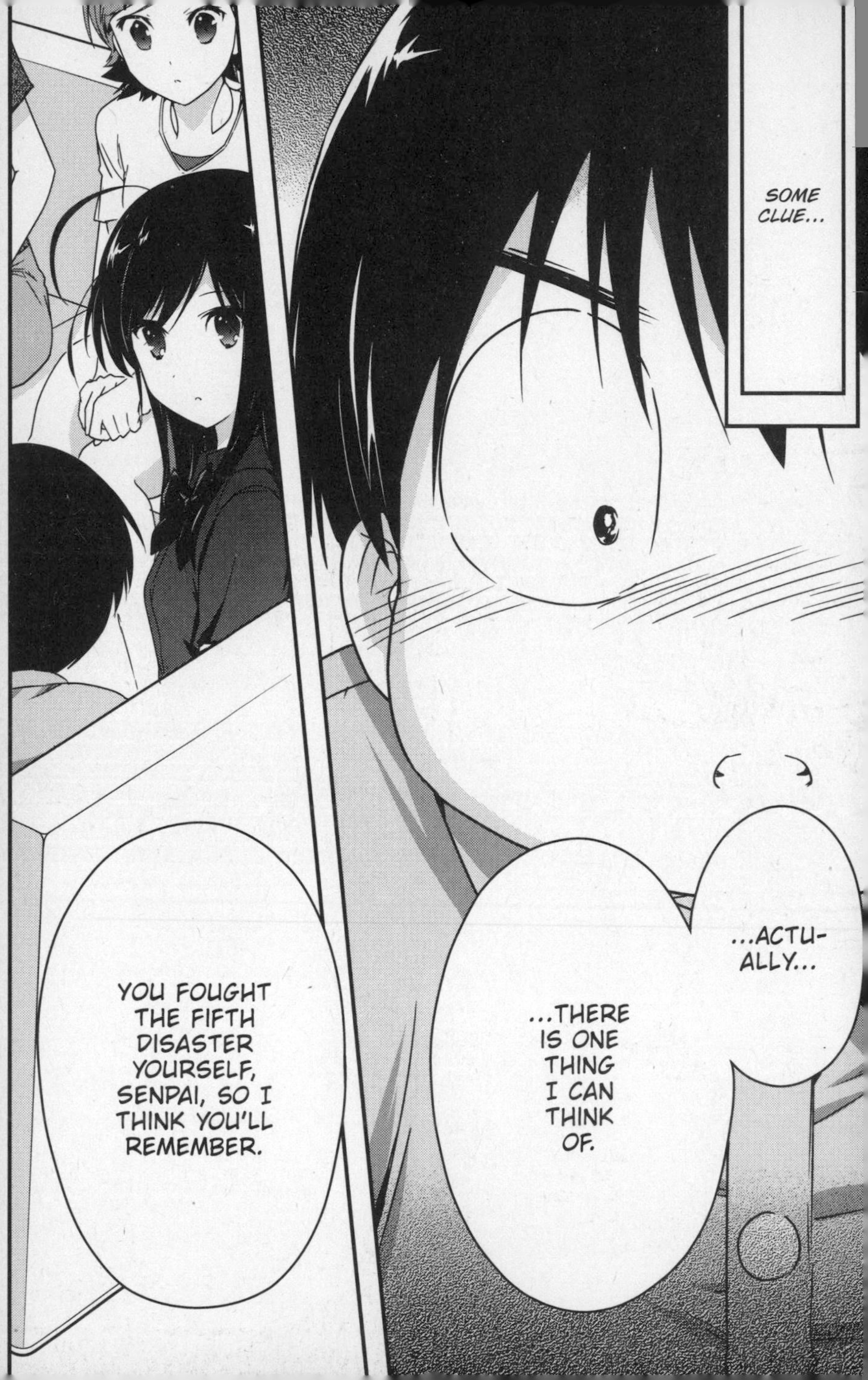
SOME CLUE...
...ACTU-ALLY...
...THERE IS ONE THING I CAN THINK OF.
YOU FOUGHT THE FIFTH DISASTER YOURSELF, SENPAI, SO I THINK YOU'LL REMEMBER.

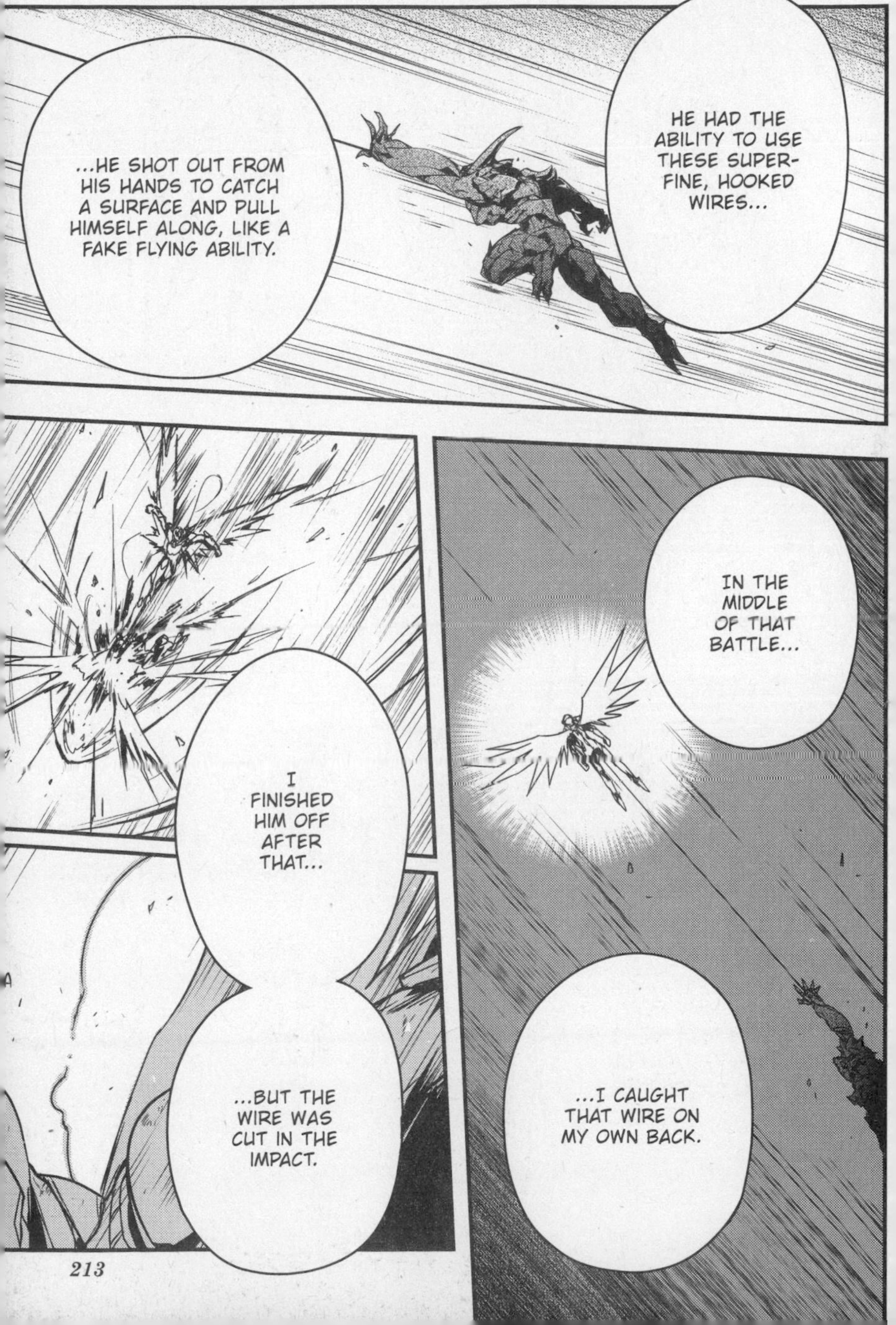
HE HAD THE ABILITY TO USE THESE SUPER-FINE, HOOKED WIRES...
...HE SHOT OUT FROM HIS HANDS TO CATCH A SURFACE AND PULL HIMSELF ALONG, LIKE A FAKE FLYING ABILITY.
IN THE MIDDLE OF THAT BATTLE...
...I CAUGHT THAT WIRE ON MY OWN BACK.
I FINISHED HIM OFF AFTER THAT...
...BUT THE WIRE WAS CUT IN THE IMPACT.

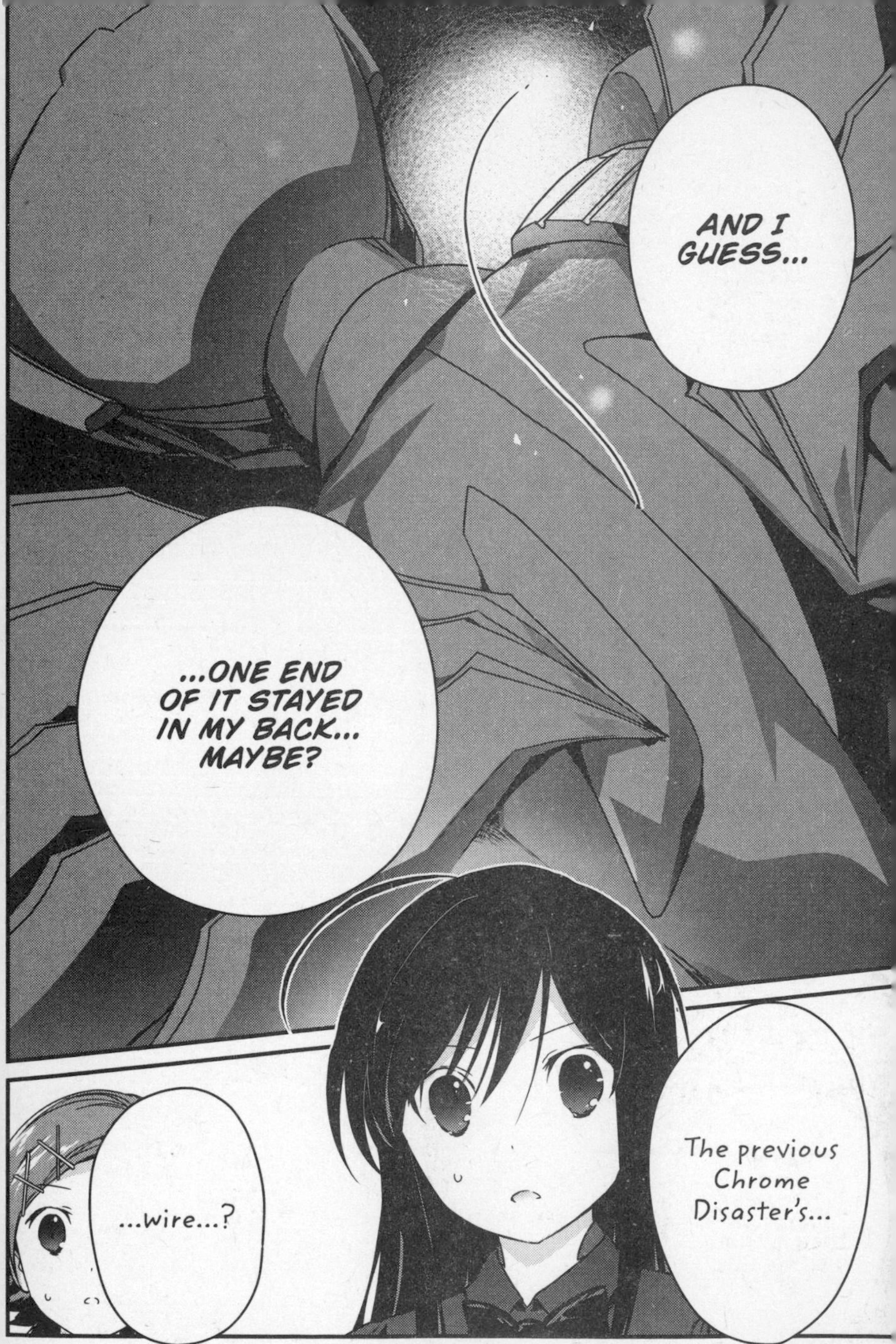
AND I GUESS...
...ONE END OF IT STAYED IN MY BACK... MAYBE?
The previous Chrome Disaster's...
...wire...?

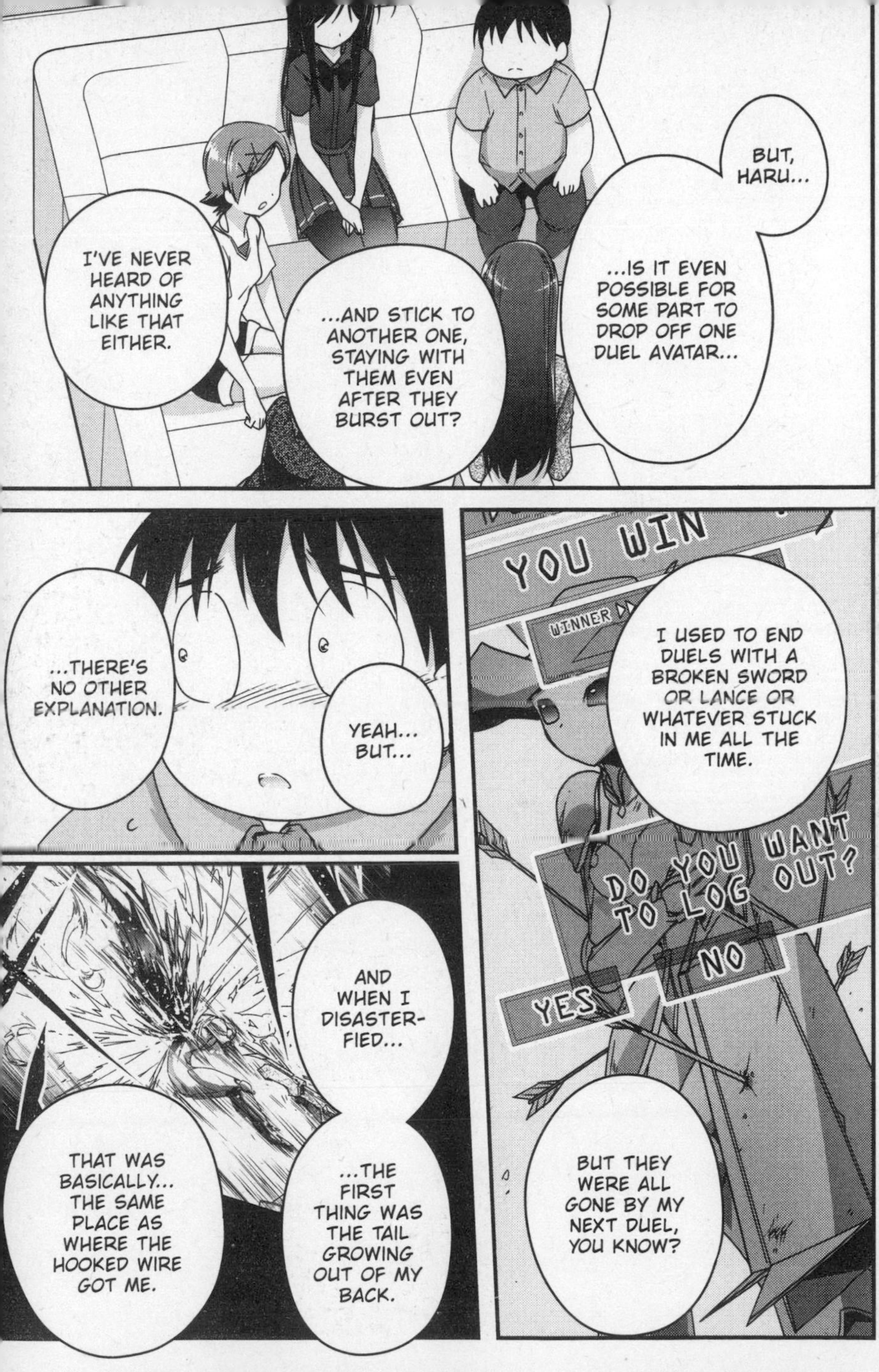
BUT, HARU...
...IS IT EVEN POSSIBLE FOR SOME PART TO DROP OFF ONE DUEL AVATAR...
...AND STICK TO ANOTHER ONE, STAYING WITH THEM EVEN AFTER THEY BURST OUT?
I'VE NEVER HEARD OF ANYTHING LIKE THAT EITHER.
YOU WIN
WINNER
I USED TO END DUELS WITH A BROKEN SWORD OR LANCE OR WHATEVER STUCK IN ME ALL THE TIME.
DO YOU WANT TO LOG OUT?
NO
YES
BUT THEY WERE ALL GONE BY MY NEXT DUEL, YOU KNOW?
YEAH... BUT...
...THERE'S NO OTHER EXPLANATION.
AND WHEN I DISASTER-FIED...
...THE FIRST THING WAS THE TAIL GROWING OUT OF MY BACK.
THAT WAS BASICALLY... THE SAME PLACE AS WHERE THE HOOKED WIRE GOT ME.

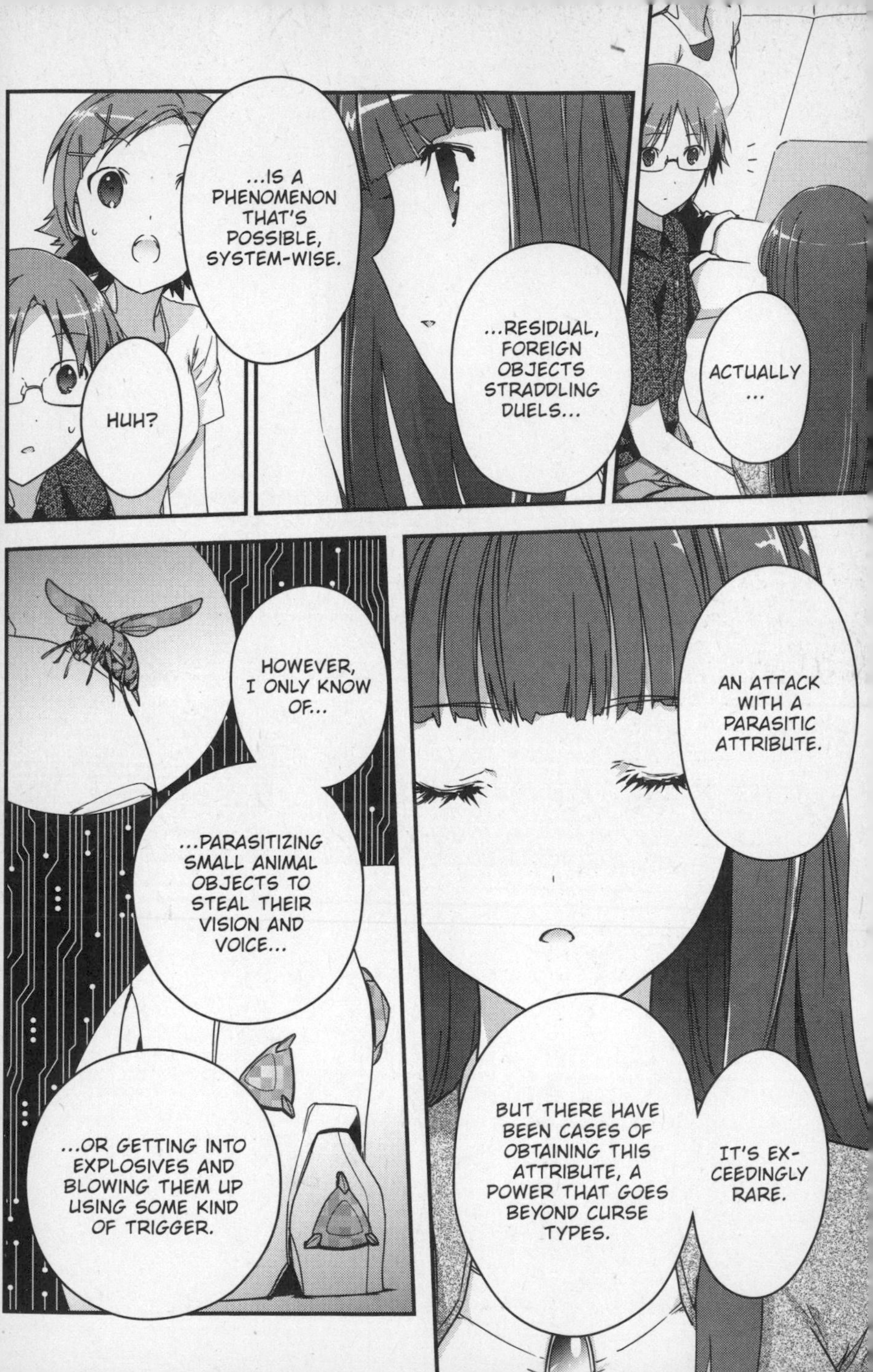
ACTUALLY ...
...RESIDUAL, FOREIGN OBJECTS STRADDLING DUELS...
...IS A PHENOMENON THAT'S POSSIBLE, SYSTEM-WISE.
HUH?
AN ATTACK WITH A PARASITIC ATTRIBUTE.
IT'S EX-CEEDINGLY RARE.
BUT THERE HAVE BEEN CASES OF OBTAINING THIS ATTRIBUTE, A POWER THAT GOES BEYOND CURSE TYPES.
HOWEVER, I ONLY KNOW OF...
...PARASITIZING SMALL ANIMAL OBJECTS TO STEAL THEIR VISION AND VOICE...
...OR GETTING INTO EXPLOSIVES AND BLOWING THEM UP USING SOME KIND OF TRIGGER.

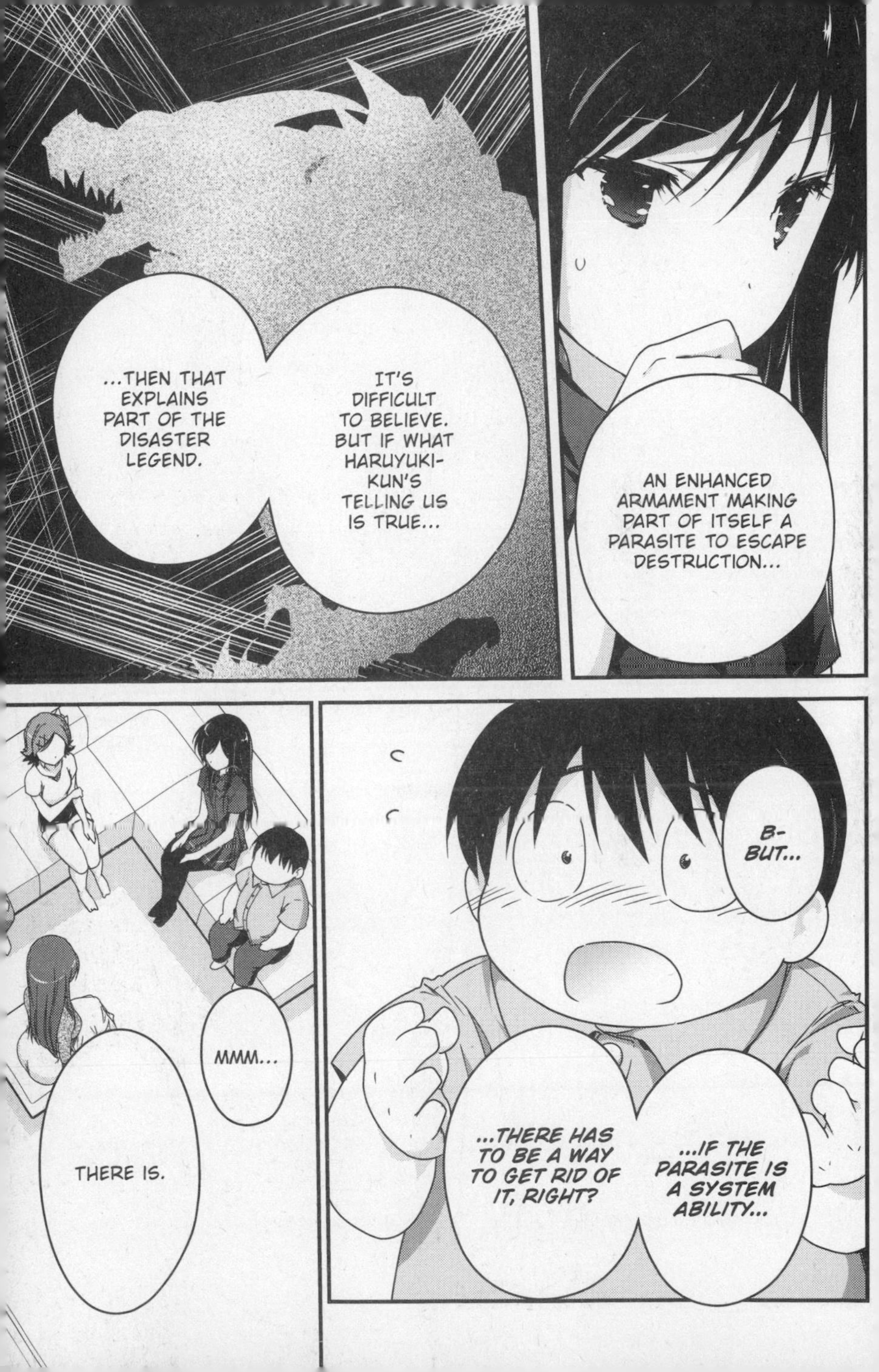
AN ENHANCED ARMAMENT MAKING PART OF ITSELF A PARASITE TO ESCAPE DESTRUCTION...
IT'S DIFFICULT TO BELIEVE. BUT IF WHAT HARUYUKI-KUN'S TELLING US IS TRUE...
...THEN THAT EXPLAINS PART OF THE DISASTER LEGEND.
B-BUT...
...IF THE PARASITE IS A SYSTEM ABILITY...
...THERE HAS TO BE A WAY TO GET RID OF IT, RIGHT?
MMM...
THERE IS.

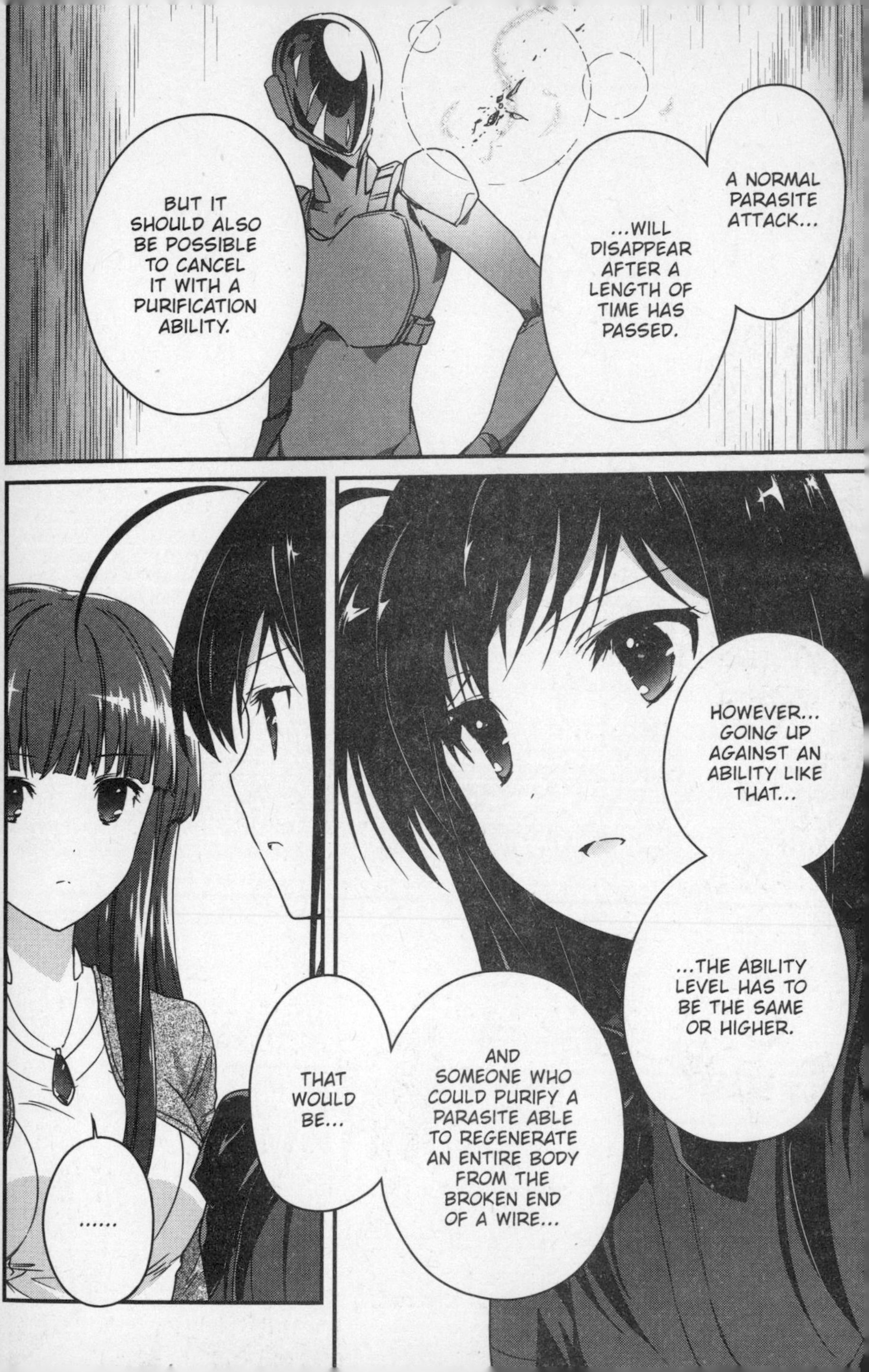
A NORMAL PARASITE ATTACK...
...WILL DISAPPEAR AFTER A LENGTH OF TIME HAS PASSED.
BUT IT SHOULD ALSO BE POSSIBLE TO CANCEL IT WITH A PURIFICATION ABILITY.
HOWEVER... GOING UP AGAINST AN ABILITY LIKE THAT...
...THE ABILITY LEVEL HAS TO BE THE SAME OR HIGHER.
AND SOMEONE WHO COULD PURIFY A PARASITE ABLE TO REGENERATE AN ENTIRE BODY FROM THE BROKEN END OF A WIRE...
THAT WOULD BE...
......

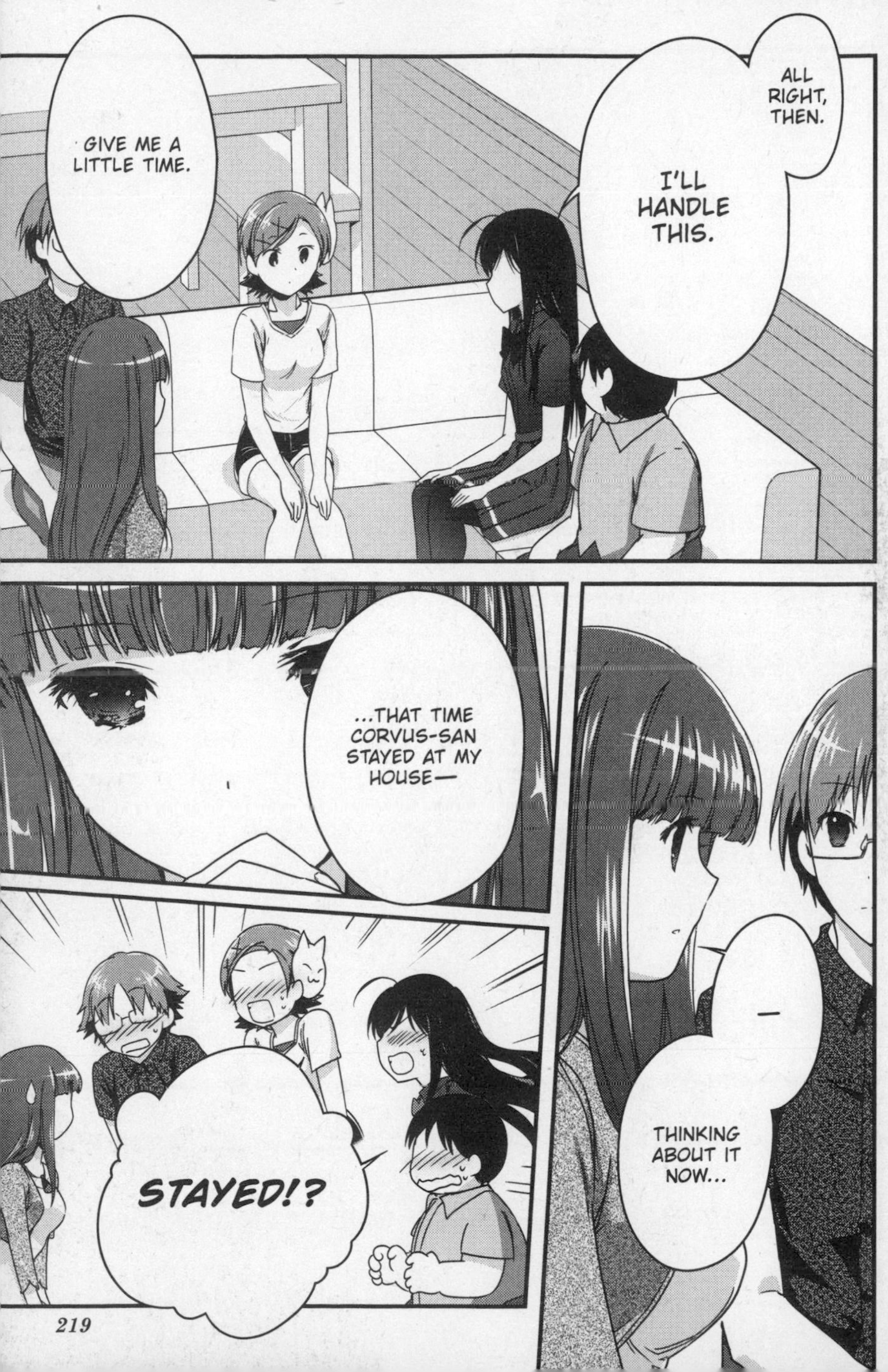
ALL RIGHT, THEN.
I'LL HANDLE THIS.
GIVE ME A LITTLE TIME.
—
THINKING ABOUT IT NOW...
...THAT TIME CORVUS-SAN STAYED AT MY HOUSE—
STAYED!?

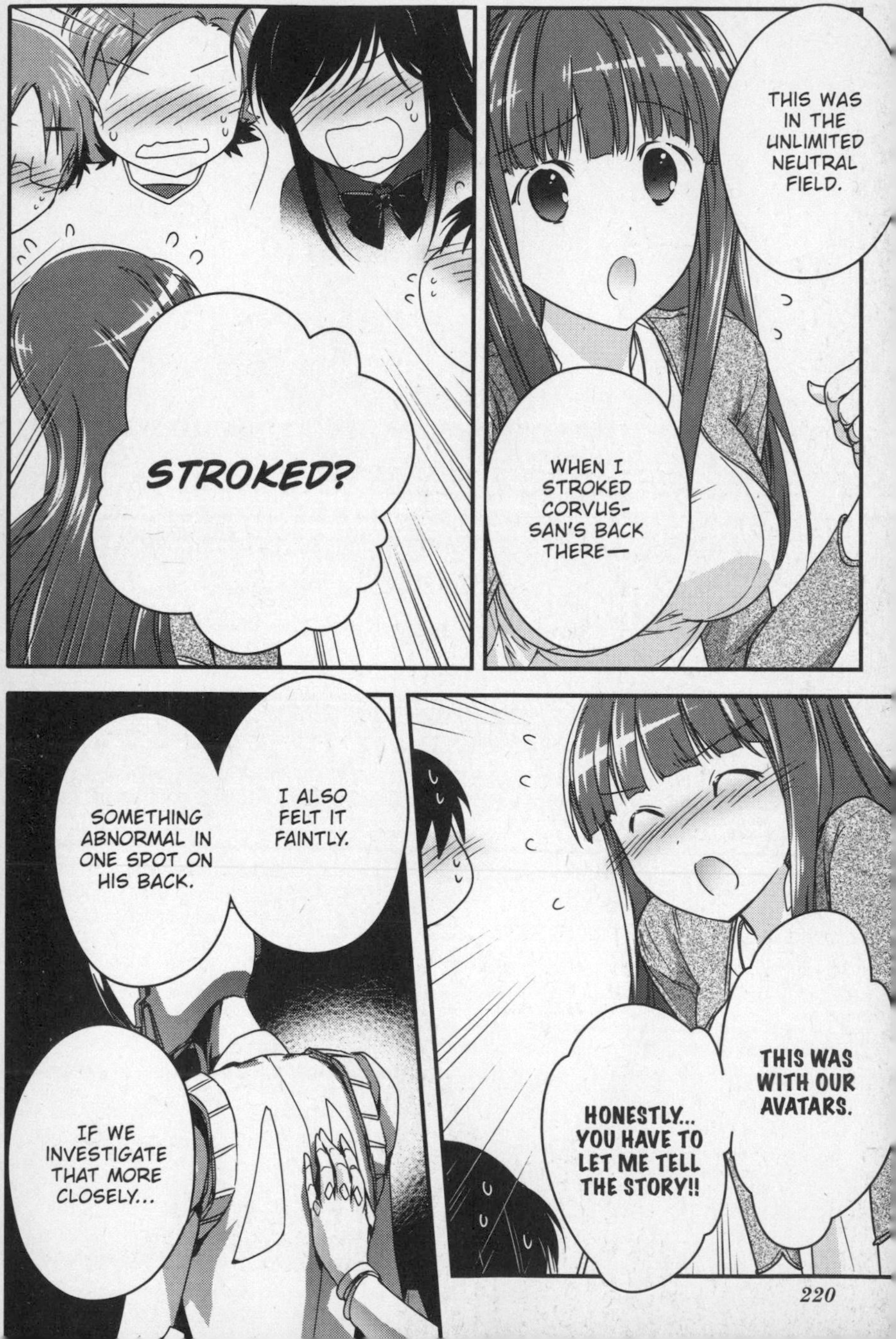
THIS WAS IN THE UNLIMITED NEUTRAL FIELD.
WHEN I STROKED CORVUS-SAN'S BACK THERE—
STROKED?
THIS WAS WITH OUR AVATARS.
HONESTLY... YOU HAVE TO LET ME TELL THE STORY!!
I ALSO FELT IT FAINTLY.
SOMETHING ABNORMAL IN ONE SPOT ON HIS BACK.
IF WE INVESTIGATE THAT MORE CLOSELY...

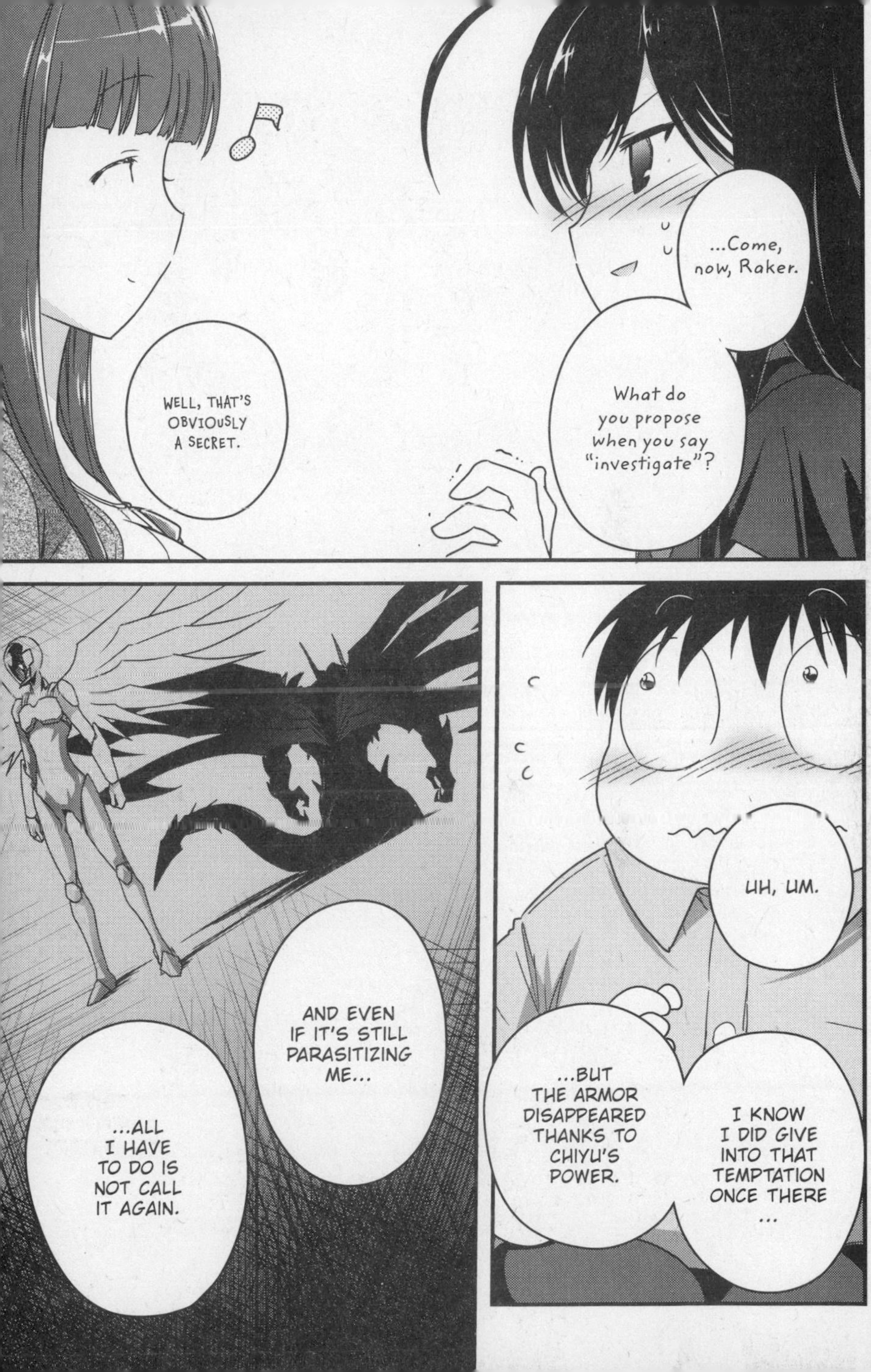
...Come, now, Raker.
What do you propose when you say "investigate"?
WELL, THAT'S OBVIOUSLY A SECRET.
UH, UM.
I KNOW I DID GIVE INTO THAT TEMPTATION ONCE THERE...
...BUT THE ARMOR DISAPPEARED THANKS TO CHIYU'S POWER.
AND EVEN IF IT'S STILL PARASITIZING ME...
...ALL I HAVE TO DO IS NOT CALL IT AGAIN.

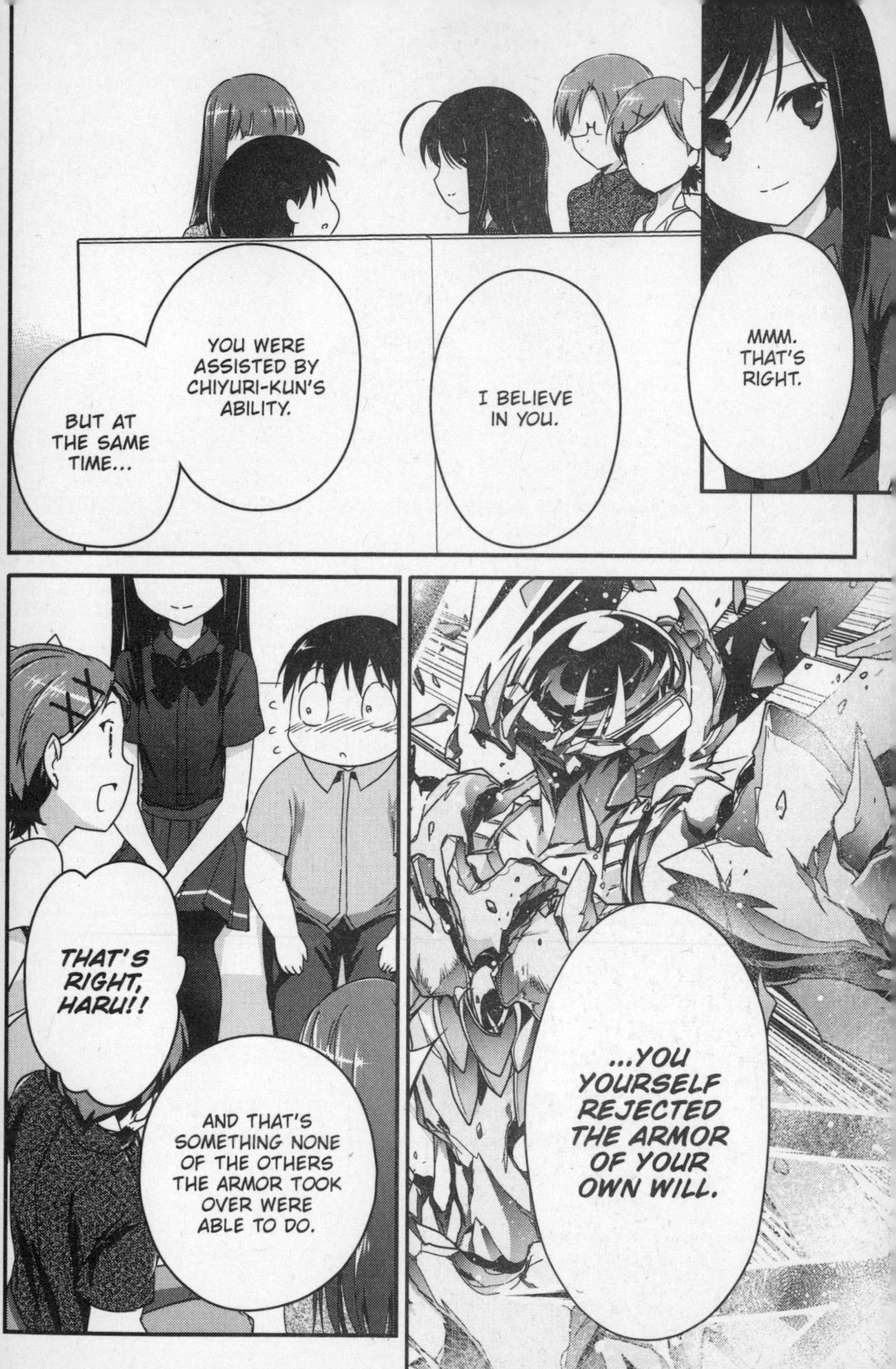
MMM. THAT'S RIGHT.
I BELIEVE IN YOU.
YOU WERE ASSISTED BY CHIYURI-KUN'S ABILITY.
BUT AT THE SAME TIME...
...YOU YOURSELF REJECTED THE ARMOR OF YOUR OWN WILL.
AND THAT'S SOMETHING NONE OF THE OTHERS THE ARMOR TOOK OVER WERE ABLE TO DO.
THAT'S RIGHT, HARU!!

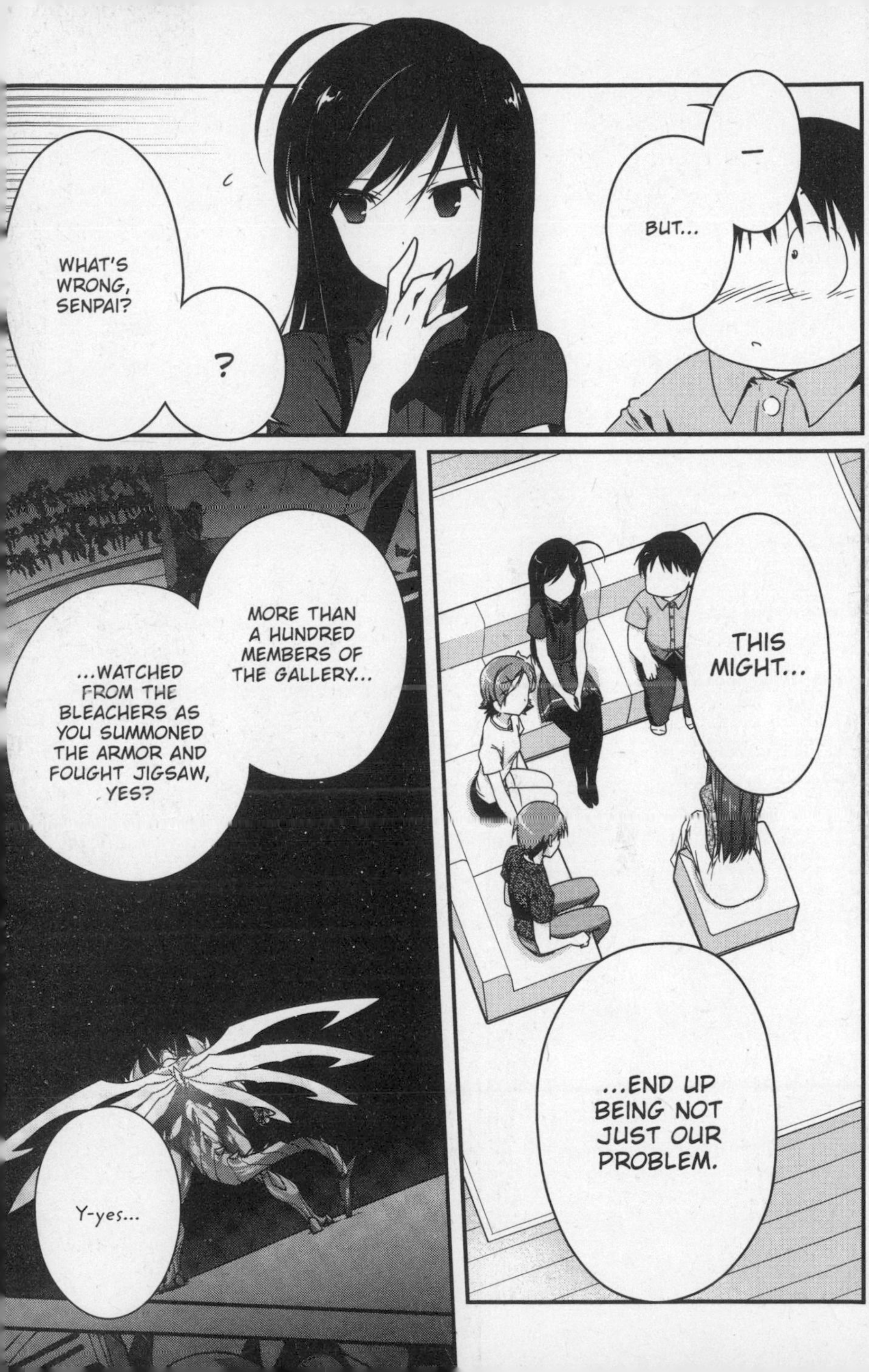
BUT...
WHAT'S WRONG, SENPAI?
?
THIS MIGHT...
...END UP BEING NOT JUST OUR PROBLEM.
MORE THAN A HUNDRED MEMBERS OF THE GALLERY...
...WATCHED FROM THE BLEACHERS AS YOU SUMMONED THE ARMOR AND FOUGHT JIGSAW, YES?
Y-yes...

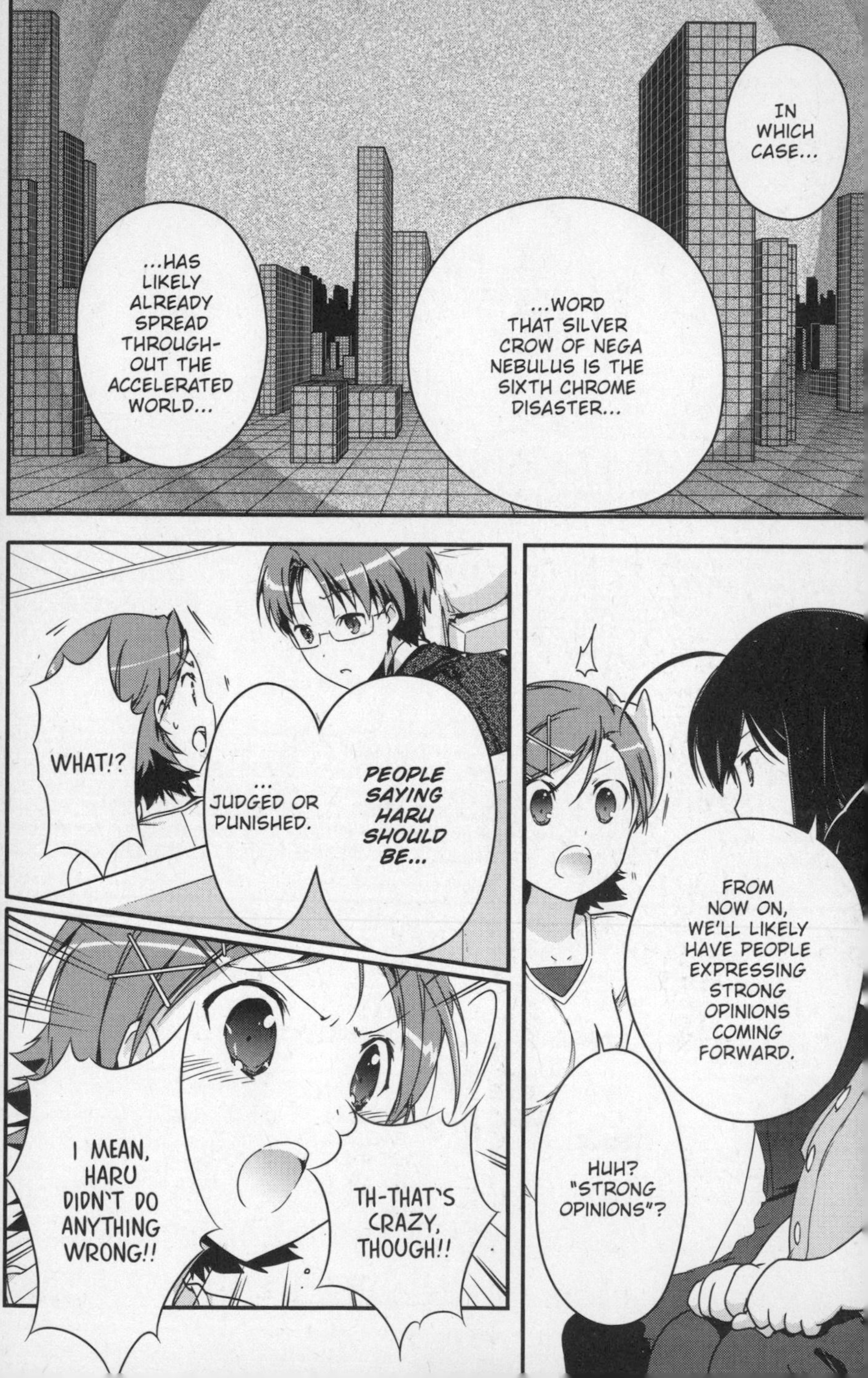
IN WHICH CASE...
...WORD THAT SILVER CROW OF NEGA NEBULUS IS THE SIXTH CHROME DISASTER...
...HAS LIKELY ALREADY SPREAD THROUGHOUT THE ACCELERATED WORLD...
FROM NOW ON, WE'LL LIKELY HAVE PEOPLE EXPRESSING STRONG OPINIONS COMING FORWARD.
HUH? "STRONG OPINIONS"?
PEOPLE SAYING HARU SHOULD BE...
...JUDGED OR PUNISHED.
WHAT!?
TH-THAT'S CRAZY, THOUGH!!
I MEAN, HARU DIDN'T DO ANYTHING WRONG!!

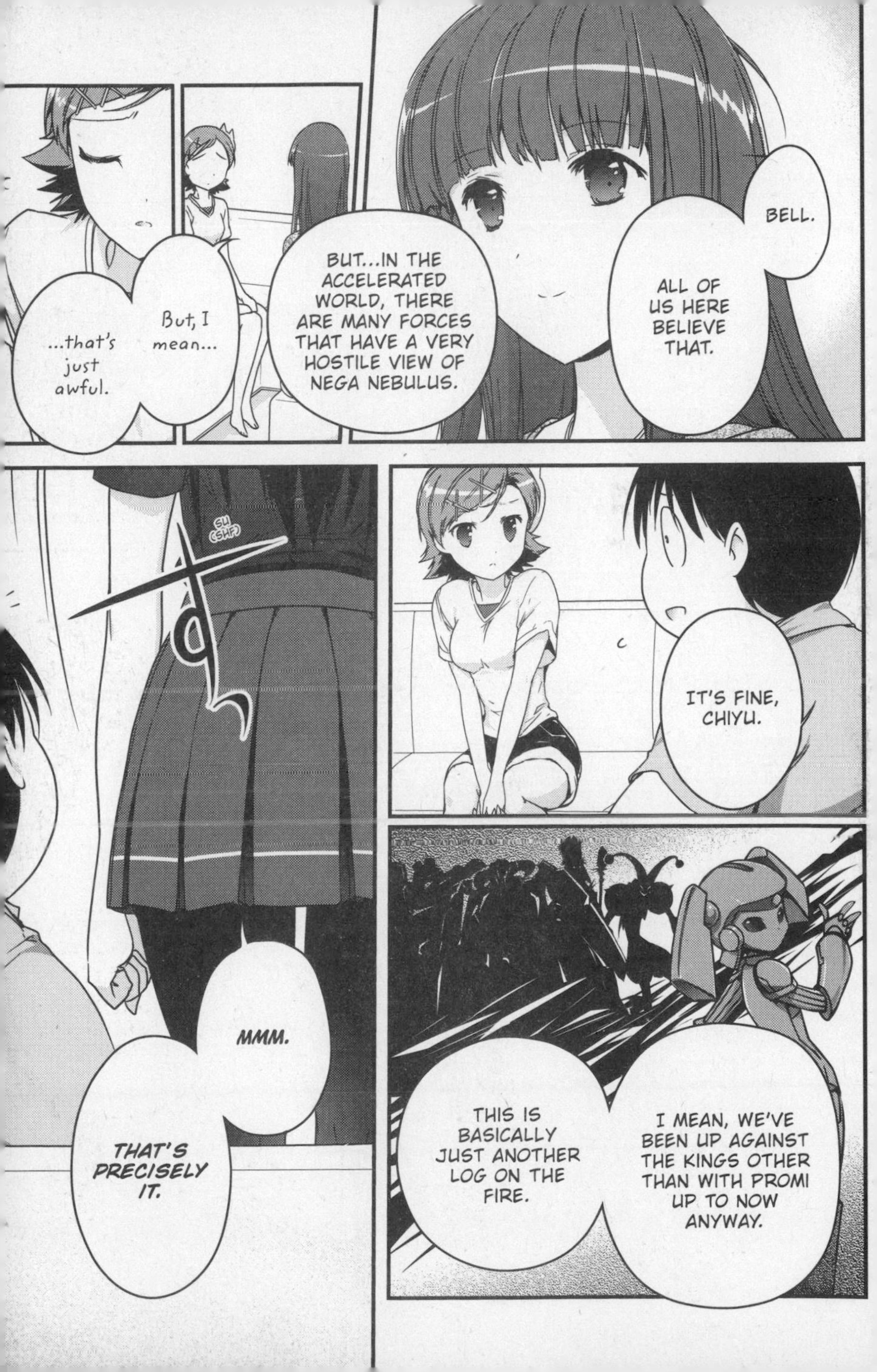
BELL.
ALL OF US HERE BELIEVE THAT.
BUT...IN THE ACCELERATED WORLD, THERE ARE MANY FORCES THAT HAVE A VERY HOSTILE VIEW OF NEGA NEBULUS.
But, I mean...
...that's just awful.
IT'S FINE, CHIYU.
I MEAN, WE'VE BEEN UP AGAINST THE KINGS OTHER THAN WITH PROMI UP TO NOW ANYWAY.
THIS IS BASICALLY JUST ANOTHER LOG ON THE FIRE.
SU (SHF)
MMM.
THAT'S PRECISELY IT.

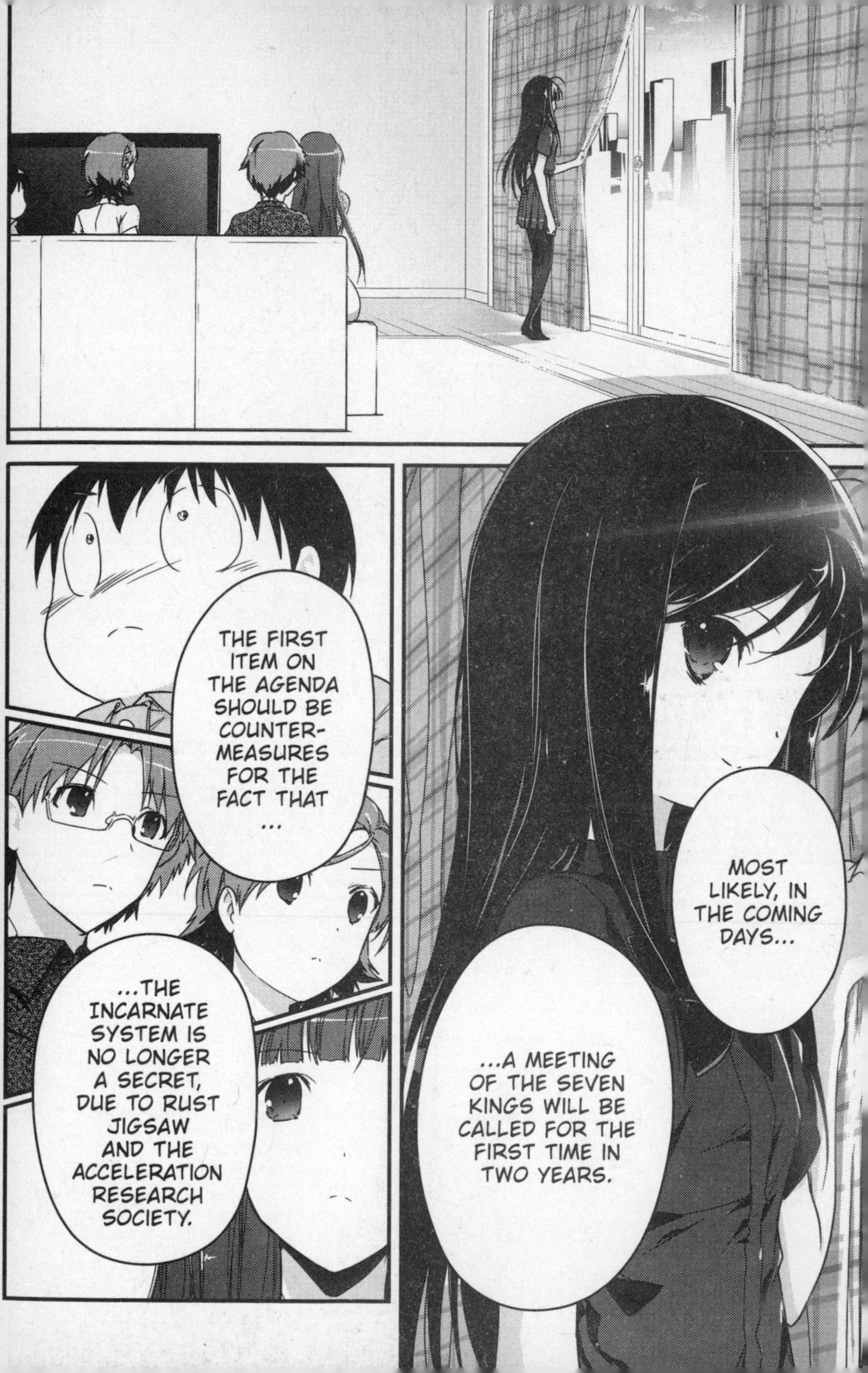
MOST LIKELY, IN THE COMING DAYS...
...A MEETING OF THE SEVEN KINGS WILL BE CALLED FOR THE FIRST TIME IN TWO YEARS.
THE FIRST ITEM ON THE AGENDA SHOULD BE COUNTER-MEASURES FOR THE FACT THAT ...
...THE INCARNATE SYSTEM IS NO LONGER A SECRET, DUE TO RUST JIGSAW AND THE ACCELERATION RESEARCH SOCIETY.

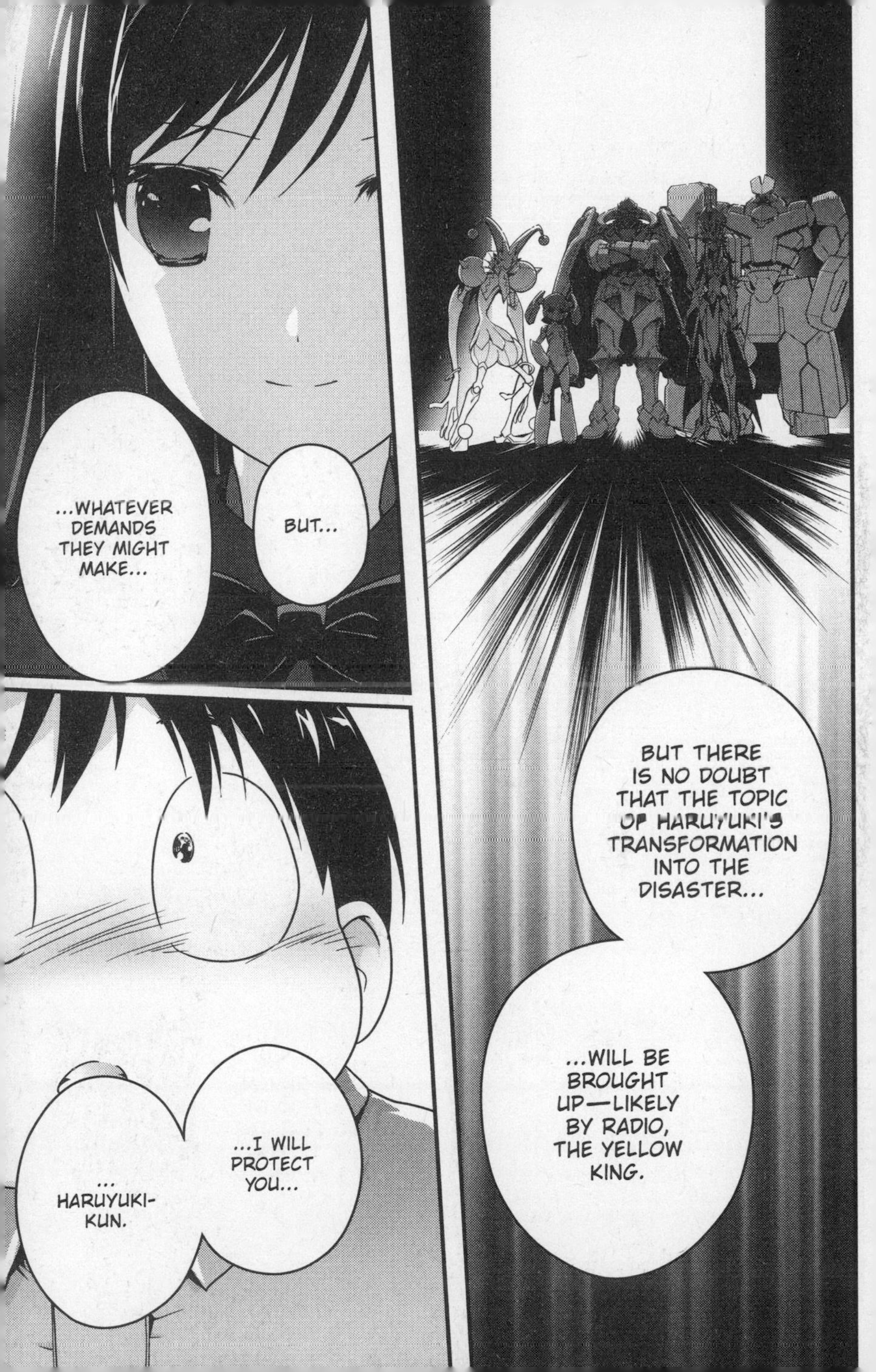
BUT THERE IS NO DOUBT THAT THE TOPIC OF HARUYUKI'S TRANSFORMATION INTO THE DISASTER...
...WILL BE BROUGHT UP—LIKELY BY RADIO, THE YELLOW KING.
BUT...
...WHATEVER DEMANDS THEY MIGHT MAKE...
...I WILL PROTECT YOU...
... HARUYUKI-KUN.

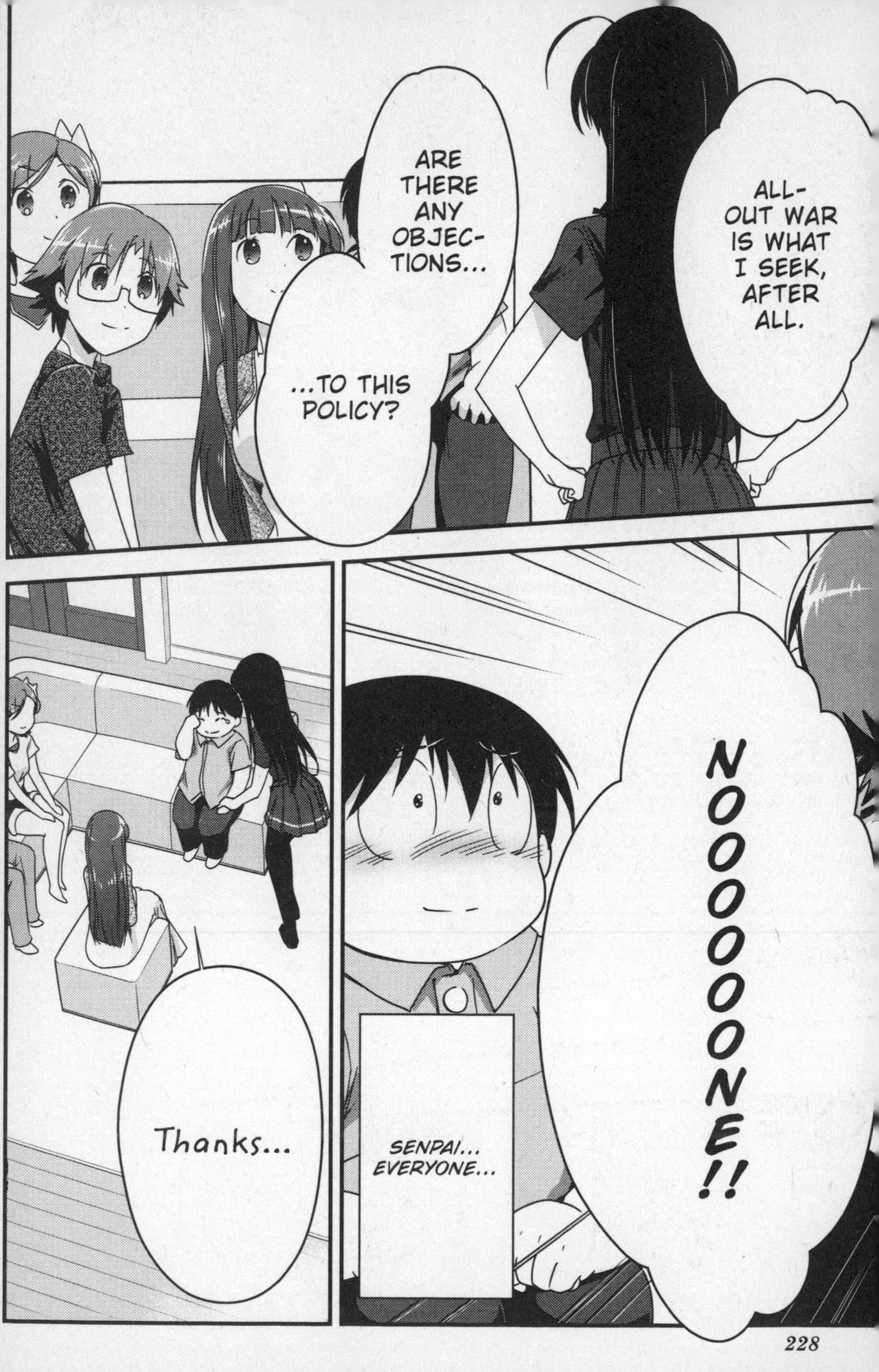
ALL-OUT WAR IS WHAT I SEEK, AFTER ALL.
ARE THERE ANY OBJECTIONS...
...TO THIS POLICY?
NOOOOOOONE!!
SENPAI... EVERYONE...
Thanks...

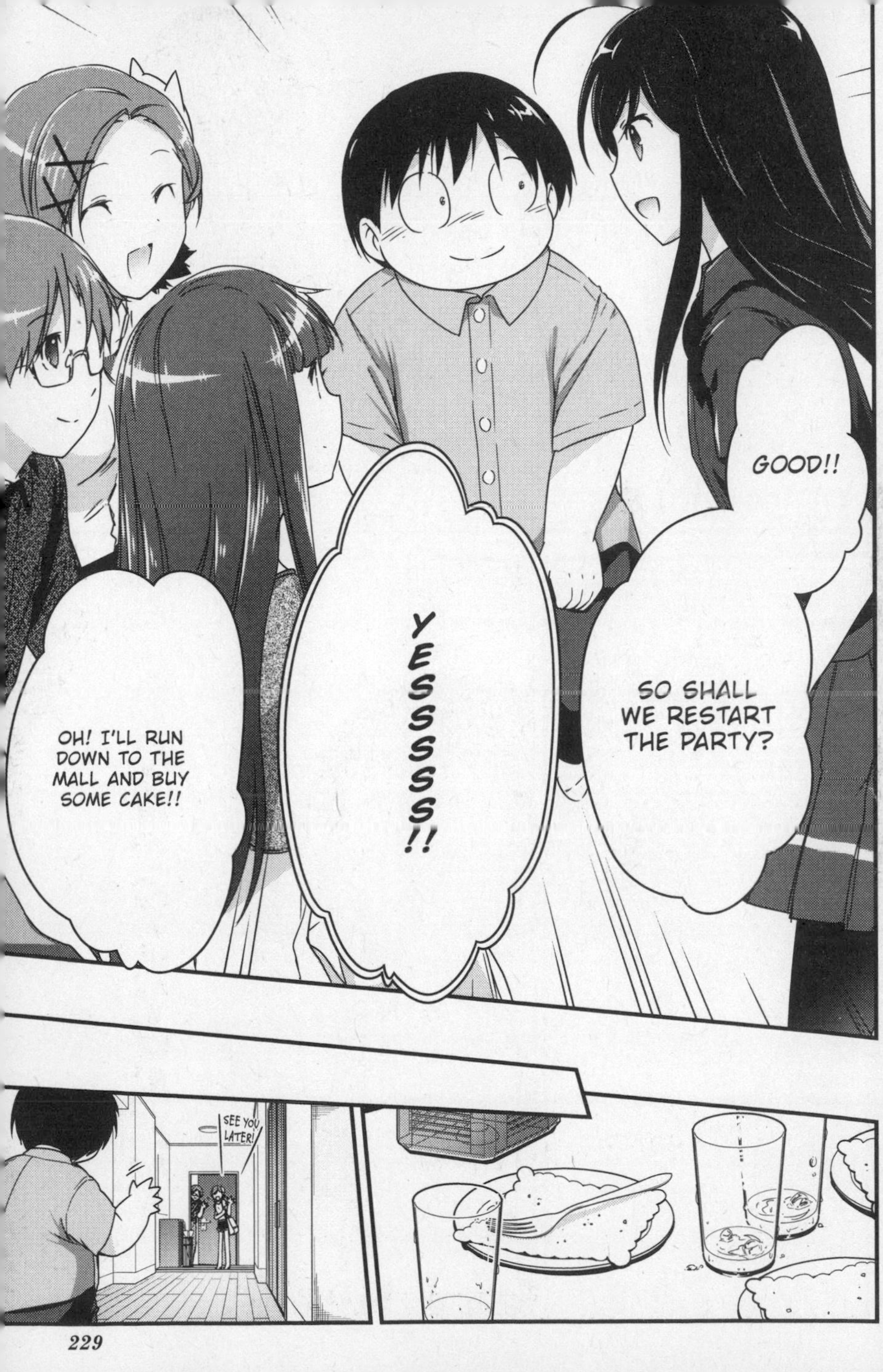
GOOD!!
SO SHALL WE RESTART THE PARTY?
YESSSSS!!
OH! I'LL RUN DOWN TO THE MALL AND BUY SOME CAKE!!
SEE YOU LATER!

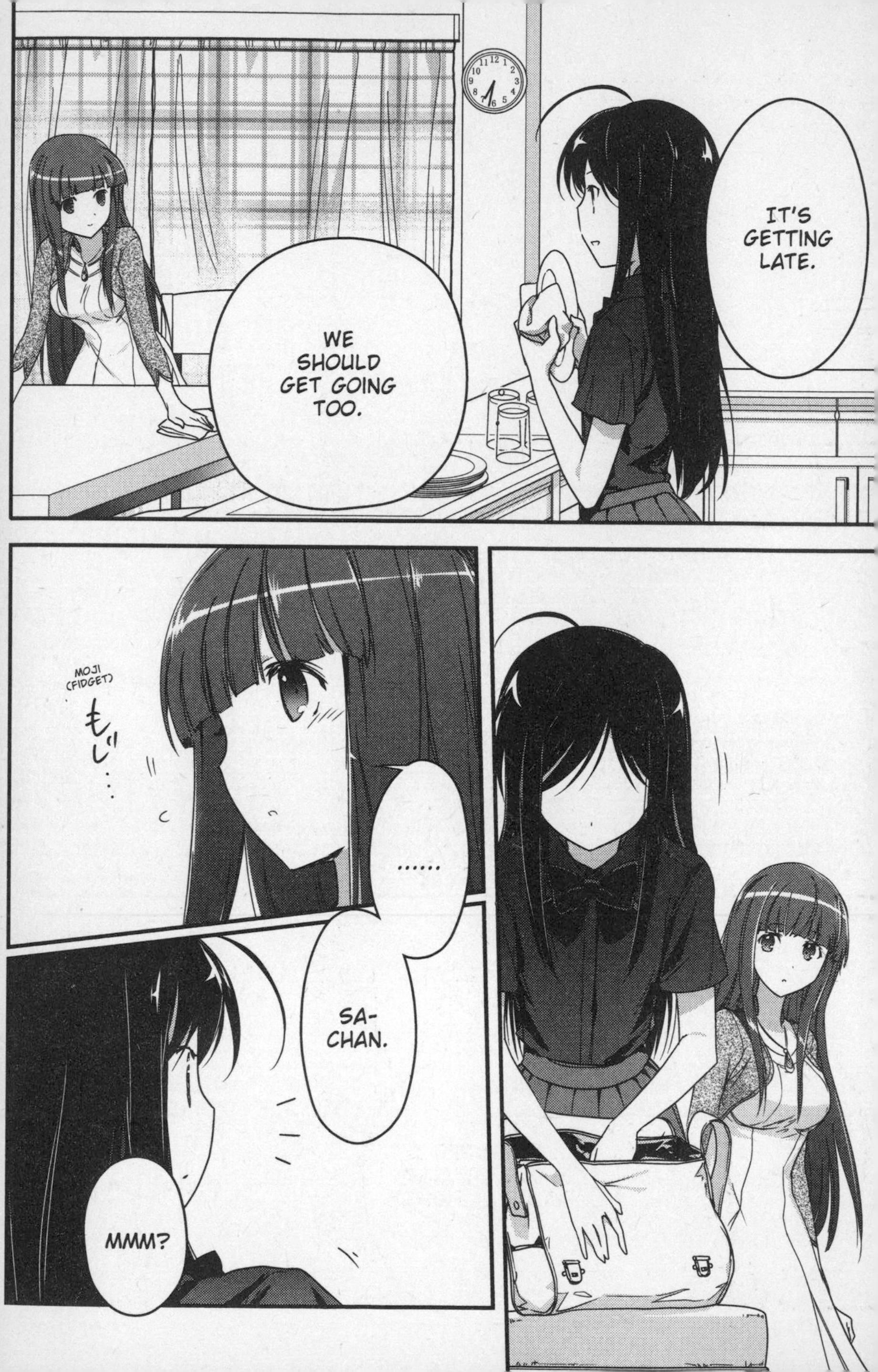
IT'S GETTING LATE.
WE SHOULD GET GOING TOO.
MOJI (FIDGET)
もじ…
......
SA-CHAN.
MMM?

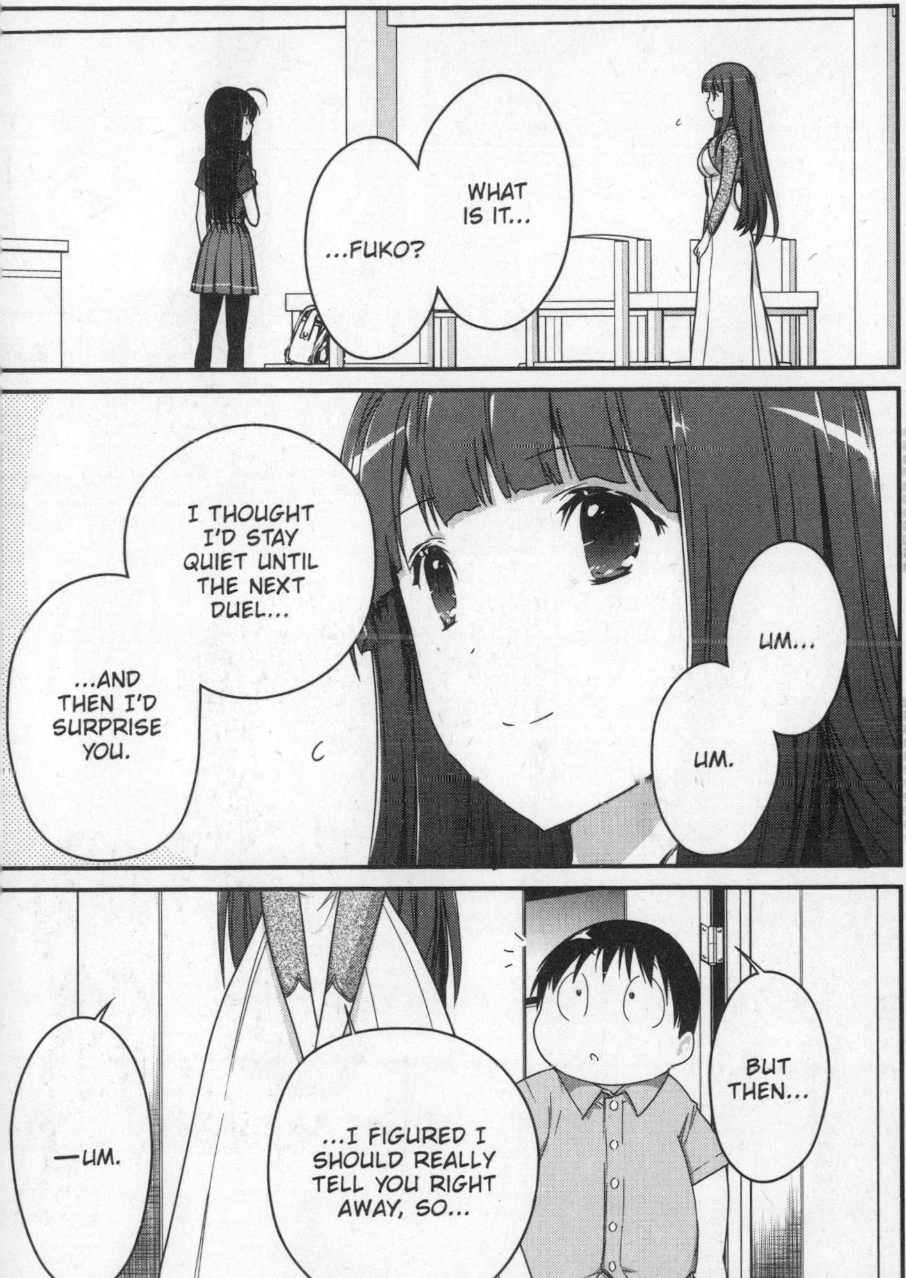
WHAT IS IT...
...FUKO?
UM...
UM.
I THOUGHT I'D STAY QUIET UNTIL THE NEXT DUEL...
...AND THEN I'D SURPRISE YOU.
BUT THEN...
...I FIGURED I SHOULD REALLY TELL YOU RIGHT AWAY, SO...
—UM.

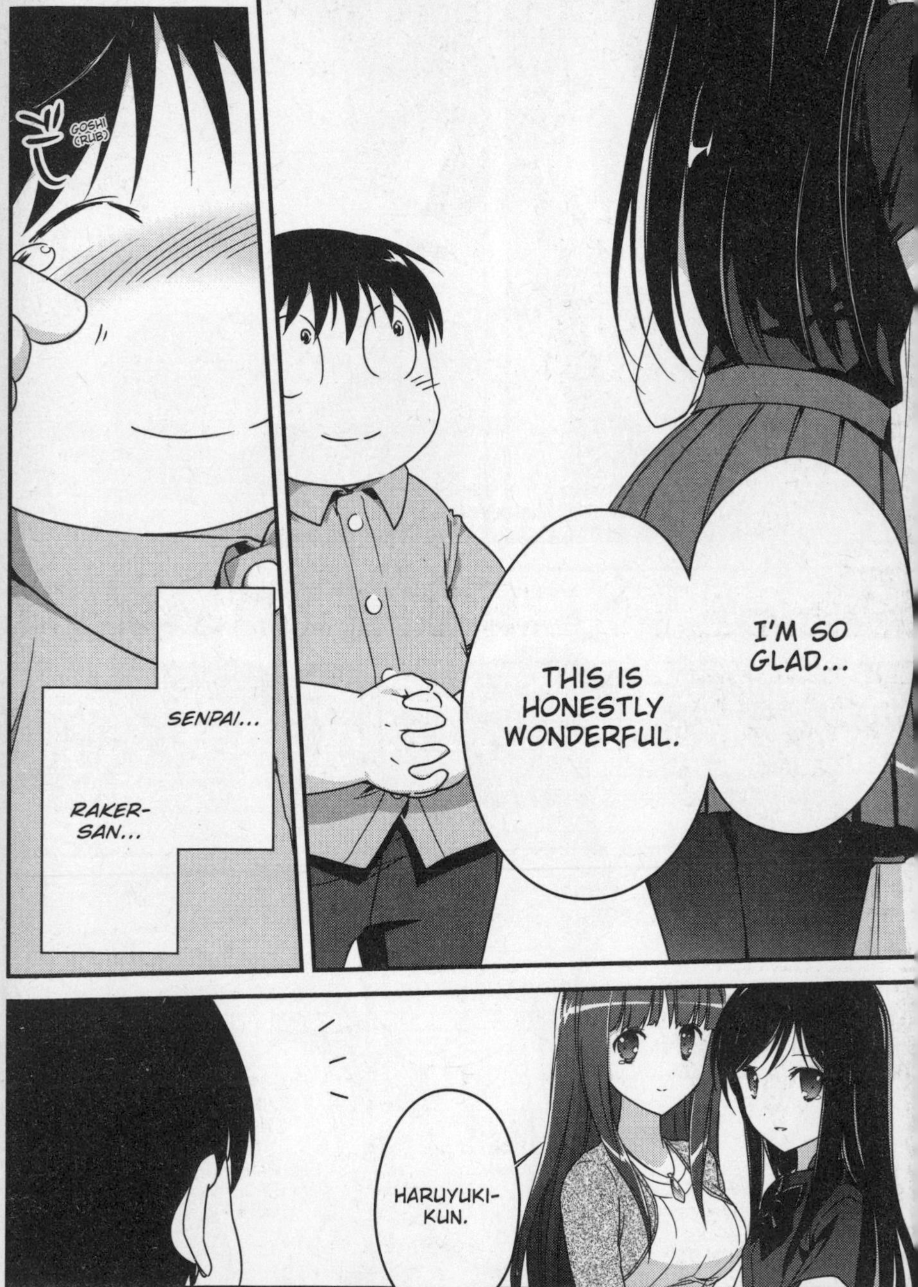
I'M SO GLAD...
THIS IS HONESTLY WONDERFUL.
SENPAI...
RAKER-SAN...
GOSHI (RUB)
HARUYUKI-KUN.

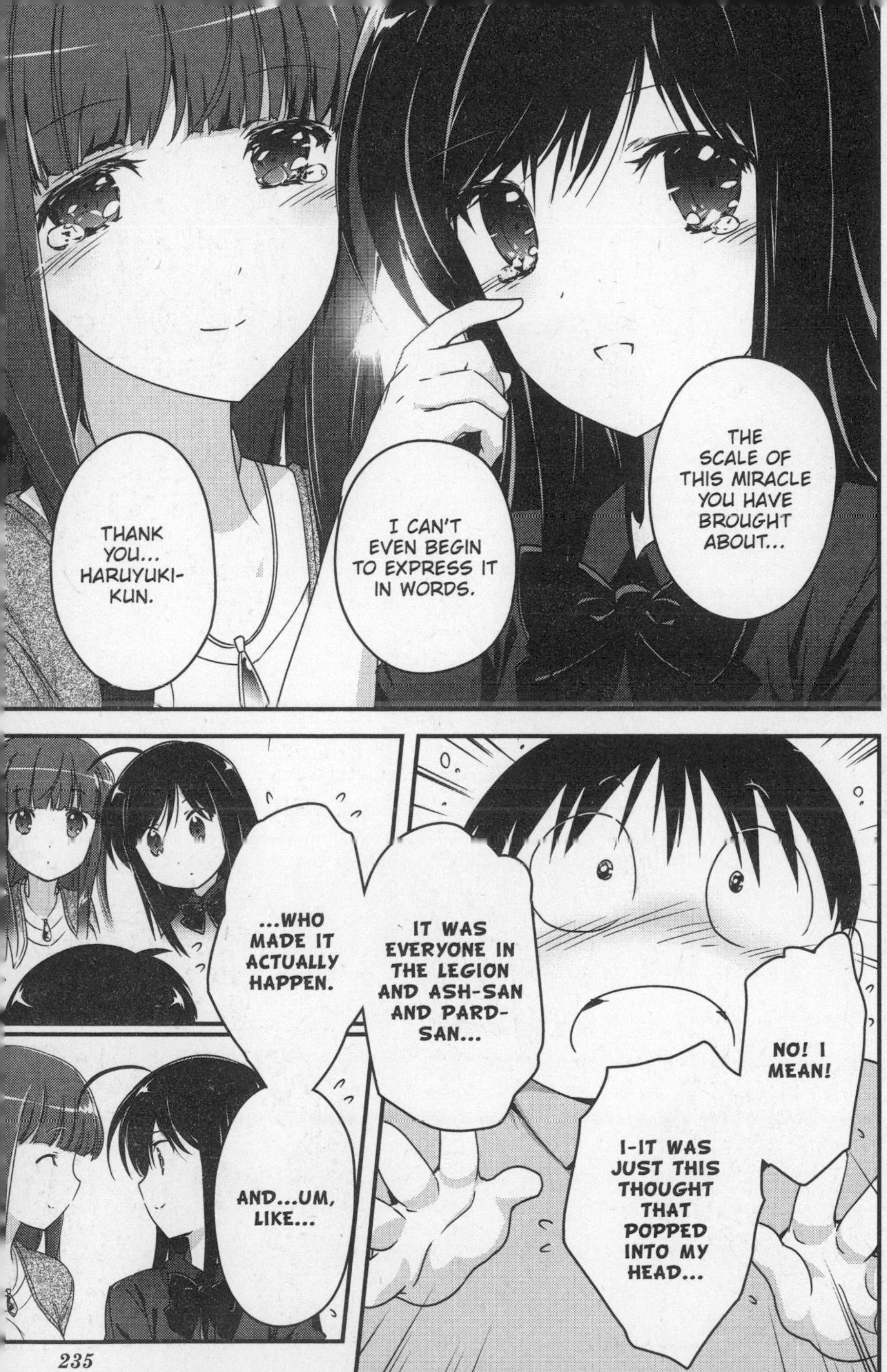
THE SCALE OF THIS MIRACLE YOU HAVE BROUGHT ABOUT...
I CAN'T EVEN BEGIN TO EXPRESS IT IN WORDS.
THANK YOU... HARUYUKI-KUN.
NO! I MEAN!
I-IT WAS JUST THIS THOUGHT THAT POPPED INTO MY HEAD...
IT WAS EVERYONE IN THE LEGION AND ASH-SAN AND PARD-SAN...
...WHO MADE IT ACTUALLY HAPPEN.
AND...UM, LIKE...

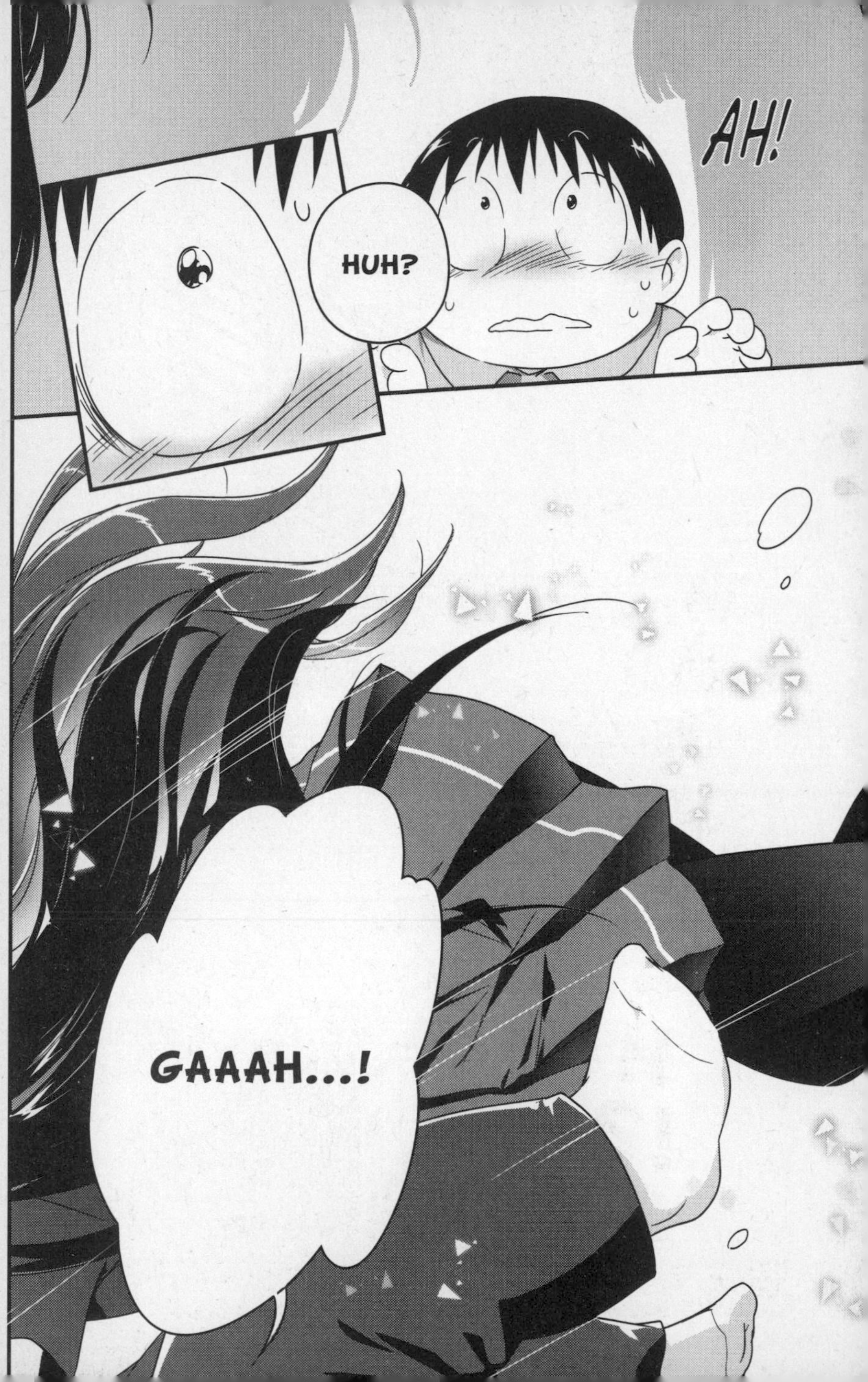
AH!
HUH?
GAAAH...!

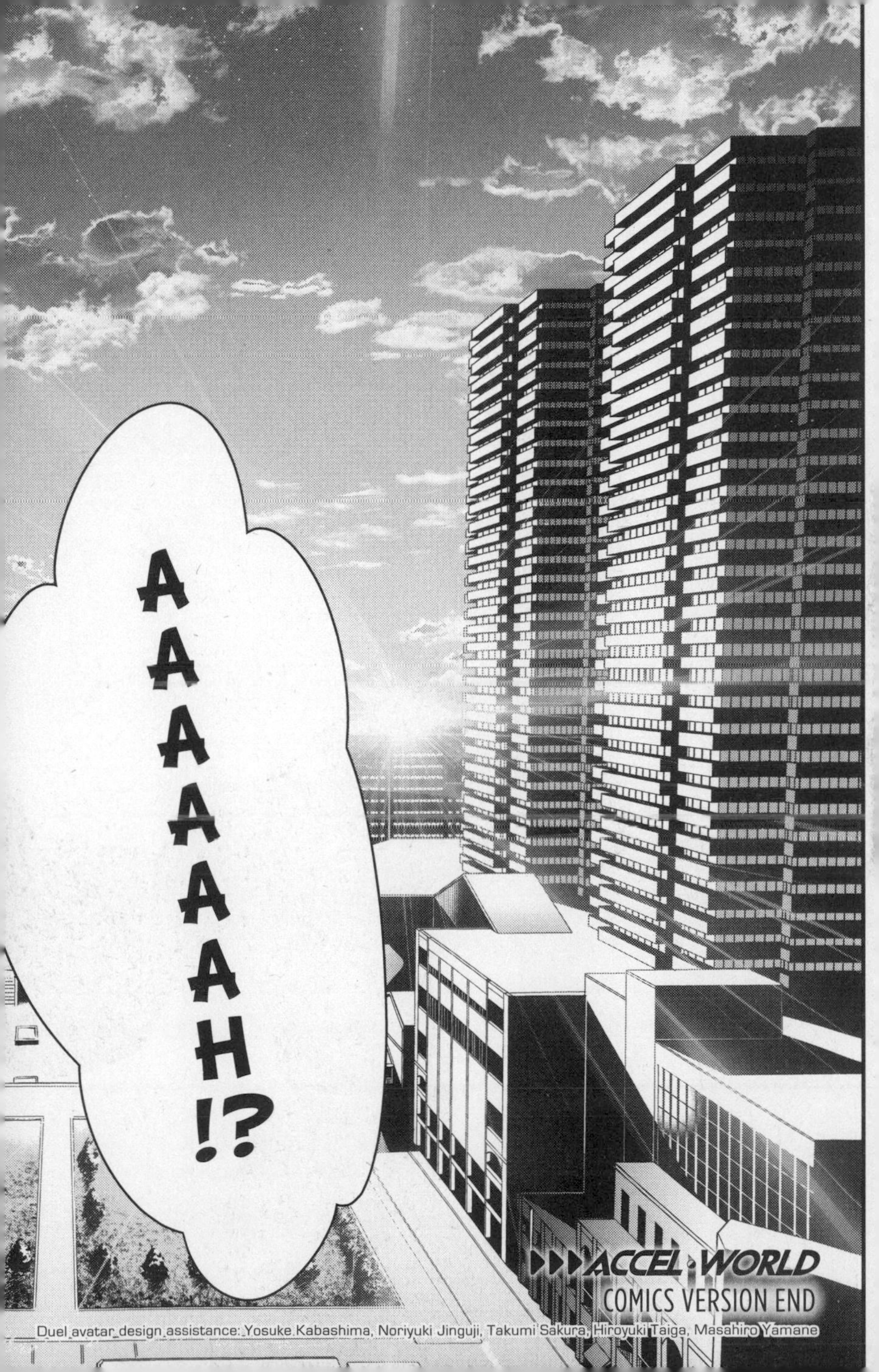
AAAAAAH!?
ACCEL WORLD
COMICS VERSION END
Duel avatar design assistance: Yosuke Kabashima, Noriyuki Jinguji, Takumi Sakura, Hiroyuki Taiga, Masahiro Yamane

Afterword

Thank you so much for picking up Volume 8 of the comics version of *Accel World*! This volume finally brings the story to a conclusion. In the blink of an eye, the series had been running for a full seven years, and I can really see now how far we've come.

The fact that I've managed to keep going until now is because the author of the original series, Reki Kawahara-sensei, HIMA-sensei, editors Kazuma Miki-sama and Chie Tsuhiya-sama, and all the anime staff helped me out enormously every step of the way. In particular, my editor, Tsuhiya-sama, followed up with me in extreme detail——it was almost like we were running a three-legged race together. She really gave me the support I needed.

To my assistants who helped with these pages, my family and friends who kept me going, all my work friends, and all the readers who stuck with the comics version right up to the end, you have my heartfelt gratitude. Once again, I would like to take this opportunity to thank you all.

Thank you so, so very much!

■ALL ASSISTANTS■

Hio-sama
Tsukikaname-sama
Sakuraba-sama
Motoko Ikeda-sama
Momoto-sama
Inoue Mk-II-sama
Eika Sorano-sama
Kumiko Morita-sama
Tatsuki Edo-sama
Yui Ito-sama
Ao Esaka-sama
Sayoko Kamimoto-sama
Hanimaru-sama

Kusasora Yamano-sama
Haru-sama
Kana Shibusawa-sama

■Special Thanks■

Reki Kawahara-sama
HIMA-sama
Ryuryuu Akari-sama
Ayato Sasakura-sama
Everyone on the Sunrise anime staff
abec-sama
Chie Tsuhiya-sama
Kazuma Miki-sama

Now, the story in the comics ends with Volume 5 of the original novels, *The Floating Starlight Bridge*, but the novel series continues long after that. I would be delighted if you would follow the continuation of the story of Haruyuki, Kuroyukihime, and their friends.

I hope we can meet again sometime somewhere else!

Sincerely,

Hiroyuki Aigamo

THE CHART-TOPPING SERIES THAT SPAWNED THE EXPLOSIVELY POPULAR ANIME ADAPTATIONS!

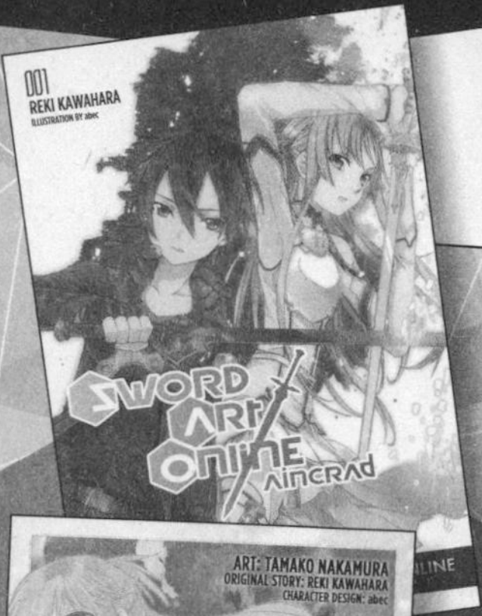

001
REKI KAWAHARA
ILLUSTRATION BY abec
SWORD ART ONLINE
AINCRAD

SWORD ART ONLINE, VOL. 1-14
LIGHT NOVEL SERIES
SWORD ART ONLINE © REKI KAWAHARA
KADOKAWA CORPORATION ASCII MEDIA WORKS

SWORD ART ONLINE, PROGRESSIVE, VOL. 1-5
LIGHT NOVEL SERIES
SWORD ART ONLINE: PROGRESSIVE © REKI KAWAHARA
KADOKAWA CORPORATION ASCII MEDIA WORKS

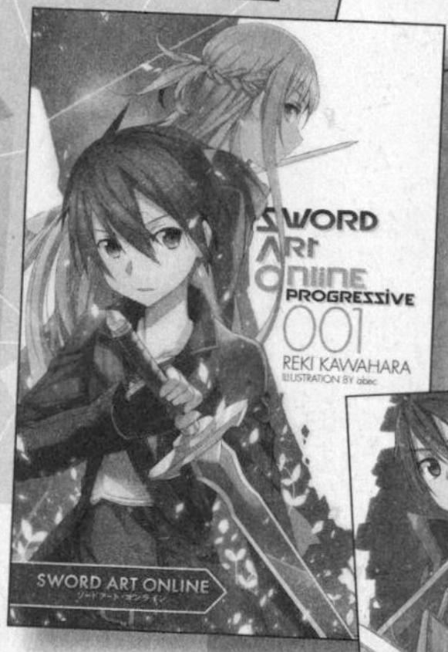

SWORD ART ONLINE
PROGRESSIVE
001
REKI KAWAHARA
ILLUSTRATION BY abec
SWORD ART ONLINE
ソードアート・オンライン

SWORD ART ONLINE, PROGRESSIVE, VOL. 1-6
MANGA SERIES
SWORD ART ONLINE: PROGRESSIVE
© REKI KAWAHARA / KISEKI HIMURA
KADOKAWA CORPORATION ASCII MEDIA WORKS

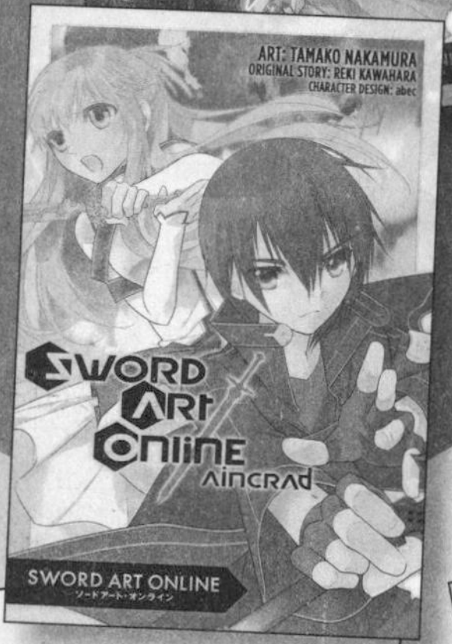

ART: TAMAKO NAKAMURA
ORIGINAL STORY: REKI KAWAHARA
CHARACTER DESIGN: abec
SWORD ART ONLINE
AINCRAD
SWORD ART ONLINE
ソードアート・オンライン

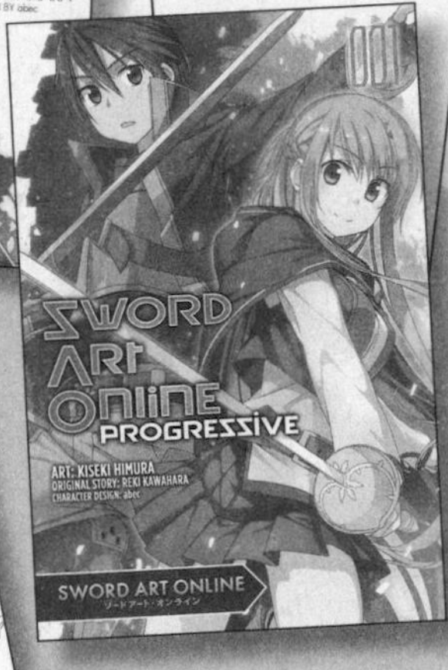

001
SWORD ART ONLINE
PROGRESSIVE
ART: KISEKI HIMURA
ORIGINAL STORY: REKI KAWAHARA
CHARACTER DESIGN: abec
SWORD ART ONLINE
ソードアート・オンライン

SWORD ART ONLINE, VOL. 1-12
MANGA SERIES
SWORD ART ONLINE: AINCRAD
© REKI KAWAHARA / TAMAKO NAKAMURA
KADOKAWA CORPORATION ASCII MEDIA WORKS

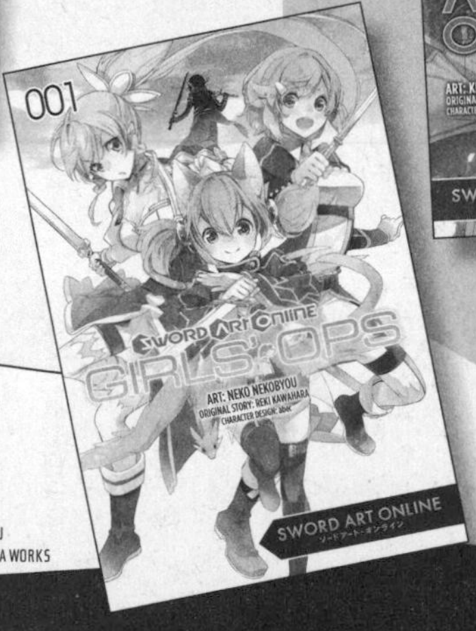

001
SWORD ART ONLINE
GIRLS' OPS
ART: NEKO NEKOBYOU
ORIGINAL STORY: REKI KAWAHARA
CHARACTER DESIGN: abec
SWORD ART ONLINE
ソードアート・オンライン

SWORD ART ONLINE, GIRLS' OPS, VOL. 1-4
MANGA SERIES
SWORD ART ONLINE: GIRLS' OPS
© REKI KAWAHARA / NEKO NEKOBYOU
KADOKAWA CORPORATION ASCII MEDIA WORKS

VISIT YENPRESS.COM
TO CHECK OUT ALL THESE TITLES AND MORE!

YEN ON
Yen Press
www.YenPress.com

ACCEL WORLD 8

ART: HIROYUKI AIGAMO
ORIGINAL STORY: REKI KAWAHARA
CHARACTER DESIGN: HIMA

Translation: Jocelyne Allen
Lettering: Brndn Blakeslee

ACCEL WORLD
© REKI KAWAHARA / HIROYUKI AIGAMO 2017
First published in Japan in 2017 by KADOKAWA CORPORATION, Tokyo.
English translation rights arranged with KADOKAWA CORPORATION, Tokyo, through Tuttle-Mori Agency, Inc., Tokyo.

English translation © 2018 by Yen Press, LLC

Yen Press
1290 Avenue of the Americas
New York, NY 10104

Visit us at yenpress.com
facebook.com/yenpress
twitter.com/yenpress
yenpress.tumblr.com
instagram.com/yenpress

First Yen Press Edition: December 2018

Yen Press is an imprint of Yen Press, LLC.
The Yen Press name and logo are trademarks of Yen Press, LLC.

The publisher is not responsible for websites (or their content) that are not owned by the publisher.

Library of Congress Control Number: 2015952578

ISBNs: 978-1-9753-2913-6 (paperback)
       978-1-9753-2914-3 (ebook)

10 9 8 7 6 5 4 3 2 1

WOR

Printed in the United States of America